# BRANCH POINT

# POINT

## MONA CLEE

*For Janet - hope to see you again some time. Maybe lunch in Palo Alto on a weekend? Best, Mona 1-20-96*

**ACE BOOKS, NEW YORK**

This book is an Ace original edition,
and has never been previously published.

BRANCH POINT

An Ace Book / published by arrangement with
the author

PRINTING HISTORY
Ace edition / January 1996

ISBN: 0-441-00291-9

ACE®
Ace Books are published by The Berkley Publishing Group,
200 Madison Avenue, New York, NY 10016.
ACE and the "A" design are trademarks
belonging to Charter Communications, Inc.

PRINTED IN THE UNITED STATES OF AMERICA

10  9  8  7  6  5  4  3  2  1

Thanks to Mary Clee, Mark Willard, Deborah McIntyre, David Keith Arctur, and Ardath Mayhar for their support and encouragement; Russell Galen and Laura Anne Gilman; the Oregon Science Fiction Society and the Susan Petrey scholarship fund for enabling me to attend Clarion '83; and Yana Ratmansky, for her Russian language assistance.

# Prologue

From the Journal of Anna Leah Fall-Levchenko
April 1836

It is hard to be so old when the world is now so young.

I am the last of our merry band; Jeffrey and Daria are gone. While I do have cherished friends here in the past, I will never stop missing the comrades of my youth.

Age is not a ridiculous thing in this culture, the way it was in my lost America. I am respected by all, and loved by many. There are lots of children in the Presidio now, though of course I never got to have any. They call me *abuelita*, *babushka*, and give me little presents—a shell, some preserved fruit, a set of carved wooden nested dolls, a delicate lace mantilla.

My dear Nikolasha and the Arguello family have been very good to me. I have an estate on what was once called Russian Hill, and now will never be. My little house sits on bedrock where our apartment building was once located, and now will never be. On spring mornings I go to my patio, lay the diaries I have kept since girlhood before me on a table, and gaze at the majestic outlines of land and bay I have loved since first I left my concrete prison near Livermore: the mighty sweep of the Golden Gate, now denuded of its beautiful bridge; the slopes of the east bay hills (startlingly thick with virgin redwoods which I never allowed to be cut); the looming presence of Mount Diablo to the east; and to the north, the misty outlines of what I once knew as the Napa Valley, and Sonoma, the Valley of the Moon.

Already there is a great city stirring to life around me, which will not be called San Francisco. On what used to be Telegraph Hill, there is no Coit Tower, no monument to the quake that is coming in the year nineteen-six. Instead, a gold-encrusted onion dome, strayed hither from Byzantium, glitters in the bright sunlit sky. Many of the city's other hills are topped with golden-domed churches. Their brilliance hurts my eyes.

Well—I was just about to start bawling, when my little maid, Consuelo Mikhailevna Akhmatova, brought me some good English tea. We got it last month from a battered Yankee trader that limped through the Gate after a rough voyage around Cape Horn. It is such a treat after that cursed chocolate the Spaniards drink night and day that I cheered right up, and forgot all about crying.

Since the machine is all used up, I will have to do my time traveling on paper. No matter. I look forward to writing a chronicle of the four alternate histories of Earth. In this way, they will all be kept alive.

The first part of my memoir consists of a journal I kept as a girl—it chronicles our voyage back in time from the year 2062 to the year 1962, and how we saved the world from nuclear war. I kept that journal religiously almost through the end of 1962, not wishing to forget a single detail of our great adventure. However, I soon learned that life in twentieth-century America was so hectic, no journal could possibly keep up with it. So the rest of my story has been written here, in my last years, overlooking the glittering bay of Novaya Moskva.

To paraphrase what Bette Davis once said—in another world that will never be—Fasten your seat belts! It's going to be a bumpy ride.

# PART I

October 2062–October 1962

From the Journal of Anna Leah Fall-Levchenko
October 31, 2062; 6:00 P.M.
Salamander Bunker, in an unnamed canyon below the northeastern face of Mount Diablo, near
the ancient site of Livermore, California

When one path is chosen, all others must be forsaken.
Every day men and women weigh possible courses of action
and choose one above all others. So do towns and cities and
peoples and nations; so do empires. In the moment before
such decisions are made, many possible worlds hang
suspended on the razor's edge of being. Julius Caesar went
to the Senate on the Ides of March, against his better
judgment, and one future was born. Had he only heeded
Calpurnia's warning, the course of Western history might
have been vastly different.

Accident also leaves its mark upon the world. One story
tells us that Alexander the Great sailed with his engineers
down the Euphrates River, seeking to divert its flow for the
city of Babylon. The hat he wore to shield himself from
the sun blew into the water, which was foul with sewage.
The hat was returned to him, and soon thereafter he
sickened and died; had he lived, the future of civilization
would have been greatly changed.

In every road there comes a fork, where multiple paths
present themselves to the traveler. Our interest is in this
place, which we call a branch point—the spot where one

5

possible future comes into being, and all others perish stillborn. For if one could journey back in time to such a branch point, one could change a mistaken decision or prevent an accident of fate, and alter significantly the shape of the world to come.

Some branch points are dramatic, readily apparent to the untrained eye. Others carry the potential to change history just as thoroughly, but are so subtle, so obscure, that they only become apparent through detailed study of the past— and here Fate is not without humor. A young man from Illinois applied to enter West Point, but when it was found he had six toes on each foot, that august institution rejected him and accepted in his place a student named Ulysses S. Grant. Had the first young man possessed only ten toes, there would have been no General Grant, no President Grant, and no modern history quite as we know it.

In October 1962, the President of the United States was confronted with a choice. In that moment of choice was a branch point of staggering proportions. The survival of the very world hinged on his making the right decision.

Sorry to say, the bastard got it wrong.

Attachment to the Journal of Anna Leah Fall-Levchenko (Entry of October 31, 2062) [translated from the Russian]

April 30, 1963
Dearest Lara,

Since arriving in San Francisco last October I have missed you more than words can say. Now I would give anything never to have come to America. But that is hindsight speaking. We both knew I had to go—two weeks in the United States, only a madman would refuse such a trip! Besides, the Party asked me to go, to represent the Academy. They knew I'd come back. How could I not, with you waiting for me in Moscow?

"The City," the locals called San Francisco, using capital letters—as if it were the first city in the world! Yet when I was struck by its beauty on a clear, cool afternoon at the foot of the golden bridge, when the air was sweet and the sunlight as bright as crystal, I could understand why its people could fall victim to such bourgeois arrogance. Remember, Nikita Sergeyevich himself liked The City. Its people cheered him in 1959, which is why he allowed our own tour to stop here.

On our third day, there came a group of citizens who called themselves soldiers for peace, who gave us money. They said they knew we had been allowed to bring no hard currency out of the Motherland, and wanted us to have "a little splurge," as they put it, while we were in San Francisco. At first I turned the money down, as did we all, except for Kirilenko, our political officer, whose eyes lit up as if for a May Day parade. Seeing us hesitate, the citizens said we should not spend it on ourselves; since the money was a gift to us, we should spend it on gifts for our loved ones. Again I started to refuse, knowing I should set a good example for the others. But when I saw Kirilenko pocket his envelope, I succumbed to temptation, and accepted.

No retribution was forthcoming. And no, they never asked me to tell them our atomic secrets—*o gospodi!*— why would they have, they who were so far ahead of us! These soldiers for peace put us on a bus and took us to a place in The City called Union Square. There they took us to two department stores, each smaller than GUM in Moscow, but filled with many riches. The name of one would have amused you. It was not GUM, but GUMP! It was like a museum of china and crystal and lovely things for the apartment and *dacha*—they even had some of our own Russian lacquer boxes from Palekh, for prices you would think could buy a whole house in America. The other was a magnificent store primarily for women, called City of Paris, which boasted a titanic domed ceiling made of stained glass, portraying a ship in full sail. I remembered how you had always wanted to visit the real city of Paris, and resolved to spend all my money on gifts for you in that store.

Oh, Larisa, if you could only see what beautiful things I chose for you. First I bought a bottle of Chanel perfume, No. 5. The salesgirl said that was the very best number of Chanel. Then I saw silk scarves for sale—brilliant, gossamer, airy things, as delicate and weightless as a spider's web. I bought two, both in bright colors that would go so well with your dark hair. Next I found a quilted purse with a gold chain, made of fresh and supple leather that itself smelled like perfume. They had food there too, and I bought a dozen little cans of things you would never see back home—"pâté" and "cocktail onions" and "maraschino cherries" and "escargot" (I did not know what all these were; I hoped we would find out together). And a box of chocolates shaped like seashells. I almost bought you a pair of silver-colored shoes, but they did not look sturdy and were very expensive, so I looked further. By then my money was almost gone, but another salesgirl said I could find inexpensive gifts in the bath department, so I bought sweet-smelling soaps and bath powders and little embroidered linen towels that I knew you would like.

[Illegible]. These gifts are with me now, in my concrete refuge—my prison for life. I have been here six months. Each morning, in the instant before full consciousness comes, I pray I will find it has all been a nightmare. But it is not.

The American women here look at me with too much interest. They are heartless—they don't care that a man is grieving. Oh, Larisa, I would gladly trade this "haven" for a cell in our own Lubyanka prison if it would bring the world back, and I could know that you were alive somewhere in the Moscow streets outside!

How could it have happened? How could it have

escalated so? From very the beginning, we only did what was right. Lara, men *must* defend what they hold dear. Cuba's bold socialist experiment in the New World was in grave peril from the "Colossus of the North." We knew it, everybody knew it! The United States detested Fidel Castro and everything he stood for. The Americans would not stomach a Communist Cuba on their doorsteps for long. It was only a matter of time until they moved against it.

Cuba was our first fraternal socialist brother in the Western hemisphere. We had to protect it from the corrupt capitalist empire next door! But how were we to do so, we whose Motherland lay on the opposite side of the globe? By diplomatic protests? By angry statements from Tass?

Our brilliant Nikita Sergeyevich hit upon a plan. We would place nuclear missiles in Cuba, each equipped with a warhead many times more powerful than the ones the Americans had used to destroy Hiroshima and Nagasaki. Then we would train them on major American cities. Getting the missiles in place would be easy. Cuba possessed so many palm trees, the natives assured us, that the missiles would never be spotted by American planes. Once they were in place, we would announce their presence to the entire world, and the imminent American attack would be instantly deterred. It was a bold move, yes—but the only one that would dissuade the American tiger from its inevitable invasion.

With missiles positioned ninety miles from American shores, we were certain young Kennedy would not dare move against us. Early on Nikita Sergeyevich had judged the boy to be a bungling amateur, unsure of himself in the international arena. And last spring the Bay of Pigs incident had confirmed Kennedy's weakness in front of the entire world. Furthermore, the American people *understood* what nuclear war would mean. They thought about it night and day. They portrayed it in their movies. Silly metal bomb shelters were sold at their shopping malls. No, once the missiles were operational, the Americans would not dream of letting their leaders harm Cuba.

We would never have attacked first. Dear God! We were the standard-bearers of Marxism-Leninism, the bringers of light to a dark world! Besides, what were a few missiles in Cuba compared to America's atomic might? Hadn't the United States already encircled the *Rodina*, the Motherland, with its own necklace of nuclear missiles, more numerous and powerful than our own?

We only wanted to scare the Americans, to teach them a lesson, to put ourselves on a halfway equal footing with them. But Fidel was a fool. He never understood our strategy. And he had no idea what war would really mean. He wanted Nikita Sergeyevich to go in and obliterate the Americans once and for all, like the blood-mongering actor John Wayne did with the Indians. And when Nikita Sergeyevich would not, when he said in fact he wanted to withdraw the missiles, Fidel called him a coward.

They had been like brothers, and Fidel knew how to play on Nikita's pride and vanity. Fidel exhorted him to stand tall and crush the Americans. Strike quickly and silently, said Fidel, and the Americans could never retaliate in time. They were only a paper tiger; surely the Soviet Union was not afraid of them.

Despite Fidel's goading, Nikita Sergeyevich was still not swayed: he was no fool. Larisa, I knew the man well, and I tell you he did not want to die! He wisely told Fidel that the paper tiger had atomic teeth, and he must abandon then and there any foolhardy thoughts of a "first strike."

But then the unthinkable happened. Like a madman, Kennedy lashed out at us. From what we have been able to piece together, he sent an air strike that laid waste our missile sites in Cuba and killed thousands of our Soviet countrymen. Then Fidel must have called Nikita Sergeyevich a fool. So must have the Red Army generals and colonels, the Politburo, and the KGB. Then the Premier was cornered, and badly wounded, like a wild bear before the huntsman.

He matched Kennedy, taking an eye for an eye. We launched our battlefield nuclear weapons in Cuba against the invading American soldiers. Simultaneously, our bombers struck with all their might at the American missile bases in Turkey. So the Americans, bound by treaty to Turkey, attacked Soviet missile bases in the heart of the *Rodina*.

Then, like wildfire, it escalated out of control. Inevitably, the surgical strike of the American air force had missed a handful of our medium-range missiles in Cuba, and as the invading Americans landed upon Cuban shores, we fired at them. At America. America fired back with hundreds upon hundreds of nuclear bombs, turning Cuba and the *Rodina* into an inferno. In retaliation, from Soviet soil and from submarines we launched our forty long-range missiles that could reach America, and the many hundreds that could reach the closer countries of NATO.

It was enough to do the job. At first the Americans, who had not lost all their major cities, thought they might still survive as a nation. (Our missiles, you see, were grievously inaccurate.) But they had not counted on what such a war would do to the Earth—to the air and wind and sunlight, to all the plants and animals. It completely destroyed the [illegible; here the paper is torn].

Good-bye, Larisa. May God have mercy on us all.

Your husband, Sergei Makarovich Kharitonov

From the Journal of Anna Leah Fall-Levchenko (continued)
October 31, 2062; 7:00 P.M.

On October 31, 1962, most life on Earth was destroyed by a nuclear war between the United States of America and the Union of Soviet Socialist Republics. Earlier today, on the hundredth anniversary of that war, the citizens of the Bunker voted to send three of us—two of my comrades and me—back in time to try to avert it. They did so knowing full well that success could mean the death of us all, for if we changed history, our own world would never come to be.

But there was no other choice. For a century, backed by the enormous resources of the Bunker, our people have labored to preserve the last remnant of our ancestors' culture. We have lived in hope that one day the land outside would become fertile and habitable again, and we could leave our concrete fortress to build a new world. We have endured in solitude, like the cloistered monks who preserved the learning of Greece and Rome for more than a thousand years. We have endured, trusting that we were carrying the seeds of civilization forward in time in order to one day begin a new renaissance.

But after a hundred years of struggle, we were forced to acknowledge that we were losing our battle to survive, that there would be no outlasting this spell of bad weather. We were almost certainly doomed; nothing would save us from the consequences of our race's madness.

A month or so after the holocaust, men and women from the Bunker donned protective suits and ventured into the dark and cold to assess the damage to the world outside. They also searched neighboring towns for uncontaminated supplies and foodstuffs to bring back to the Bunker; despite the massive stores of necessities already on hand, more food and supplies meant our people could hold out that much longer.

These forays were continued for about a year, until they were judged no longer of any use. At first the reconnaissance teams encountered many survivors, and were hopeful that some remnant of civilization might yet endure in the Bay Area. After all, San Francisco had taken no direct hits; The City lay out of range of the Cuban missiles, and was

missed completely by the inaccurate ICBMs launched from
Soviet soil. So it escaped all the deadly primary effects of a
nuclear strike: the initial radiation, the intense heat, the blast
wave, and local fallout.

Therefore, it took almost half a year for the Bay Area's
population to die from the secondary effects of the bombs.
No one had counted on these, which were far less dramatic
than the primary effects: the worldwide fallout of fine,
radioactive ash from the troposphere, the lofting of count-
less tons of dust and debris into the stratosphere, which
blotted out the sun and plunged the entire Earth into a winter
that lasted nearly a year, and the almost total destruction of
the Earth's ozone layer.

What a joke it was! And how pitifully unprepared were
the American people!

Within weeks after the bombings everything collapsed,
because everything was connected. Hospitals were overwhelmed with victims of radiation sickness and refugees
from other parts of the state. Sanitation systems failed, and
epidemics of disease became rampant. With the nation's
economy and transportation network in ruins, there were no
deliveries of food, clothing, medical supplies, energy, or any
other basic necessities. People died by the hundreds of
thousands from the cold. Cities and towns, their fire-
fighting capabilities destroyed, burned to the ground. Food
could not be grown in the dark, so once local stockpiles
were used up, the survivors of these earlier perils starved to
death. Many were killed by their fellow men, themselves
seeking food and shelter; in fact, in early 1963 a jeep from
the Bunker was ambushed near the town of Walnut Creek
and its crew was eaten.

Months later, when the sun finally emerged, it shone
down upon an Earth stripped of its ozone shield. Then
ultraviolet radiation wiped out those plants and animals that
had not already been killed by cold and fallout. With its
vegetation gone, the land was not rejuvenated by rain-
storms, but eroded so that it could no longer sustain a

mature community of plants. Minerals and nutrients flowed out of the soil into streams, rivers, and lakes, which were themselves degraded when the growth of algae and microscopic organisms, spurred by this new supply of food, depleted the water of its oxygen.

In about fifty years the ozone layer partially restored itself, and the last of the global fallout settled. The climate finally began to warm a little, and there even was something like seasons again. Even the atmospheric nitrogen dioxide from the bombs dissipated, so that the sky, which had been brown for half a century, turned blue once more.

At last men and women from the Bunker could walk in the sunlight and live to tell of the experience. But that was little consolation, for by then all but the hardiest living things had been wiped out. Outside the Bunker there was literally nothing but a wasteland of insects, moss, and grass.

Now, in our lifetime, the machines that control the Bunker's air and water and recycling systems are beginning to break down. The nuclear generators are failing, and there are no more spare parts to fix them. Over the years, California's earthquakes have wreaked further havoc upon the very foundations of the Bunker. Our once-tremendous stockpiles of food are running out, and cannot be replaced. Soon we will have to go outside and try to grow crops, with the help of what little fertilizer was stored in the Bunker. If it can even be done! The resiliency and recuperative powers of the Earth are not yet known. Millions of years may need to pass before the planet is sufficiently rehabilitated to bring forth new life forms, or to support even the smallest organized settlement of human beings.

So you see, in 2062, our community has little in the way of a future to look forward to. Therefore, once the time machine was finished, it was not a difficult decision for the citizens of the Bunker to send three of their children into the past on a mission that might well kill them. And my comrades and I never dreamed of refusing to go. If we stayed in the Bunker, we would have almost certainly died;

but if we went back in time, we would have had a chance to restore life to that beautiful Earth, which had been destroyed one hundred years before, and should have been our birthright.

November 1, 2062; 12:30 A.M.

I can't sleep. There's just no use in trying any longer; after all, in a few hours we may be dead. So I figure I'll just write in this journal to keep myself sane. I'll take it with me, and, if by some miracle we survive, I'll give it to my grandchildren. If I have any.

My earlier description of the Bunker was pretty sketchy. I'll add what I can here in this entry, but actually, I don't know near as much about the Bunker as I'd like to. All of us know the official story, of course—when it was built, how big and impregnable it is, that sort of thing. But nobody who wound up in the Bunker on Halloween night, 1962, was high-up enough to know the real story of its origin. Like exactly *who* was behind the damn thing from the start. It wasn't entirely clear that anyone besides President Kennedy and his closest advisors knew that. And of course there weren't any written records concerning the Bunker for us to examine after the war, at our oh-so-eternal leisure. So we can only speculate, based on the rumors that were circulating at the time.

The American public didn't know shit about the Bunker; its very existence was top secret. On the other hand, the Department of Defense knew a great deal about it—after all, they guarded the Bunker round the clock. A few of the top people at the Lawrence Livermore Lab knew about it too, as did—obviously—the support staff who worked inside it. And of course, the local citizens, who were kept out of the area, suspected something was up from the get-go.

What records we have tell us that construction was begun

on the Bunker shortly after the first nuclear weapon was dropped on Hiroshima. At that time, the Powers That Be—excuse me, the Powers That Were—must have decided it was only a matter of time until the Commies somehow got the Bomb too, so they had better start preparing. The Bunker was designed to be a war-proof repository of the totality of American scientific and technological know-how, the theory being that if war came, the Bunker, like its namesake the salamander, would survive the fire and give the country the wherewithal to rebuild.

But the Bunker was more than just a glorified storeroom. It was a fortress, a world unto itself. It was built and equipped to endure for a hundred years in complete isolation.

Perhaps you've heard of Mount Weather, that other bunker hidden in the carved-out innards of a heavily wooded Virginia mountain ridge, intended to shelter the country's leaders in the event of a nuclear attack. Mount Weather was a self-contained city. It had its own power plant, cafeteria, kitchen, hospital, gymnasium, sewage treatment plant, TV and radio station, computer network, stores of dried, canned, and preserved food, underground reservoirs of drinking water, living quarters, offices, and a direct link to the White House Situation Room. Its residents included computer programmers, engineers, fire fighters, security personnel, craftsmen, secretaries, and bureaucrats.

How did the bunkers compare? Well, let me put it this way. Salamander came first. Next to it, the Mount Weather bunker was just a cheap Japanese knockoff. It didn't even make it through the war; afterward we never once heard from those guys.

Salamander differed from Mount Weather in another way. It was not built to serve as a haven for the government, but as an ongoing scientific facility. It was the site of an extraordinary amount of research and development activity. For almost two decades, the shadow men who designed and implemented the Bunker culled the country to recruit a particular kind of scientific mind to conduct that research—the kind that loved research for its own sake and would be happy in a place like the Bunker.

In her own diary, one of the female secretaries trapped inside the Bunker on the day the world was destroyed described these individuals thusly: "Think of every skinny little geek you knew in high school. You know, the ones with crew cuts, black glasses, pimples, and incredible college entrance exam scores. The ones who carried slide rules and understood everything about those enormous new computers but could never explain anything about them to anyone using the English language. The ones who never went to a dance or dated a girl and would rather work in a morgue like this where they never had to deal with people. Got it? Now you have a picture of every last man in this concrete mausoleum, except for those visiting Russians. Well, thank God for those Russians! And thank God they go for American girls!"

As an aside, I think I have just explained why (as you will shortly notice) two out of the three of us time travelers have Russian last names, even though we are all Americans, born on American soil, and would be United States citizens if there were still a United States. You will be more fully introduced to us in a moment.

Anyway, here you had the Bunker—built like the granddaddy of all tanks. It was stocked with enough chips and dip to last several lifetimes, staffed by brainy scientific types with all the time in the world on their hands and nothing to do but invent things, and loaded to the gills with enough supplies and scientific equipment to conduct research on the cutting edge of everything for the more-than-foreseeable future.

So whose idea was it, anyway? And who paid for it?

There were all sorts of rumors. The CIA, the FBI, the Mafia, the military-industrial complex that Eisenhower had warned about. Some bandied about the name of Howard Hughes. Others said that the man who could bankroll the

Bunker would make Hughes look like a financial peanut. Some thought the Bunker was the brainchild of a secret international cartel of incredibly important shadowy people; "They" knew an atomic war was coming and "They" meant to ensure the survival of humankind and Western culture in a latter-day nuclear Noah's Ark. (Of course, you've got to wonder why "They," if "They" were so smart and powerful, didn't just pull strings and prevent The War to start with.)

Some said the Livermore Lab itself was only a front, that the *real* work was being done in the Bunker, which was actually the most important research facility in the country. Some said it was a joint effort of American and Soviet visionaries—how else could you explain that, when the missiles flew and that tour group of Soviet scientists and astronauts-in-training hightailed it out of San Francisco for the Bunker, we let them in?

What was the secret of the Bunker's origin? You tell me. If we get back to 1962 and by some miracle aren't killed, maybe someday I'll find out. On the other hand, maybe I'll never go near this place again as long as I live.

## November 1, 2062; 2:30 A.M.

I'm still here. I still can't sleep. Rereading my first entry, I think I erroneously made it sound like we were all going to die on this expedition no matter what. Actually, that *is* a distinct possibility. All sorts of horrible scenarios present themselves to my sleepless mind. The machine may malfunction and blow us up. Or we may make it make to 1962 and be unable to persuade Kennedy to stop the war. The machine is supposed to be good for four hops total, but what if it breaks? Then we'll have a ringside seat at the biggest bonfire in history.

Or, let's say we get to 1962, it turns out the past actually *can* be changed, and we succeed in doing so. Then the future that gave us birth will cease to exist. We'll be snuffed out right then and there like puffs of smoke. We won't be able to continue hanging out in the year 1962, no matter how much we'd like to.

But there is another possibility I think about a lot. There's one school of thought that says the past can't be changed. That it's futile for us even to try to convince President Kennedy not to go to war. Yet what if we somehow do convince him? Then we will have changed the past, right? But you can't change the past. Ta-da! Contradiction!

Well, right again. But since the past can't be changed, according to this theory what we've actually done is generate a whole new world, one existing in a dimension parallel to our own.

On this new Earth, Kennedy's more hawkish advisors didn't sway him following the disastrous events of Saturday, October 27. Kennedy didn't launch an air strike against the Cuban missile bases on October 30. Consequently, there wasn't a Soviet strike against the American Jupiter missiles in Turkey on Wednesday the thirtieth, followed by American retaliation against bases inside the Soviet Union. The Cubans didn't launch their few surviving missiles against the United States, and on Halloween the conflict didn't escalate into all-out, total, global nuclear war.

We've jumped ship, in other words. Of course, our poor original Earth still exists somewhere, off in its own dimension, doomed to be annihilated no matter what; no power in the universe can change that. But we are safe, in a world that won't burn up, with our whole lives ahead of us.

As we jump, our comrades back at the Bunker will be holding their breath, waiting to see whether their own lives will be snuffed out of existence when we change the past. If they aren't, they'll know that one of the following things happened: (a) the machine screwed up, (b) we screwed up, or (c) we brought Kennedy around, but our own world's past can't be changed, so we're alive and well on an alternate, unreachable, second Earth where they still dance the Twist.

Unfortunately, there is only one time machine. This is

because building such a contraption was almost impossible. In fact, I wonder whether it could have been built in any environment except the Bunker.

When the bombs fell, recall, the Bunker suddenly became home to much of the cream of the American and Soviet scientific communities, who now found themselves with an eternity of time on their hands, and access to equipment and supplies that were state-of-the-art in 1962. For a couple of decades, these scientists kept hoping that they—or even their children—might one day be able to walk on the surface of the Earth again. But around 1982 they began to see the writing on the wall, felt that old icy tingle start to creep up and down their collective spines, and started working like mad on Plan B—preventing the damage in the first place.

There was so much work to be done, so much basic research, that eighty years was not one day too long to build the working model. In fact, by 2042 it turned into a race to see whether the machine could be completed before the Bunker broke down. Remember, the Bunker's life-support systems and generators had already begun to fail in my lifetime. By the time the machine was finished, food was being severely rationed.

The point of all of this is that there is only one machine, which was barely finished and tested in time. So if we blow it in 1962, there's nothing our comrades can do to help us. Talk about pressure!

Why, one wonders, don't we just hop back to ancient Rome or Greece, change history by the introduction of our technological prowess, and direct the planet's future down a path of peace and plenty like good little masterminds? Why bother with 1962 at all? A good question but, you see, we have to bother with it. We love 1962. It's the only world we know. We cut our teeth on it. There was so much beauty in that last year of the world, so much good, which was all preserved here in the Bunker.

Throughout the years, we studied the records of the

period and extracted from them every drop of its richness. Think, dear reader, of what we represent—a hundred years' worth of children who could not go out and play, who had to turn inward and explore every book and magazine on file, every film, musical composition, work of art, and play available in the archives. We know everything in the world about 1962 because, inside the Bunker, there was nothing to do one's whole life long but learn about the world that was denied us. We have to go back to try to save it. What kind of people would we be if we did not?

## November 1, 2062; 4:00 A.M.

I am so tired! To kill time, I'll keep writing. A word would be appropriate here about our merry band. We have, tongue-in-cheek, nicknamed ourselves "the Butterflies." Not that we are lightweights or puny or anything like that. It's just that back in Great American Literature class we had to read Ray Bradbury's classic short story "A Sound of Thunder." We feel we have a lot in common with that seemingly insignificant insect in the story whose death changed the future so drastically.

We are all eighteen, or so close as makes no never mind. Jeffrey Kharitonov is blond, six feet tall, with a crew cut and a good smile, and could pass as a fraternity boy at the University of California, or maybe as a young Mercury astronaut. He's decent but tough when necessary. Though he's our team leader, he needs a lot of help from the power behind the throne—me.

I'm the group's flaming redhead, the Jill-of-all-trades; I'm the one with the overview, the common sense, the one who pulls it all together—the synthesizer, the den mother, the nanny. I think that I have the team's hardest job.

Daria Burnet Connell, small and dark despite her Scotch-Irish blood, comes across as rather madcap at times. It makes you think she read more well-preserved issues of

*Teen* magazine than was prudent, or watched Sandra Dee in *Gidget* too many times while in an imitative frame of mind. But she tests out significantly more intelligent than Jeffrey and I. More importantly, she has the ability to think in a nonlinear fashion, to break the invisible rules that condemn most of us to rigid patterns of thought and unimaginative solutions to problems. Hence, her unique value to the team.

And the fourth, most important member of our team, The Time Machine. It's an innocuous-looking thing, a deceptively simple black box the size of a fat wallet. It can fit into Jeffrey's backpack with room left over. Yet that small box can generate a force field strong enough to tear open a hole in time and space and catapult into the past three people, plus suitcases full of money, gadgets, historical records, copious quantities of precious stones, and an assortment of really nasty weapons. And after our 1962 caper, it's good for three more hops, which——God willing——we'll never need.

If our elders have taught us anything, it's that these additional hops must not be frittered away on unimportant things. They are insurance——insurance for the world. A week ago our biological parents sat us down with the science director-general and a Bunker governor and administered a lecture of monstrous proportions on this subject. It practically made me feel like a criminal, even though I haven't done a damn thing wrong . . . not yet, anyway. But I guess they felt it was more important to beat the lesson into us than to spare our feelings.

Our mandate goes like this. Even if we succeed in preventing the nuclear war that sprang from the Cuban missile crisis, there can be no guarantee another such war will not occur in the future. After all, the weapons will still be there, and human nature will still be as cussed as ever. No matter what the circumstances, we cannot ever let ourselves be tempted to use the time machine to prevent anything short of another nuclear war. Even if one of us is killed, we cannot use the machine to go back in time and prevent our deaths. The machine may only be used to prevent another atomic holocaust, which could occur at any time in the powder-keg of a world we're going to. And if there's no second holocaust in our lifetimes, we're responsible for finding somebody trustworthy enough to take over stewardship of the machine after we're gone.

A tall order, huh? When Daria asked if they wanted us to pick up some fries while we were at it, I thought her mother was going to slap her.

Last night my comrades and I went on two pilgrimages. First, we paid a visit to our beloved Father Chuck Alexeyev. As background, you must understand that our population is so small, we can spare only one man for religious duties, so he must be an ecclesiastical eclectic. Although no true men of the cloth happened to be in the Bunker on that fateful Halloween night, our forefathers figured God would not object if one of them assumed the duties of sacred office, so long as he also put in a full work shift during the week. And, given the recent humongous reduction in the size of the Earth's human gene pool, even the Catholics thought the Almighty could not really object if the guy were allowed to procreate, too.

In our generation, the Bunker's spiritual leadership had fallen to Chuck Alexeyev. He was a very busy man; each week he was called upon to perform Russian Orthodox, Catholic, Methodist, and foot-washing Baptist services for our motley citizenry. Our guys have gotten along quite well over the past century, considering how people used to kill each other over religion in the Outside world. I think it's because in the Bunker, everyone knows that survival depends on mutual cooperation and support; I would revise that old saying to read, "There are no atheists—or religious bigots—in foxholes." When you're up to your ass in alligators, you don't really care whether your neighbor crosses himself starting on the right shoulder or the left.

When we got to Father Alexeyev's quarters, he served us tea from a samovar one of our metalsmiths had made, along with some little protein cookies. He blessed each of us and said the prayer for those undertaking a journey. Then we chatted for a while about little things, avoiding the real issue and the moment of parting.

At length he sat down on the couch under a framed reproduction of a Russian icon, one depicting the archangel Michael. It had fascinated me my entire life. The archangel had a serene, exquisitely beautiful face that could have belonged either to a man or a woman. Yet its expression was not cherubic or insipid; there was great strength in the solemn face. And behind the dark, quiet eyes, there was full knowledge of evil—and the will to beat it in hand-to-hand combat.

Father Alexeyev regarded us with a somber expression. "I am praying with all my heart that you will succeed in your mission tomorrow," he said. "If you do, never allow yourselves to grow complacent; in the future you will see battle again."

"The science director-general seems to think so," said Jeffrey. "He beat it into us with a bullwhip last week. Human nature won't change, so there could always be another war."

Daria tossed her head and rolled her eyes with an excess of drama. "You people are all so *cynical*!" she cried. "I can't imagine how, after such a terrible scare, mankind could ever play with fire again. It just doesn't make any sense!"

Father Alexeyev looked down at his clasped hands. "I hope with all my heart that you are right, child, and your elders wrong. Look, I won't repeat what the director said. I want to give you my own warning. If another war comes, you will find it difficult to hold on to your faith. I know what I'm talking about; it's very hard for me to do, here in the Bunker."

From Daria's expression, you could tell that sort of talk made her nervous. People in charge weren't supposed to lose faith, least of all priests. "Why?" she asked guardedly.

"Because there are so many questions I cannot answer. I close my eyes and cast my spirit into the dark, questing, crying for answers and understanding, but a response never comes." He hesitated, and I realized with a shock that he was on the verge of tears. "If there is a God, and you meet Him at the end of your travels, ask Him what in the world He was thinking of when He created the human race the way it is."

We were all stunned. Especially Daria. You could tell by the way her jaw muscles twitched. "How do you mean?" she asked.

He spread his hands wide in a helpless gesture. "When He made men, what did He give them? Bodies pummeled by all the drives and cravings of the animal kingdom; the emotional maturity of little children; a fundamental inability to value the welfare of their fellow living creatures on this Earth; and gigantic brains capable of splitting the atom. That's simply a recipe for disaster. I don't know what possessed Him."

"Perhaps He was doing the best He could," I said.

Father Alexeyev gave a short laugh. He wiped at one eye, and I saw his fingers come away glistening. "If you believe Christian mythology, He is quite capable of doing better. In fact, once He even did so. Look at the wall."

None of us understood. Father Alexeyev got to his feet and gestured to the icon of the archangel Michael. "See, His work is not always shoddy!" said Father Alexeyev. "But in our case, He created twisted, pitiful creatures, incapable of governing their lives in harmony with the Earth and their fellow men, yet cursed with the desire to. Why? *Why?*"

I shuddered, as if someone had walked across my grave. I had a horrible feeling Daria was wrong, and the graybeards were right. Even if we succeeded in saving the human race back in 1962, the story would not end there, for men would be as self-destructive as ever, and would still possess nuclear weapons.

We put our arms around him. "I'm sorry," the priest said, weeping. "I should have counseled and encouraged you and instead I've weighed you down with all my doubts. I despair, you see—for even if you succeed, we're done for here in the Bunker!"

When we left Father Alexeyev's quarters, Jeffrey was attempting to look stoic and I was trembling, blinking over and over in an attempt to stifle tears. Daria, however, seemed to be in another world. She was wearing an expression that I called "Gidget attempting to grasp a complex concept."

"Listen," she said at last. "I think I have it. God is not omnipotent and He knows it. So He's afraid to create another race of archangels, because the last time He did there was hell to pay, literally. Even though the failure rate per unit was quite low, if a single archangel screwed up, the consequences were dire—and on a cosmic scale. I'm talking about Lucifer."

Jeffrey and I were speechless. Daria continued, "Remember all those courses we had to take on Bayesian analysis, risk management, and insurance companies? Think about what we learned. When God created us, he did make us inferior to the archangels . . . on purpose. While more of us go bad than archangels, when we screw up, at the very most it only trashes one planet, not the whole cosmos."

Jeffrey took a deep, shaky breath. "Well, personally, I think if you can't do the job right, you shouldn't do it at all."

After that we were in no shape to go to sleep. So we walked the corridors of the Bunker and performed a familiar ritual one last time. We took a look at the world outside through the Bunker monitors we call the "periscope."

It was still dark, of course, and cold, as it has been come nightfall ever since the bombs fell. There was a sickly sliver of moon overhead, barely illuminating the fold between two hills in which nestles the entrance to the Bunker. Those hills were barren except for the trunks of long-dead oak trees and a coating of icy moss that looked ghostly white in the moonlight. Otherwise there was absolutely nothing. We were the very last people on Earth—utterly alone, in a way no other human beings in the history of the world had ever been.

We shivered, and were glad to say farewell to that aspect of our world. "What if we have to go out there?" asked Daria, putting our deepest fear into words.

She meant, of course, that if we succeeded in our mission but got kicked into an alternate world, we would have to do something absolutely terrifying: go out of doors. Outside.

Jeffrey indicated the cold, empty night and the waning moon. "Don't be afraid. If we have to go out, it won't be like that."

"I know," said Daria, her voice miserable. "I'd almost rather it was. Then I'd know what to expect."

"No, you don't. Trust me." Jeffrey said. We put our arms around her. Together, we turned away from the wasteland in the periscope, and went back to our rooms for the last time.


## November 1, 2062; 5:00 A.M.

How, you ask, did the three of us get mixed up in all this? Well, it's complicated. The science director-general and the others who govern the Bunker had known for years that time was running out for our little enclave. So, a couple of decades ago, they put together this plan to select a pool of the healthiest babies born in the next few years and, when said babies got old enough, test their IQs and adaptivity scores. Daria, myself, and Jeffrey scored highest, in that order (and don't you forget it). We were then put through an incredibly rigorous course of training which essentially was concluded yesterday.

We were taught history, logic, political theory, basic medicine, the use of firearms, the techniques of espionage, a variety of martial arts, the art of debating—to win—and automotive repair. We studied economics, finance, and every aspect of business administration. We understand the workings of most commonplace technological items prevalent in the era that ended in 1962: Jeffrey can fix small electrical appliances, air conditioners, typewriters, televisions, cash registers, washers, dryers, you name it, and Daria and I can both type eighty words a minute, tend bar, and take shorthand.

And lest you go away unimpressed, let me mention this. When the bombs fell and the Bunker doors swung shut with a big thud, inside were more than a few representatives of the two best spook outfits on Earth. Anyway, the descendants of those Spy-vs.-Spy types imparted to us state-of-the-art skills in laundering money, discreetly converting *many* precious jewels to cash, and placing large amounts of genuine 1962 big bills in bank accounts without attracting undue attention. Suffice it to say that if you pressed me for details, I could give them.

Why all this preparation in the nitty-gritty skills of life, since if we succeed tomorrow we may just melt into nothingness, like the wicked witch in *The Wizard of Oz?* Well, if we end up in an alternate world, we could run short of cash. Or maybe history *can* be changed—but our persuasive skills turn out to be less than stellar and we can't change Kennedy's mind. Then we'll have to beat a hurried retreat from the Oval Office and jump back a year or two in time. We'll regroup, and look for another way to influence the course of events, perhaps from the Russian end.

In all this confusion we might be forced to go to ground in a major urban area. We may lose our stash of money and jewels. In either case, we can assume anonymous, low-profile jobs and survive economically while waiting for another opportunity. In a word, we're as well prepared to meet the real world of 1962 as any three kids who have lived indoors their entire life could possibly be.

Why, you wonder, would the Bunker's governors send teenagers back in time instead of adults, given the importance of the mission? Daria gave away part of the answer in her worries last night. At eighteen, we are still young enough to cope with the concept of Going Outside. By age thirty or so, the first generation of children born in the Bunker began to report feelings of acute anxiety at the mere thought of leaving the confines of the Bunker. The next generation developed a virtual phobia concerning the notion. They got the shakes just thinking about it by age twenty-five! The third generation started getting fruit-loopy at the prospect around age twenty-two.

Anyway, while the thought of Going Outside is somewhat discomfiting to my generation, we could still do it at age eighteen or so, if necessary. Our elders just plain couldn't.

That's one reason. The others are more obvious. At eighteen we're at the peak of our physical powers, and with proper maintenance, we can stay there for many years. The time machine has enough juice for three more jumps, and we're young enough to manipulate events and save the world from several additional nuclear wars should we need to use those jumps.

Father Alexeyev had his own opinion as to why they chose teenagers for the mission. It was rather cynical. "Eighteen-year-olds," he said, "don't really believe they can be killed."

We three are close. There is affection, but little attraction between us. There's not much mystery associated with the opposite sex in the Bunker; I mean, it's hard to get a crush on the guy who's occupied the next dorm room for fifteen years.

Also, the Bunker is not the most conducive place in the world for romance, period. Because of the limited gene pool, if you're a woman, you can't just marry anybody you like. You are required to have two children, each with a different father, chosen by the computer. It compares your genetic profile to those of all the men in the Bunker, and then fixes you up on a big fat double-date with the two lucky guys whose profiles—when paired with yours— maximize the Bunker's genetic diversity.

Don't worry, it's not all *that* bad; there is a God, and He invented artificial insemination! Anyhow, if you're in love with Guy #1, all this tomfoolery with Guys #2 and #3 tends to put a cramp in your love life. It really spoils the mood—especially since if you conceive a child with Guy #1, it's off for a D&C.

Needless to say, this arrangement also plays hell with family ties and parental bonding. So, if you detect a certain flatness of emotion in my references to our parents, do try to be understanding. In the Bunker your biological parents almost never live together—and may not even like each other. You're raised by your mother and, if you're lucky, the man she does love, does live with, but must never have a child with.

In any case, no matter who you live with, your guardians' duties in the Bunker will take them from their assigned room for most of the day, so you will spend most of your time with the handful of individuals charged with raising Salamander's latest crop of children. Again, so much for family bonding.

I guess romance was just one more casualty of World War III. Well, at least we have movies and tapes of TV. I swear Daria hopes we get bounced into an alternate world just so one day she can go to Los Angeles and meet Rod Taylor.

Me, I want Rod Serling.

## November 1, 2062; 6:30 A.M.

At 6:30 we were scheduled to assemble in the Green Lab, on level six of the Bunker, to begin our journey. I had finally gotten to sleep and then almost overslept, so when I arrived Jeffrey and Daria were there before me.

We were all scared to death, though our college-kid period costumes were diverting. These clothes were the real thing, preserved in a deep freeze or super mothballs or something for a hundred years. Daria and I both wore slim-cut gray wool skirts, pink cashmere sweaters with strings of real pearls, garters and hose, and pumps of soft black leather. We wore our hair teased, styled in a flip, and pulled back behind the ears to show off our genuine little pearl clip earrings. Jeffrey wore nice slacks and shoes, an oxford shirt, and a crewneck sweater.

Only a handful of people were there to see us off: our parents, the science director-general, and a few friends. No staff was needed to oversee the jump; the hardware and required juice were already in the machine in Jeffrey's backpack.

It was a quick leave-taking. Everyone knew that prolonging it could only undermine our nerve. So we kissed our parents and friends good-bye forever, shook hands with the director, and turned our backs on them. We took up positions in a Stonehenge-like circle, entwined our arms, and waited. Our destination? Thousands of miles to the east in the Oval Office of the White House. The time? Three o'clock the morning of Saturday, October 27, 1962, which would soon prove to be the most dangerous day of the Cuban missile crisis. There we would lie in wait for John Kennedy; it is a matter of historical fact that during the crisis he always went to his office first, even when Excomm (the Executive Committee of the National Security Council) was meeting in the Cabinet Room.

Jeffrey mumbled a few words from a Russian Orthodox prayer. Though his ancestors were dedicated Commies, you'd be surprised how quick the old religion came back once they were stranded in the Bunker. The old no-atheists-in-foxholes bit, you know.

Then Daria reached over and threw the switch. I thought my heart was going to pound clear out of my chest. I braced myself and closed my eyes. The transition was supposed to be quick—so quick, a mere thousandth of a second long, that no physical protection was needed for the time traveler.

For a brief moment it looked like nothing was going to happen. Then I became aware of a giddy, swimming, disoriented feeling, like when the first shock waves from an earthquake shake the Bunker. This was followed by a plunge into darkness and a wrenching sensation that seemed to turn my guts inside out. I hung onto Daria and Jeffrey for dear life. A force slammed my whole body and knocked me against my companions. The floor seemed to vanish from under my feet, but just as quickly reappeared. Then all was silent and quiet.

After a moment I raised my head and opened my eyes a tiny bit. "Well, guys," I whispered, "we're somewhere."

I was in a large oval-shaped room, looking right at a bookcase built into a wall. This was topped by a beautiful plaster shell motif and had four shelves of photographs, knickknacks, and handsomely bound books. So far, so good. I turned my head to the left and caught a glimpse of a wooden cabinet on top of which rested a model of a sailing ship. There was a very large, shiny carved wooden desk, flanked by a couple of flags and three tall windows hung with heavy, rich-looking drapes. Behind the desk was a display table with still another model of a sailing ship. Whoever worked there definitely liked ships. It was all very reassuring; I could hardly believe our luck.

Then, to my consternation, I realized the room was brightly lit. That was no good; at three in the morning, the Oval Office should have been deserted and dark.

The others opened their eyes too. "Oh, damn," I whispered, "something's really wrong."

# 2

Saturday, October 27, 1962; 3:00 A.M.

Jeffrey and I drew breath, let go our stranglehold on Daria, and straightened up. Then we turned and looked around.

We saw the two men—and recognized them—at the same time. One was sitting in the famous rocking chair, the other in the ordinary wooden chair of a mere mortal. They seemed to have been in deep conversation quite recently. Apparently they hadn't been able to sleep that night any better than I. Both were staring at us in utter amazement.

Seeing as how things had not gone according to plan, Jeffrey had an attack of nerves and cried, *"O chort! O gospodi!"*

The younger man, Robert Francis Kennedy, jumped to his feet. "Jack, that's *Russian!*" he exclaimed. He strode over to the table and started to reach for a telephone.

"Please, no! Stop! Wait!" I screamed. He paused for an instant. "We're Americans!" I cried. "We're here to help you!"

Robert Kennedy shook his head and began to dial a number.

"Listen to us!" bellowed Jeffrey. "If you don't, there's going to be a nuclear war!"

He hesitated for a fraction of a second. In desperation, I appealed to the older man, John Fitzgerald Kennedy.

33

"Please, Mr. President, listen to us, I beg you! You've got nothing to lose."

He favored me with a cold, assessing look. Despite all his idealistic speeches of record, he looked like one tough cookie, not so easy to convince. And yet, I sensed we'd just told him something he was very much interested in hearing.

"Hold it, Bobby," he said to his brother, his tone more than a little sardonic. "It's not every day visitors pop in out of thin air. Let's hear what they have to say."

"For God's sake, Jack, the boy was speaking Russian!"

Kennedy leaned back in his chair and continued to size us up. "Bobby," he said, "if they're Russians, they sure as hell don't need those Cuban missiles."

He grinned, so cool he should have had a big Havana cigar to light up right then. "So," he asked, taking his time, "where are you kids from?"

I suppressed a hysterical laugh. He had balls. Great, big, fat shiny ones, made of brass. I wanted to kiss him, because now I knew we had a chance.

Jeffrey drew a deep breath, squared his shoulders, and looked back at Kennedy. "From the Bunker, sir. Salamander Bunker, on Mount Diablo, near Livermore."

That got to him. His eyes widened and he exchanged an incredulous glance with his brother.

Robert swallowed. "That's impossible!" he snapped.

"Oh, I don't know," said John, with the barest hint of a smile. "Now you see 'em, now you don't? So far I could buy it."

Robert scowled. "Any magician at the Magic Castle could put on the same show!"

Hearing that, Daria gasped out loud. *The Magic Castle!* In spite of the head-splitting tension of the moment, her eyes shone at the mere mention of a Hollywood treasure, and she looked to be on the verge of asking Robert Kennedy when he had last gone there and what he'd eaten at dinner.

"For Christ's sake, shut up, Daria!" I whispered.

"What's this?" asked John.

"Nothing," I said in disgust. "Actually, it's Hollywood. She idolizes it; she's read all about it in books and she's gone 'round the bend. She'd give anything to meet Rod Taylor."

Both Kennedys looked astounded. But, more importantly for us, they looked disarmed. Momentarily, anyway. Cleverly seizing the opportunity, Jeffrey stepped forward. "Mr. President, Mr. Attorney General," he said, "we *are* from the Bunker, so please hear us out and let us show you the exhibits we've brought. Later today you will receive a lot of bad news, which will make it seem that war with the Soviet Union is inevitable. When that happens, you must not give in to the hawks on Excomm. You must stand your ground and resist those who wish to launch the air strike and the invasion. If you don't, the world will be destroyed."

For what felt like a very long time, John Kennedy eyed us. Then Robert went for the phone again.

"Drop it, Bobby!" John ordered.

"Drop it? I'm going to call security and—"

"No, you're not. You're going to listen to what these kids have to say."

"Are you crazy?" Robert was outraged. "We're in danger!"

"Yes, you are," said Jeffrey, "but not from us."

John digested that. "Sit down, Bobby," he said. "Maybe you can explain their popping out of thin air with this Russian business, but how the hell do they know about the Bunker?"

Jeffrey caught the ball and ran with it. He picked up one of the suitcases we'd brought and said, "Mr. President, we've brought some exhibits to show you. May I put them on the table?"

"In a minute. First, explain about the Bunker."

Jeffrey looked at him solemnly. "We were born there."

The President frowned. "That doesn't make any sense. It's just a lab. No one lives there now."

"Not now, sir. But they will, after the war."

He shook his head. "You still can't have been born there."

"Not yet, sir. But we will be, in a hundred years."

Kennedy stared at him. He had the remains of a summer Hyannisport tan, and so you could really see it when he turned white underneath. He was a smart man, possessed of a great capacity for vision. He almost believed Jeffrey.

"Oh-kay. Right. Holy Jesus, you're from the future. Shit, why not Mars?" He waved in the general direction of the table. "Five minutes. Don't jerk me around."

Jeffrey scrambled and began unpacking the suitcase. First he took out a copy of the letter that I had attached to my first journal entry—the one from Jeffrey's ancestor, Sergei Kharitonov, to his wife Lara. He gave that to Kennedy and told him to read it. Then he set about putting the exhibits in order.

Kennedy spent a long time reading the letter. By the time he had finished, he looked as if we had slugged him in the nuts, hard.

When he raised his eyes, Jeffrey struck like a cobra. "If you're done, sir," he said in a smooth, professional voice, "let me direct your attention to these documents." Kennedy and his brother approached the table and examined them. They included transcripts of key White House communications with the Joint Chiefs of Staff and the Strategic Air Command from October 26–31, 1962, which, of course, had been sent electronically to that ultimate repository of historical records, the Bunker. We had included material from the day just past, the twenty-sixth, so that Kennedy would recognize in our transcripts his own secret communications with those august entities over the past twenty-four hours, and be convinced of the validity of the whole package. Then we brought out a little battery-powered TV monitor, no bigger than your hand, and a little video player, both developed in the Bunker, which made the President's eyes bug out of his head. Using these, we showed him a tape of the live TV coverage—from an aircraft—of the bombing of Washington, D.C. Then we laid out numerous still photographs of what the city looked like afterward. In color. There were some close-ups taken by people who knew they were going to die anyway, and went out into the ruins to record it all for posterity. These were real stomach-turners.

"They're fakes. They've got to be fakes," said Robert Kennedy, getting up and pacing around the room.

"If so," said John, gray-faced, "they're the best I've ever seen. Somebody went to incredible trouble to prepare them."

Bobby rolled his eyes. "They're still fakes, Jack. These jokers aren't from the future. They can't be. It's impossible."

"Oh?" said John, his voice caustic. "Then kindly tell me where this fucking fake miniature television came from and this fake thing that plays these—what did he call them?—videotapes!"

"Sure!" said Robert Kennedy, with a sidewise dirty look in our direction. "You can buy a little tiny battery-powered Sony television right now at Abercrombie & Fitch for two hundred dollars. The kids were begging for one last weekend."

"I've seen those," replied John. "They're three times the size of this one. And I don't see the name 'Sony' on the front!"

Robert Kennedy paused in his pacing and nailed Jeffrey with a hard gaze. "Sorry to sound like a broken record, son, but when you first popped in here, you were speaking Russian. I'd like you to explain that right now."

"Very well," Jeffrey answered. "There was a goodwill tour of Soviet scientists in San Francisco when the missiles were launched. No bombs fell directly on San Francisco, so the scientists had time to drive to the Bunker near Livermore. Since we are descended from Americans and Soviets, we are taught both English and Russian as children. I endeavor to speak Russian just as well as I do English, since I'm proud of my heritage."

"Okay, okay. He's got an answer for everything, doesn't he?" said Robert, and sat down again.

John nodded. "I know that tour. In fact, I know just where it is right now. Which one of those guys was your ancestor?"

"The scientist Kharitonov, of course," said Jeffrey, his nose in the air. "The one who wrote the letter we showed you. It belongs to me, as do all his precious books and papers."

John whistled. "Sergei Kharitonov! One of their best, to be sure. Knows Khrushchev personally." He sat back in his chair and looked at Jeffrey. "Okay, tell me your version of what's going to happen. But I warn you, it's going to be hard to convince me. Khrushchev just sent us a conciliatory letter, and even now we are close to an agreement."

Jeffrey gave him a knowing smile. "On October 20," he said, "your Executive Committee of the National Security Council voted eleven to six to blockade Cuba, rather than launch an air strike. The possibility was left open for an air strike at a later date, if the blockade did not result in the missiles being removed from Cuba. On October 22, you announced the blockade on national television. On the twenty-fourth, you received good news—a dozen Soviet vessels bound for Cuba had turned back. Yesterday, the twenty-sixth, you received very good news indeed. John Scali, an ABC diplomatic correspondent, had been contacted informally by Alexander Fomin, a Soviet embassy counselor whom you suspect of being the local KGB chief of Soviet operations. This led to the delivery of a letter from Khrushchev calling for normalization of relations and removal of the missiles in exchange for your pledge not to invade Cuba. Your Mr. Acheson judged from the tone of the letter that Premier Khrushchev was either 'tight or scared.'"

The Kennedys glanced at each other. "Either he's the real thing," John said, pointing at Jeffrey, "or else he's their top spy, and he's in our bag. Either way, we're looking good."

"Here is what will happen today," Jeffrey went on, ignoring the comment. "This morning Robert Kennedy will receive a memo from J. Edgar Hoover stating that Soviet personnel in New York are preparing to destroy all sensitive documents in preparation for war. Then you, Mr. President, will receive a second letter from Premier Khrushchev, contradicting the one received yesterday, which will demand that you trade your missile bases in Turkey for the missiles in Cuba. At ten-fifteen in the morning Major Rudolph Anderson and his U-2 spy plane will be shot down over Cuba by a newly operational Soviet surface-to-air missile."

"There!" cried Robert. "There! They may have a notion one of our planes will be shot down later today. They may even know what time the Soviets will be gunning for it. But so help me God, they can't know who will be the damn pilot!"

Jeffrey gazed at him, cool as a cucumber. "Quite true, Mr. Attorney General. Therefore, logically, if a Major Rudolph Anderson is shot down at ten-fifteen this morning, that will prove we're the genuine article, won't it?"

"Well, yes. I shall wait for the news with bated breath!"

"Be my guest," replied Jeffrey, and continued with his story. "The members of Excomm, pressured by your Joint Chiefs, will conclude that Soviet actions have now entered a military phase. There will be almost unanimous agreement that the United States must bomb the Cuban missile sites no later than Tuesday, which action must be followed immediately by an invasion. You will assert that the Soviets should be given more time to consider their position before the United States attacks Cuba, but you will allow yourself to be overruled, because you are worried about being impeached if you don't act, and by that time you will no longer be completely convinced that your more cautious position is the correct one.

"You will launch an air strike and invasion on Tuesday, the thirtieth. From then on it will happen just as described in Kharitonov's letter. Soviet commanders in Cuba will fire their short-range battlefield nukes at the American forces landing on the beaches. Soviet bombers will—"

"Wait!" cried the President. "There aren't any battlefield nuclear weapons in Cuba!"

"Yes, there are," said Jeffrey. "You just don't know it yet. Furthermore, the on-site Soviet commanders have the authority to fire them. Only the longer-range missiles are under Khrushchev's personal control."

Kennedy's face turned ashen. "How can you know this?"

"As you well know, the Bunker is a national information repository," replied Jeffrey, with just a hint of impatience. "We continued to receive transmissions concerning the progress of the war until the very end, when Washington was destroyed and our communication links with the Strategic Air Command were severed."

There was not a peep from either Kennedy. "There's even more stuff you don't know," said Jeffrey. "For example, you've grossly underestimated the number of Soviet troops in Cuba. There are forty thousand of them."

Robert Kennedy swore. John said, "Go on. Finish."

"Soviet bombers will strike your missile bases in Turkey on Wednesday morning, the thirty-first. You, of course, will then attack missile bases inside the Soviet Union by late afternoon. By the afternoon of October 31, it will escalate out of control. No surgical air strike is 100 percent effective. You will have missed a few missiles in Cuba, and they will be fired at New York and Washington. You will respond with your own long-range missiles—all of them—and lay waste the Soviet Union. Then the Soviets will launch all their missiles at the U.S. and its NATO allies."

"*All* the missiles? Both of us? You're sure?" John Kennedy interrupted. Jeffrey nodded.

"But that's insane!"

We didn't say anything. What was there to say?

Kennedy put a hand to his face, and then lowered it. He made a fist, and opened and closed it several times, seemingly unaware of the motion. Jeffrey, encouraged, proceeded to lay it on with a trowel. "Even though a few cities, like San Francisco, will not be hit by the missiles, they will be destroyed later. Fallout will be borne across the planet and decimate those population centers not already levelled by the bombs. A cloud of dust and debris will cover the Earth, blocking out sunlight and preventing plants and crops from growing. The atmosphere's ozone shield, without which most forms of life cannot exist, will be destroyed. Except for the Bunker, civilization will vanish from the face of the Earth.

"Mr. President, the Bunker has endured for a hundred years. In all that time there has not been one shred of evidence that a single other human settlement survived the war! I tell you, Mr. President, *everything is gone*—plants, animals, forests, people, cities, *everything you can think of!*"

Kennedy said nothing. He looked ghastly. I mean, how would you look under the circumstances?

Jeffrey smiled. "It took a full hundred years to develop a working time machine. As you know, such a project is under consideration at Salamander even now."

Kennedy cradled his head in his hands, as if he had a massive headache. "Yes, as a matter of fact it is."

"It was very fitting the war culminated on Halloween, Mr. President," said Jeffrey.

Kennedy looked up, his face drawn. "Why is that?"

"In pagan times the ancient Celts also celebrated Halloween, though they called it Samhain. Then the onset of winter and the death of the fruitful Earth were marked by the lighting of great bonfires and the slaughter of animals for food. Such a festival might mark equally well the coming of an atomic war, don't you think—given its celebration of fire, cold, and death?"

Kennedy actually shuddered. "You are speaking to one already convinced of the folly of war, young man. Now let us be practical. What should I do?"

"Stand your ground," replied Jeffrey. "Believe the message of the first letter. Khrushchev doesn't want to die, and he doesn't hate America! I mean, he loved San Francisco when he visited there three years ago. Everyone in Moscow knows he went to hear Benny Goodman's opening at the Red Army Sports Palace last summer and went crazy over the King Porter Stomp, even though he's too fat to dance. He's just in over his head, and he wants out. So give him a way out, no matter what Excomm says."

"I see," said Kennedy. With a pensive look, he got to his feet, clasped his hands behind his back, and looked at Daria and me. "I haven't heard from you ladies yet," he said. "What do you think I should do?"

I took a chance. I walked over to meet him, and stood very close. I looked up into his face and said, "Mr. President, you may still doubt us, but later this very morning, when everything we've predicted comes true, right down to the identity of the U-2 pilot Major Anderson, you will believe. Then you will do what is necessary to save the world."

He looked right back into my eyes. He nodded, and smiled. And for that moment, he made me feel like I was the most important person in the world.

Stop! Anna Leah calls time out!

There were a number of things we didn't like about the President. I mean, he was the one with the itchy trigger finger, who launched the Cuban invasion at the moment things were about to cool down . . . and got our world blown up in the process.

Also, enough intelligence had filtered back to the Bunker by the end of 1962 for us to draw a pretty good bead on the President's off-duty character. We knew about his many peccadilloes with women, his reputed underworld connections, his sharp dealings with political competitors. Rest assured, there was plenty in our archives to paint a damn clear picture of John F. Kennedy, shitheel.

I knew all that then. To this day I don't contest it. Yet there was much more to him than that. There have been

people like him all through history. In such individuals, a
great capacity to inspire comes part and parcel with their
darker side. When they use their abilities to kindle the best
in others, the very angels sing. Or ought to, at any rate.

Kennedy was one of those people—wonderful and vital
and full of magnificence, like Henry the Fifth must have
been on St. Crispin's Day. I remembered what Jackie had
written in a magazine article about their first meeting: that
Kennedy was like a walking fountain of youth. Looking at
him in the Oval Office that night in October 1962, I
understood what she meant. Young and full of energy, he
was not a symbol of the country's accomplishments, but of
its potential, of glory yet to come.

Think back. When you were eighteen you had achieved
little; it was, as yet, too early. Yet your whole life was lit up
with a golden glow, because the horizon was still wide and
bright and very far away, and you could still achieve
anything within the reach of humankind.

Kennedy made lots of people who were long past
eighteen feel like that. He embodied youth and hope and
promise. When his countrymen looked at him, they felt that
all the possibilities of life still lay before them. He made
them believe they could change the world—and so, for a
short while, they could.

In such rare and precious times, the Land of Oz is near.
One who inspires faith can really make your heart's desire
come true, because that faith makes you believe. And strive,
and keep on striving, long past the point where any sane
person would throw in the towel. And, more often than you
would think possible, such foolish effort ends by bearing
fruit.

"Fair enough," Kennedy said. "If your predictions come
true, then I will stand my ground, and there shall be no air
strike." He turned away from me, and paused. "Or perhaps,"
he said in a low voice, "I will stand my ground no matter
what." He took a deep breath. "I'll need you kids to hang

around here for a while, if I'm going to put you to the test. You look like you could use some sleep. Bobby, call security and have them ready the cot room."

At the word "security," Jeffrey and I tensed up. "Oh, don't be alarmed," said Kennedy. "I won't double-cross you." When we did not visibly relax, he added, "Really, it's not my style!"

When the President commanded, people hopped to it. In less than five minutes the Kennedys and a White House security guard were leading us out of the Oval Office and down a corridor to a plain, unmarked locked door. Once opened, it gave onto a spacious room containing a large square wooden table flanked by chairs, half a dozen cots with sheets, blankets, and sumptuous pillows, and a separate bathroom and wet bar. We checked out this last immediately, and found it came complete with glasses, cups, a pot for heating water, and an eye-popping assortment of exotic instant coffees, teas, soups, broths, and cocoas in a plastic box. We all went over to the bar and took the mixes out of the box and handled them, passing them back and forth among us. Then Daria figured out there was a miniature refrigerator under the sink and opened it. Inside were lots and lots of little glass bottles—fruit juices, vegetable juices, milk, and mineral water.

"Oh!" said Daria, like Marilyn Monroe being kissed.

"Sleep well," said the President, giving us the grandfather of all strange looks. "I'll be back before you know it."

We nodded. All we could focus on, by that point, were the drinks—and the cots. Kennedy jabbed his brother with one elbow and grinned. "Go wake Rene," he said. "I've got a job for him."

I looked at Jeffrey. "Who's Rene?" I hissed.

"Damned if I know," he replied.

I grunted, and joined Daria beside the wet bar. Before we went to sleep, we had tasted all its contents, and the bar looked like a tornado had hit it.

Saturday, October 27, 1962; 8:00 A.M.

Kennedy himself knocked on our door at eight in the morning. He swept into the room, followed by his brother and a stranger dressed all in white, who sported a large cylindrical hat, much like a chimney. This man was grinning like it was Christmas and carried an enormous silver tray laden with covered dishes. With a flourish, Kennedy draped a damask cloth over the wooden table next to our cots. "My friends," he said, "may I present the White House chef, Monsieur Rene Verdon."

"So pleased to meet you," said the Frenchman, sounding exactly like Charles Boyer in the beloved movies we used to watch in the Bunker as children. "Breakfast is served!" He set the tray down and motioned for us to approach the table.

We had not gotten near enough sleep. In fact, Jeffrey almost fell over himself getting out of bed. But sleep mattered no longer; nothing mattered except the incredible, intoxicating, and utterly unfamiliar smells coming from the tray. We drew round it like moths to an open flame, and stared like so many Ray Bradbury boys at a carnival sideshow on a cold October night.

*"Bon appetit!"* said Kennedy, grinning, and begun humming to himself. He looked as jolly as Monsieur Verdon, but his eyes never, ever left us. Robert stood slightly behind him, to the right, and watched us too.

I wondered briefly what was on their minds, but then forgot all about it, for Monsieur Verdon put great snowy napkins in our laps and placed before us silver knives, forks, and spoons, and beautiful ivory-colored bone china dishes like we had seen in books. He picked up a large silver pot with a long spout and inquired of Daria and me in turn, "Coffee, mademoiselle?" As if in a dream, we nodded, and he filled our cups.

How can I describe the smell of that first coffee? We had

read about coffee, like we had read about everything else in the world that made life worth living, that we could never have. And of course, we were completely unprepared for it. I bent over and sniffed the air above my cup; I was afraid to lay even a finger on that delicate thing because my hands were shaking so.

"Cream, mademoiselle?" said Verdon, appearing at my elbow once again. He proffered a lovely white saucer on which there was a little pitcher of rich cream, so cold that a film of water had condensed on its outside surface. I raised my hand and started to take it, but I knew I would drop it, so I just nodded as hard as I could. He poured cream into my cup until the coffee turned a beautiful light brown color, and then went on to Daria.

I did not want to embarrass us. I thought I should wait, but by the time he was serving coffee to Jeffrey, I could sit still no longer, and broke. I bent over, grasped my cup with both hands so they wouldn't shake as much, and gulped the steaming coffee like I was starving. I have a fleeting memory that the Kennedys looked startled, but I'm not really sure whether I actually saw this, or just imagined it later. Verdon refilled my cup with coffee and cream, and then, with more grand flourishes, removed the covers from several of the dishes.

Great clouds of steam rose up, as did a host of aromas from foods that no longer existed in our world. It was like scenes of fine dining in the movies, only the food was real and we could smell it. There was a heaping stack of pancakes, dripping with dark blue syrup that appeared to have berries in it. On another plate there was a pile of hot, tender biscuits, accompanied by a little round porcelain dish of chilled whipped butter and another of sweet red jam. On still another there was a Lucullan assortment of meat and meat by-products. I could identify each and every one of them because I had read all the cookbooks in our library: bacon, fried ham, little cylindrical sausages, and flat sausage patties that looked like they had a lot of pepper in them.

There was a large bowl of fresh fruit, cut up, and another
plate piled high with triangles of bread, toasted and already
brushed with yellow butter. "Ladies and gentleman," said
Verdon, "because we did not know how you preferred your
eggs, we prepared several varieties." With that, he removed
the covers from the last remaining dishes.

Daria gasped. Jeffrey just looked stunned. I wanted to die.
There were four different egg dishes, all of them like something out of a fairy tale. "This is called Souffle Marthe,"
said Monsieur Verdon. "A very simple dish, merely eggs,
butter, milk, and a little flour, poured over tender tips of
fresh asparagus and baked in the oven until golden brown.
And here we have Scrambled Eggs Carmaux—we take
eggs, butter, a touch of sweet heavy cream, a little curry
powder and paprika, and scramble them together with some
delicious cooked lobster meat from the state of Maine. Over
here we have prepared an Omelette Louis, which you see is
a little pouch of eggs folded over spices, parsley, onions,
and Gruyère cheese. And last of all, you may choose Eggs
Benedict—"

Daria let out a funny, gulping cry and lowered her head.
I looked up at Verdon and nodded again with all my might,
which seemed to be the only response I could make. It
seemed to dawn on him then that there really was something
wrong with us, that we were not your ordinary White House
breakfast guests. With an expression of chagrin, he quickly
set to filling our plates with tastes of each and every one of
the offerings.

"Rene, they've been away," said John Kennedy, softly.
"In the Peace Corps."

I picked up my fork, and then put it down, thinking a
spoon was all I was good for. I hunkered down, getting my
face as close to my plate as I dared, and began to spoon food
into my mouth. At first I tried to go slowly and taste
everything, but then I got overcome, and began to shovel
everything down like I thought it would run away from me
otherwise.

"Juice?" said Monsieur Verdon gently. "Milk, anyone?" But nobody seemed to hear him. After a moment he began to move around the table, silently refilling our plates.

I ate until I felt dizzy. Then all the chickens came home to roost, so to speak. I began to tremble, and I knew I was going to start crying. We had not been in 1962 more than a few hours, and already we had discovered so many incredibly wonderful things that the war had denied us. How many more were there? If we had to stay in 1962, there would be hundreds or even thousands of such discoveries to come. How could we bear them?

For a moment I really hated Kennedy, because he was the man who had failed us, who had brought down the world and taken away such treasures from the survivors in the Bunker. A great rage welled up inside me, and I could hold in my tears no longer. I began to sob. I reached for my cup of coffee, thinking maybe a swallow would make me stop, and this time I did knock the cup to the floor and break it. Utterly humiliated, I looked over at Jeffrey for support, but he hadn't even noticed. His face was full of misery, and he was just looking down at a piece of bacon he was holding, as if it contained all the secrets of the world. I looked at Daria, and saw she was crying too, dribbling tears all over the front of her sweater.

I raised my head. Both Kennedys were staring at me.

You read in books how people turn white when something horrible happens; well, it's true—both of them did. Robert also looked mortified, while John's expression was more complex: a jumble of pity, of chagrin, of realization, and of profound embarrassment at having done something—I couldn't tell what—that he was very ashamed of.

Then I figured it out. This grand breakfast had been a test. Until then he hadn't really believed we were from the Bunker or the future. And to be fair, we hadn't expected him to believe for another couple of hours, until the new Khrushchev letter came over the wires and Major Anderson got shot down. So, in a prospecting frame of mind, he had sprung the food on us to observe our reactions, hoping to glean a clue or two as to our real origin and our mission at the White House. Instead he had gotten more than he bargained for. Playing games, he had ripped aside our dignity and exposed our poverty for all to see. And now he felt like a first-class prick.

At that very moment, something strange happened. It reminded me of the sensation of traveling through time—it had the same familiar giddy, swimming feeling, and produced the same momentary disorientation. But this time there was no shock wave, no wrenching apart of the fabric of time. Instead I experienced a singular perceptual shift. The whole tableau before me seemed to transform, as if a black-and-white photograph on a screen were briefly replaced by its negative. Then it righted itself again.

Only later, upon reflection, would it dawn on me that that was the precise moment the future changed. A couple of hours on, around ten A.M. when the second Khrushchev letter came and Kennedy heard the news of Major Anderson's death—all that was only icing on the cake. Kennedy first believed us, in his heart of hearts, when the food made us weep at breakfast. That was the moment when he resolved to stand firm against an air strike; that was the moment when history changed, and the world was saved.

Well, *this* world, anyway—*this* alternate world. For when President Kennedy made up his mind against the air strike, the course of history took an alternate route, into a second world where the Bunker would never exist. The fact that we three weren't snuffed out was proof that we had jumped ship into a new Earth, one where our very existence was not an impossible contradiction.

Only later that night, talking in the dark before sleep, would it really come home to us that we hadn't stopped the destruction of our own world. It couldn't be done. By going back to 1962, we had only forced a branching in the path of time and brought about the birth of a new, alternate world, in a parallel dimension—one in which the terrible future we

knew did not exist. In that new world we were now
safe—and marooned.

Anyway, after breakfast the Kennedys withdrew to meet
with Excomm in the Cabinet Room, leaving us alone. About
an hour later they rushed back into the room with a copy of
Khrushchev's second letter, which had just clattered in over
the teletype. I must say Robert Kennedy looked remarkably
subdued. And a few minutes later, more bad news arrived.
Just as we had foretold, poor Major Anderson had been shot
down over Cuba.

Both Robert and John came over to us, pulled up chairs,
and sat down. Robert took a deep breath, sighed loudly, and
said, "For the sake of argument, I'm willing to proceed as if
you're the genuine article. We can't do anything about
Major Anderson, but what the hell do you kids suggest we
do about the letter?"

"In the past weeks, I've been severely criticized for not
being tough enough on the Soviets," said John. "Now it
looks like my blockade isn't working. Khrushchev—or
whatever Commie committee wrote this letter—has become belligerent. The Soviets appear to have escalated the
confrontation into a military phase. The brass hats, particularly that bomb-fucking jerk Curtis LeMay, are on my ass to
respond in kind and knock out the Soviet missiles. If I do
that, I have no choice but to follow up with an invasion.
Now that you kids have proven yourselves, you can damn
well help out. Where do we go from here?"

"Yeah. The second letter completely contradicts the first,"
said Robert. "We're stumped."

So were we. Except for Daria. "Just ignore it," she said.
"Reply to the first one."

"What? That's crazy!" said Robert.

"Sure. But it worked for me."

*"Huh?"* said John.

She laughed. "Oh, yeah. Last year this boy wrote me
these notes about going steady. In one, he got carried away,

and wrote all this mushy stuff he was ashamed of later. He followed it up with a second that said he didn't mean any of it. I pretended I didn't get the second one, and we ended up going steady for a while. Just apply the same principle, Mr. Kennedy. You guys just pretend you didn't get the second letter."

John crossed his arms, looked at her, and sighed. "Sweetheart, the Russians *know* we got the second letter!"

"Sure they do. But this isn't about reality. It's about feelings, and saving face. You'd be amazed what people will pretend to believe, if you only let them."

Robert looked at John. "I don't know."

John frowned. "Bobby," he said, "let's take the lady's advice, unless you've got a better idea."

That's just what they did. They replied to the first letter and praised the statesmanship of Premier Khrushchev. With great relief, the Soviets accepted their terms. And so Kennedy, with the complicity of the entire upper echelon of the Communist Party of the USSR, ensured that the world lived to see another day.

Everyone breathed a gigantic sigh of relief. Before long, we're told, Christmas decorations went up in American stores (obnoxiously soon after Halloween, and way too long before Thanksgiving). Church attendance briefly increased.

Apparently the only man in America who was pissed at the way things turned out was General Curtis LeMay. This was the guy who was later said to have coined the phrase, "Bomb them back to the Stone Age." It was widely reported that he was disgusted with the overly peaceful way the crisis had been resolved.

I had a feeling we would hear more of him.


Sunday, October 28, 1962; 12:00 P.M.


Late Saturday night, when it was all over, the Kennedys thoughtfully allowed us to bathe and take another very long nap in the cot room. We didn't wake up until almost noon on Sunday. And we only woke then because Rene Verdon brought us breakfast—delicious and ample and satisfying, but, I must admit, a tad less resplendent and sadistic than our repast of the morning before.

"Better late than never," said John, drawing up a chair. "I would like to know each of your names." We told him. All the while Robert hovered in the background, looking anxious.

"Where would you kids like to go? What would you like to do?" John asked.

We had talked about this briefly the previous night, before we fell into exhausted sleep. "We'd like to go to San Francisco," said Jeffrey. "You see, we have this affinity for the West Coast. We feel we know it best."

"Very well," said John, "to San Francisco you shall go. I'll ask Pierre Salinger, my press secretary, to take you to the airport. If you like, he can also accompany you to San Francisco and help you get settled. He was born there."

"No, no. We'll take the lift to the airport, but that's all," said Jeffrey. "We've got to learn to fend for ourselves."

"Do you have money?"

We exchanged glances. "Yes, we have some money," Jeffrey replied. "It's real money from 1962. And we have many small jewels that can be exchanged for money."

Kennedy drew a fat white paper envelope from an inside pocket of his jacket and handed it to Jeffrey. "Here's a little more," he said. "It's poor enough reward for what you've done, but there's a limit to how much cold cash I can lay my hands on in the middle of the night without some asshole asking questions. I'm presuming you wish to remain anonymous."

"Absolutely," said Jeffrey.

"Do you have identification?" asked the President.

"Oh, yes. We have papers." Jeffrey gave a faint smile. "They say we're twenty-one."

Kennedy grinned back. "You thought of everything."

"*You* thought of everything, sir, when you built the Bunker," Jeffrey said softly. "We only continue the tradition."

"I see." John lowered his eyes at this reference to Salamander. For a brief moment, a shadow passed across the room. "Well," he asked, "what will you do in San Francisco?"

Jeffrey shook his head. "Start over. Learn how to live in a foreign country."

Kennedy gave a wry smile, as if he could empathize with Jeffrey's loneliness. "Better buy some suntan lotion if you're going to California. You kids are awfully pale."

Daria gave him an admirably wan look. "Comes from spending a lot of time indoors."

John looked at us pensively and then remarked, "Considering the events of the last thirty hours, you don't look all that happy. Why?"

"We are pleased," said Jeffrey.

"But you've just saved the frigging world! You should be jumping for joy."

I shook my head. "We've saved this frigging world, Mr. President, not the one we came from."

"What do you mean?" John exclaimed, and looked to Robert for an explanation. This time, Robert was quicker on the draw; judging from the look on his face, he got it. At once.

"If we'd changed the history of our world," I spoke up, "we'd all be dead now. We'd have disappeared in a puff of smoke. Logically, if there was no war and no settlement in the Bunker, we could no longer exist."

"But you're still here!" said Robert. "So you didn't."

I nodded. "We've created a new world. Picture a train, Mr. President. It's hurtling down a single track, which is history. Suppose you know there's a boulder on the track, and the train's going to crash, so you go back in time and try to remove the boulder. But the laws of nature dictate—as we have just learned—that the past can't be changed. So when you meddle, you don't remove the boulder—you create a second track, on which there's not a boulder, and a second train to speed along it."

"Well, what happened to the old world? The original world? Where is it?" John Kennedy cried.

"Somewhere. In that world, you and your family will soon be dead . . . as will everyone, except for our ancestors in Livermore."

"Good God! In that world, my mistakes live on. And the tragedy is real, to the people who live there."

"Yes, sir," I said.

"Your parents, your friends. . . . Is there any hope for them?"

"Probably not, sir. They'll try to make a go of it outside the Bunker, but the chances aren't good. The ecosystem's ruined and the land probably can't be farmed successfully."

"Then everything we do here is futile."

"Oh, I don't know," said Daria, surveying the room. "This World Number Two, it looks pretty real to me. Copy or not, I can't wait to see Hollywood."

Kennedy looked like he was about to have a nervous breakdown. At this point, it was not productive to have an overwrought President, so I tried to calm him down. "Like I said, sir, we can't help anybody back in the original world. So let's save this one, and make the best of it."

"Dear God." He looked at me, realization dawning. "You kids came here prepared to die. You really did."

"Of course," replied Jeffrey.

"You thought you were going to die no matter what! If you didn't persuade me to abandon the air strike, you would die in the ensuing nuclear war. If you did persuade me, you thought you would extinguish your own future, and die anyway!"

"That's right," I said. "The only way we'd luck out would be if the past couldn't be changed."

John shook his head. "You have enormous courage." He laughed; there was so much tension in his voice that the laugh came out as a squeak. "I should publish a new edition of *Profiles in Courage*! Except I can't put you in it. I can't tell anybody about you!"

Robert cleared his throat and sidled over to the President. "On that note, Jack," he said quietly, "you can't just let them walk out of here, not yet. Think about the TV, the tapes, all the stuff they brought. Think about what they know. You've got to debrief them. Think how much they could help us."

John looked up at him. "I gave that a lot of thought last night. I decided it's time for me to start being an honorable man. They're going to San Francisco, Bobby, and no one's going to stop them, including you. Is that clear?"

Bobby swallowed, and nodded. John looked back at us. "You've set me a damn good example. And you have shamed me."

Rising to his feet, he crossed his arms and walked slowly across the room. "I was a child when I took the oath of office last January. I had no experience, and no guts. I couldn't stand up to Khrushchev in our first meeting in Vienna back in '61 when I should have. Then I bungled the whole Bay of Pigs thing and let those Cubans down. Jesus, I singlehandedly led that Russian porker to think he could get away with this missile caper! And, except for your intervention, I wouldn't have stood up to those idiots on Excomm, and would have ruined everything. All I've been good at is giving rousing speeches, so long as Ted Sorensen could put the words in my mouth.

"That's going to change. You've taught me a great deal. Pay attention to me now and then, kids, while you're out there having fun in California. I give you my word, I'm going to be a President this country will never forget."

"Thank you, sir," said Jeffrey.

"And if you *ever* need help, contact me. Use this number." He walked back and handed Jeffrey a card.

"Thank you," Jeffrey said again.

"Bobby," said John in a brisk tone of voice, "is Mrs. Lincoln still around?" At Robert's nod, John picked up a phone and dialed his secretary. "Could you book tickets for three to San Francisco out of National Airport? In a couple of hours."

He replaced the receiver and looked at us ruefully. "I wish you could have flown out of our new Dulles airport— the jet-age airport, they're calling it. Pretty soon you'll be able to make reservations by computer, and a machine will spit out your ticket on the spot. But it won't be open for another month, so you're stuck with a flight out of National."

He stood up and shook hands with each of us in turn. "Divide your money among several bank accounts," he said sternly. "Watch out, because cities are dangerous. Keep away from con men. And don't start making investments for a few months, until you know your way around the block."

"I've thought about buying some property," said Jeffrey. "A house in the city, perhaps, and then maybe a lot of acreage north of San Francisco for a retreat."

Kennedy nodded. "Pay cash," he said, pointing to the envelope in Jeffrey's hand, "and lowball 'em."

We said good-bye. Kennedy shook hands with Jeffrey and kissed Daria and me on the cheek. I promised myself that someday, somehow, perhaps when we were all very old, I would meet him again, and kiss him back.

Bobby looked wistfully at Jeffrey's backpack. "What *are* you going to do with the tapes and TV?"

Jeffrey laughed, but underneath the humor, he wasn't about to budge. "Keep them, sir. They're heirlooms now."

Bobby gave a wan smile. "Tell me one thing, kid."

Jeffrey was on guard immediately. "What, sir?"

"Can you do it again?"

Jeffrey knew exactly what he meant. He looked back at Bobby, his face as pure as your mother's, and lied like a son of a bitch. "No, sir. The machine is back in the year 2062. There's no way we could carry it with us."

John glanced at Bobby. "If I were him, and I could do it again, I sure as hell wouldn't tell you." And he gave that inimitable Kennedy grin.

## 3

Sunday, October 28, 1962; 4:00 P.M.

By late afternoon, there was no avoiding it. We were going to have to go Outside.

We all had sweaty palms and the shakes. Jeffrey and I just handled it better than Daria. As the moment of departure for National Airport drew close, Jeff and I sat down and put our arms around her, trying to steady her nerves. At first this maneuver seemed to backfire, because she burst into tears. But after a good long cry, she started to get some of the jitters out of her system.

"I know we've got to go through with this," she said. She got up and peeked out one corner of a window, as if afraid of snipers. "It just seems so big out there . . . so *wrong*."

"Come on, Daria," said Jeff. "We've gotten through the hard part. Now it's time for the payoff. I can't wait to start going to movies and restaurants. Hey, I bet once you start shopping, I won't be able to get you to stop. Think, you'll be the only woman besides Anna in the history of the Bunker to get to go shopping—and in San Francisco, too!"

It was all a big line of bull; I could hear the quaver in his voice. But I played along. "You better watch out, Jeff. With all this shopping talk, you could be creating a monster."

Daria nodded emphatically, tears once again streaming down her face. "Hey!" I said. "We can have ice cream. Chocolate ice cream, even!"

"Forget ice cream," said Jeff, "and cut to the chase. We can have chocolate, period. And booze. I cannot wait!"

Daria laughed, but she was still just this side of full-blown hysterics. "Daria," I said as comfortingly as possible, "everything I ever read said that Mr. Salinger was a really nice guy. He's been through a lot too, so let's don't upset him. Plus, he's one of the most important men in Washington, and he's personally taking us to the airport. We owe it to everybody we left behind to behave like grownups."

"Stop trying to appeal to my pride," Daria retorted. "I don't have any." But she started to smile, and I knew she was past the worst of it.

The ample and dapper Mr. Salinger appeared on schedule and took us to National Airport in a big shiny white Buick. The President didn't tell him the Peace Corps story—rather, he said, we'd just completed a special assignment, and he told Pierre to treat us with kid gloves. The soul of discretion, Salinger did not ask a single nosey question. He was quite good-humored, as if delighted to be alive, and made pleasant small talk about the excellence of Rene Verdon's sauces and smoked a stinky Brazilian cigar as we sped toward the airport—a Brazilian cigar, of course, because to smoke a Havana at that point in time would have been impolitic.

Although we were finally Outside, it really wasn't so bad, because we were really only halfway Outside. After all, we were enclosed in a car, about the size of our dorm rooms back home, so our surroundings felt somewhat normal. All told, it was a nice way to ease into the practice.

Washington was basking in a beautiful fall afternoon, the sky bright blue, the air crisp, and the leaves on all the trees a riot of colors we had heretofore only seen in old books. Mr. Salinger sang a lively French tune; we tried to be cool and not stare at all the buildings we passed, but it was so hard! After living all our lives in a concrete warren, to find ourselves speeding through a living, breathing city was too much to take. We almost overloaded. Daria, in the backseat, put her head back and closed her eyes, as if she had a headache. Jeffrey and I tried to keep the conversation animated, but ended up sounding like idiots.

I was afraid Mr. Salinger thought we were really weird and couldn't imagine what we had been doing for the President. But he was too nice, or too diplomatic, to say so. "Don't you want to know the scoop on us?" I said, for openers.

He gave a little shrug, and took a long drag on the Brazilian stogie. "Perhaps."

"Well, you can ask a question. It's okay."

"My dear," he said, smiling as if we shared a secret, "when you work for President Kennedy, you soon learn to keep your curiosity in check."

"Oh, yeah?"

He grinned. "Yeah."

"So you're not going to ask us about things, no matter what?"

He nodded. "The last time I asked Jack to tell me the 'scoop,' as you put it, I got the scare of my life. I've decided to mind my own business for a little while."

"When was that, Mr. Salinger?"

"Just before he went on television about the missiles."

He wasn't going to be more forthcoming unless I really pushed. "Go on."

"The President was off giving a stump speech when suddenly he canceled all his plans and we went rushing back to Washington. He instructed me to tell the press that he had a cold. Well, about halfway through the flight I found myself alone in the President's cabin with him, and I said, 'Mr. President, you don't have a cold. Is something else going on?' He nodded and said, 'Yes, and when you find out, grab your balls.'" Salinger shot me a sheepish look, as if he feared such language might offend me.

"He's pretty earthy, huh? What did he do then?"

Salinger gave a deep, growly laugh. "He handed me an

envelope containing the evacuation instructions for my family, just in case. I'm still getting over the shock."

So that was how we eventually found ourselves in a terminal at National Airport and then in the first-class section of an airplane bound for San Francisco. We were by ourselves; everyone else was in coach. No sooner had we sat down than the stewardess came by and offered us something we had only seen in pictures until then: glass bottles, shaped like a woman's silhouette, full of ice-cold Coca-Cola.

Jeffrey gazed at his serving and sipped it with a look of intense absorption. "Quite exotic," he pronounced.

I murmured my assent. But Daria paid no attention to the Coke. "Are we allowed to buy alcohol?" she asked. "I would like to try my first martini now."

But Jeffrey had greater things on his mind. "Do you know how much money was in the envelope?" he whispered. Of course, neither of us did. "A hundred thousand dollars!"

I whistled. "We won't have to dig into our principal for quite a while."

"How much is a martini?" asked Daria.

"Oh, for God's sake," Jeffrey said, heaving a sigh.

Just then the stewardess came up with a stack of magazines, and gave Daria a *Photoplay* and a *Silver Screen*. *Photoplay* had an article about Rod Taylor possibly getting engaged to Anita Ekberg. Daria went into a frenzy, and would have forgotten the martini, if I hadn't ordered it for her. During the rest of the flight she read both magazines cover to cover. Twice.

We arrived in San Francisco many hours later, long after nightfall. It had been like a dream to stare through the window as the golden landscape of America flew by and gradually darkened with the retreating sun. Now we found ourselves moving over a never-never land of moon and stars and black velvet countryside, adorned with bright shining dots that were cities and towns, and a network of veins made of car headlights on the many highways.

When the plane at last approached our promised land, we were beside ourselves with excitement. Jeffrey almost busted a gut when we got a brief glimpse of the glittering city through the window. A sense of unreality set in a few minutes later, when the stewardess opened up the door and set us free. In Oz.

Everybody else from the plane seemed to know where to go, and disappeared immediately. We stood around in the busy terminal, having not the faintest idea what to do next. I felt unexpectedly confused and lonely. There we were, the three of us and our luggage, in the middle of a strange city, with no friend in the world but the President of the United States, three thousand miles away.

Resourceful Jeffrey collared a young blond stewardess. "What's a good place to stay in San Francisco?" he asked.

"Well," she replied, "what kind of a budget are you on?" I noticed then that her speech sounded different than our own.

True, the Kennedys had rather strange accents, but I'd just attributed that to their being from Massachusetts. Now I realized there was more to the story. Despite our being raised on 1962 movies and TV, we of the Bunker apparently had developed our own subtle off-brand of speech, and it didn't sound exactly like mainstream American. We would have to work on that.

"Budget?" asked Jeffrey. "Money is no object."

She looked at him quizzically. "Oh. Try the St. Francis."

"How do we get there?"

This time the look was even more quizzical. "By taxi."

"You mean we're not in The City right now?"

"No, we're not," she said, her voice turning slightly acid.

"Well, how do we get a taxi?"

Now she was sure he was woofing her. "You go out the main entrance of the airport, find a taxi stand, and wait there," she said coldly. "Or you see one driving around and wave at it."

"How much does it cost to go to The City?"

She shrugged. "Five dollars, maybe."

"Can the driver change a twenty-dollar bill?"

"Are you for real?" she cried. "Where are you people from?"

"The Peace Corps," said Jeffrey.

"Please excuse us," I added. "We've been away a long time."

"Oh," she said, embarrassed. "Well, where have you been?"

I don't tolerate fools well and looked away with a sour expression. But Daria, the movie nut, said, "We've been with the Morlock tribe in Africa!" She had just finished reading about Rod Taylor and had clearly been thinking about the classic movie he had recently starred in, *The Time Machine.*

"Oh," said the stew again, flustered. "You know, I heard about them somewhere!" Her look grew thoughtful, and she said, "You must be starved for fun."

"Yes, we are," replied Jeffrey.

"Have you ever come to the right place!"

Jeffrey extended his hand, and after a puzzled moment, she did likewise. They shook. "Thank you," said Jeffrey.

I spied a promising sign with an arrow pointing to "Ground Transportation," and quickly herded the group toward it, lest the situation with the stew grow more involved than it already was. Halfway there, Daria grabbed my arm and pointed to what seemed to be a brightly lit, glassed-in store, right there in the airport. "Wait, Anna," she said, "we've just got to look in the window!"

"The sign says 'Closed' and the door is shut, Daria," I pointed out. "There's nobody inside."

"I don't care! I just want to look!"

She pressed her hands against the glass and stared for a long time at the contents within. Jeffrey and I joined her, and took to staring too. "Lucky Strike," said Jeffrey. "Camel, Viceroy, Salem, Pall Mall, L&M, Chesterfield,

Benson & Hedges." He might have been reciting a Russian Orthodox litany.

"Look at all the candy!" Daria said. It was tantalizing to see all that sweetness in shiny wrappers, just out of reach.

"There's clothes, writing materials, books, a transistor radio—this store has everything," said Jeffrey.

"Look at all the magazines!" Daria sounded like she was about to cry. "*Life, Post, Look*. . . . Oh, God, there's the same copy of *Silver Screen* I read on the plane." She drew a slow breath. "Jeffrey, please, can we come back here in the morning?"

"Of course we can." Jeffrey, the fearless leader, looked pretty weepy himself. "We can do anything we want now, Daria."

Though it was so late the airport was practically deserted, we did manage to hail a taxi for San Francisco. We had a bad moment when we got to the St. Francis Hotel, because we didn't have a reservation, and they couldn't understand why we hadn't phoned ahead to get one. But at length they took our money, and showed us to a two-bedroom suite.

We had a magnificent room that faced a square containing a statue atop a tall pedestal, just like in Europe. We all went to the window and looked out for a long time at the glittering city. "Is everybody all right?" Jeffrey asked at length.

We eyed each other, making comparisons. How scared is he? How scared is she? How scared can I get away with being? "Yeah, we're all right," Daria said. "But just by a hair."

"In the other world, they're getting ready for the air strike," I said.

"But not here," whispered Daria. "Not here."

Jeffrey drew a deep breath and went over to the telephone. "We'll want to explore tomorrow morning. I'll order breakfast."

He sat back in a plush chair, balanced a leather-bound folder on one knee, and perused it for a long time. Then he picked up the receiver. "Room service?" he said. A pause, and he began to order a king's ransom of food for the morning.

"Get a load of the Czarevitch over there," said Daria, when Jeffrey hung up.

"I beg your pardon?" Jeffrey exclaimed. "In the movies, they always order room service. What's wrong with that?"

Daria glared at him and walked over to the plush chair. "Here you sit, living it up like a lord," she said bitterly, "while back in our own world, everybody is getting ready to die!"

Jeffrey stood up and glared back at her. "I know that, and I was willing to give my life to change it. But the laws of nature wouldn't let me! Now I'm alive and marooned in a very strange world I've only read about in books. I have to start making my way in that world tomorrow. Before I do, if you don't mind, I'd like to have a nice breakfast!"

"Don't be a butt, Daria," I said. "Go easy on him. It's going to take a while to get our bearings."

Daria nodded, though a bit sullenly. Jeffrey, endeavoring to show that he could be of some use to the mission, went off to figure out how the bathtubs worked. Each of us then bathed and changed into our usual plain khaki pajamas. I finally plopped down in a big chair and started leafing through some magazines.

"I hate these pajamas," Daria said. "And I need something else to wear besides that damn sweater and skirt. We can go shopping tomorrow, can't we?"

Jeffrey nodded. "Yes, but let's not go wild."

"Is there a clothing store around here?" Daria asked.

The truth beginning to dawn on me, I looked up from my tourist brochures. Then I walked over to the window. My jaw dropped, bounced on the floor a couple of times, and rolled to a halt. "Comrades," I said, "but especially Jeffrey, you're going to die when I tell you this. Do you know where we are?"

"Where?" cried Daria, eyes suddenly wide. She was jumpy.

I caught Jeffrey's gaze. "We're right down the block from the City of Paris! That big department store! The place that you-know-who wrote about in his letter!"

He digested that bit of information. "My God," he said at length. "Kharitonov!" He clasped his hands in his lap. "I don't know exactly what day he shopped there. It didn't say in his diary or in the letters. It could have been as late as the thirtieth, and tomorrow is only the early morning of the twenty-ninth."

"We could go hang out there and watch for him," I said.

Jeffrey shook his head. "No, no, it doesn't feel right."

I stood up. "Look, everyone, we're all exhausted, so let's turn in. After all, breakfast will be here in just a few hours."

I didn't get any argument. Daria and I took one bedroom, and Jeffrey took the other. To my surprise, though I was dead tired, I couldn't fall asleep immediately. The enormity of the unknown world around us, and a sense of our utter aloneness began to sink into me. Before long I heard Daria trying to cry without making noise, but I didn't razz her about it like I would have back home. I couldn't—I knew all too well how she felt.

## 4

## Monday, October 29, 1962; 8:00 A.M.

At 8:00 A.M., after only a few hours' sleep, I was rudely awakened. Daria was kneeling by the side of my bed, shaking me. Her hands were cold as ice, and she was fully dressed.

"What is it?" I asked, not in the most charitable of tones.

"Come with me," whispered Daria, "I need your help."

Alarmed now, I sat up and glanced around. Outside the hotel a cloudy morning apparently had just broken, for the room was lit with a gray, suffused light, most peaceful in nature. Nothing seemed the matter. Yet Daria was trembling.

"Tell me what's wrong," I said, no longer mad at her.

"I want you to come downstairs with me, now."

"Okay." I got up and groped about for my wool skirt and cashmere sweater. I was starting to hate them; in rebellion, I resolved to go the first chance I got to one of the cafes in North Beach and figure out how to dress like a beatnik. "Why?"

"I woke up an hour ago. I'm so afraid, I almost don't think I can leave this room."

I pulled on my garter belt and stockings. "Don't be silly."

"If I don't face this now, it'll get the better of me. I want to go downstairs before there are many people awake and just walk around the lobby. Will you please come with me? Then we can come back here and eat breakfast."

"Yeah, that sounds great."

She hung her head and looked ashamed. "The two of you are so brave, I feel stupid. You just pop back a hundred years and fit into this world like you were born here. You start swimming around in it, happy as guppies in a fishbowl."

"Don't kid yourself," I said, looking in a mirror to put on my pearl earrings. "We're all a little crazy, even Jeffrey. We're just going to show it in different ways—you wait and see." I picked up the little leather clutch purse full of ID and money that I knew I was supposed to carry now that we were in 1962, and turned to face her. "Let's go."

"Okay!" said Daria. She took a deep breath and we walked into the main room of the suite toward the door. We turned the handle slowly and quietly, as if we were afraid of being caught, and tiptoed into the hall.

Daria stood up straight, her posture perfectly correct but rigid as a ramrod. She flinched when we got to the elevator, but we scurried inside, pushed the appropriate button, and survived the descent to the lobby.

The place was almost deserted. "Try to look relaxed," I said. "If you look scared, someone is sure to notice."

Daria nodded and assumed a stiff, frozen little smile. We ambled slowly around the lobby, awed—but trying not to show it—by the beautiful plush rugs, the chandeliers, the elegant wallpaper, and wood paneling. "I cannot believe any place could be so beautiful," Daria whispered. "I know I saw it all last night, but somehow it just didn't sink in."

We passed the registration desk, crept up a short flight of steps, and peered into a large room filled with tables and chairs. The hour being so early, it was dark. There were rich velvet curtains, a gleaming black grand piano, and a harp. In the background, solid and reassuring, there was a long, sweeping bar made of polished wood. Behind it were glass shelves stacked with literally hundreds of bottles of liquids— alcoholic liquids. I recognized this sort of establishment from picture magazines.

"Let's do come back tonight and have martinis," I suggested. Daria actually smiled. We continued on our rounds, and at length discovered a jewelry shop, whose display windows flabbergasted Daria and me. Many of the shop's wares appeared to be missing, as if they had been put away for safekeeping, but what was left was mind-boggling enough.

"This must be the finest jewelry shop in The City," said Daria. "Of course, this is one of the best hotels."

We walked on and came to a large dress shop. There was a wonderland of clothes inside; rows upon rows of suits, evening gowns, dresses, hats, scarves, blouses, skirts, and coats. Daria frowned, and appeared to be losing ground in her battle with her nerves. "I don't understand, Anna," she said to me. "This is kind of how I pictured the City of Paris."

"Maybe the City of Paris is even bigger."

"Oh, no!" exclaimed Daria. She almost seemed offended. "It couldn't be. I mean, how could it possibly be?"

She turned away from the window and squared her shoulders, just like a soldier preparing for battle. "Let's go a little bit farther," she said in a strong, clear voice.

I squeezed her hand and followed her down the corridor. But after a few steps, she gasped and stopped dead on the carpet. When I caught up with her, she clutched my arm and pointed to the source of her consternation: a shop door, flooded with light.

"Can it really be open?" she whispered.

I checked my Timex watch. "Could be. It's eight-thirty."

Daria pulled me forward and we came to a stop. The shop was indeed open, and there was a little old lady in a black dress and pearls at the counter. She had frosted hair and looked to be of good breeding and background.

"Act normal!" I said to Daria in a furious whisper.

"So what's normal?" she hissed back.

"Don't stare at everything. To Americans in 1962 all this is perfectly ordinary."

"Good morning," said the little old lady as we walked in.

"Good morning," I replied.

Daria made a beeline past the little old lady to the back of the shop. "Excuse me," I said, and followed Daria to a large display of magazines, from which she reverently extracted a copy of *Silver Screen*. "This," she said in a soft voice, "is the same one I read on the plane."

"Get it," I said. "I brought some money."

Daria never took her eyes from the magazine. "You're so smart, Anna." Her voice quavered.

"Don't even think of crying," I ordered.

She blinked. For the first time, she seemed to become aware of the rest of the store. "Anna," she said, sounding puzzled, "this shop is just like the one at the airport!"

I looked around. It had pretty much the same selection of wares. "Yeah, you're right." I walked over to the candy display and did a bit of staring myself: Three Musketeers, Mars, Butterfinger, Tootsie Roll, Jawbreakers, Payday, and Big Hunk. I picked up a handful and asked the little old lady, "Would you hold these for me while I look around?"

"Yes, dear," she said, looking puzzled. Then she added, "You should eat a good breakfast, you know."

"Yes," I said, "I will. Room service arrives at nine."

She smiled, though clearly still puzzled. "Which paper would you like?"

I fumbled it. "Uh . . . which ones do you have?"

She raised her eyebrows slightly. "Here is the *Chronicle*," she said, "and over there is the *New York Times*."

"Both, please." I got out my purse. "My friend's buying stuff," I babbled. "Let me pay for our purchases all at once."

"Certainly," said the little old lady.

My eyes fell on the *New York Times* and all thought of candy and magazines and silly treats went out of my mind. Like a slap in the face, the world reasserted its reality, and the headline reminded me of the horror we had just escaped.

"U.S. AND SOVIET UNION REACH ACCORD ON CUBA; KENNEDY ACCEPTS KHRUSHCHEV PLEDGE TO REMOVE MISSILES UNDER U.N. WATCH"

Snatching up the paper, I pored over the smaller headlines. "RUSSIAN ACCEDES—TELLS PRESIDENT WORK IN BASES IS HALTED—INVITES TALKS," said one. "CAPITAL HOPEFUL; PLAN TO END BLOCKADE AS SOON AS MOSCOW LIVES UP TO VOW" said another.

I had forgotten all about the little old lady. My face must have betrayed my deep emotion, for she reached out and touched my arm. "This morning I thanked God that I was alive," she said, "that it was Monday, and I had to come to work."

I grabbed her hand and squeezed it. It was small and delicate, and the skin was cool and thin and fragile. "I knew our wonderful young President would pull us through," she said. She drew a deep, raspy breath.

"Yeah," I said. "We're very lucky."

I rejoined Daria, and together the two of us lost our minds. She bought a stack of magazines a foot high. I bought candy, Salem and Camel cigarettes, matches, pens, a transistor radio with batteries, and writing paper, even though I didn't know anyone to write to but the President. We needed two shopping bags. When we got back to the room, Jeffrey looked disgusted.

"We don't even have a place to live yet," Jeffrey said, his voice hectoring. "We haven't even been out of the hotel, and already you've bought half of San Francisco."

I just gave him a dirty look and emptied our bags on the bed. He got all pop-eyed, shut up, and picked up the package of Camels and some matches. Then he sat down opposite a mirror, opened the package of cigarettes, and lit one. He went through all the motions of smoking he had ever seen in the movies—right in front of our eyes he turned into Edward R. Murrow, Yves Montand, Charles Boyer, and Bogie, all in rapid succession. He would have done Marlene Dietrich, but he didn't have the cheekbones. Then he tried inhaling. It was pretty funny.

In the midst of Jeffrey's death throes, there was a knock on the door, indicating breakfast had arrived. Jeffrey ran into one of the bathrooms to conceal his humiliation from the hotel staff. While he regained his composure, I let in the room service guy and found some money to tip him.

We ate breakfast, nobody talking, just savoring the food. It wasn't quite as good as Monsieur Verdon's cuisine—for us, nothing ever would be—but it came pretty damn close.

"Well," said Jeffrey, when we were all stuffed, "we have to do some serious planning. We have to find a place to live, we have to buy an automobile, and we have to establish our identities here and begin learning all about this society."

"Could we please enjoy ourselves for just a minute or two before you start in with all that stuff?" demanded Daria. "I want to go explore the city! I want to have fun!"

Jeffrey responded with a stern, reproachful look. "Another nuclear war could occur at any time. We must be ready."

"Oh, for God's sake, lay off!" she cried.

She was over her attack of nerves, all right. "Jeffrey," I put in, "we should plan. Let's plan to plan—two days from now. In the meantime, let's frolic a bit. We've been through hell. We deserve a vacation."

Jeffrey looked pissed. So I tossed him the pack of Camels, and he started to laugh in spite of himself. "Okay."

"Soon as you've got the knack of looking cool," I said, pointing to the cigarettes, "we'll start planning."

He got up, went over to the bed, and picked up the Salems. "I'll try these next. Maybe they're milder."

After breakfast Jeffrey put the pack with the time machine, our documents, our hardware, and our jewels in a dresser drawer. He sealed the drawer shut and rooted the piece of furniture and its contents firmly to the floor with a protective force field generated by another little technological gem designed just for us by the brains in the Bunker. Using the remote control, Jeffrey activated a beeper alarm which would notify him if anyone tried to mess with our stuff. It was as safe as safe got. Jeffrey tucked his wallet into his inside jacket pocket, and Daria and I took a firm grip on our handbags. On impulse, I snatched up the *San Francisco Chronicle* to take with me.

It was the moment of truth. "Well," said Jeff, "are we ready?"

"Yeah," I said. "I guess we should get started."

"Yes," said Daria, almost inaudibly. "I guess we should."

"Wait," said Jeffrey, "I have to go to the bathroom."

When he was out of earshot, Daria shot a withering glance in his direction. "Coward! He just went ten minutes ago, for God's sake!"

I nodded. "As long as he's doing that, I should check my hair," I said, and went over to a vanity table. "I'm not used to these hairdos yet," I said. "Even if I've got it right, it doesn't feel right." I picked up a rat-tail comb with fingers that were starting to shake, and fussed with my hair some more.

"For God's sake, let's just *do* it!" cried Daria. "Let's go! All this fooling around is driving me crazy!"

"Of course, of course, just as soon as Jeff gets back."

We heard the sound of a toilet flushing. "Fearless leader, my you-know-what!" hissed Daria.

"Look, you and I went downstairs earlier, so we've already had a little introduction to going outside. Jeffrey stayed here. So go easy on him."

Jeffrey emerged from the bathroom. "I should buy one of those effective remedies for acid indigestion they are always talking about in the magazines," he said.

"Come on!" cried Daria. I thought she was even going to stamp her foot. "Let's go! It has got to get easier!" So, marshalling our energies and our nerve, we trooped downstairs to check out our brave new world—October 1962.

We made it through the lobby and down the front steps of the hotel. Then, disoriented, we bunched together in a knot under the awning that protected the entrance. Standing under that awning, next to the street, was a very large colored man with a whistle in his hand, apparently employed by the hotel. He was dressed in a most ornate uniform, resplendent with gold braid and tassels. "Taxi, sir?" he called to Jeffrey.

Jeffrey shook his head, looking bewildered. Even though it was only a quarter of ten on a Monday morning—a slow time in The City, we were to learn—the hustle and bustle outside the St. Francis was overwhelming to us. Cars whizzing every which way, hordes of people walking up and down the street, whistles blowing, horns honking— why, just in Union Square alone there were literally more people than I had seen in my entire life. I would have suggested going back to the room to regroup, but I was afraid to set a bad example for the others.

Daria kept eyeing the man in uniform, the whites of her eyes showing the way they do when she's spooked, and didn't stop until I kicked her. "I'm sorry, Anna, but I've never seen one before," she whispered, her look reproachful.

"There were some in Washington, in the airport!" I hissed.

"I guess I wasn't paying attention then."

"Well, don't stare. It's rude."

I should explain here about one of the suspected skeletons in the Bunker's closet. Daria hadn't ever seen a Negro until we got to 1962 because there weren't any in the Bunker. Of course she knew what a Negro was, as did we all, because of movies and books and things like Chuck Berry records. Now, I did some research on this once and it appears from some records and accounts that there actually were some Negroes employed at the facility in 1962 on the janitorial staff. Also there were a couple of secretaries. Officially, however, none of them seemed to have been in the Bunker on October 31, 1962 even though it was Wednesday, the middle of the work week. And so, curiously, none of them seemed to have survived the war.

Although there was never anything in writing to confirm this, rumor has it that when that tour group of top Russian scientists and good-looking, healthy young astronauts-to-be arrived, the Bunker was almost—but not quite—full. The same rumor goes that the Bunker higher-ups, like my ancestor Leo Fall, kicked out certain people, so there would be room for the Russians. Which people? No one I ever talked to would speculate. I've always suspected, though. The Russkies might have been dirty filthy God-hating immoral Red Communists, but they were white, and had great resumes.

Anyway, I digress. Miffed at me, Daria beckoned to our group to follow her, crossed Geary Street, and towed us to the door of Macy's. "Oh, no!" she cried, spying the store's posted hours. "It won't open for another fifteen minutes!"

I could tell Jeffrey was preparing to give us a lecture on saving money again. In a fit of brilliance, I opened up the San Francisco paper to the very back and quickly scanned it for the real estate section. "Look at this, Jeffrey," I said, shoving it in his face. "We could buy three houses with what Kennedy gave us. And that's just pocket change compared to the cash we brought. So it's okay to do a little shopping, don't you think?"

Jeffrey looked at each of us in turn. "Two days," he intoned. "Each of us gets a thousand dollars. Make it last."

"How much are dresses?" Daria demanded, practically snatching the paper out my hand. She came upon a Macy's ad for a really cute little number—a navy princess-style coat dress with pleats kicking out from hipbone pockets, for twenty-five dollars. It was accessorized with twenty-five dollar pumps, a twenty-dollar Balenciaga scarf, and a twenty-dollar bag.

"No, Jeffrey, two thousand!" said Daria. "We need lots of boring things that run up the bill, like socks and underpants."

Jeffrey swore in Russian, garnering a glance from a passerby. "All right, two thousand, but not a penny more until we are settled in our house and have purchased an automobile *and* have inspected land prices."

Daria and I exchanged glances, allies once again, and marched off down the sidewalk with Jeffrey in tow.

We made the circuit of all the stores: The Emporium, Roos Brothers, Livingston's, Macy's, I. Magnin, the White House, and the City of Paris. As we approached this last, my watch showed that it was past ten o'clock, so the store ought to be open. Right then Daria tapped me on the shoulder and whispered, "Anna, do your feet hurt?"

I hadn't focused on it until then. Once she pointed it out, though, I realized my feet did hurt. A lot. I nodded.

"These shoes aren't made to walk in," Daria said. "Why didn't they tell us that back home? My toes are killing me."

"Let's buy some shoes without these heels, then."

"Okay. But what would you wear them with?"

For the life of me, I couldn't answer her. I'd always worn our sensible Bunker jumpsuits with sturdy flat-soled shoes. As far as I was concerned, our 1962 cashmere-and-skirt getups were just costumes they gave us back at Salamander. I couldn't imagine how to put a current wardrobe together on my own.

"We'll have to observe people, then."

Daria nodded. Right then we arrived at the front door of the City of Paris. "Oh, God, it's open!" she said.

Jeffrey began to look extremely uncomfortable. "Let's go to a different store," he said. "I can't get anything here. It looks like it's just for women. Plus, it's so expensive."

"My feet hurt," Daria replied, "and we're already here, so I'm going in." And she did.

I thought I knew what was the matter with Jeffrey. He was afraid of going in there, for fear of who he might meet. But to my surprise, he meekly followed Daria right through the door, though his posture drooped and he actually sort of slunk inside.

Jeffrey cast a quick, furtive glance around the interior. There were hardly any shoppers. A look of great relief crossed his face, and he relaxed a little.

"Oh my God, look up," said Daria, her voice reverent.

I craned my head and followed her gaze. There, overhead, several stories up, was the stained-glass dome of a ship in full sail described by Kharitonov in his letter. Thanks to the bright morning sunlight outside, it glowed like a ceiling of jewels. To my overwrought emotions, the sea seemed to move, the wind to fill the ship's sails, and the cresting tips of the waves to glitter.

Tears filled my eyes. We were standing in the middle of San Francisco looking up at a beautiful thing that had long been ashes in our world—a thing we felt we already knew, because of Sergei Makarovich's letter. It was October 1962, an ancient time, and we were alive and the world was alive. It was too wonderful to bear.

"Okay," I said to Daria, wiping my nose, "find the shoes."

We crept through the aisles cautiously, like little mice, taking sidewise peeks at the jewelry and perfumes and cosmetics and scarves and purses. Daria consulted a store directory, and took us to a place where they sold casual clothing, which hopefully could be worn with comfortable shoes. There she threw herself on the mercy of a saleslady.

"We've been out of the country," said Daria. "What is everybody wearing now when they want to be casual? Especially when they want to wear flat shoes?"

We learned about pedal-pushers and capris. We gleaned by observation that these were not worn in the City of Paris, although, said the saleswoman, one might get away with them at a place like Macy's. We ended up buying some very nice wool gabardine pants and some lovely sweaters to go with them.

"Now for the shoe department," said Daria.

"Oh, no," said the saleslady, "it might still be closed."

"Closed?" asked Daria. "What do you mean? The store's been open since ten."

"It was supposed to be off-limits until ten-thirty for a private showing," said the woman. "There's been a special tour group in the store since nine this morning, and they were going to wind up in the shoe department at ten-thirty."

"I don't understand," said Daria.

The woman raised her eyebrows and leaned over toward

Daria, as if to tell her a secret. "I'm not supposed to tell anybody this, so please don't quote me," she said in a low voice, "but it's so exciting I can't help myself. It's a tour group of *Russians*. They brought them here to shop."

Jeffrey gasped as if someone had slapped him. The woman, misunderstanding the source of his surprise, gave him a knowing look. "Imagine, *Communists* right here in the City of Paris! What must they think of all our lovely things? I do so wish they'd come by my department. I'd give anything to see them."

Daria and I took our packages. "Well," I said, trying to remain calm, "I think it's time to check out the flat shoes."

We headed toward the shoe department as fast as decorum would allow, our high heels and aching feet notwithstanding. To our disappointment, when we arrived we found the place deserted. Apparently the tour group had moved on.

"Oh, shit," said Jeffrey.

"I thought you didn't want to see Kharitonov," I said.

Jeffrey shook his head, looking like he was on the verge of tears. "I don't know."

Then Daria put a hand to her mouth. "Look over there," she said, her voice barely audible. In one corner, by himself, stood a man holding a pair of women's silver evening slippers.

We barely recognized him from his brave official photograph. In person, he looked thinner and much less substantial. His hair was gray and receding, his posture faintly stooped, and his clothes were the faintest bit shabby.

"Oh, God," said Jeffrey in a whisper, "it's really him. He's alive in this world. I can't believe I'm actually looking at him."

"Look," I said, "he's holding the shoes—the ones he wrote about in the letter, that he wanted to get for his wife."

The tour had apparently moved on to another section of the store, but Kharitonov had remained behind with the silver shoes, as if unable to put them down. Despite the bravado of his letter—you remember, the part about his not buying the shoes for Larisa because they weren't sturdy—I figured out in an instant that he thought they were incredibly beautiful and wanted more than anything to get them for her, but his money had run out.

As we watched, another man approached Kharitonov and clapped him on the back. "Who the hell is that?" whispered Daria, her voice resentful. "The local KGB goon?"

I shook my head, recognizing the man from Bunker archives—my own ancestor. "He's American! That's Leo Fall! In the other world, he was the first head of our Board of Governors!"

We exchanged disbelieving glances. "What's he doing here? On this tour?"

"Hosting it, probably," said Daria. She whistled under her breath. "Those scientists types sure stick together. No wonder the Russians made it out to the Bunker."

Kharitonov looked up at the man, laughed, and seemed to indicate he would catch up with the group in a moment. The American scientist sauntered off, smiling.

Jeffrey reached over and took my copy of the *New York Times*. "This time, she has to get the shoes," he said, pale-faced. "He's going to go back to her in Moscow, and I want him to have the shoes. Stay here—I'll be back."

We followed him anyway. He went over to Kharitonov and gave him a strained smile. Then he said in calculatedly terrible, execrable Russian, "*Zdrastvuyte*. Hello. I am American student. I study Russian language." He showed the front-page headlines of the paper to Kharitonov and said, "Good news, yes?"

Kharitonov smiled back, being polite. Jeffrey pointed to the shoes. "For your wife? You want?"

Confused now, Kharitonov said no and started to put the shoes down. "Please," said Jeffrey, "I rich boy, from Hollywood. I want to give you gift, for goodwill, good luck." He put a hundred-dollar bill into Kharitonov's hand. "You buy shoes."

Kharitonov was totally bewildered. At that moment a salesman hurried up, and Jeffrey simply gave him the money and told him he was paying for the shoes and to keep the change. With stunning swiftness, the salesman wrapped and bagged the shoes and presented the package to Kharitonov.

"*Spasiba*," said Kharitonov, still nonplussed. "Thank you."

"*Pazhalasta*," replied Jeffrey. "My pleasure."

The American scientist, Leo Fall, surfaced once again, this time eyeing us suspiciously. I was awed, and stared at him with devouring curiosity from the shadows; I was, after all, his direct descendant.

Kharitonov edged away from our group, still puzzled, but smiling. "*Spasiba*," he said again, waving, as he joined Fall.

"*Pazhalasta*," we echoed.

Daria gave Jeffrey a sweet, sweet smile. "You've only got nineteen hundred dollars left, baby."

Jeffrey looked as if he were going to collapse. "Sit down," said Daria, putting him into a chair. She and I bought our flat shoes, and the three of us then retreated in disarray to our hotel room. Since it was past noon by then, we ordered up lunch from room service: hamburgers and french fries, coffee, several flavors of ice cream, chocolate cake, and apple pie. Then we took a long nap to rest our poor shattered nerves.

## 5

Tuesday, October 30, 1962; 9:00 P.M.

It is embarrassing to report how we spent the rest of Monday and most of today, but I am attempting to be historically accurate, so I must confess the truth. After the stress of our first foray outside and the enormous lunch from room service, we ended up sleeping until well after dark. By then it was too late to do any more shopping, so we went to the bar and had a number of martinis. After that, we went back to the room to recuperate. All would have been well, except that I was too excited to sleep, and turned on the transistor radio.

All at once sound came blasting out of that tiny black box. It was Little Eva, singing "Do the Locomotion"! Suddenly we weren't hearing a scratchy reproduction from an old, incredibly beat-up record in the Bunker, but the real thing, coming right over the airwaves into our room from a radio station right there in San Francisco. A hundred years in the past, and the song was new and fresh. Little Eva herself was alive somewhere in the country, and about the same age as us. I started dancing.

The tunes came rolling out of the radio, one after another. We couldn't believe it. Soon the others got up and started jumping around and behaving like crazy people. We danced to Del Shannon singing "Runaway," to "Please Mr. Postman" by the Marvelettes, and "Twist and Shout" by the Isley Brothers. Jeffrey called room service and ordered up several bottles of champagne. We drank them and danced a lot more.

Sometime after midnight I went into the bathroom and threw up, as if I were ill or had eaten spoiled food from the Bunker storehouse. Oddly enough I felt better afterward, and was able to dance some more. After that it got a little murky for me.

None of us woke up before noon on Tuesday, the thirtieth. Even then we felt wretched. The literature of the period frequently mentioned hangovers, but since no alcohol was served in the Bunker, except once a year in small quantities on October 31, none of us had ever had one. Besides, none of the advertisements for alcohol in magazines preserved from the era ever showed people feeling bad. So it was quite a surprise to us to feel, as it is put in the vernacular, like hammered dogshit.

We ordered a lot of hot, soft, comforting food from room service. I went down to the lobby and returned with Kaopectate, which helped, though not as much as we'd hoped. But we were young, and by four o'clock that afternoon we felt reasonably recovered. Then we took stock of our situation.

"We've inadvertently wasted most of our second play day," said Jeffrey. "Under the circumstances, I think it is only fair to take tomorrow off. On Thursday, we can get down to business."

"That's a very good idea, Jeffrey," I said. "Especially considering that tomorrow is the anniversary. I don't think I could settle down and focus on much of anything important."

"Yeah," he said glumly. "It's going to be a rough day."

I heaved a sigh. "Yesterday we launched the air strike against Cuba. Earlier today Soviet bombers struck our missile bases in Turkey. Right about now, we're attacking missile bases inside the Soviet Union."

"Will you *shut up*?" Daria cried. "Have you got ice water for blood? You're talking about real people!"

That brought me up short. "You're right," I replied. I looked inward, and tried to examine my feelings. "I'm distancing myself from the other world, Daria. I can't keep dwelling on it, and suffering. I have to live in this world."

"And protect it," said Jeffrey. His voice was deadly quiet. "We can't assume this world is now safe from atomic war, any more than ours was. It may happen again."

Daria rolled her eyes. "No. It won't! It can't!"

"It could. And if it does," said Jeffrey, "we are the only people who can do anything about it." He cleared his throat. "I can't emphasize this enough. On Thursday, we have to get very, very serious. We must establish a secure base in this world. We must buy property. We must maintain an inventory of precious jewels that can be transported back in time with us if the need arises. And we must make money. Money will give us security. It will give us power and access to information and tools. We have a responsibility to this world that we must not shirk."

Daria finally broke the silence. "Shit. One more day of play," she said. "Then we have to grow up. Forever."

"Right," said Jeffrey. "And we have to visit Russia."

"What?" cried Daria, practically screaming.

"You know there could be another war. If there is, the key to its undoing may not be found here, but in the USSR."

"You mean Russia may start the next war?" I asked.

"I don't know," replied Jeffrey. "I just have this feeling that the fates of our two Motherlands are bound together. Until the rivalry between Russia and America is stopped, we'll never be completely safe. We have to understand Russia well enough to know when, and how, to intervene if a new branch point turns up there."

On that serious note, I went to the newsstand and brought back the very last copy of the day's *New York Times*. "Get a load of this," I said to Jeffrey and Daria. " 'EUROPEANS HAIL KENNEDY AS HERO, BUT KHRUSHCHEV ALSO GETS PRAISE FOR EASING CRISIS.' "

Jeffrey surveyed the front page and shook his head

ruefully. "Now everybody in the world is going to think that mankind is smart enough not to start a nuclear war!"

I raised my eyebrows in what I hoped was a supremely sardonic fashion. "Get this, guys: 'AIR ATTACK ON CUBAN BASES WAS SERIOUSLY CONSIDERED.'"

Jeffrey smirked. "No shit!"

Daria took the paper and gave it a sullen look. "People are so stupid. If new evidence gets uncovered tomorrow about Marilyn Monroe's death, *it* will get top billing." Angry tears ran down her cheeks and dropped onto her new oxford cloth shirt. "I mean, in two weeks everybody will have forgotten all about the crisis."

Jeffrey shook his head. "Every kid in America has been scared for weeks. They'll never forget."

"Yes they will."

"No, think about it. All month their parents have been terrified. At school there have been air-raid drills and those stupid Civil Defense films! Cities have tested their sirens. Kids twelve and up are old enough to *understand* what it's all about, and they've been puking into the toilet every night in sheer terror. They won't forget. Around 1990 they'll be running the country—at which time I foresee a significant improvement in our chances of survival."

I regarded the two of them thoughtfully. "This is a switch. Back in the Bunker, Daria was the optimist. Now you've turned into Little Mary Sunshine. What gives, Jeffrey?"

He gave me a dirty look. "I'm merely extrapolating from my observations of the behavior of people in this new world of ours. Nothing is graven in stone here, Anna. Nothing."


Wednesday, October 31, 1962; 11:30 P.M.


The next day Jeffrey thought we should honor Kharitonov by retracing his footsteps, so we hailed a taxi and went to the Golden Gate Bridge, Daria clutching a guidebook to her bosom.

I was not prepared for the effect that vista would have on me. Until then, I had not truly been Outside, although I thought I had. But in truth, since leaving the Bunker we had spent our days in a succession of halfway houses: offices, cars, planes, hotel rooms, and city streets lined by comforting, enclosing buildings. Now the magnificence and boundlessness of our new world were brought home to me with the force of an earthquake.

A brisk, cool wind was blowing off the Pacific, and the day was perfectly clear, without a hint of fog, smog, or cloud. The sky overhead was an immense bowl of pure, deep blue. The sunlight was as bright as a steel knife. The water in the bay, and in the ocean to the east seen through the Gate, glittered and sparkled as if it were an undulating cloak adorned with hard, bright diamonds. Directly before me, the bridge reared skyward out of the rock of the Presidio, coming to earth again only when it reached the Marin headlands, which loomed barren and majestic out of the sea like a misplaced piece of Cornwall or the Scottish Highlands—those headlands that, even now, hid Nike missiles pointed at the Soviet Union.

There were boats with white sails in the Bay. On every distant shoreline, settlements were visible. Seagulls moved effortlessly in the air, their cries shrill and harsh, and in the background traffic hummed as it sped across the bridge. This world was like an immense, shining, sentient thing, with lungs breathing in and out, heart beating time, and blood pumping vital and swift through its body. It bore no resemblance to the world I knew from books, from videotapes, perused to kill the omnipresent boredom of the Bunker. It was as real and immediate as my right hand; it was *alive*.

I felt like screaming, like running and dancing, like weeping, like covering my eyes and hiding from all that life and light. Until that instant I had not grappled with my grief for that other world of ours, which had been murdered— that parallel world, traveling through space and time beside us, unseen but ever near. That other world, at that very instant, was engulfed in a nuclear inferno. Yet here I stood, alive and well, privileged beyond reason, allowed to stretch in the sunshine and breathe clean air and gaze upon a spectacle of terrifying beauty.

I walked away from the others and sat down next to a flower bed, protecting my clothes with several pieces of Kleenex from my purse. Although it was the last day of October and winter should have been coming on, the bed was bursting full of impossibly large and colorful blooms. I cried. I didn't lower my head; I looked into the wind, straight at the Golden Gate, and let the tears run down my face as they would.

It took twenty, thirty minutes to burn itself out. When it was over I felt as if someone had beaten me with their fists. Although I was grateful for this beautiful world, there still remained the hateful, ugly knowledge of the death that had come to our own. I had the taste of ashes in my mouth; I would never be able to escape it.

I rejoined the others. They were sitting down, their eyes red, their faces cowed. My brief illness had been catching.

"It is the anniversary," said Jeffrey. "It is."

We sat in a tight circle and clasped hands. In those minutes we aged a great deal. We grew up, we grew sober. At last Jeffrey spoke. "It may happen again. If it does, we are the only people who can prevent it. For the rest of our lives, we will bear that responsibility."

I nodded. "This is our world now." Daria just sniffled.

The human organism can only take so much heavy emotion. We were very young, and the world was still very new, and so we soon rebounded. In the wake of my grief came one of the purest moments of happiness in my life. Daria and I started laughing and shoving each other, and then we kicked off our flat shoes from the City of Paris and did cartwheels in our wool gabardine pants at the foot of the Golden Gate Bridge. We ran and screamed and played in sheer joy at being alive—a joy that would not have been so delicious and razor-sharp without the ongoing horror in the world next door.

"Oh God, oh God," said Daria, when we had calmed down again. She looked into the wind and stretched on tiptoe to her full height. "Can you imagine what this must have looked like to the first Spaniard to sail through the Golden Gate?"

"Or to the first Russian," said Jeffrey. The look on his face was envious, musing, and wistful, all at the same time.

"Huh?" said I. "The Russians never came here. They settled up north for a while in Fort Ross, and then split."

He didn't seem to hear me. His eyes, fixed on a spot somewhere in Marin County, had a faraway look. "If things had gone differently, this entire coast could have been Russian."

I favored him with a skeptical look and said, "Didn't you pay attention in history class? During the early nineteenth century, the Russians could have occupied the whole West Coast. There was no one around who could have stopped them. They just didn't figure it out in time."

He favored the ocean with a brooding look, and said, "Perhaps—"

"Don't even think of it," I interrupted. "We're staying right here where they have novocaine and antibiotics."

Daria, meanwhile, had begun to study the guidebook. "Guys," she said, "this history stuff is really interesting, you know, but I was just wondering, can we go to the Blue Fox for dinner? It's really famous—a real San Francisco institution. I bet its food is as good as Mr. Verdon's."

# PART II

## 1963: Russia, and a Death

## 6

## November 1962–June 1963

We got on with our lives, hoping they would be normal—and peaceful. Jeffrey called up a realtor, discovered that two units making up the entire eleventh floor of a co-op on Russian Hill were for sale, and grabbed them. Although the purchase just about wiped out the nest egg Kennedy gave us (well, there was enough left over for a '63 Ford Fairlane 500 Sports Coupe with bucket seats, and a '63 Oldsmobile F-85 Cutlass), Jeffrey said the units were an excellent investment, so we had not been profligate.

I should mention here that Jeffrey, Daria, and I had grown up in a world whose view of proper sex roles was descended directly from the year 1962. For those in the Bunker, human culture had been frozen, like a fly in amber, exactly as it had been on the last day of October 1962. While men and women in the Bunker might share work as necessity dictated, when Jeffrey, Daria, and I returned to 1962, we assumed that men handled the money stuff, and girls went along with it. And we were right, for the most part; people hadn't yet heard of women's lib. I wish I had. It would be years before I could begin to exert proper control over our financial well-being.

Although Daria and I were a bit taken aback by all this haste, Jeffrey waxed eloquent over the view and the cultural significance of the area. Russian Hill, he said, after a hard bout of library research, was the "artistic Olympus" of The

City's poets and writers. On Russian Hill George Sterling had written his verses extolling the "cool grey city of love." The poet Ina Coolbrith was reputed to have served tea to Mark Twain and Bret Harte in her digs there on the Hill. Besides that, it was close to the Chinese restaurants in Chinatown, and the bohemian bookstores and espresso places in North Beach.

We installed a safe in Jeffrey's apartment that could withstand everything but a direct nuclear strike, and put the time machine and all our money, jewels, and documents in it. As in the St. Francis, Jeffrey then affixed the safe firmly to the building with a protective force field and activated our personal beeper alarms. Only then did we feel really secure.

The moment we were settled, Jeffrey once again brought up the subject of an imminent visit to Russia. I was really annoyed. We had just averted a nuclear war, and here he was worrying about the next one before we even had a chance to draw breath. I mean, no normal person could go around worrying about nuclear war every waking second, or they'd go nuts! Jeffrey was just *so paranoid* about there being another war, he couldn't let go of it, even for a minute. He was convinced that the key to understanding the genesis of one or more future wars, not to mention the fate of the world, was all bound up in the gloomy millennia of Russian history.

He was dead right, of course. But it would be many years before I would understand that myself.

Jeffrey perfected his contemporary Russian accent by studying with local emigres, amassed a sizable library on the Cold War circa 1963, quietly converted some jewels to cash, and proceeded to make an obscene amount of money by dabbling in venture capital and the stock market— guided, of course, by the Bunker Theory of Parallel Technological Development.

This was Jeffrey's own pet theory. Our ancestors in the Bunker had developed eye-popping marvels of technology in their scientific hothouse, starting with only the knowledge, concepts, and tools of the trade available in October 1962. Thereafter the substance of their discoveries had progressed in a discernible, predictable pattern. Jeffrey thought the development of technology on our new Earth over the coming years would follow roughly the same pattern as the Bunker discoveries, since they both started from the same point; he thought he knew which infant industries to back, and which to ignore.

Some of his investments I could approve of, like those in certain Japanese and domestic companies specializing in television, musical reproduction technologies, and that sort of thing. Anything that had to do with entertainment looked like a sure bet to me. As a worshipper of early 60's popular culture, I was sure that taking people's minds off their misery would always be a well-compensated activity. I mean, look how rich Elvis was.

But Jeff risked frightening amounts of money driving down to little towns like Palo Alto, Mountain View, and the like, spending endless hours pow-wowing with nerds and geeks not much older than him who were into the new computers, and backing their first baby steps toward corporatehood, usually out of their garages.

One day Jeffrey even came home convinced that in the future everyone would have their own small household computer. I told him he was crazy. What on earth would they use it for? Naturally in the Bunker each scientist had needed one. And if we were to continue in our role of self-appointed nuclear holocaust watchdogs, *we* could certainly use one, because we needed a handy way to keep track of a lot of data on megatonnage and stuff like that. But most American consumers didn't exactly share our private agenda. Of course, he didn't listen.

For my part, I bought a prodigious amount of black clothing, practiced smoking Gauloises, wore out Bob Dylan's new album, and hung out a lot at North Beach cafes and clubs, getting jazzed on espresso and listening to folk music. I learned that Victorian mansions in need of a facelift were selling dirt cheap in an area of The City around Haight and Ashbury streets, and that the neighborhood was expected to appreciate in value. I passed this on to Jeffrey, and he bought a dozen of them. Soon I became very popular among the denizens of North Beach, as the font of many a gig patching up these houses—for which my rich brother paid a magnificent dollar-fifty an hour.

As for Daria? She complained bitterly that the only boys there were to meet in The City had beards or were otherwise weird, and incessantly agitated to start college in the fall.

Sure, we had all intended to enroll. Someday. Soon. I had hoped to put it off a year, the better to acculturate in the meantime. But Daria was adamant. She wanted to go *now*.

She could be a big pain in the neck when she tried, so I reluctantly began my investigation. Before long I hit a brick wall. How was I going to get the three of us enrolled in a good college or university in only six months? Specifically, what the hell were we going to do about the paperwork?

As covers go, ours was pretty good. We had the best fake birth certificates and passports that talent and time could buy. We had real drivers' licenses—doctored to suit us, of course—from California and half a dozen other states in 1962. We had lots and *lots* of real 1962 greenbacks. However, what we did not have was some high school in the Midwest from which Cal or Stanford could actually get our transcripts. We had no grades, no pep squad background, no science fair awards. In other words, we had no paper trail and no means of independent verification of our identities. And thus, no history.

I was really stumped.

Then around the middle of March we got this note in the mail. It was hand-written on paper of impeccable quality and lacked any sort of letterhead whatsoever. It read:

Dear Daria, Anna, and Jeffrey,
      You're probably wondering how I got your address.

Well, my little brother is on my ass all the time not to lose touch with old family friends. So, while bowing to the inevitable, I'm dropping you this note to say I hope you are well and are savoring the delights of California as only kids your age can do.

As long as we're keeping the lines of communication open, you might as well benefit. I'm enclosing three pre-paid tickets to a thousand-dollar-a-plate celebrity benefit in Los Angeles next month. It's for a worthy cause—which escapes my weary brain just now. Lots of stars will be there—Charlton Heston, Lauren Bacall, Richard Burton, Elizabeth Taylor, Marlon Brando, Gregory Peck, Rod Taylor . . . etc., etc., etc. Have a good time. (Especially you, Daria.)

Remember, if you need any help, *call me.*

Jack

"Son of a bitch! We're under surveillance!" cried Jeffrey.

Daria looked thoughtful. "Well, if we have to be under surveillance by somebody, I'm glad it's him."

"It's not just *him*, stupid," said Jeffrey. "If it were just him, there'd be no problem. It's *them.*"

She snorted. "Well, *they* aren't the KGB, so spare me!"

Jeffrey glared at her. "Don't single out the KGB. Intelligence agencies are all the same, including the CIA."

"They are not!"

"Daria," he sighed, "you're just being naive."

"No, I am not naive! You're the one who's naive, believing all that Commie propaganda."

"Such as?"

"You know, where they find *one* sneaky thing the American CIA did, and then say there's *no* difference between it and the KGB. Like the concept of *magnitude* has no meaning to you whatsoever!"

"Daria, you mean it doesn't make you uneasy that government goons are watching us?"

Daria sniffed and turned away. "It's benevolent surveillance. I, for one, can't wait to meet Rod Taylor."

She had a point. And that gave me an idea. In April, having thought the problem through, I decided to write to Jack myself. If he was going to keep tabs on us, well then, I was going to milk the situation for all it was worth. I wrote:

Dear Jack,

I have decided I would like to start college at the University of California, Berkeley this fall. However, I have no high school transcript to send them. And I have no high school to list when I sign up for the college entrance exams. My two friends are in the same boat. Can you help?

I see our friend Nicki has settled down and become a good global citizen. We're all very grateful.

California's a kick. When you retire, you should check it out. By the way, thanks for the tickets. I thought Daria was going to faint when she met Rod Taylor.

Your friend,
Anna

Not long thereafter, each of us got a letter from Cal Berkeley awarding us a full university scholarship—tuition, books, and living expenses—starting in the fall of 1963. It referenced (a) our outstanding college entrance exam scores, (b) the excellent job our missionary parents had done educating us despite the lack of public educational facilities in Africa, and, incredibly (c) the glowing letters of recommendation submitted on our behalf by our Peace Corps supervisors regarding our good works among the Morlock tribe.

The rogue! His minions had even talked to the stewardess at San Francisco airport!

It gave me the willies. The bad kind, but the good kind

too, the kind that sends a delicious quiver through your gut. Our man Jack was nothing if not good.

By then I was on a roll, and decided to use Jack to solve another one of my problems. Jeffrey kept whining about how important it was to visit Mother Russia, but was always too busy investing our money to do anything about it. He clearly wanted me to do all the homework, and would not shut up until I did.

So, I figured if Jack was willing to play tooth fairy to assuage his guilt, then I had another agenda item to take care of. In June I wrote to him again.

Dear Jack,

Thank you so much for your university recommendation. It really did the trick. I was wondering if you could help me with one more thing. Jeffrey wants very much to visit the Soviet Union and rediscover his roots, as I do also. But right now—*as I'm sure you know*—he's all tied up investing in real estate like you told him to, and so I get stuck with the social planning. Would it be possible for Jeff and me to visit Moscow this summer as part of an American student delegation or something? If you could expedite this I would be very grateful. Daria isn't really that interested. She's not as fascinated by things Russian as Jeffrey and I. Also, she's boy-crazy . . . but just for American boys who go to American parties and dance to American songs, just like in *Gidget*. Heck, she doesn't even speak Russian that well. I, for my part, would really dig a chance to do my part for world peace. It gets to be habit-forming, you know?

I enjoyed your speech at American University yesterday. Do you *really* think one day the Soviets will join us in banning nuclear weapons testing? Well, I guess it never hurts to ask.

Best,
Anna

A week later he came through. He was obviously enjoying this.

Dear Anna,

We're getting to be regular pen pals. Yes, I can help you and Jeffrey visit the Soviet Union. We just happen to have a group of students going to Moscow for a goodwill visit in mid-July. You may join them. Now that the crisis has cooled, the Reds have become rather cuddly, and they are welcoming such delegations with almost-open arms. You will have to attend some rather wearisome official functions, but you will hopefully have plenty of time to tour the city.

I foresee an imminent end to the Cold War. We have definite plans to establish a telephone hot line linking Moscow and Washington, and the first week of August we—and the Brits—are scheduled to meet in the Kremlin's Great Palace and sign the Partial Test Ban Treaty. In fact, here is something that will gladden your heart: The moment the treaty is signed, our nuclear scientists have promised to set back that doomsday clock in the *Bulletin of the Atomic Scientists* to twelve minutes before midnight. Twelve minutes, I'm told, is doing quite good; the clock has been hovering around the two-minute mark for the last few years.

On a droll note, the Soviets have scheduled some sporting events on the grounds of the Kremlin after the signing. Our very own Dean Rusk is scheduled to play Cousin Nicki at badminton. In the interest of world peace, I've instructed Dean to let the fat boy win.

So, when you return from your trip, Bobby and I would be very, very interested to hear your impressions of the USSR. You know better than anyone the dangers of our rivalry with the Soviets, and the ease with which our two nations can blunder into war. Hopefully, you wear fewer blinders than we do. You have a very real incentive to see things in the Soviet Union as they truly are, not as the prevailing political climate dictates you see them.

When you get back, we'll have a lot of questions for you, such as the following. (Yes, I have already received a baker's dozen of answers to these questions from members of the American security apparatus. Screw 'em. This time around I want *your* input.)

We're awfully intimidated by these people. Should we be? I often suspect we've fallen for a lot of hype. Surely the Soviets don't think they can take over the world. The very idea is insane. To get any good out of the venture, they'd have to occupy the countries they conquered, and they don't have the manpower. (For that matter, neither do we; I dread the day we get sucked into "stabilizing" even that piss-pot third world kingdom, South Vietnam.) Alternatively, they could set up puppet regimes in conquered countries. But my spies tell me the client states they've already got are bleeding them dry. Furthermore, the Soviet economy is currently producing ninety percent guns and only ten percent butter; in other words, there ain't that much butter left to cut out, no matter how many more guns they'd like to buy.

Find out, my friends, how long are the Soviet people going to put up with this? Do they have any gumption? Will they ever rebel?

The Russians are so good at some things. Today, no less, they sent the first woman into space, Valentina Tera-what's-her-name. How the hell do they keep it up? What's it costing them? Is the emperor wearing any clothes? Can the Soviet Union last? What ails Russia, anyway?

(As long as we're going for broke, Bobby instructed me to throw in "What is the meaning of life?," but I preferred to keep it simple.) Anyway, plan on dropping by the house for lunch on your way back to San Francisco.

As always,
Jack

## 7

## July 1963: San Francisco to Moscow

We flew from San Francisco to Helsinki, where we were to link up with our tour group at the airport and fly to Moscow.

The entire time Jeffrey was on the edge of a nervous breakdown. He paced up and down the plane like a caged panther, drank too many cocktails, tried to sleep in his seat but only twitched and muttered, and generally made my life miserable.

Why all this suffering? Well, imagine, if you can, the mental state of a lover of fantastic fiction who suddenly finds himself on the way to Barsoom or Pellucidar. To Jeffrey, Russia embodied everything magical, dark, and exciting in the world. He felt drawn to it like a snake to the charmer. To him it was the fabled land of ancient times, the other side of the moon.

You have to understand: In the Bunker, the language, the customs, the mores, the fabric of our everyday life all came from America; but the shadows we cast were Russian. Every one of us had been thrown out of Eden when our two peoples clashed; and yet every one of us was the product of their mating. Most of us, like good amphibians, managed to · cope with this duality on a day-to-day basis. We went about our business and didn't think about it. Everyday tedium is a great leveller of men. But a few, like Jeffrey, could never turn their backs on it for long.

Certainly Jeffrey idealized Russia. He read into its people
the noble, passionate, melancholy nature of his ancestor
Kharitonov. As a child he drank in all the violent, colorful
tales our elders told us of firebirds, snow maidens, witches,
murdered princes, and czars gone mad. He cut his teeth on
the splendid, brooding music of Mussorgsky. Listening to
Borodin, he absorbed the grandeur and loneliness of Russia's vast steppes. He listened to Tchaikovsky, and was filled
with love for the marvelous bastard Russian mind that
sprang from the overlayering of paper-thin European finesse
upon the ancient barbarian.

Because of his feelings for Russia, Jeffrey (who at heart
was the biggest idealist of us all) completely discounted the
1950's Cold War propaganda directed against Russia by our
other parent nation. Granted, the stuff was pretty extreme,
but he refused to believe that there might have been a grain
of truth in any of it—even though Kharitonov's own papers
were full of terrified allusions to his watchers.

In the Bunker, many had written about the great differences between our two countries. America was like a
laboratory experiment in which everything had been rigged
to go right beforehand. The country's European settlers
blundered into a vast continent, bulging at the seams with
natural resources, and peopled only by Indians who could be
disposed of with great ease. Colonial America was like a
BankAmericard with no credit limit.

You would think at first glance the early Europeanized
Russians were just as fortunate. They, too, had settled in a
land possessing a significant fraction of the Earth's natural
wealth. Hell, it was even bigger than the future United
States, covering one-sixth of the world's land mass. As in
America, only a few puny squatters barred the early
Russians' path to empire—in this case primitive Asiatics,
nothing to be reckoned with, for all that they were descended from the Golden Horde.

There the similarities stopped. North America was settled
by educated aristocrats and yeomen with worldviews

shaped by the Renaissance, the Enlightenment, and the Industrial Revolution. The traditions of democracy soon took solid root in the land. Furthermore, the Founding Fathers, those brilliant and most cynical of men, imposed upon the fledgling country a fascinating experimental form of government: one that acknowledged the evil, selfishness, and corruption inherent in human nature, and by its very design attempted to curb those tendencies through a system of checks and balances. Face it, Washington, Jefferson, and all the other good ol' boys were realists. They shared none of Marx's dream of a Utopia where everyone would pitch in and work, not for personal gain, but because they were such great team players; where goodies would be produced by each according to his abilities, and be allocated to each in accordance with his needs. Marx, a social recluse, had spent way too much time reading in the British Museum. Didn't the idiot ever sit down and really ask himself why he avoided people so assiduously? Before he set out to change the world, he should have spent a couple of hours in a kindergarten observing basic obnoxious human behavior. It would have saved the world a lot of trouble.

But I digress. Russia, unlike America, was blessed with no diabolically clever governmental system. In earlier times its people, many the product of Viking rapes, had enjoyed the rule of such teddy bears as Ivan the Terrible and Boris Godunov. In the late seventeen hundreds Russia wound up not with the cerebral American Founding Fathers in charge, but Peter the Great, a royal pain in the butt. It was Peter who built his great city, his window to the West, on a swamp covering the bones of hundreds of workers. It was Peter who shut up his pesky rebellious sister in a Moscow convent, and, to annoy her, hung the dead body of her lover outside her window to ripen in the sun. In later years, each time the poor Russians got a reform-minded czar, he either went off his rocker or got shot. When they finally exploded into revolution, they ended up with Lenin and his gang for leaders.

By the twentieth century, America was defined by her achievements and her limitless possibilities. Russia was defined by her history of subjugation and her limitless capacity for suffering. As a child in the Bunker, I had read most written material available on Russia, and heard everybody's family history more times than I cared to count. Still I could not share Jeffrey's worshipful obsession with our other homeland. Of the two countries, Russia was certainly the more majestic—but not the one where you'd want your kid to grow up.

We made it to Helsinki, briskly deplaned, and made our way to the Aeroflot gate. There we met up with our tour group and the supervising professor from American University, Mr. Sergeyev.

The Moscow-bound passengers were directed to the tarmac and shepherded toward the waiting plane. A chill ran down my spine as I identified the Ilyushin-18 prop plane and spelled out the airline's name in Cyrillic characters on its side: A           о        .

Then I noticed something rather odd. As if someone had waved a magic wand, all the ruddy-cheeked Finns from our flight over had disappeared. In their place were a hundred new people stampeding toward the airplane, all with a morose and Slavic tilt of eye. They all looked like Kharitonov. They were, every last goddamned one of them, Russians.

They had all been shopping, and were weighed down with many unwieldy parcels—how they were going to get all that stuff on the plane, I could not fathom. When they reached the metal staircase that fed into the plane's belly, they began to push and shove to get aboard. We were jostled and elbowed and I, for one, complained loudly, but no one paid any heed.

Eventually our group found our assigned seats, and sat down. I had a window seat, Jeffrey the middle seat, and on the aisle was a fat, swarthy, fragrant fellow, probably from one of the southern Republics of the USSR.

I was flabbergasted by how plain the cabin was. There were no overhead compartments with doors that snapped shut, only open metal racks which were rapidly being filled with packages. The fabric covering the seats was dingy and dirty, the walls were scuffed, and the seat belts were frayed. In fact, mine never would buckle, because the catch was broken. The ventilation was either malfunctioning or wasn't turned on yet, because the interior of the cabin was hot as hell and stank like a ripe cheese. As I stared at my surroundings, there was a high shrill whine next to my right ear. In disbelief, I slapped at—and missed—a fly.

"Jeffrey," I whispered, "did you see that?"

"Yeah," he mumbled. He looked mortified, as if the shabby condition of the plane reflected on him personally.

"I don't get it." I was bewildered. We both knew there were supposed to be shortages now and then in the Soviet Union, and that accommodations could be a bit spartan, but this was just crazy. Jeffrey did not reply.

"And here I thought the Soviet Union was supposed to be a superpower," I said. "They've just been fooling all this time."

He shook his head, and still didn't answer.

I studied the rows and rows of people in front of me. Was it the government's policy to let them out once in a while for a shopping trip in Helsinki, if they were good? Suddenly I remembered someone's old diary in the Bunker saying that when Americans went abroad, they visited museums; but when the Russians got out of Russia, they went shopping.

I endured my suffering like a true stoic, except when they neglected to tell us to bring our seats to an upright position during the takeoff. I squeezed my eyes shut and comforted myself with the thought that despite this safety omission, we weren't going to die. If we went down, so would the pilot; even in Russia, pilots surely prized their lives.

At length I noticed Jeffrey kept looking at his watch, as if waiting for something. Finally the tension built up to a point where he had to speak to me—after all, I was the only one within earshot who could possibly understand what he was going through.

He glanced at his watch still another time and said in hushed tones, "We just passed over the border into Russia."

I looked out of the window. The bright sunlight of Finland had disappeared under high clouds. We were flying over a land that was flat, shadowy, and mysterious.

By now I was annoyed beyond appeasement at the slovenliness of our surroundings. "Yep, it's ground," I said sourly. "Yep, dang sure is ground. Flat ground. Hell, it could be Texas."

"Fuck you!" Jeffrey muttered. He crossed his arms over his chest and turned toward the aisle seat, as if he would find superior companionship there. Instead, he came face-to-face with the interested countenance of the smelly southern fellow.

"You want to sell your sport shoe?" the man asked in thickly accented English. "You want to sell your jeans?"

Jeffrey fixed him with a horrible blue gaze. "No. What would I wear in the airport?"

The guy just shrugged and grinned. No harm in trying, he seemed to say. He leaned across Jeffrey and gave me an ingratiating smile. "You want to sell clothes, miss? You have ballpoint pen?"

I shook my head and waved him away. "So, Jeffrey," I said. "The New Soviet Man is quite interested in consumer goods!"

He ignored me, and I turned back to the window. Although I wouldn't admit it to Jeffrey, a chill had run down my spine at this early glimpse of Mother Russia, vast and gray.

We landed in Moscow about an hour later. When we finally came to a stop outside the terminal, we couldn't deplane; first an official had to come on board and check all our passports against a manifest of some sort. Then we had to wait while one guy unloaded everyone's baggage from the belly of the plane. Then each of us had to collect his own luggage and drag it into the terminal.

As we traipsed across the tarmac toward the gate, I bundled up in my jacket and shivered with cold. I was so tired I felt absolutely no apprehension at walking right into the maw of the Iron Curtain. All I wanted to do was sleep.

An interminable time later, we were directed to a passport control point. Professor Sergeyev went through first, without incident, and then I approached the booth and showed my passport.

The guy behind the glass was young, probably in his early twenties. He took my passport and looked repeatedly from the picture to my face and back to the passport again. His eyes, which were dark brown, were cold and hard. For what seemed like an hour he stared at me, until I began to feel furtively guilty. At length my nerves could take no more, and I began to giggle.

With a final measuring look, he returned my passport. His face remained completely impassive. "*Spasiba*," he said.

Then I was over hurdle number one. Ahead was number two: customs itself. I told myself it would go quickly; after all, we had filled out the required declaration forms on the plane, and they had already been turned over to the proper officials.

Again, Professor Sergeyev got through quickly, but the Russian official, a heavyset guy in an untidy gray uniform, went through his baggage in a way that made me uneasy.

Jeffrey had learned the ropes from somewhere. When the official went through his suitcase, Jeffrey looked dreamily into space, and tapped two packs of Marlboros absentmindedly on the counter. The guy took them and whisked Jeffrey on through.

I began to sweat. When my turn came, I laid my suitcase on the table in front of the official and waited. The official fumbled through its contents and then snapped it shut. "How many traveler check?" he barked.

I had already put on my form the total amount I'd brought with me, but I choked. "A couple hundred?" I asked.

He scowled. "You bring Soviet currency?"

"No."

He eyed me and then pointed to my purse. "Open."

A second official, younger and with a sprinkling of pimples on his cheeks, appeared at his side. He also stared at me. I hadn't done anything wrong, but I knew I had turned pale. When people looked at me as if I were guilty, I tended to feel guilty.

I put my purse on the table and they pawed through it. Finding nothing in it to interest them, they still wouldn't let me go. "Any food?" they asked, pointing to my carry-on suitcase.

"Yes," I replied. I was carrying all the cans of tuna fish, dried beef, and sardines that Jeffrey and I had brought as possible picnic provisions.

"Give!" ordered the first official.

"Why?" I asked. They didn't answer.

Jeffrey caught my eye and nodded. Pissed, I turned over the goodies, which the officials stuffed into a sack and put out of sight under the table.

The older official was not through with me yet. "Any newspapers, magazines?" he demanded.

"None of your fucking business," I said in Russian—or words to that effect.

I know, I shouldn't have sassed them. And I sure paid for my crime. They went *hog-wild*. I won't go into all the excruciating details here. Suffice it to say that they tore my luggage apart and confiscated my pair of good blue jeans, with the lame excuse that I must be intending to trade them on the black market. They stole all my reading materials and all the cheap cosmetics I actually *had* brought to trade on the street.

Because of me, they detained our group for an hour, leaving me in tears, Jeffrey in a rage, and the rest of the tour really unhappy with me. It was a wonderful welcome to the Soviet Union.

And that was not the last of it. Not only were my fellow tourists pissed at me, but so was Olga, our Intourist guide.

Olga was exactly what you'd picture, given her name—a big, square buffalo of a woman, born the year of the Great October Socialist Revolution, and fiercely patriotic. She wore a dowdy blue woolen suit, cut in a mannish way. Her only concession to fashion was a bright scarf, draped rather incongruously around her neck. She tucked her gray hair into a bun on the nape of her neck, had a steel front tooth, and sported a pair of hideous black glasses that were no doubt provided free by the state.

You think I'm kidding? You think I'm cheating in my diary and reciting a stereotype, don't you? Well, a lot of stereotypes have a basis in reality—how else do you think they get started?

She was fervently proud of her Party membership. Whenever anyone on the tour asked her what she thought about the United States, or any Western country for that matter, she would shrug and invariably reply, "*U nas luche*"—"Everything is better here."

Olga was not at all happy with me for having razzed the authorities and thrown our group off schedule. She lectured me in Russian about my bad attitude and lack of moral fiber. She speculated that I was the spoiled granddaughter of a bunch of corrupt White Russians who, like rats, had deserted the Motherland during the Revolution. And she expressed pleasure that I would soon learn just what a workers' Eden had been created in my absence, in which I could never have a place.

Having fixed me but good, she proceeded to take every-body's passport away—a routine matter, she assured us, for our own protection. Not that I felt all that naked without it. I had other ID. Distrustful of the Soviets from the start, I had encased my California driver's license in durable plastic, punched a hole in it, and strung it on a chain around my neck under my clothes.

Then she herded us onto a bus that would take us to the city and our hotel. Through the window, I watched the lead-colored landscape of Russia pass by.

My heart sank under the weight of a horrible, growing disappointment. This dreary country was not the Utopia the Reds made it out to be. (Deep down, I had wanted to believe in that dream, if only just a little.) The highway, devoid of billboards, was also empty of cars; I had read that few Russians owned an automobile, but now it really came home to me. Though we were still in the countryside, there were no real farms to speak of. Every once in a while the ubiquitous skinny white birch trees would thin out, and you saw clusters of small, tin-roofed houses, each with its own fenced yard. But the houses were invariably dilapidated, weeds choked the yard, the fences were falling down, and nothing looked prosperous. It was incredibly depressing— nothing like what Soviet publications had led us to expect.

Russia was a mess. Just like in the fairy tale, the emperor was buck naked. The Great and Powerful Oz had at least turned out to be a dapper little man; Russia, unmasked, was a pauper.

I knew we had reached the outskirts of Moscow when I spotted a row of enormous, grim-looking apartment houses, so alike they might all have come off the same assembly line. Their concrete grayness was broken only by the green of overgrown grass. There weren't even any flowers, on the ground or in the windows.

I drew a deep, shaky breath and thought to myself: I hate this place.

## 8

## July 1963: Moscow

Our hotel, the Ukraina, barely five years old, was a giant granite wedding cake of the ornate "Stalinist gothic excess" school of architecture. The place bore quite a resemblance to the main building of the University of Moscow, which figured prominently in every Moscow guidebook; American visitors were fond of referring to this latter as "Big Brother U."

By the time we got to the Ukraina, I wished to heaven that I'd just doused myself with a whole bottle of perfume and used the stinky bathroom on the airplane. I was in such agony, it defied description. Enhancing my newfound reputation as a tour troublemaker, I refused to wait until we had been "processed" and sent to our rooms to use the toilet, for I had this sneaking feeling that said processing would take a long, long time.

Russians do not like to deviate from programs, itineraries, or schedules. None of us was supposed to use the bathroom until we had been shuttled to our own private rooms. So I encountered considerable resistance in my quest until I told Olga, our Intourist guide, that I was on the verge of having an accident right there in the lobby of the Ukraina, and what's more, if I did, I would give the story to the newspapers when I got back.

Now, Olga didn't know whether to believe me. And she personally didn't really give a damn what the capitalist papers might say. However, she was not willing to call my bluff. She did not want to Make a Mistake in handling her charges. If she Made a Mistake, she would look bad to her bosses. And face it, having a female tourist engage in antisocialist behavior in the lobby of the Ukraina on Olga's watch would definitely be a Mistake. So, even though she wasn't sure I would go through with my threat, I had her undivided attention.

She excused herself to the rest of our now-glowering group, and led me twenty whole feet down the marble-lined lobby from the reception desk and pointed at a door labeled "Women" in Russian. It was opposite the entrance to a hotel restaurant. Radical though the notion seems, the bathroom was clearly intended for use by women visiting the hotel who did not have time to return to their homes elsewhere in the Soviet Union to perform their natural functions. I thanked Olga and dashed inside.

Words cannot describe my chagrin when I opened the first stall and found that the entire toilet fixture apparently had been removed, leaving only a hole in the concrete floor.

Hurriedly, I went on to the next stall. There, too, the toilet was gone. I found this to be the case in the third and the fourth stall, and suddenly it dawned on me that there never had been any toilet fixtures at all. What you saw was what you got. Sanitary arrangements in the tradition of Genghis Khan.

Then I noticed a separate stall, set aside from the others, that was somewhat bigger. I yanked open the door and saw, to my delight, a lone white porcelain apparition fit for the gods.

It had once possessed a toilet seat. But that had been removed. Neither was there any toilet paper. However, in a corner behind the toilet I saw a pile of what looked like large cotton balls or hunks of cotton wool, stained with blood. For a moment I couldn't for the life of me figure out what they were, or what they were doing there.

Then light dawned. *Many* consumer goods were hard to

come by in the Soviet Union, even those that Western women considered indispensable. (Although, strangely, there seemed to be plenty of smelly *papirosi* cigarettes for the men.)

I gave an exclamation of outrage and disgust, relieved my bladder, and returned to the group, where the processing took an hour and a half. Then, mercifully, we were allowed to take the elevator halfway up the twenty-nine-story skyscraper to our room, where we were expected to freshen up for twenty minutes before reconvening downstairs for supper. On the way up I hissed at Jeffrey, "This is *not* the worker's paradise. It is not anybody's paradise. It is just plain *shabby*!"

Our room ran true to form. It had narrow little twin beds and looked like it had been furnished from an S&H Green Stamp store in 1955. At first I thought we had been given this dump because we were passing as brother and sister; later I learned that the one married couple in our group had been given the same wretched little twin beds too.

However, the view from the tower was magnificent. From the fifteenth story, our window overlooked a hairpin turn in the Moskva River and Kalinin Prospekt, the broad, modern street that led due east to the Kremlin.

The view was thrilling, and at last I began to feel impressed. Then something odd happened. As I took in the scenery, my gaze fell on a nondescript, empty piece of land directly across from the hotel. Try as I might to focus on more impressive sights, my eyes kept being drawn back to it. Each time I looked at the spot I felt weird as hell. It was like time shivered; it was most bizarre. Nonplussed, I turned to my guidebook, and discovered that particular spot was part of the "Krasnopresenskaya Embankment." Not very helpful.

"Jeffrey, look down there," I said, pointing to the vacant patch of land. "Do you feel anything strange?"

He frowned. "Looking at it makes me dizzy. Weird."

I figured we must have low blood sugar brought on by

starvation since leaving Finland, so I hurried Jeffrey back
down the elevator to our designated dining room. When I
heard we were having roast chicken, my mood greatly
improved. I even sat back and downed a bottle of strange-
tasting but cold beer, and started joking with some of the
other students. Then the feast arrived.

"Roast chicken" turned out to be a desiccated drumstick.
We also got half a pickle, some very greasy fried potatoes,
wilted cold cabbage, and a salad of onions and pale pink
tomatoes.

I was just *this far* from throwing a major temper tantrum.
Here's why. Although I am part Russian, I am also American in ancestry, and after living in San Francisco, I had
come to worship America. Well, California anyway. Now,
back in America all we ever heard out of the Soviets was
how hard they worked, how much they suffered, how
superior socialism was, how their kids could read and ours
couldn't, how they were going to bury us or get to the moon
first, and how they were the friend of oppressed peoples and
we weren't. To hear them talk, all they needed was five
more years, and they'd build heaven on earth.

Well, we'd been had. If they couldn't even put on a good
show to impress visiting American running-dog tourists,
that meant they were hard up as hell.

To pay for the military, and for all the hardware the
Soviets sent into space and trotted out to Red Square on
May Day and Revolution Day, the ordinary citizen was
doing without basic necessities that were simply taken for
granted in America. This country and all its propaganda
were just plain frauds.

Jeffrey was quiet throughout dinner, barely touching his
food. He had the same look on his face as when Kharitonov
had shown up at the City of Paris in shabby old clothes. He
was also starting to realize we'd been misled, and it hurt.

After dinner, we retreated to our room. I tried to sleep, but
Jeffrey kept me awake, tossing on his little twin bed across
the room. Finally he got up, turned on the light, and dressed.

"I'll be back," he said darkly—pure Matt Dillon to Kitty, before the big gunfight. He took some dollar bills and a package of Marlboros and disappeared. In less than twenty minutes he returned, grinning, bearing an ice-cold bottle of lemon-flavored vodka. A few shots each, and we slept like babies.

The next day was a horror. Breakfast was revolting: a bowl of tepid stewed grain, called *kasha; kefir*, a fermented milk drink; and fried potatoes, fried egg, fried beef, and fried sausage. Then we were bused to the famous Palace of Congresses on the grounds of the Kremlin. This was a big modern building which contained offices, meeting rooms, and a huge auditorium with Lenin's head on the backdrop, where the Communist Party held all its meetings. The decor of that auditorium brought to mind a peasant's notion of luxury, or maybe a whorehouse—there were excessive amounts of red velvet upholstery and gold trim. It clashed in every way imaginable with the rest of the stately, ancient Kremlin structures.

In a wood-paneled conference room at the palace, we were subjected to a three-hour address on Soviet-American relations by a guy with an accent just like Boris on *Rocky and Bullwinkle*. Halfway through, desperate for a break in the boredom, I told Jeffrey I was going to the ladies' room, and fled.

I was all braced for another unpleasant experience. But this time the bathroom was splendid—a regular palace within a palace. It even had a separate lounge with magazines and soft chairs for relaxing. Clearly, the Party did not spare the horses when it came to the comfort of its own.

I settled down in a plush chair and picked up a freshly printed copy of a magazine called *Soviet Woman*. It had a variety of articles, which I perused at my leisure: "The Greatness of Lenin"; "A Message from the Soviet Premier"; and "Rumania's Liberation from the Fascist Yoke." I would rather have had my stolen fashion magazines back, but even so, it was a chuckle.

After about fifteen minutes I heard heavy footsteps outside. I must have had a guardian angel, for something told me to throw the magazine down and feign serious illness. I slumped down in the chair, put a hand to my tummy, and clapped the other one over my brow—the Lady of the Camellias herself, the very image of suffering. All this saved me from brutalization at the hands of Olga, who had grown suspicious, and come to check up on me.

"You are ill?" she demanded.

I looked up at her and sighed like I was dying. "Woman's trouble," I said in Russian.

"You have no American medicine?"

"Only time can ease the pain," I replied. I agree, it suffers in the translation.

She actually looked sorry for me. "You Americans don't know everything. If only my grandmother were here, she could make a tea for you that would stop all the pain."

I examined her closely, thinking she was being a jerk, but her face was suffused with an expression of sympathy.

"Your grandmother is still alive?" I asked.

"Eighty-five years old. She has survived everything."

That meant she had been born around 1878. She really had seen it all. "Wow," I said.

"You stay here," said Olga, "until you are well."

I was flabbergasted. Underneath that gray steel exterior there lurked a human being.

I did get better, right around lunchtime. Funny about that. I was contemplating the prospect of another rancid meal, when to my surprise they led us in a big room lined with buffet tables. I almost fainted with shock.

These tables were the length of a city block. They groaned with Beluga caviar with lemon and onion and sour cream for garnish, smoked salmon, sturgeon, chicken and jellied meats, fruit, lavish salads, and enough vodka and wine for an army.

Jeffrey and I exchanged outraged glances. "These Party guys are living like kings," he said, loading up on the caviar.

"Hypocrites," I said, chowing down as fast as I could.

The rest of the day consisted of an escorted tour around the Kremlin, with Olga droning on and on with facts about the sites we visited. I swear, nice person underneath or not, she could make even the bloody dark tapestry of Russian history seem boring—a really heinous crime.

"Jeffrey," I said at last, "I can't take two weeks of this. We've got to get away from her."

Back at the hotel, dinner dragged on forever, thanks to the damn lackadaisical waiters—as employees of the state, they couldn't be fired. By the time we were finished, it was dark outside. Jeffrey and I wanted to go exploring, but everybody else was still jet-lagged. "Let's sneak out," I suggested.

We had little Ukraina guest cards that would allow us to get in and out of the hotel. We said we were going to our room, slipped away from Olga and the group, and struck out on our own.

You find it surprising we could do this? Admittedly, by 1963 most Americans who visited the Soviet Union thought they would be followed wherever they went by relentless, malevolent, bloodless human robots who worked for the KGB. And I'm positive some people were followed . . . even harassed. But as I got to know the Soviets, I came to appreciate the sheer magnitude of effort required for them to get their shit together and do anything right. If they'd tried to tail everyone in our tour group, it would have absorbed the available resources of the entire Moscow branch of the KGB. We simply weren't worth it.

So, off we went. The hotel sat right on the south bank of one twist and turn of the Moskva River, hard by one of the many bridges that spanned the river as it wound its way through the city. We hopped across said bridge to Kalinin Prospekt, which would take us straight to the Kremlin and Red Square.

Now, at last, I began to be mildly impressed. Kalinin Prospekt was wide, spacious, and brightly lit, just like in a real metropolis. On the right side of the boulevard stood brand-new office towers; on the left side more were being built. Seeing them, you could almost believe in socialist progress.

As we crossed the bridge, I got that strange feeling again. I looked to my left and focused on that empty spot of land on the river's edge—the same spot that had given me the willies from my window. Then the most extraordinary sensation passed through me. It reminded me of time travel. It was like I was on a train, moving swiftly down the track of history, and had hit a bump.

I felt giddy and disoriented, as if there had been a small earthquake—one that jostled not the ground I stood on, but the fabric of time itself. "Did you feel it?" I asked Jeffrey.

"Yeah," he said uneasily. "What was it?"

I didn't have a clue. So I buttonholed an old guy passing by and asked him in Russian if there was something special about that spot. Was it the site of some ancient battle or massacre?

He favored us with a beady-eyed, mistrustful, unblinking stare, like we were creatures from a UFO. This was the "Russian stare," with which all foreigners soon became acquainted.

I repeated my question. Now the old guy began to look nervous. It was one thing to stare at us; talking to us was another matter entirely. He might be seen.

I was about to remind him that Comrade Stalin had been dead for ten years when he pointed at me and asked, "*Amerikanka*?"

I looked at Jeffrey. "How does he know? Is my accent that bad?" Jeffrey shrugged.

"*Da*," I said, and repeated my question a third time.

Reluctantly, the old man answered. "That is the place where one day they will erect the new parliament building for the Russian Soviet Federated Socialist Republic."

"When?"

He shrugged. "It has been planned for many years.

Perhaps in twenty more it will be built. I don't make the decisions."

"*Spasiba*," I said. He took off at a brisk trot.

"I feel very uncomfortable," I stated. "That is simply an empty field. Nothing is happening there at all."

"Yet," said Jeffrey, looking like he'd been goosed.

Light dawned. "Yes! That's it! Jeffrey, *something* is here. In the future. The answer to something—or the site of something. But what?" At a loss, he only shook his head.

We walked on toward the Kremlin. In moments we were on a pedestrian overpass crossing another major artery, the Garden Ring Road, which circles the entire inner city of Moscow. I glanced right, and got whacked again by that strange shuddery feeling. When I looked down at the pavement, the patches of oil and grease left by passing cars looked like blood. Lots of it.

"Damn," I muttered, "there are ghosts here or something."

Jeffrey took a very deep breath. "Yes. Something's going to happen here in the future. That's the only explanation."

"But we've *changed* the future. So it hasn't happened yet! Like you said that time, nothing is graven in stone here."

His expression grew thoughtful. "You know, we like to think of time as a continuum, but that doesn't mean it is one. We're beings of extremely limited intellectual capacity. The nature of time may be totally beyond our comprehension."

I shivered. "Oh, blah," I said, to give myself courage.

"I once read something to the effect that, in the mind of God, all moments in history are eternally present. It stands to reason that we, being more limited of vision, can't see the big picture like God does. Think about it: What if this spot is the site of a major future branch point? Or even a *possible* major future branch point? If all times and all possible worlds *are* eternally present, no wonder the spot feels weird to us."

"I didn't know you read such high-minded books, Jeffrey."

"I don't make a habit of it," he said defensively. "If you must know, I stayed up and read lots of philosophy and religion the night Father Alexeyev got so upset."

"You mean you took on John F. Kennedy and his brother with no sleep?" He nodded. "You idiot," I muttered, even though I had done the very same thing.

We stayed on the right side of the boulevard, so we could look at the shops we passed. They were all closed, of course, but we still got a kick out of reading off their names. Russians have this remarkable inability to bestow appealing names upon their shops. Secondhand books are found at Bookstore Number 14, foreign books at Bookstore Number 18. If you want bolts, it's off you go to Bolt Factory Number 9. On Kalinin Prospekt, a lady in search of new clothing would visit the Shop of Ladies' Garments. If she desired a meal, she would descend upon the Pre-Cooked Foods Cafe. Then she might hop on down the street and visit her husband or paramour at work at the "Central Research Institute of Health Resorts and Physiotherapy."

Enough funning at the expense of the Soviets. We pushed on, past the darkened Arbat District, and shortly came to Karl Marx Prospekt, where we found ourselves gazing up at the Kremlin's high brick walls and turreted gates, topped by glowing red stars. The whole tableau was sinister and impressive as hell.

There was a full moon that night. It must have made us bold, because we began hurrying, then running. We headed to the Alexandrovsky Gardens, at the foot of the Kremlin's western wall, and turned left. A short way farther, by a dark red granite building that was a historical museum, we found a narrow entrance into Red Square.

In old Slavonic, the square's name was *Krasnaya*, which meant not only "red," but "beautiful." There it was, just like in all the books, only this time real and grand and awe-inspiring.

Now, I must confess to you, my heart began to hammer. Before me, completely deserted, bathed in cold moonlight,

lay the square I had heretofore seen only in pictures and
newsreels, in which so much history was made—the square
through which, each May Day, were paraded the weapons
that had destroyed my world.

For centuries Red Square had been the center of Russian
life. There was iron here, and blood and power. It was vast;
as I walked, my footsteps echoed and died too quickly. On
my left was the long Victorian facade of GUM, the
department store, now deserted and ghostlike under the full
moon. On my right was the low, forbidding mausoleum that
housed the remains of Lenin himself. Inside, his mummified
body lay in state in a glass casket; there visitors wept, knelt,
and crossed themselves.

But ahead . . . oh, ahead lay a great marvel. Ahead lay
St. Basil's Cathedral, the violently colored fantasy of
twisted onion domes built hundreds of years before by Ivan
the Fourth, called the Terrible, to commemorate the destruction of the Khanate of Kazan. To most men and women, it
was the symbol of Russia. I could feel that some of my
ancestors had sprung from this thousand-year-old city, and
that part of my own life and being were rooted in that very
spot.

There was no lighting on the cathedral that night, except
for the moon. Its vast bulk rose up in front of us like a
barbaric Joseph's coat in stone, its riot of colors softened
and grayed by the pale light, but not its sinister majesty.

Over the centuries, in Red Square below the cathedral,
there had been fires, massacres, markets, rebellions, decrees
by the czars, and marches of victory and of sorrow. Near the
south end was a stone platform known as *Lobnoye Mesto*, or
the Place of Skulls, where executions and burnings were
carried out. The stones of the square had run with blood
more times than anyone could count. In 1917, the Bolsheviks
had stormed the Kremlin, and many died. Here, in 1945,
German flags and Hitler's personal standard were dragged
through the dust in a great parade. Here, more recently, Yuri
Gagarin was welcomed back from outer space.

To me, the very earth under Red Square was different from the rest of the city. In my mind's eye it glowed, as if radioactive, from the centuries of human despair and desire that had been trapped within its confines. I did not know how long I would be able to stay there.

I think there must be a malady that affects time travelers. We cannot stay long in a place where too many people have lived, or died, or prayed, or hoped. Truly, there are ghosts in the world, and we, who have broken the laws of nature, are forever afterward too aware of these spirits for sanity's sake. We are as Poe's poor Roderick Usher, exquisitely sensitive to the slightest sound, the slightest trace of their vanished lives. In such places, the walls that confine us to one time and one place, and protect us from the emotion of other ages, do not hold as they do for other people.

I had to get out of there. I could hear the ghosts whispering. If I stayed there much longer, I might actually start to understand what they were saying. I turned to Jeffrey, and found to my astonishment that he had sat down on the cobblestones and was crying.

He raised his head. He didn't look at me, but at the cathedral, and said, "Anna, everything's gone so wrong here."

I crouched down beside him. "What do you mean?"

"This could have been the greatest country in the world," he continued. "Instead it's just . . . pathetic."

"No, no," I said, pointing at St. Basil's, "not everything."

He shot me a reproving look. "Russia sucks, and you know it. You haven't stopped wrinkling your lip since we arrived."

He had me. "Yeah, the country is in pretty poor shape."

Jeffrey lowered his head again. "I guess you can kill anything, if you keep after it long enough."

"What? What's killed?"

"The Russian spirit. It was in all their old music and poetry and books. Kharitonov had a spark of it. Solzhenitsyn still believes in it. But I think they've killed it—the

Mongols, the Vikings, the Poles, the French, the Germans. Lenin and Stalin and the Communists. Anna, in the eleventh century, Kiev was one of the richest cities in Europe. It had paved streets a hundred years before Paris. Then the Mongols came and wiped out two-thirds of the people. It's been like that ever since. Every time the Russians got to their feet, somebody came along and cut them off at the knees. Now they've just given up."

I sat beside him, in the shadow of the moonlit cathedral, gripping his hands in mine. He cried for a while longer, until he got it out of his system, or was simply too wrung out to continue. "God!" he said at last. "I feel like an old man."

"Jeffrey," I said thoughtfully, "maybe we're zeroing in on the problem. If things had ever gone well for Russia—even one time—think how different our world would be."

At that moment we heard a footstep. We looked up to see a pale, thin Russian youth with a black leather jacket and a ducktail hairdo reminiscent of the last decade.

"Oh, for God's sake, not now!" I cried. "Go away!"

"*Amerikanka*? You sell cigarette, pen, clothes?" he asked.

This was the ultimate blow. Jeffrey started laughing like a crazy man. It wasn't nice laughter, not at all.

I glared at our visitor. I had to save this situation somehow. "How did you know we were Americans?" I asked in Russian. "Tell the truth."

He seemed quite taken aback. "By your shoes, of course, and your clothes. I could tell from the other end of the square."

"So you want to buy our clothes?" I inquired.

"Yes, yes. I will give you many rubles for them."

I was starting to have a *great* idea. Jeffrey and I were going to go searching for that vanished Russian spirit—incognito. "Stand up!" I hissed at Jeffrey.

"Okay, look," I said to our visitor. "What's your name?"

"Yevgeny," he replied.

"Okay, Yevgeny, you take a real good look at my friend and me. We'll meet you here tomorrow night at this exact same time. I want you to bring complete sets of real Russian clothes and shoes that will fit both of us. In return, we'll give you these clothes."

He looked at me like I was crazy. "You want *Russian* clothes?"

"Yes, we do. No more questions, or the deal is off."

He responded well to the authoritarian approach. "*Khorosho,*" he said. "Okay."

"Are you out of your mind?" Jeffrey demanded.

"No," I said. "With Russian clothes, we'll blend in. We can go anywhere we want and see what we want. Maybe we'll find slumbering sparks of that Russian spirit you're mourning."

He gave a sour laugh. "I doubt it."

"Now *you're* talking like a Russian! 'No, it won't work. No, I won't try.' Shit, Jeffrey, there's always hope."

The Russian guy gave Jeffrey a very nervous look. "It's okay," I said quickly. "We'll meet you here tomorrow and you can have all these clothes plus some dollar bills. Is it a deal?"

"*Da, da, da,*" he said, nodding emphatically.

"See you then. Bye."

He disappeared into the shadows from whence he had come.

"I can't wait until tomorrow," I said, insufferably smug.

## 9

## Moscow (cont.)

With our drab new Soviet clothes, we could go anywhere. As a courtesy to our tour, each day Jeffrey and I hung around for (a) breakfast, (b) the boring official function that was unfailingly planned for the morning, and (c) lunch—where we ate as much as we could and stole rolls, sausages, cheese, and the like to nibble on later. This last was a vital necessity, since those Nazis in Russian customs had taken all our canned food. Then we would ditch the tour and split.

Permit me a digression here. We *had* to load up with supplies at lunch if we wanted to eat. See, the Soviet Union is not part of the normal world. In the normal world, you can go to a store or a restaurant and buy food. It's that simple. This equation holds whether a country is rich or poor, accessible or remote, Western or non-Western, so long as you have money. But in Russia, things don't work that way.

The usual tourist on a budget in a foreign country heads for the grocery store. There he buys practical items like bread, cheese, cooked meat, or canned fish. (I'm told that in France being poor like this can be a fabulous treat.) However, our one and only venture into a Russian *gastronom*, or food store, didn't quite turn out as expected.

One day we broke away from the tour before lunchtime. When our stomachs started to growl, we went into a grocery store in the heart of Moscow and were stopped dead in our tracks by a rank, stinky, fishy smell. Still, driven by hunger, we pressed onward. To our astonishment, there wasn't much in the store to buy at all. In the meat department there were no sausages, cold cuts, pâtés, or the like—just a few chunks of rotten-looking uncooked beef. Where one would expect to find cheese, the shelves were bare. The only ready-to-eat food available was a loaf of bread and some tins of evil-looking fish.

"I don't get it, Jeffrey," I whined. "What is the problem here?"

"I don't know, but we'll have to make do with the bread and fish." We steeled ourselves and bought them. But when we finally got out of the store and sat down on a stoop somewhere to eat, the fish tasted so vile we couldn't swallow it, and the bread must have been a week old.

So we went to a restaurant. There, another surprise awaited us. Even though the sign said OPEN, the workers refused to serve us. When we asked to order, they just shrugged and walked away.

"What's the matter, you won't serve us because we're Americans?" asked Jeffrey in Russian. His blood sugar was quite low by this time and he was spoiling for a fight. Most of the waiters laughed, but one of them came over to us.

"You have dollar bill?" he asked with great interest.

"Several," replied Jeffrey.

"Then we'll serve you."

"We'd rather pay you with all those rubles they made us buy at customs," Jeffrey replied. "This is Russia, after all. I assume you do accept rubles."

The waiter shrugged and started to go away. "Wait!" said Jeffrey. "We'll pay in dollars. Only explain why you won't take rubles."

The waiter was at our sides again in a flash. "You can actually buy things worth having with dollars," he said, as if explaining the matter to a small child. "Rubles are worthless. Why should we work for them?"

"But aren't you afraid of getting fired if you don't serve customers with rubles?"

The waiter laughed, as if Jeffrey had said the stupidest thing in the world. "We can't be fired. We work for the State."

Jeffrey and I exchanged puzzled looks. "As the saying goes," the waiter added, " 'The State pretends to pay us, and we pretend to work.' "

"I see," said Jeffrey.

The waiter seated us and, motivated by real spending money, rustled up some food in the kitchen. "I don't see how this society manages to function," I whispered.

"I don't either," replied Jeffrey.

The answer was, of course, that it didn't.

Thanks to our dollars, we were able to get a decent meal at that restaurant. The problem was, the staff demanded so many dollars, we would have gone broke within a week. So we were forced to filch food at breakfast and lunch to get through the trip.

According to my reading, Russians actually had worked hard back in the early days after the Revolution, when they still thought they were building the new Utopia, and food and basic supplies were available in Russia just like in other civilized countries. But nowadays people slid uncaring through their jobs, doing as little work as possible. After all, why exert yourself if you couldn't be fired, and if you wouldn't be rewarded for trying harder? Consequently, in Russia you couldn't buy any of the ordinary goods you take for granted in the West. Consequently, Russia itself was a mess.

In a couple of days, Jeffrey and I had learned our way around the Moscow subway, the Metro. Then we began to realize that our interests sharply diverged. True as ever to the spirit of our mission—and Kennedy's instructions—Jeffrey spent his afternoons skulking around the university, the Arbat District, and the Gorky State Park of Culture and Rest, getting exposed to as big a slice of Russian life as possible. I should have done so as well, but I wanted a small break from the World Savior detail. I wanted to see some art galleries. So we agreed to disagree, and went our separate ways.

Free at last of the tour and Jeffrey, about to bust with excitement, I headed for the world-famous State Tretyakov Gallery. In the Bunker our Russian ancestors had always referred to the Tretyakov as the glory of Moscow, so I was cranked up to see it.

Actually it had a few high points. I got goose bumps from the picture of Ivan the Terrible holding the body of the son he had just murdered. There was a good gruesome one of a maiden standing on a bed in a prison cell; lots of water is streaming into the cell from outside, and there are all these rats jumping onto the girl's bed to escape it. As you study the picture, you realize they're all going to drown. And the Tretyakov's first-floor collection of icons was great. But as for the rest—"Yecchh!" as Alfred E. Neuman always said in *Mad* magazine.

Ever heard of "Socialist Realism?" If not, lucky you. Let me give you a small sample of some of the works I saw on display that summer afternoon.

—A portrait of Maxim Gorky.

—A portrait of I. P. Pavlov (he of salivating dog fame)

—A painting entitled "Lunch Hour." It showed young women construction workers in Central Asia during—yep—their lunch hour. According to the legend, the artist, "in her rendering of abundant air and light, the unconstrained movement of the figures, and the wealth of colors, successfully conveys the merriment, vigor, and spontaneity of young Soviet women."

—And, finally, "J. V. Stalin at the Ryon Hydro-Electric Power Station," painted in 1935.

I tore out of there in a hurry and headed across town to the Pushkin Museum. While the Tretyakov clearly labored under a burdensome propaganda mission, surely a museum named after one of the world's great writers could not suffer the same fate.

Well . . . to be fair, the Pushkin does boast works by

Picasso, Cézanne, Van Gogh, Renoir, Monet, El Greco, Rivera, Rembrandt, and Rubens. I made it a point to see them all. But the Soviet mundane was everywhere intrusive. Most notable—and annoying—was a rendering of a young man and woman working on an electric power tower in the Caucasus Mountains. It was noted that "the artist conveys the enthusiasm of the younger generation of Soviet workers, the self-sacrificing builders of Socialist industry, to whom work is a matter of joy."

Then, to my surprise and delight, I discovered an out-of-the-way room full of pre-revolutionary portraits, including one by Valentin Serov. Understand, Serov was not the greatest painter in the world, but one of our ancestor Russians had brought some copies of Serov portraits from Leningrad's Russian Museum to the Bunker. In his luggage. These had been consigned to our Bunker museum and I had been very fond of them as a child.

Now here was a new and unfamiliar Serov portrait, of a young girl named Lydia Kardovsky. She was sitting at her dressing table on a spring morning, with sunlight pouring through French doors. Outside there was a garden full of flowers and apple trees in bloom. A breeze came through the window and stirred the curtains in the room, as it did her long, riotous red hair, which she was apparently trying to comb. The wind made this task extremely difficult; the artist had painted her laughing.

What gave me the creepy crawlies was that she looked a very, very great deal like me. Now, it was not beyond the bounds of possibility that this Lydia was a remote ancestor of mine. But still, for her to look so very much like me, so many generations removed—the notion was just wild.

Eventually I tore myself away. I was museum-ed out and wished to pursue pleasure elsewhere in the city. I figured somewhere there had to be somebody playing decent jazz. As I left the room, a man in a Red Army uniform passed me, going in.

Seeing a soldier in the museum was not so remarkable;

after all, the city was crawling with them. There were army guys everywhere you looked, usually carrying briefcases. The Soviet Army appeared to be the country's largest employer. But this particular soldier came to a screeching halt in front of Lydia Kardovsky's portrait and stood there as if bewitched.

I watched him for some time as he stared, apparently enraptured, at the long-dead aristocrat. I was really touched. Here was this guy, practically a Martian, gazing spellbound at the same portrait that had captivated me not so long ago. I considered asking him why he liked it so much.

Then I got this harebrained thought, this idea for a prank, and nothing in the world could have stopped me. Satan himself got into me and made me do it. There was no way I could have turned back; it was just too delicious.

Russians are big, slobbering romantics. Actually, so are Americans, but they usually have the cool to hide it. But here this guy was, mooning over this czarist portrait as if he'd never seen a woman before, and I was going to fix him.

I'd done up my hair (which was long, kinky, and inordinately red) in sensible braids, to keep it out of my way while I pursued High Culture with a low profile. Now I turned it loose, fluffed it up nice and sexy, and undid one button on my blouse. I composed myself, tiptoed over silently, and stood behind him. Then, in as sultry a voice as I could muster, I said in Russian, "My darling, I have been waiting a lifetime for you."

He turned. He was wearing one of those annoyed expressions that attractive men get when a mere mortal woman has the cheek to ask for a bit of their attention. Then he got a good look at me.

It was most gratifying. He gasped. He truly did look as if he'd seen a ghost. He turned white and stepped back and put out an arm as if to ward me off. Then he looked confused and walked right up to me and put his hands on my shoulders and gripped them tightly. For a minute I thought he was going to kiss me. If he had, my prank would have backfired, because I would have come unglued.

Explanation time! In five more years, in 1968, the Russians were going to come out with a fabulous six-hour version of *War and Peace*. A famous Russian heartthrob named Vyacheslav Tikhonov would play the hero, Prince Andrei Bolkonsky. I swear, I would have killed, or at least committed mayhem, to get my mitts on that guy for five minutes. Well, this army fellow was gorgeous in exactly the same way as ol' Slava Tikhonov, and I fell for it in 1963, just the way I would come 1968. Coal-black hair, fair skin, dark eyes, aquiline profile, and a bearing that—until right then—had been just a tad haughty.

I knew Russians mostly had bad teeth. I waited for him to open his mouth or smile. If I could only see his bad teeth or smell his bad breath, I knew it would break the spell.

I started to laugh. He looked from me to the portrait and back to me, and threw back his head and laughed too. He had beautiful teeth. What had he done, I wondered—wandered through the forest cleansing them with birch twigs when he was a boy?

No matter. I was in love. No, not in love—I've never been good at that. I was greatly, thoroughly in lust.

Jesus. He was really old, maybe even thirty, like Prince Andrei. His uniform looked really neat on him. I know this is fascist, but I grew up around so much military memorabilia, the sight of a man in a nice-fitting uniform just did things to me.

"You startled me so," he said in Russian. Yeah, yeah, he had a beautiful voice too. "I was so struck by the beauty of the girl in the painting, I forgot where I was. And then you . . ."

We started laughing again. *"Kak vas zavut?"* I asked.

"Lavrenti Borisovich Zorin," he replied. "What is yours?"

Woops. This was going to blow it. The minute he found out I was an American, he'd be gone. After all, he was an army officer—in fact, a major, or else I didn't know my Russian uniforms. "Anna Levchenko," I said.

He looked puzzled. When Russians introduce themselves, they always give their first name and their patronymic, their "son of" or "daughter of" middle name. His father's name was Boris, so he was Lavrenti Borisovich. Had my father's name been Dmitri, I would have been Anna Dmitrievna. But my father's name happened to be Charlie, so it just didn't work.

*"Ya amerikanka,"* I admitted.

He looked utterly amazed. "But your clothes . . . ?" he said.

"Bought, so I could explore Moscow incognito."

His eyes narrowed. "Let me hear you speak some English."

He didn't believe me, the scum. "Sure, baby!" I said, talking fast. "I'm from San Francisco and I have been to City Lights bookstore and every espresso joint in North Beach and met all the beatniks, even Allen Ginsberg. I am *cool.*"

Now he looked just the least bit dazed. "All right, you have convinced me. How long have you been in Moscow?"

"A week," I replied. "I have one more week to go."

He smiled again, showing those beautiful white teeth. "Moscow is not my home either. I am on leave here, also for one more week. Then I must return to my unit at Krasnoyarsk."

"Where were you born, if not Moscow?"

"In a small town in the Stavropol district. But I have been to Moscow many times. I received my schooling at Moscow State University, and now I visit the city whenever I have the chance."

"Then you've seen all the sights?" I asked.

He grinned. "Yes, but not on this visit. Not yet." And then, just like in a Harlequin romance, he offered me his arm.

## 10

## Moscow (cont.)

I have never been capable of losing my heart over a man. Perhaps it was my Bunker upbringing, or perhaps something within me. But I have been very capable of losing my mind, and that I did over Lavrenti.

It was pretty mutual. To Lavrenti I was foreign, exotic, tantalizing . . . as he was to me. Each of us epitomized the other's fantasies. And we only had a week in which to realize them.

I kept up my masquerade as a Russian, and nobody but Lavrenti and his friends ever knew the difference. With me looking like a local chick he'd picked up, we walked all over Moscow together. No one could tell us from any other soldier and his vacation girl.

Contrary to my first impression, the city actually had a pulse. We saw all the monuments of the czars, walked the city's showy streets, and ate delicious vanilla ice cream at the grandiose Exhibition of Economic Achievements. We went to Gorky Park and Serebryany Bor, or "Silver Forest," the park that is an island in the middle of the Moskva River. On sunlit summer afternoons, with my arm around Lavrenti, Moscow suddenly seemed fabulously beautiful—a cross between an elegant Italianate city and a vibrant, color-mad pagan capital straight from the pen of the American literary giant, Robert E. Howard.

Lavrenti knew underground clubs where they played the

latest rock and jazz, right under the nose of the Kremlin bigwigs. Like all Russians who had learned to work the system, he was very good at forming useful networks of acquaintances and friends. He knew a dozen kids in their twenties whose fathers were rich Party hotshots, and as many movers and shakers his own age who were scaling the Party ladder under their own steam. Lavrenti's friends threw a lot of shindigs, and he took me to all of them.

The first time we walked into a luxurious apartment and I saw a bunch of Russian kids jitterbugging to Elvis, I was stunned into silence. I was not myself again until they made me drink a large shot of ice-cold pepper vodka. I had only just recovered when they put on Jerry Lee Lewis and "Great Balls of Fire."

"What are you doing?" I cried to Lavrenti. "You're playing American rock and roll! I thought you hated America! Aren't you afraid the authorities will catch you?"

Amused, Lavrenti asked the host, Sasha, to show me his collection of jazz and pop records. Sasha was so proud. He had Benny Goodman, Nat King Cole, Louis Armstrong, Bing Crosby, Frank Sinatra, Duke Ellington, Woody Herman, Dizzy Gillespie, Charlie Parker, and even Peggy Lee.

Then I realized that if I hadn't known better, I'd have been sure I was at a party in America. Everyone was smoking Camels and had on nice, expensive American clothes. The flower of Communist youth, as they wallowed in Western corruption and rock and roll, looked more American than the kids I knew back home.

Dressed in my shabby Russian duds, *I* was the one who looked like a drip. People stared down their noses at me until Lavrenti explained I was a real American in clever disguise. Then I was mobbed with admirers. When they found out I was not only from America, but California, their hospitality knew no bounds.

"I really was under the impression that you Russians hated America," I said to Lavrenti in a plaintive tone of voice.

He laughed. "What a foolish idea."

"But the Party says we're evil," I replied.

"The Party says many things, but only children believe them."

I grew nervous, hearing such a sentiment voiced by a Red Army major. He had a career to ruin, after all. "Shh," I said. "What if somebody is listening? What if the room is bugged?"

Lavrenti laughed again. He was really amused. "Believe me, Anna, there is no one spying on *this* party."

"How do you know?"

"Sasha's father is a colonel-general in the KGB, and this is his apartment."

"Oh. So, you actually like America?" I asked.

"Yes. We very much admire American culture." No shit. He produced a pack of Pall Malls and offered me one. I accepted gladly. "Elvis Presley and Chubby Checker are Americans," he said. Then, after a wistful pause, "So was Marilyn Monroe."

"Well," I countered, "when Nikita Khrushchev visited California four years ago, he said Marilyn was the epitome of American decadence."

Lavrenti laughed. "That's what he *said*. That old woman-chaser would've given all our military secrets for one hour in her bed."

"My God. Red Army or not, you're a regular dissident."

"No, no! Most young people would share my opinions." Lavrenti narrowed his eyes and looked at me. He puffed on his cigarette and for a time said nothing. Then he said, "Tell me, Anna, did President Truman or President Eisenhower put your father in jail and then kill him?"

I was caught off guard; I couldn't imagine where this conversation was leading. "Of course not!"

"You say, 'Of course not.' You sound indignant. So, things like that don't happen in America, do they?"

"Well, if they do, they aren't very common."

"I was born in 1932," Lavrenti said. "In 1938, Comrade

Stalin sent my father to a camp and I never saw him again. In 1945 and 1946, when we were starving in my village, the only things I had to eat were yellow egg powder, canned ham, and concentrated milk, all from America. They were delivered in a car that had a name from a Wild West movie. What was it? Ah, yes—Dodge, like Dodge City. America is not my enemy."

With my heart in my mouth, I skated onto real thin ice. "Lavrenti, nine months ago we almost got into a nuclear war."

I was no mind reader, but I would have staked my life his surprise was genuine. "Don't be silly! Are you referring to that incident in Cuba?"

"Well, yes," I replied, trying to keep my voice neutral.

"There were many rumors at the time, but no one seriously thought there would be a war."

"Why not?"

"What would have been the point?"

A slow chill took shape at the base of my spine and crept upward toward my brain stem. He was a major in the Red Army, and even he didn't know how close it had been.

"Didn't your papers say anything about the crisis?" I asked.

"Yes. They said the Americans wanted to invade Cuba because it had embraced Communism."

*"Well?"*

"You Americans don't like Communism, but you wouldn't invade a peaceful island like Cuba unless there was a good reason."

"Whew," said I, mainly to myself, and took a deep, steadying drag on my cigarette.

"Some say Nikita Sergeyevich is impulsive, and a fool," continued Lavrenti, in utmost confidence, "but your President Kennedy would never let such a thing happen."

My eyes wanted to bug out on long, skinny stems. "What?"

"Your President Kennedy is a good man, a true leader. He would never go to war over something so silly."

"I have just crossed over into the Twilight Zone," I said. "I need a nice strong drink."

"What? Please, I do not understand."

I shook my head. "Just a joke. Would you get me a vodka?"

He jumped up and fetched me a glass liberally filled with lemon-flavored vodka. "So, you really like President Kennedy?" I asked, when I had chugged half of it.

He nodded. "My mother put his picture on the wall at home."

Only great personal discipline kept me from spewing lemon vodka all over the carpet. "If I had a picture of Khrushchev on my wall and the neighbors saw it, they wouldn't speak to me!"

He raised his eyebrows in a knowing look. "Perhaps your country is not as free as you think. But seriously, Anna, to us the President and Jackie are very exciting. They are so young and dashing and glamorous. And though they are rich, they work hard and seem to care for the American proletariat."

"Uh, yeah," I said faintly, "they do."

"To be fair," went on Lavrenti, "since Stalin died life in Russia has improved greatly. I have made fun of Nikita Sergeyevich, but he has opened as many windows to the outside world as Peter the Great—witness the visit of your student group. We have much more freedom, and these days the secret police rarely pound on one's door at midnight. I am grateful."

This was certainly a new perspective on Khrushchev. "I didn't realize that," I said.

Lavrenti waved his Pall Mall at the darkened room, where couples were now necking to the strains of "Johnny Angel" by Shelley Fabares. "Ordinary Russians, peasants, do not believe things will ever get better. But I'm biding my time. In twenty years, the people you see here will be heading the government. My comrades and I will have attained high rank in the army. Then, as says my far-seeing friend Misha from Stavropol, we can tear down the walls. Our two countries will be friends again, as when they met at the Elbe River at the end of the Great Patriotic War and shared vodka. Would you like some caviar?"

"Huh?" I said. "Yes, please."

He led me over to a linen-bedecked table. On it was an enormous cut-glass bowl, nestled in an even larger bowl of crushed ice, that was brimming with caviar. "The finest beluga," said Lavrenti. There was noticeable pride in his voice; even he could not resist bragging in front of an American. He told me that it was permitted to spoon up the caviar and garnish it with lemon, tiny bits of shaved onion, sour cream, or tiny little chives before eating; but that the purist took his caviar straight, crushing the eggs against the roof of his mouth and downing a chaser of ice-cold vodka. I tried the caviar every which way I could; I can testify that it was heavenly no matter what you did.

When I had only four days left in Moscow I got desperate. Lavrenti had been a perfect gentleman, and had not once made a pass at me. Maybe he figured he could get a girl for sex anywhere, but he wasn't likely to stumble across another stray disguised *amerikanka* any time soon, and he didn't want to blow it. God, maybe he *respected* me! So I had to kiss him long and passionately in Gorky Park before he saw reason.

I knew it would speed up my acculturation process to experience sexual intercourse, and there was going to be no better time in the world than now, with this incredible man. Unfortunately, Lavrenti was staying at an army barracks outside town. Though he had local friends, they lived in small flats with their families. And he didn't want to ask the others, the rising luminaries, the Party kids, for an apartment. Afterward they would snicker and ask him questions; he said he was getting too old for that, especially where somebody like me was concerned. So there was no place we could go to be alone.

Except the forest. I soon learned that one of the many Russian euphemisms for having sex is "to go for a walk in the forest." Well, in a land with few cars, no motels, and little private housing, that's what you had to do.

Having been well prepped for our Russia trip by San Francisco emigres, Jeffrey and I had brought all sorts of stuff to trade for Russian goods. As you know, they robbed me of my stash at customs. But Jeffrey still had a lot of goodies, including rubbers, of which I swiped half a dozen. Lavrenti was thunderstruck; in Moscow, they would have cost half a year's wages. But I was an American—that is, an Alien—and it was a proven fact that Aliens could do anything they wanted. He didn't ask questions. And he didn't think me evil and wanton for wanting to have sex. Anyone with the least bit of culture had seen American movies and knew it was okay for Americans—that is, Aliens—to have sex, because they did it all the time.

I had read a great deal about sex and had gleaned that it could be a messy and unpleasant—and even painful—business the first time. I figured that I was so intoxicated and infatuated with Lavrenti, I would never notice. I was mostly right.

It was a beautiful, warm, sunny afternoon when we took the Metro to the end of the line, northwest of Moscow. We had food and drink which we carried in a couple of sacks, since Lavrenti owned no picnic basket, and several blankets and a small pillow.

We came up out of the subway and walked a couple of miles past blocks of ugly gray apartment complexes. Then, abruptly, the city stopped, and were surrounded by skinny birch trees.

We walked another mile or two. We were both pretty nervous, so walking was sort of the natural thing to do. When we were way out of town and the sun was threatening to set, Lavrenti spotted a cozy little grove way off the road, and we went for it.

The vodka he'd brought helped a lot. We drank about half of it and had some of the picnic goodies and laughed and acted silly. Then we got down to it and crawled between the blankets.

This is really none of your business, but I will tell you a little bit anyway.

In the Bunker, living a sort of death, we had learned to dampen the vividness of our feelings. Emotions should be painted in oils, but, confined as we were, we could not bear such brightness; we stripped it out until nothing was left of life but its watercolor shadow. When something threatened to move us or hurt us too much, we emasculated it. True, that way lay misery, but—listen carefully—that way also lay sanity and survival.

This strategy would not do for Lavrenti. Flat on my back, with the fading sun shining into my eyes, the birch trees in motion above, and a beautiful man on top of me, I forgot all that Bunker shit. I wasn't observing life anymore; I was part of it.

I suffered some discomfort, but I just swigged more vodka and we made love two more times in spite of it. I was determined to extract every last drop of intensity from this experience. In my entire life, I had never been so close to another human being in body or spirit, and it was not likely to happen again any time soon. Not until long past midnight did Lavrenti and I pack up our belongings and head back to the Metro and civilization. Around 2:30 A.M., I bribed the Ukraina doorman with some of Jeffrey's Marlboros to let me in and sneaked into our room.

Jeffrey woke up the minute I opened the door. He sat up in bed and cried, "Where have you been? I have to talk to you!"

Before I could even reply, he continued, aggrieved, "You came in late last night, and then you ran off after lunch before I could get two words out of my mouth. Anna, I don't know what's going on, but I really needed you today and you weren't there!"

"Ain't life a bitch?" I replied. "What happened?"

He ignored my sarcasm. "I met a girl!"

"Wow! Russia's got all the modern conveniences!"

"Anna," he said in a hurt voice, "this is really important."

I felt ashamed. He was clearly nuts about this unnamed girl, and his closest friend wouldn't even listen. "I'm sorry," I said. "You tell me all about it. Then I've got something to tell you."

"I was over at the university, and heard there was going to be an avant-garde art show all day tomorrow at this park in the Lenin Hills. I started talking to some of the students, and met this wonderful girl, Rima, who is one of the artists!"

"I didn't know you cared for art," I said. After all, he hadn't been particularly wild to visit the Tretyakov with me.

"This is different. It's people's art—political art, I mean, not bowls of fruit and naked baby Jesuses," he replied, a bit of the old haughty Jeffrey creeping into his tone. "These artists are risking a great deal to put on their exhibition."

"Are they? And here I thought the iron grip of Stalinism had loosened under Cousin Nicki!"

Jeffrey shook his head emphatically. "Rima says that Khrushchev absolutely hates modern art. Anna, won't you come with me after lunch tomorrow and meet her? Please, Anna!"

It really meant something to him. I nodded. "Sure, sure I will. Only I can't get there until later."

Jeffrey looked up at me, completely mystified. "Why?"

"Well, I met somebody too."

*"What?"*

"I met a man. I have a date."

"You? *You* have a date?"

"You don't have to sound so fucking incredulous. I met him at the Pushkin."

Jeffrey looked dazed. "What does he do?"

"He's an officer on leave from the Red Army."

*"The Red Army?"* Jeffrey fairly screamed the words at me. "My God, Anna, you can't associate with army people!"

"Why not?"

He sputtered. "Well, they're on the wrong side!"

"Not Lavrenti. He's very well-educated. He's critical of the Soviet government, and he's even crazy about JFK."

"Anna, you are out of your frigging mind."

I bristled. "No, I'm not. He comes from a small town and speaks fondly of his mother. Besides, we don't really talk about politics. We drink, listen to music, and have sex a lot."

That stopped him dead in his tracks.

For a time we didn't speak. Or rather, he didn't speak to me. I spoke to him, pointing out repeatedly that it was absolutely unfair for it to be okay for him to have sex, but not me. After about an hour, I wore him down and he resumed normal relations with me. He didn't have much choice.

"When does the exhibition shut down?" I asked.

"Dark," he grunted.

I laid down the law. "I'll come to the exhibition and meet Rima. But not until five or six." Lavrenti and I were heading right back to the forest after I ditched the tour at noon. No way was I going to miss that to meet Jeffrey's artsy girlfriend.

"That late? I'll bet I know why."

I drew myself up indignantly. "We are having tea with a friend of Lavrenti's, a poet," I said.

Jeffrey looked so disappointed, I began to feel guilty as all hell. "I'll be there by six. You can count on it. Just promise that if Lavrenti comes along, you guys will be nice."

He shrugged. "The exhibition is open to everyone. But if he turns out to be a snitch, you're going to be very sorry."

Of course he wasn't a snitch. If he'd been a snitch, he would have jumped at the opportunity to infiltrate a gathering of modern artists. Instead, when I asked him to accompany me to the exhibition, his expression at once grew guarded and strained. "Anna," he said, "I am embarrassed to tell you this. Going to your friend's art show would not be a wise thing for me to do."

"Why?" I asked.

"If there were any trouble, and I were arrested, it could ruin my career."

He wasn't kidding. "So," I said, "it really hasn't gotten all that much better since Stalin, has it?"

Lavrenti lowered his eyes. "Truly it has, in some ways. But with Nikita Sergeyevich, you are never entirely sure which way the wind is going to blow. Last year he personally approved the publication of that new book by Solzhenitsyn about the prisoner Ivan Denisovich. Yet he has never allowed the publication of *Dr. Zhivago*, and five years ago he would not even let Boris Pasternak leave to accept that great award he won."

"My friend Jeffrey says he hates modern art."

Lavrenti clasped his hands together, and still did not look at me. "The situation is not that simple. It has to do more with power than art. You see, the USSR Academy of Arts is made up of *apparatchiks*, or Party bureaucrats. They say that any new trend in art competes with Socialist Realism and poses a grave threat to our society and therefore must be suppressed. I don't know whether they really believe this; perhaps they are just using this as a way to increase their influence within the Party.

"This past December they steered Nikita Sergeyevich to an exhibition of the Union of Soviet Artists at the great Manezh exhibition hall. They showed him all the new innovations in Soviet art, and convinced him that these were deviations from orthodox ideology and were dangerous. Thereupon, he began a campaign against 'liberal tendencies' in Soviet culture. None of the new artists may any longer exhibit their paintings in galleries or museums supported by the state."

"So artists put on exhibitions in the parks," I said. "And you don't want to go, because you think there may be trouble."

He looked at me helplessly. "I cannot judge."

"Lavrenti, if you decide not to go. I won't be angry. I'll just go for an hour to make Jeffrey happy, and then take the subway and meet you somewhere downtown."

Lavrenti took a deep breath. "I feel like a coward."

"Bullshit!" I cried.

He had just learned this new word from me, and almost smiled. "I don't know the best thing to do. One can fight society directly, as the artists are doing, and be destroyed. Or one can join society, and change it from the inside."

"If it doesn't change you first."

"Yes," said Lavrenti. He made a fist and slammed it against the palm of his hand. "Your artists have the better idea."

"Not necessarily. Khrushchev came up through the ranks. Then, when his turn came, he de-Stalinized the whole country."

"I admit, that is true. My friend Misha would agree also."

"Listen," I said. "There's nothing to be gained by your going to the exhibit. I'll meet you afterward."

"I don't know, I don't know."

"Lavrenti, forget about it. They don't need you. One less spectator will make no difference."

Oops. That was the wrong thing to say. "Anna," he said, sounding very much like John Wayne, "I've decided to go with you."

## 11

## Moscow (cont.)

We didn't actually get to the exhibition until six-thirty. See, it was a beautiful summer day, and a Friday at that, so the forest was full. Lavrenti and I had to walk forever to find a private place for ourselves. Then it turned out he had not brought vodka, but two bottles of sweet Georgian champagne, called *Igruskoye*, which by some miracle was still nice and cool. It made us silly and we kept lolling about in the grass and fooling around. At first I was uncomfortable and sore, since I had just done it for the first time in my life the day before. But after the champagne took effect I started having a wonderful time. Not until after five o'clock could we tear ourselves away. Sweaty and disheveled and smug, our clothes a mess, we made a run for the faraway subway line and hoped it wouldn't be too obvious to Jeffrey that we hadn't been having tea with a poet.

But Jeffrey had eyes for no one but his inamorata, Rima of the beautiful name. I expected her to be pale, delicate, and green-eyed, perhaps even a touch consumptive. It was not to be. She was a quiet, solemn, fleshy girl from sterling peasant stock. If she lived long enough, she might come to resemble Olga, or perhaps even Madame Khrushchev. I wasn't too clear what Jeffrey saw in her; even her paintings weren't all that good. But I kept my thoughts to myself and studied her, giving Jeff the benefit of the doubt. Before long, I thought I had it figured out.

Rima wasn't in the least "cool." She wasn't blasé. She wasn't sophisticated or quick to make fun of anyone who wasn't, like so many of the hip people Jeffrey and I had met in the cafes of San Francisco—or for that matter, like so many of Moscow's "golden youth" whom I had met at parties that week. Rather, she was a friendly, serious, straightforward girl, who believed wholeheartedly in the importance of what she was doing.

It was quite a big show, considering that it was illegal as hell. However, once the novelty wore off I grew a tad bored, as the art did not generally reflect great talent. I had demonstrated my support for Jeffrey by showing up; now I wanted to slip away with Lavrenti and find more Georgian champagne.

The artists had arranged their pictures in a single long row in an open space between two groves of birch and fir. Doggedly, I worked my way down this row, and Lavrenti humored me. But then we got to this guy who was next to last. He had attempted some soft, dreamy portraits faintly in the Serov style, and Lavrenti, seeing them, came to a halt and simply couldn't be budged for love or money. So I went on to the last artist myself.

Until then I wouldn't have described any of the art as radical, subversive, or even all that political. The stuff could only be considered avant-garde by Soviet standards, i.e., because there were no paintings in the vein of "Stalin at the XVIth Congress of the Communist Party." In U.S. terms, the art show was pretty mediocre. It could have been an exhibit by any bunch of dilettante students at a Bay Area university.

However, the last artist blew my complacence to smithereens. On a small canvas he had painted a lovely, pastoral scene, set right there in the Lenin Hills, of men and women and children who had been picnicking on the grass. The tiny figures were so perfectly detailed that they might have leapt from one of the famous lacquer boxes from Palekh. In the background was a panorama of Moscow, its ancient buildings bright and sharp and clear against the sky, its onion domes radiant with gold.

Only problem was, there was a ghastly mushroom cloud in full flower over the city. In its billows of smoke and debris floated the faint, almost subliminal patterns of a hammer and sickle, and a flag with many stars and stripes.

The people on the ground were portrayed seconds after the Bomb went off. Those at the edge of the picture, farthest from the Bomb, were human torches set on fire by the Bomb's intense heat. The men and women and children in the center, closest to the explosion, had been likewise set ablaze; but on the heels of the Bomb's searing heat had come its blast wave. The painting had captured these poor wretches at the instant the wave ripped their bodies apart in an explosion of flesh and blood.

I can't even remember what the artist looked like, only that he was young. He saw me staring at the painting and came running over. When I looked into his eyes, I thought that he was haunted by the same monster that threatened to follow me to my grave.

I showed him the laminated California driver's license that I, ever paranoid, had been careful to carry on a chain around my neck. "*Ya amerikanka.* How did you come to paint this?"

"I saw it in a dream," he replied. "Last October."

My flesh crawled. "How much do you want for it?"

"I cannot sell it."

I reached into my money belt and got out a twenty-dollar bill. It was a lot, but right then money was no object. His eyes widened, but he shook his head. I added another twenty. He struggled harder. When I added a third bill, he took the money.

"Why do you want my painting so much?" he asked me.

I pointed to the canvas. "This almost happened."

That shocked him. "Please say you make fun of me."

I shook my head. "We know these things in America."

He turned away, and started to weep. "*Nyet, nyet,*" he said. He was glad I was taking the painting away.

Then Lavrenti came up to me. "What did you buy?" he asked. I showed him, and he practically recoiled. "That is horrible."

I nodded. "Yes. And as accurate as a photograph."

"It is an awful thing," he whispered. "We must wrap it in paper or you cannot take it on the subway."

I rolled my eyes. We were about to have our first argument.

Lavrenti took my elbow and ushered me back to the starting point of the exhibition. "We must say good-bye to your friend Jeffrey and be on our way," he said, his voice urgent. "So far there has been no incident. Let's not press our luck."

I *never* say things like that, because they tempt Fate. Nervously, I scanned the throng of people around us, and was struck by how the crowd had grown in the last half-hour.

A moment later I heard shouting and my heart sank. People moved back in a wave from a scuffle up front. "It's the *militsia*, the police!" cried Lavrenti. "And probably the KGB too!"

To my shame, when I heard the commotion and suspected the exhibition was being busted, I thought first of my picture. This was selfish of me, but sometimes I am just a foolish, selfish person. We were right by that grove of firs and I dashed into the middle of it, stowed my painting in the crotch of a tree where it was safely out of sight, and hurried back to Lavrenti's side. The whole business took about ten seconds.

My first thought was for my precious painting, because I was still so silly and naive. I didn't realize that real people were going to get hurt. In the Bunker, I had read accounts by our Russian ancestors of many Soviet barbarities. But they weren't truly real to me until that moment. I just hadn't grown up in a world where that sort of behavior was possible.

See, in the Bunker, each citizen was as precious as an unflawed diamond. Each new child was cherished by our clan with a fierce love born of the terror of extinction; we knew that in our sons and daughters lay our only possible future. When push came to shove, I just could not envision a world where a state could grind its children into the dirt with a giant boot.

When the shouting escalated into screaming, Stupid here got a ghost of a clue. Then I dashed into the crowd, Lavrenti in tow, and started frantically searching for Jeffrey and Rima.

It all happened so quickly. Wherever you looked, there were police and men sporting the sword-and-shield insignia of the KGB. People in the crowd I'd taken for gawkers and browsers turned into undercover thugs. They were everywhere, beating people with fists, brass knuckles, and short, ugly clubs. They slashed paintings with knives, kicked them out of their frames, and set fire to them. They also brought up a truck with a fire hose, and turned it on the artists and their poor amateurish pictures.

In less than a minute, the childishness I had brought across time from the Bunker was destroyed. I saw an enraged, terrified Jeffrey struggling to stay between Rima and three KGB bastards. Caught off guard, he couldn't get his balance back; he seemed to have forgotten all the martial arts he had learned back home.

I tried to go to Jeffrey's aid, but I couldn't get through the crowd in time; it was like that dream where you try with all your might to reach somebody, but you're weighed down like a fly in hardening amber, and cannot move fast enough.

One of the men hit Jeffrey in the mouth with all his strength. Blood flew, along with some white specks which were his front teeth. Another blow, and Jeff was on the ground, knocked out cold. Then they turned on Rima—the artist, the real offender. Two of them moved forward, each grabbing an arm, and they stretched her tight between them, as if she were to be crucified. Then the third took careful aim and kicked her with all his might in the stomach. He did it a second time, and a third.

Years later it became the fashion to say, "So-and-so went ballistic." I did then. Lavrenti cried out and, to his credit, started for Rima. But I had lost all reason and outran him. I shoved and kicked and made people get out of my way. And I didn't forget one iota of *my* combat training from the Bunker.

Since neither of those KGB sadists was paying any attention to me, I managed to land a blow on the closest one that forever curtailed his reproductive capacity. Before the other one could recover himself, I pulled out my California driver's license on its chain and screamed that I was an American and I was going to tell all the papers about what I had seen that day. He was disconcerted just long enough for me to get in position to deliver a kick that would have taken his face off. I didn't get to, though, because Lavrenti came up behind him and pretty much bashed his fucking brains out with one side of a picture frame.

Jeffrey, still on the ground, had curled up into a ball and was moaning. From what I'd seen, he wasn't mortally wounded, so I jerked him to his feet and shook him. He took a good look at Rima and shrieked like he was going to die. Lavrenti barked an order to him and together they put their arms under her shoulders and pulled her into the protection of the forest.

"Where are we going?" I screamed.

"There is a major roadway on the other side of this wood," Lavrenti said, struggling for breath. "Do you have any money?"

"Ten, maybe twenty rubles!"

"No!" he yelled. "*Dollars!* Do you have dollars?"

In a moment of panic, I thought I'd spent it all on my painting. Then I remembered I had a little bit left. "Yes!"

"When we come to the road, take out the biggest bill you have and wave it at the cars."

We crashed through underbrush, and the trees and land and setting sun circled round me like pieces in a kaleidoscope. I didn't remember seeing that many taxis in Moscow. "At the cars?"

*"Da, da!"* Lavrenti cried, his voice breaking. "Idiot, your American money will work wonders—you will see!"

In moments we were out of the forest and sliding down a dirt bank toward a paved road. Following Lavrenti's instructions, I waved my last ten-dollar bill at the traffic, and waited.

Not for long. A passing auto, a ratty old Volga, stopped so fast that it skidded twenty feet on down the road, and backed up at fifty miles an hour. Then I saw that the driver was a Soviet naval officer, apparently moonlighting for some American bucks.

"We're dead, Lavrenti!" I cried. "He'll turn us in!"

Lavrenti looked at me like I didn't understand a goddamned thing. He shepherded all of us into the car and babbled something to the officer about how his girlfriend was being molested by some street punks, and he and Jeffrey got into a fight with them. The officer bought it. His run-down excuse for a car didn't even have a radio.

The officer asked where we were going. Lavrenti, so reluctant to call in favors for our lovemaking comfort, now cashed in a big one. He didn't give the navy officer the address of a hospital, but the apartment of this thirty-year-old rich kid whose father was a general in the Red Army. This particular kid owed Lavrenti a lot, and Lavrenti had been keeping his gratitude on ice, saving it for something really important. Now he was blowing it on Rima.

Mercifully, when we got to the apartment, the kid was home, and his parents were not. He took us in and even slipped the naval officer a bottle of Stolichnaya vodka, the good kind the Soviets usually saved for export. Freaked though he was, the kid had the presence of mind to write down the navy guy's license plate; he explained that if the fellow decided to try his hand at blackmail later, he would soon be made to lose the taste for it.

Oh, God. I shall summarize, and get this over with quickly. I can deal with big tragedies, like a whole planet exploding into flame; there's something sickeningly beautiful about it. Little tragedies involving helpless, innocent creatures are just sickening, period. I can't deal with them at all; I hate the movie *Bambi*.

Lavrenti's friend said that with his connections we could get Rima into a hospital, but people would have to be bribed or else she'd be arrested. So Jeffrey headed back to the Ukraina, and passed the hat among the kids on our tour.

We did get Rima to a hospital. But those ferocious kicks in the Lenin Hills had so seriously injured her that she died in the hospital, in great pain, with all of us at her bedside.

Right before our student tour left the country, I went back to the park with Lavrenti to retrieve my picture. It was right where I had left it; the thugs had left the forest alone.

"Do you want to get out of here?" I asked Lavrenti. "Do you want to come to America?"

"Yes, but it would be selfish," he said.

"You mean you haven't given up on Russia, even after what happened?" He didn't answer. "We could get married here and now," I offered. "I have a lot of money, and some damn good connections. Eventually they would let you go."

Still he wouldn't say anything. "You can't stay here," I pressed. "This is a system that kicks innocent girls to death."

"It's changing," he replied. "What you saw was . . . a backslide."

"Yeah, endorsed wholeheartedly by the government."

He shook his head. "Some party official gave the order to break up the exhibition. Whoever he was, I do not believe he meant for anyone to be killed; why kill the artists and risk trouble with the West, when mere intimidation would achieve the same goals? But the men of the KGB are like bad dogs; once you remove their leash, no one can answer for the result."

"So you think if you stay here you can reform the system?"

"Reform has already begun. Nikita Sergeyevich means to lead us away from Stalinism."

I wanted to cry. I'd nurtured this hope he would come back with me and I could show him San Francisco and all of California, and maybe we would even stay married. But it was pretty obvious that wasn't going to happen. Therefore, this was good-bye.

"My country is at a turning point," Lavrenti said quietly. "What would happen to it now, if everybody like me left?"

"Mother Russia," I said bitterly, wiping away tears. "I heard all about how you people love your country even though you hate its government, but I never understood till now." As I cried, my nose began to run, and I felt ugly and grubby.

Lavrenti knew it was good-bye too. He wrapped his arms around me and we cried together. Russian men are raised thinking it's okay to cry, so they do it all the time, even their leaders, even in public.

"Lavrenti," I said suddenly, "listen to me." My voice was so grim that he almost stepped back from the embrace. "If you're going to ruin my life, you sure as hell better do some good here. You'd better do all you can to change Russia, or I'll haunt you."

"I will do my best," he whispered. "In fairness, you must remember I am only one man."

"In the right place, at the right time," I whispered back, "one man can make all the difference in the world."

He called in another favor and we spent my last night in Moscow together, sick at heart, but in a comfortable bed.

## 12

July 1963: Washington, D.C.

"Drop by the house for lunch," Jack had said. So we did.

I felt terrible. We had flown out of Russia early in the morning of the previous day. Jeffrey and I started drinking to blot out our misery the minute we picked up the Finnair plane in Helsinki. Fortunately Jeffrey had already reserved rooms for us at the Watergate Hotel in Washington, D.C., so when we got to America we only had to collect our luggage, clear customs, pour ourselves into a taxi, and get a bellhop to guide us to our rooms. Once in our lair, we ordered room service and kept drinking until, jet-lagged and sick to my stomach, I finally passed out.

It took lots of coffee and soft, buttery oatmeal the next morning before I felt human enough to face Jack. Until a couple of days ago I'd thought of this lunch as the crowning glory of our trip; now I was afraid I'd walk through it like a zombie.

We found the President running around like a chicken with its head cut off, trying to fit us into an unbudging schedule, so great was his desire to talk with us about Mother Russia.

"Come on into the Rose Garden with me," he said at last. "I've got to greet some delegates from Boys Nation, but after that we can hide in a basement somewhere and talk."

"Boys Nation?" Jeffrey asked. "What's that?"

"It's an American Legion thing. A youth program." When

153

Jeffrey seemed puzzled, Jack added, "They campaign for it or compete somehow. Every one of these kids is a real hot dog."

Dutifully, we followed him into the Rose Garden and the hot, muggy summertime of Washington, D.C. I was so hung over I thought I was going to throw up right there. The garden was full of a gaggle of young, coltish teenage boys, who looked to be from all over the place. "What a bunch of kids!" I exclaimed. I had recently turned twenty and felt infinitely older and superior.

"The cream of the crop," Jack replied. "Outstanding high school students from every corner of the country. And I have to try to shake hands with every one of them."

He looked so frazzled, I didn't know if he would last. "Just say a few words and kick 'em out. You're in charge here."

"Now, now, be nice," Jack replied, with a hint of a grin. "When I'm gone, your future might depend on one of them."

I felt unbearably frustrated, standing there in the blazing sun watching Jack press the flesh with a lot of gawky pubescents, cameras flashing all around like firecrackers. I had traveled halfway around the world and gotten my heart severely bent, if not broken. I had earned my lunch with Jack, so it griped me beyond words to watch him waste time shmoozing with a mob of awestruck kids.

And awestruck they were, all right. As Jack waded into their ranks, I saw their eyes light up with pure, unadulterated hero worship. They gazed upon him like acolytes, their love and idealism naked, unprotected, and plastered across their faces for all the world to see. There was terrifying power in the air; I was reminded of old newsreels of Hitler with his *Jugend*.

But Jack, though powerful, was not corrupt like Hitler. When he touched these children, they were not filled with dreams of world domination; in the future forming above our heads right then, no blood ran in the gutters. Rather, the kids were chomping at the bit to run home, beat poverty and racism, and then go build hydroelectric dams in the Third World with far too few power tools.

They went into public service. They went into the Peace Corps. They dreamed of doing battle with the forces of evil and injustice, and never thought to question whether the good guys always won.

I was unexpectedly amused by a big kid near the front of the mob. This guy, a six-footer at least, seemed about to expire with anxiety for fear Jack would pass him by. As I watched, the kid squared his shoulders, muscled up, and got himself right out there in front, so no way in hell Jack could miss him.

I got a real kick out of this mini-drama and turned to Jeffrey to point it out. As I did so, I was goosed by a sudden ripple in the fabric of time, just as when we had stood by the Moskva River on that moonlit night a few weeks before.

Jeffrey felt it too. Like cobras, we nailed Kennedy with our twin gazes, determined to trace the ripple to its source.

There was nothing much to see. He was still passing down the line of picture-perfect all-American kids, flashing that smile, shaking their hands, inspiring the bejesus out of them, and probably changing the future every time he drew breath.

Then Jack made contact with the big kid. The ripple came again, this time stronger.

"What the fuck is *with* that guy?" I whispered.

"God, I don't know," said Jeffrey.

The kid was not particularly remarkable to look at—just a rawboned, slab-faced boy in a T-shirt, cute in a sort of football-playing way, who looked like he came from Texas or Oklahoma or some equally godforsaken place. I mean, there was *no way* he came from California. But his eyes followed Kennedy, full of love and inspiration. He looked as if he had found a long-lost father, and his life's calling to boot.

I squinted against the unpleasantly bright sun. All the

boys had itty-bitty name tags designed to torture the eye at a distance. I couldn't read the kid's tag for love or money.

Kennedy passed on, and the kid saw me staring at him. Our eyes locked. I'd caught him off guard, and for a moment he looked startled. Then he regained his composure, squared those shoulders again, and gave me a cocky, lopsided grin, one worthy of Jack himself.

Embarrassed, I looked away. Jeffrey nudged me hard. "Anna, the future just changed. The torch got passed— again."

"Huh?" I said, a mite overwhelmed.

"We saw it! We saw the torch pass!" Jeffrey hissed. "To a new generation, born in *mid*-century." His eyes grew soft and reverent. He might have been H. G. Wells, speaking in tremulous tones of the shape of things to come. "Whoever that kid is, he's important in the future. One possible future."

"For better or worse?"

"Idiot," said Jeffrey, the quintessential big brother. "You know there's no way to tell."

At last we saw Jack heading back into the White House. He signaled us with a quick jerk of the head, and we dutifully threaded our way toward him through the crowd, Jeffrey leading.

As I started up the stairs, I felt a hand on my arm, and turned. There, detaining me with a firm grip, was the kid himself.

This was no pickup, no flirtation. He had given me a jaunty grin before, but now he was dead serious. "Excuse me, ma'am," he said. He sounded like he came from someplace in the South. "Why did you stare at me so when I shook hands with President Kennedy? You looked as if you'd seen a ghost."

I looked at his name tag. I stalled. "Maybe I had."

"Who *are* you?" he asked.

"A friend of the President."

"Please . . . you looked like you knew something."

What could I say to him? His eyes looked into mine. His will insisted on an answer.

That answer came to my lips from another place, maybe a world still forming. "Somebody has to pick up where he leaves off," I said, pointing to the doorway through which Jack had gone. "Maybe it's you. Don't blow it."

The boy turned dead white. Then, like one of the rolling waves off our beloved California coast, there came a new ripple through time. It slapped me so bad, it temporarily made me forget all about my hangover. I broke away, and fled up the steps.

Back inside the White House, where sanity prevailed, I realized that for the first time in my life, somebody had called me "ma'am." And I was only twenty! It was a real shock.

Thank heavens, Jack chose that moment to round us up for lunch. He wiped his face with a handkerchief and said, "You know, sometimes meeting kids like that is all that keeps me going."

Coming from anybody else, it would have sounded so cornball. Given the time slip I'd just been through, it freaked me out. "I keep wishing I'd chosen a nice stress-free vocation," Jack went on. He sounded exhausted. "Something like brain surgery. At least then only one person would die when I fucked up. See, I never know for certain I'm doing the right thing. My advisors split down the middle and scream at each other, and I gamble. I'm that one-eyed man who's king in the country of the blind. And now, on top of everything else, just when I'm hitting my stride, I've got to drop everything and worry about getting re-elected in 1964. Christ, it never ends!"

It all piled up and got to be too much for me, and I started snuffling. He put his hands on my shoulders and made me look at him. "I love getting together with kids like those Boys Nation guys—and you and Jeffrey and Daria. When I talk to kids like you, I feel like I can touch the twenty-first century, though I probably won't live to see it.

"I'm like a vampire. I take away a little bit of your energy and enthusiasm and utterly indefensible belief that the world will work out after all. At the very moment I'm running dry, you make me believe in such a silly thing as hope. Hope is a hard thing to hang on to if you're a politician—shit, if you're over forty. So when you can get a dose of it, you treasure it. Live long enough, guys, and one day you'll know exactly what I'm talking about."

I started crying in earnest then. Jeffrey looked mortified, but I didn't care, because Jack suddenly looked stricken and started patting my arm. He was afraid he'd said something wrong.

"I'm going to tell you something," I gasped.

"What?" said Jack.

"I can't explain why, but ever since the time travel we sometimes become supersensitive about—perfectly ordinary people or places. It's a weird feeling, like the earthquakes out in California. We felt it several times in Russia. We think it means the person or the place or the thing is going to play a role in history in the future—in one possible future, that is."

He gazed at me, hanging on my every word. "What does this have to do with me?"

"It happened again out in the Rose Garden. You shook hands with this kid and we got another bleep on the radar. You made some kind of mark out there. Something in the future changed because you were out there shaking hands."

"Which kid was it?"

For some reason I didn't want to say the kid's name. I felt like I was protecting him. "I could point him out if you got them all together again," I said reluctantly.

Jack laughed. "That won't be necessary. Who the kid was doesn't matter—only that he was there."

"Yeah, I guess so." I wiped my nose on the back of my hand.

Jack remembered his handkerchief, and handed it to me. "Thanks," he said. "I really need to hear that kind of thing."

Jeffrey couldn't bear to stay out of it. "Of course, we don't know whether you affected the kid for better or worse."

Thankfully, just then Rene arrived with lunch. He was very friendly and greeted each of us by name. Thanks to the good food and the superficial chatter required at a lunch like that, we all had a chance to decompress.

When we were finishing dessert, Robert Kennedy sidled into view and joined us at the table. "So, what's the word from the Soviet Union?" he asked. "Hope I haven't missed anything."

"Yes, it is time we talked about your trip," Jack said. He sat back in his chair and looked at each of us in turn. "Judging from experience, my friends, you both have a hell of a hangover. What went wrong in Russia?"

"Nothing," Jeffrey muttered.

"Jeffrey met a girl, an artist, and she got killed accidentally when the KGB busted an exhibition," I explained, striving for succinctness. "Me, I met this army officer and had to leave him behind. We're both in bad shape."

Jeffrey speared me with a look of rage. "It was not accidental! Those bastards meant to kill her!"

"I just meant the Party didn't give orders to kill her, or anybody else. The KGB went overboard because they're thugs and they can get away with it. That's what Lavrenti said."

"He would," replied Jeffrey, his tone venomous.

"Whoa," said Jack. "I'm sorry for both your sakes. Can I do anything? Anna, does your fellow want to come over here?"

"No," I replied, "I already asked him. He would defect but he wants to stay behind and make Russia a better place."

Jack digested that for a moment. "What an idealist!"

"Yeah. A big idealistic fool. Like most Marxists."

It went right over Jack's head. "How old is this man?"

"Thirty."

Jack glanced at Bobby. They were floored—and pleased

as punch. "He really thinks reform is possible?" Bobby asked.

"Yes. He thinks Khrushchev has been very good for Russia," I said. "He thinks the country will loosen up even more in the future. I guess he wants to be there if it happens."

Bobby shook his head. "Well, I'll be goddamned."

"He'd better be right," said Jeffrey, "because if Russia keeps on the way it's going, it will explode!"

"They're in a bad way," I said. "We should help them."

Bobby laughed outright. "When pigs fly."

"Haven't you learned anything?" I cried. "You idiots!"

Jeffrey slammed his fist on the table. "You are bankrupting Russia with the arms race! Why, ninety percent of its production must be going to the military, just to stay level with us!"

Bobby just looked more pleased. "Good."

"No! Not good! The ordinary citizens have nothing. Russia's bleeding to death. The only reason the people don't rebel now is the jackboot on their necks. But it *can't* go on. Someday they'll explode, and we'll be dragged down too!"

"We're bound together like Siamese twins," I added. "If we don't somehow transform Russia into a peaceful, stable country, we're going to pay for it dearly. Maybe not this year, maybe not for decades. But someday. When I'm still alive, but not you."

"You're trying to blackmail me," said Jack with a grin.

I shrugged. "Whatever works. Jack, think of Russia as a big, scruffy, hungry bear. With nukes. Since we seem to be stuck on the same planet with the beast, feed it, would you?"

Jack looked at Bobby. "We're winning. We really are winning." Then they asked, "How long do you think they can hold out? How long before they collapse? Ten years? Twenty?"

They sat there like hound dogs, tongues hanging out, waiting for my answer. They hadn't heard one word we'd said. I got so mad I cried, "Is that all you can think about? *Winning?*"

"No," said Bobby with a toothy grin, "but it's definitely in the top three."

"What about the poor Russian people?" I cried.

Jack regarded me without blinking. "We're sorry for them."

I stammered and sputtered and then said, "Oh, yeah? Well, listen to this! Little old men and women in small Russian towns put *your* picture up on the wall, because to them, you stand for something! You're the young, glamorous leader of a young, glorious country. *They look up to you*—I'm glad they don't know you're just a fucking cynical son of a bitch!"

I rendered him absolutely speechless. I was so proud of myself, I almost broke my arm patting myself on the back.

"Jack, you asked what you could do for me," I said. "Well, I'll tell you. Give Nikita some breathing room. Call off the race. Stay strong, but support his reforms loudly. Give all the people in Russia like Lavrenti the chance to make a difference."

Jack looked thoughtful. "What's in it for me?"

"The fate of your immortal soul."

He threw back his head and laughed. "Playing on my Catholic upbringing, are you?"

"Sure, why not? And if that's not enough for you, try thinking how you'll fare in the history books." He looked thoughtful, but clearly expected me to say more. So I did. "Jack, to this day, each Tuesday noon when they test the air-raid siren in San Francisco, I jump out of my skin. Spare the next generation that terror, will you?"

Jack, serious now, said, "You are wise beyond your years, Anna darling. You always give me something to think about."

"Don't just think about it, *do something*," I replied.

He smiled, grimly. "I'd have to be very careful how I implemented your advice. This is not a dictatorship. I have to get re-elected. The minute I started looking soft on Communism, you'd see Barry Goldwater sitting here next year."

"Oh, God," I replied sadly. "I hadn't thought of that."

So we concluded our lunch on an amicable note. Jeffrey and I went back to San Francisco to lick our wounds, start college, and pick up the thread of our lives again.

## 13

## November 1963: San Francisco

I had to hand it to Daria. School was actually fun. What with the trip back in time and the two weeks we'd spent in the Soviet Union, the weight of the world had been on my shoulders lately. It was an incredible relief just to take classes and be twenty years old for a change.

Boys were a big disappointment, though. After Lavrenti, no one else would do. They all had pimples or a stupid laugh or were just so young and green I got impatient with them. Plus, Lavrenti was still in the picture. Since returning from the Soviet Union I had gotten several letters from him.

The first one came from Finland. They let some army friend of his out on a long leash, and the saint was able to mail it to me from Helsinki. I immediately wrote Lavrenti back. Before I left Moscow, he had given me detailed instructions how to do this without endangering his life and/or his career. To supplement this drivel, we thought up our own private little code.

I penned a missive that, on the surface, had to be the world's most innocuous letter. I talked about the nice weather in San Francisco. I told him that I was working hard in school, and had volunteered in soup kitchens to feed all the poor and oppressed working people in California (a total lie, at least the latter part). But I also said I'd gone hiking *in the forest*, a subtle reminder of the sylvan moments we'd spent together. I said I loved football and had been following with delight the exploits of the University of Southern California *Trojans*. I said I had introduced my friends to the pleasures of picnics with caviar and ice-cold vodka, and maintained how committed I was to *continued peaceful intercourse* between our two nations.

His reply (this time somehow postmarked in Stockholm) was even spicier. After that I lived from letter to letter. Needless to say, no normal American boy had a chance.

I didn't have any girlfriends either, at least not from the mainstream set. Remember, in 1963, two out of three girls were married by age twenty. A lot of the ones I met at Cal worried all the time about their clothes, their looks, their sorority, and catching a husband. They loved songs like "Chapel of Love" and "It's My Party and I'll Cry If I Want To." I, on the other hand, had lately taken to toting around a new book called *The Feminine Mystique*.

The only people I really had something in common with were the serious geeks in history or philosophy class, the folk singers on the plaza, and the students who put up ironing board stands by Sather Gate and the steps of Sproul Hall. They handed out information on the Peace Corps, or got people to sign petitions to "please save just a smattering of California's ancient redwoods," or "put an end to the nuclear arms race." In the wake of the march on Washington, demonstrations against racism were big, and were constantly being organized on the plaza.

Campus interest in events in South Vietnam became intense. I didn't think a post-Cuba Jack would let this situation escalate into something really serious, but a lot of people didn't agree with me. They said, to my never-ending disgust, that he was always trying to prove he was the biggest guy in the bar—like in the Cuban missile crisis. I got into a lot of arguments those days.

That fall was a nonending succession of beautiful, crisp blue-sky days in Berkeley. One gorgeous November morning I decided to skip my eleven o'clock class. Thanksgiving break was almost upon us, and I just couldn't get into studying.

I had this favorite lunch routine. First I would get a cup of coffee from one of the places on Bancroft Avenue that had a view of San Francisco. If the city's fog had burned off, I could look straight down the road at the beautiful bay and the Golden Gate Bridge. Once I had finished my coffee, I would head to the plaza by the Student Union Building and Sproul Hall, where I would buy something interesting from one of the many vendors there. The lineup was my idea of heaven: bagels and lox, tacos, pita bread stuffed with falafel, vegetarian sandwiches with lots of nice fattening avocado, Chinese potstickers and egg rolls, and Armenian shish kebab. See, Berkeley was one big melting pot, and the pot was full of food. After that, I would make the rounds of the various people I knew who hung out on the plaza.

Well, anyway, I had my coffee early, wolfed down some falafel, and then ambled through the brilliant sunshine toward Sproul Hall. My normally sensitive disaster antennae must have been drugged comatose by the splendor around me; I had absolutely no premonition that anything horrible was on my plate that day.

Then I realized that the usual hubbub of voices in the plaza was hushed. As always, people were standing around in tight little groups, but they weren't moving at all, just like in that Twilight Zone episode where the man finds himself in a world where time runs incredibly slow and everybody seems to be frozen.

I looked over and saw this folksinger girl I knew. She was sitting on the ground cross-legged, her head lowered, her face completely hidden by her long hair. Her hands were clasped in front of her, the knuckles white, as if she were holding onto something for dear life. Somebody else in the crowd was crying.

Anything could have been wrong. In all likelihood, it was something minor. But this cold, dead feeling washed over me out of nowhere, and I knew something terrible had happened.

You really can be so scared you shiver. I clapped suddenly icy hands under my armpits and walked up to a group that had a transistor radio. "What happened?" I asked a guy.

"Somebody shot at President Kennedy in Dallas," he replied.

For a second I couldn't believe it. It just couldn't be true. Then I realized there was a way out. "They didn't hit him, right?" I cried.

The boy looked away. "Yeah, they did."

"But he's not dead?"

"We don't know."

I closed my eyes for a moment. There was still a chance. "When did it happen?"

"About thirty minutes ago."

"Did they catch the guy who did it?"

"Nobody knows."

I started shaking like I had a fever. I had to find out more. Remembering there was a place in the Student Union where they had a black-and-white TV, I took off running.

The place was mobbed, of course. I wormed my way through the crowd and got close enough to see the screen if I stood on tiptoe. Rumors were flying through the crowd at the speed of light. A Russian agent had shot at Kennedy, one boy said. Another guy said it was an American who had been to Russia. A third said they didn't have any idea who it was; he ended up in a shoving match with a bearded fellow who said it was the CIA.

I didn't know what to do next. First I thought I should find Daria, who had a literature class on campus, and get back to San Francisco as soon as possible. We all had our orders: If anything explosive happened on the global scene, something that could possibly set off another nuclear war, we were to hightail it back to home and the time machine as soon as possible.

But if there was the slightest chance the Russians were behind this horrible turn of events, I couldn't afford to go looking for Daria. There might not be time. If the bombs were on their way, whoever got to the car last was expendable.

The TV screen jumped, and there was Walter Cronkite. To the frightened people around me, his was a familiar, comforting face; they had grown up hearing Cronkite deliver the evening news in that deep, cultured, utterly professional voice. They fell silent; they waited for him to say everything was all right.

Cronkite put on a pair of black reading glasses and said, "From Dallas, Texas, the flash, apparently official. President Kennedy died at one P.M. central standard time."

He removed his glasses, and looked up at something beyond the camera, perhaps a clock. "Two P.M. eastern standard time. Some thirty-eight minutes ago." He put on his glasses again, as if to hide his eyes, and looked down at his desk. We saw his lips clench, once and then twice.

He tried to go on. "Vice President Lyndon Johnson—" he said, and stopped. There was a horrible pause when his voice almost broke. He went on, "Vice President Lyndon Johnson has left the hospital. Presumably he will be taking the oath of office shortly and become the thirty-sixth President of the United States."

All around me, people burst into tears. I shoved my way out of the crowd and took off down Telegraph Avenue to the car. I sped down Bancroft to University Avenue, and picked up the highway to the Oakland Bay Bridge and San Francisco. Traffic was very light, as if everyone was in hiding. I drove seventy or eighty, weaving back and forth between lanes, not thinking about anything but getting home. When I got to Union Street I didn't bother with the garage. I just left the car on the street and took the elevator up to our floor.

Jeffrey was the only one home. Poised like a runner waiting for the pistol shot, he was monitoring radio and television broadcasts. The time machine was still locked up safe and sound.

"Are you out of your mind?" I cried. "Get out the machine!"

"That won't be necessary, Anna."

"Jeffrey! People on campus are saying the Russians did it!"

Before our trip to Russia, he would have exploded with impatience or yelled something at me like "Bullshit!" But after Rima's murder his personality had changed. He had grown older, in a sad way. He rarely showed emotion, and went from one day to the next melancholy, remote, and practical. Now he only said quietly, "That's nonsense."

"Not necessarily. Somebody said an American did it, who'd been to Russia. Maybe he was in cahoots with the KGB."

"Anna," he said with a heavy sigh, "*it wasn't the Russians*. It would be poor business practice."

I stared at him, speechless. "International politics is nothing but business on a grand scale," Jeffrey continued. "The Russians had everything to gain from continued friendly relations with us, like grain to feed their people. They'd never do something so completely against their self-interest."

"Then it was a madman," I said.

He shook his head. "Anna," he said, his voice low, "will you ever grow up?"

"Stop being so condescending. What do you mean?"

Jeffrey stared at me for a moment, as if debating whether to answer. At length he said, "Whether or not he pulled the trigger, the guy the cops are chasing is a patsy. I'm sure he's been to Russia, and that's why the perpetrators chose him. He's an excellent red herring, guaranteed to throw everyone off the trail! Right now the KGB must be pissing in their pants for fear the Americans will think they really were behind it."

"So who is responsible? Tell me that!"

Jeffrey gave me a withering look. "Somebody home-grown."

I sat down. "God! Things were starting to go so right. For us, and for Russia. With five more years of Jack at the helm, we might have been okay. Now we're just plain screwed."

When Daria trailed in an hour later, panic-stricken, Jeffrey and I didn't reproach her for her tardiness. Rather, the three of us stayed up all night, listening to the news and grieving.

Most of the world grieved too. There was even an outpouring of shock and sympathy from the Soviet Union, far beyond the official condolences sent by Khrushchev. Not long after the assassination I got a letter from Lavrenti, mailed from Stockholm, which had tear stains on it; remember, in Russia, it is not considered unmanly to weep. Also enclosed was a crude little handwritten note, full of misspellings, from his mother. She said what a terrible thing it was that our young leader was dead, and she would never take down his picture from her wall.

Late that following Sunday we had a visitor, not altogether unexpected. Curiously, no one buzzed either apartment from the ground floor, although we lived in a security building. We were in Jeffrey's living room and heard nothing at all, until there was a footstep outside, and someone knocked softly.

I got up and opened the door. I had a feeling who it was. "Hello, Bobby," I said.

"Hello, Anna."

"Are you by yourself?"

He shook his head. "Of course not. One guy's by the elevator. Another's downstairs in the lobby. There's more outside. We can't afford to take chances."

He was nothing like the Bobby I remembered. He looked devastated, as if he had lost everything. He had given his whole life for his brother; now he seemed to be in actual physical pain. My heart softened toward him, and I invited him in.

Jeffrey brought out some crystal brandy snifters and a bottle of Remy Martin. It was the sort of thing Jack would have done, and he wanted to be hospitable. We sat in the living room and had a quiet drink together, while Bobby asked spiritless questions about the weather, our courses, and our life in San Francisco. At times he did not seem to be all there; his pain had given way to shock.

When he had finished his brandy, he put down the snifter and looked at Jeffrey. "I know you can do it again," he said.

Jeffrey looked back at him, and did not answer.

"I'm not going to force you to help me," said Bobby. "I could do that, you know. But Jack wouldn't have approved." At that, Jeffrey nodded. "Instead, I've come here to ask you to use your machine again. Go back and save my brother's life."

Jeffrey couldn't meet his eyes, and looked down at the floor. Bobby turned to me. "Please, Anna. I beg you."

"We can't," I replied, my voice hoarse.

Bobby stood up, walked over to the picture window, and looked out at San Francisco. "If you kids aren't fond of me, I can't blame you. I was real hard on you when you popped into Jack's office that night. That was my job, to play the bad cop and protect my brother. He tended to . . . rush into things."

"We don't hold any grudges," Jeffrey said.

"I'm not asking you to do this for me. Of course I want my brother back. But the country needs him even more than I do."

I could hardly stand it. "The machine can't make many jumps. Our elders made us promise only to use it to stop a nuclear war. If we make exceptions, we'll start wasting jumps, and then the machine will be used up when we need it most."

Jeffrey shot me a poisonous look for giving away the secret.

"I'm sorry, Jeffrey," I said, "but he'd guessed anyway."

"There's not going to be another close call like the Cuban crisis!" Bobby cried. "We've learned. Khrushchev's learned."

"Khrushchev, too, could be dead tomorrow," Jeffrey said. Bobby jerked back, as if he'd been slapped.

I caved in, and frantically signaled to Jeffrey. Couldn't we make one exception? I didn't have to whisper the entreaty to him in Russian; he knew what I meant. But he just shook his head, no evidence of struggle in his face. He had a duty to perform, and that was that.

I heard Bobby take a deep breath, as if he were struggling with tears. He raised his head again and looked at Jeffrey. "You little son of a bitch, you have the power to save Jack, to change the history of the world! You can't refuse to use it—you have no right to! Who made you God?"

Jeffrey looked back at him, ice-cold. "You and Jack."

"What?" cried Bobby.

"You and Jack did, when you destroyed my world," Jeffrey whispered. "I'll decide when to use the machine!"

There was a silent contest of wills between them. It didn't last long; Bobby was too tired to fight. Then, slowly, he lowered his head and rested it in his hands. There, in our living room, he wept for his brother.

He left a short time later. "We won't meet again," he said at the door. "Jack made me promise not to bother you if anything happened to him. I keep the promises I made to him."

"Will you tell President Johnson about us?" Jeffrey asked.

"That bastard? Never." I realized then how he hated Johnson.

"Not even if he picks you for his running mate next summer?"

The old Bobby would have grinned. This one didn't. "No."

"Good-bye," Jeffrey said. Bobby looked as if he were about to say something more, but thought better of it.

He was halfway to the elevator when I called out to him. "Bobby! You might see us again."

He paused and turned. "When?"

"If there's another war, and we need your help."

He walked back to the door and asked for a paper and pencil. We supplied them, and he wrote down a telephone number. "This is a Massachusetts number. You can always contact me there."

"What about the number Jack gave us?" I asked.

"Throw it away," he said softly. "The line's been disconnected."

I needn't have worried about the missiles that time. They didn't come for another five years.

# PART III
## Interim: 1964–2013

# 14

## 1964–1968: San Francisco and Los Angeles

That was the end of our youth and innocence. We had enjoyed a moment of sheer heaven, when we had been among the few people in the history of the world who had truly changed it for the better. We had clasped hands with our country's young President, and made him a partner in our hopes for a wonderful future. Now he was gone, and there was no one who could replace him.

Grieving for the dead is like a horrible, debilitating illness. You cannot escape it; you lie helpless, like an animal strapped to a laboratory table, while it works its pain on you, while it runs its course.

Overnight, the world changed. Jack was not even buried when they carted his rocking chair out of the Oval Office and threw it into a moving van. LBJ took over the White House. Soon afterward, Rene Verdon left. He said he refused to "cook Texas," and moved to San Francisco to open a restaurant.

Over the years that followed, we often called up and arranged for Rene to prepare an evening meal for "the Smith family," which we had a messenger pick up and deliver. Not that an outfit like Le Trianon was normally in the take-out food business, you understand. But we paid handsomely for the privilege, in cash so he would never know it was us. No doubt Rene took us for a band of eccentric, elderly recluses and was happy—given the compensation offered—to humor us.

One special incident during that period bears recounting. On a beautiful morning near the end of May 1964, Jeffrey and I went on a fruit-picking expedition to Brentwood, east of Mount Diablo. Daria didn't go, being into girly-girl things like nail polish and elaborately teased hairdos, and not into tacky things like wearing blue jeans or sweating.

In Brentwood you could get big ladders, climb into the trees yourself, and pick all the fruit you wanted for ten or twenty cents a pound—not counting, of course, all you could stuff into your gut. Jeffrey and I spent a delightful two hours pawing through ancient Bing cherry trees, after which we emerged with distended stomachs and twenty pounds of fresh cherries.

Well, we were on the way home when we got to looking at the highway signs, and realized just where we were. We got a wild idea and decided to see how close we could get to the Bunker. Afterward, when all the dust had settled, we never told Daria what happened. It would have been too embarrassing; she was usually the one who got into trouble for indulging in madcap escapades.

After leaving Brentwood, we had been driving west along the main highway that connected Livermore to the Bay Area. Then we turned off into a wild area called the Morgan Territory. At last, off Marsh Creek Road, we were absolutely sure we had found the narrow dirt road that led to the Bunker—but, to our disgust, a sturdy gate and a sign blocked our way.

The sign was so innocuous, you'd never dream a mammoth facility like the Bunker lay just over the hill. It read:

FIRE TRAIL
NO PARKING
NO VEHICLES

AREA CLOSED
NO ENTRY

UNTIL MADE ACCESSIBLE
& SAFE FOR PUBLIC USE

EAST BAY REGIONAL PARK DISTRICT
FIRE TRAIL

"Shit!" said Jeffrey, and banged his fist on the steering wheel. We couldn't even get near the place. It was so disappointing.

"Let's go in anyway," I said.

"Are you crazy?"

"Look, we can just wander in there, like a couple of stupid kids. If we get caught, we can just play dumb."

"Oh, why not!" he said. "What's the worst that can happen? We get chased off."

Prophetic words. We parked the car off the road, hopped over the gate, and were on our way. The dirt road climbed sharply, and we kept turning around and craning our necks as hilltops and ridgelines came into view, hoping we'd spot a familiar landmark hitherto glimpsed only through Bunker periscopes, a hundred years in the future.

I had to admit it was a stupid idea. We didn't get very far at all. Just as we started up a really steep switchback, a man appeared in the road ahead of us, holding a great big shotgun. As we froze and stared, he took the safety off.

"What the hell do you kids think you're doing?" he asked. He was dressed like a local cattleman or farmer type, but he smelled like Fed all over.

Jeffrey blinked. "Going for a hike. Isn't this the East Bay park district?"

He had cold, mean eyes. "Sign back at the road says 'No Entry.' Can't you read?"

Jeffrey looked down at his feet and rubbed the tip of one tennis shoe back and forth in the dust. "Oh, yeah, well, we thought it was okay and nobody would really mind since it was the park. We were just looking for a place to be alone, y'know?"

The man-to-man stuff didn't work. "I asked you if you could read, mister. Can you?" said the Fed.

"I guess not, sir," whispered Jeffrey. "Sorry."

The man's eyes just bored into us. I started worrying that maybe Jeffrey hadn't gotten rid of enough of his Bunker accent yet, and the man had guessed we weren't just a couple of geeks, but something really off-key. When I got to thinking about what a mess we'd be in if they questioned us and started trying to figure out who we really were, I got rattled in the extreme, and did what came naturally; I started crying. Since I couldn't stop it, I exploited it, and cried as dramatically as possible.

The man with the gun seemed mildly amused—and contemptuous. Jeffrey told me to shush, and then assumed the most magnificent look of youthful mortification you ever saw.

"Stupid little punks," said the man. "You walk back down the road, get in your car, and get the hell out of here. Don't try anything funny. I'll be watching you every step of the way."

We went. And we never looked back, or went back. They clearly didn't want anybody going in there unannounced, and it became our fervent belief that we should respect their privacy. We had closed the door to the Bunker when we left it in 2062; we needed no more convincing that that particular door should remain closed for the rest of our lives.

Under that philosophy, I slogged my way through Cal Berkeley and graduated. That done, I kept on restoring old San Francisco houses. I enjoyed it, and I was good at it. Ironically, my business was a capitalist's fantasy come to life. I never had to pay much for labor, because I hired beatniks and hipsters—and, as the Sixties wore on, hippies and radical carpenters. They liked me, because I worked alongside them and got my hands dirty. I paid better wages than the other jobs they could get. And when they worked for me, they weren't enriching "The Man." I was even known to have good dope on occasion. Plus they thought it was cool that I wanted to save all the old buildings, instead of just plowing them under and putting up twelve-plex apartment houses. I made good money.

Jeffrey had really gotten his heart broken over Rima. He was not as resilient in that respect as I was. Or perhaps he just wasn't as able to detach himself from his feelings, so when he got badly hurt, it was like a bomb had gone off and left a big, gaping hole in his personality. He no longer cared anything for romance. I think he kept a girl or two on the side for times when the hormones got to him, but he never stuck his neck out again for any woman. It was almost like he didn't have feelings anymore, except an abstract sense of loyalty and a mild affection for Daria and me.

Having suppressed his feelings, or whatever he did to them, he was able to concentrate his energies and become the financial star of our group. He made contacts early on in the infant computer industry—slobberingly grateful contacts, in view of all the capital he lavished on them. They broadened his network into a nationwide spiderweb that boggled the mind. Now, coming from the year 2062 as Jeffrey did, he didn't *exactly* have twenty-twenty hindsight when it came to the developmental path of American technology in the late 1900's, but it was close enough, like maybe twenty-nineteen. He figured out that computers were destined to serve many more masters than the Bell and Livermore labs of the world. He foresaw a day when computers would be as common in the business world as typewriters, and went into partnership with guys of like vision. Jeffrey had evidently picked a winning horse for, over the years, he and his buddies got filthy fucking rich. That was okay; the money served an important purpose.

Jeffrey had practically filled his apartment with computers and surveillance equipment and mind-boggling data-bases and similar paraphernalia when a third unit became available in the building, right below our floor. Daria and I insisted that Jeffrey use a tiny fraction of his newfound wealth to buy it (even though property values had risen outrageously by then) and store all his Agent 007 gear there, as it was becoming logistically impossible to visit him without falling over something. He crumbled under peer pressure and complied. Soon the third unit looked like a set for *Dr. Strangelove*. But I'm not complaining; in the future, all that equipment came in handy.

Daria never finished college. She couldn't seem to focus on her courses long enough to get through them successfully. It's like the mainspring of Daria's very being was busted. Something essential was missing in her life, and neither Jeffrey nor I could figure out what it was or how to get it for her.

She threw herself into what are known as "good works." She gave away a lot of money saving cats and dogs and redwoods and sea mammals and abandoned children. I was glad for her to do it; after all, Jeffrey and I were bringing home a shitload of cash. It made me feel really useful to donate to worthy causes, and Daria was very good at picking them.

But Daria never got used to being an Alien. She hated being different; first she rebelled against it, and then she denied the fact that it was so.

Jeffrey could view the world as the ultimate chessboard, and distance himself from it. Me, I sort of water-skied across the surface of the world, had a good time, sampled its many delights, but remained essentially detached. I had missed my chance at really savoring life when I lost Lavrenti, and since then had resigned myself to living out my years as an Outsider. But Daria never stopped trying to really belong to our new world.

She had a lot of boyfriends, few of who lasted more than a month or two, and experimented with a lot of lifestyles. Around the time of the Summer of Love, she dove into the Haight-Ashbury scene and didn't surface for three whole months. Fortunately for us and for the world, there was no nuclear war during that time.

The time she spent in the Haight did harm Daria, though. It seemed to me that she had convinced herself that since she loved our new world so much, there simply could never be another war. In pursuit of the will-o'-the-wisp of belonging, she dropped out of our rather rigorous program of physical fitness, world affairs surveillance, and spymastering. She lavished far too much energy trying to break out of the prison of her Alien-ness, and on her love affair with the 1960's. And she paid for it not long after.

While we experienced difficulties, triumphs, heartbreaks, lovers, and lonely times, like everyone else on Earth, the world continued along the new path we had given it, and the next nuclear war drew ever closer.

By January 1964, the Vietnam War had claimed a hundred and one American lives. Eighteen months later, the total rose to five hundred. After that it went through the ceiling.

In June 1964, three civil rights workers were murdered in Mississippi. A few days later Lyndon Johnson rammed Jack Kennedy's Civil Rights Act through Congress. In the wake of these killings, not to mention Jack's death, Congress couldn't dodge the bill—not with everybody watching. They held their noses and signed it.

That summer of 1964 Senator Goldwater graced our fair city with his presence at the Republican convention, where he accepted his party's nomination for President. Later, on the campaign trail, he spoke with rapture of producing a Bomb "so accurate it could be lobbed into the men's room of the Kremlin." Trust me; that was *not* a good omen for the future.

In mid-July we heard strange, disturbing rumblings from the Soviet Union. Headlines suddenly proclaimed that Anastas Mikoyan had been named President of the USSR. Leonid Brezhnev, the former President, was to serve as Khrushchev's deputy in the Secretariat of the Communist

Party—the center of power in the Soviet Union. This Brezhnev had been promoted.

In August 1964, Lyndon Johnson told Bobby he would not consider him as a vice-presidential running mate. He also made sure there was no movement to draft Bobby for the presidency in November. It was rumored Bobby hoped to be appointed secretary of state under Johnson, but that didn't come his way either. Then it was said Lyndon asked Bobby to manage his campaign. Whatever the truth, Bobby ended up running for senator from New York that year, and winning. We continued to watch him closely.

In October, barely two years after the missile crisis, Nikita Khrushchev called for a radical change in Soviet economic policy, giving consumer needs priority over industry and the military. Two weeks later he was deposed.

The newspaper *Pravda* accused Khrushchev of terrible things:

> . . . harebrained scheming, immature conclusions, and hasty decisions and decisions divorced from reality, bragging and phrase-mongering, commandism, and armchair methods.

Oh yeah. From the start, I thought he should have laid off those armchair methods. And that commandism.

Reassuringly, *Pravda* promised the world that the Communist Party would continue to carry out Khrushchev's policies of de-Stalinization and economic improvements under its new leadership. At the same time, however, the Soviet Union stepped up its military backing of North Vietnam. Relations between the Soviet Union and the United States re-entered the deep freeze.

And then, suddenly, like somebody had turned off a tap, the letters from Lavrenti stopped. I wrote and wrote and wrote, used all my clandestine contacts and all of Jeffrey's, but I never ever heard anything back from him. The curtain had turned into iron once more. Later, in the summer of

1968, when the Soviet Union invaded Czechoslovakia and crushed the brief flowering of Prague Spring, it was clear that Russia's rulers were marching backward as fast as they could. I stopped trying to reach Lavrenti; I figured if he had any kind of a life or career left by then, I should not jeopardize them further.

That same month, October 1964, Lyndon Johnson said we were not about to send American boys ten thousand miles away from home to do what Asian boys ought to be doing for themselves. He lied like a yeller dog. The following February, eight Americans were killed as mortar shells landed in a U.S. military base at Pleiku. Within hours, Johnson began a massive bombing of North Vietnam. Later evidence revealed he had used Pleiku as an excuse to launch a long-planned American offensive against the North Vietnamese.

It got even worse after that. More and more troops went to Vietnam. In March 1965, an elderly woman burned herself alive in Detroit to protest the growing war. Six months later, a twenty-one-year-old seminarian soaked himself with gasoline and set himself afire in front of the UN to protest "all war," and a thirty-two-year-old Quaker burned himself to death in front of the Pentagon. In April 1965, twenty-five thousand people demonstrated in Washington in protest. The Students for a Democratic Society organized the first national mobilization against the war.

None of that stuff helped. In July, Johnson ordered fifty thousand more men to Vietnam, for a total of a hundred twenty-five thousand. To avoid sending the reserves, he doubled the draft. By the end of 1965, there were a hundred seventy thousand Americans in Vietnam, and over one thousand had died.

All this time, the civil rights movement was in turmoil. In March 1965, several hundred blacks marched in Selma after weeks of futile efforts to register to vote. They were confronted by state troopers and ordered by Governor George Wallace to stop the march. The troopers tore into the crowd with bullwhips, tear gas, and clubs. There were twenty serious injuries. This display of brutality was covered on television, and beamed into everybody's living room. It was real hard to ignore. Soon thereafter the 1965 Voting Rights Act was passed.

In August came the riots in Watts; twenty-one people died, and twenty thousand troops were called into southwestern Los Angeles. Thirty-five square miles of the city were burned and looted.

By the end of 1966, our troops in Vietnam numbered three hundred twenty thousand. In California, movie actor Ronald Reagan, age fifty-five, was elected governor.

In mid-1967, the seeds were sown for the second nuclear war. On June 5, the so-called Six-Day War broke out between Israel and the Arab states. The Arabs were armed and equipped by the Soviet Union, and the Russians repeatedly blamed Israel for starting the war. Throughout its duration, superpower confrontation always lurked in the wings, and I almost got an ulcer.

The Israelis swiftly routed the Arabs, approached the Suez, occupied the old city of Jerusalem, and agreed to a United Nations' cease-fire. After several more days of "persuasion," Egypt and Syria agreed to it too, but thereafter harbored a jumbo-sized grudge, which would in due time bear fruit. Jokes were made that Israel would take over the Vietnam War for cost plus ten percent.

In August 1967, forty-five thousand more men were sent to Vietnam. By then thirteen thousand American soldiers had been killed. That month Lyndon Johnson told an audience in San Antonio, Texas, that "the tide continues to run with us."

Fat chance. In January 1968, the Viet Cong launched the massive Tet offensive, and reversed what little progress we had made. Come March, General Westmoreland requested an additional two hundred and six thousand troops. By June there would be over half a million American men in Vietnam.

The next year, 1968, would see the election of a President. Eugene McCarthy, running on an antiwar platform, ignited the idealism of the young. In February, George Wallace launched a powerful third-party campaign in the South. In March, Bobby Kennedy announced his own candidacy.

For Bobby, the Vietnam War had become a nightmare, for he had helped forge the original interventionist policy in Southeast Asia. Now he knew he had made a mistake. He broke openly with Johnson's policy of steady escalation, and engaged LBJ in a political duel to the death. Then, at the end of the month, came the bombshell—Johnson announced he wouldn't run for re-election. That meant Bobby had a good chance of winning the Democratic primary. He threw himself into the race with a frenzy.

All this time we had been keeping tabs on Bobby; we weren't stupid. He was the only man on Earth who knew the truth about us. And of late, he started to seem greatly changed.

We weren't the only ones who thought so. Years later, Arthur Schlesinger would say Bobby was engaged in a great internal struggle to reconcile his belief in God with his brother's murder. One of Bobby's advisors would describe him as someone in pain, physically, emotionally, and spiritually. In the 1990's, his son Robert, Jr. recalled that after Jack's death Bobby began to read the poets, existentialists, and heroic writers—all those who attempted to explain human tragedy.

Month after month, we watched his star rise. Histories of the time report that by 1968 Bobby had begun to draw together a great following from the ranks of the young, the poor, the dissatisfied, the disenfranchised.

Heretofore we had not been great fans of Bobby's. Once, watching TV, we heard J. Edgar Hoover call him a sneaky little son of a bitch, and had a moment of fellow feeling with that strange old man who ruled the FBI.

However, we did see much to persuade us that Bobby had

changed and grown. After all, the foundations of his life had been turned upside down, and everything he had worked for had been put to the torch. We weren't yet cynical enough to say that no human being could change under such circumstances.

In April 1968, there was a second assassination in the United States, when Martin Luther King, Jr. was murdered. Just hours later, Bobby was scheduled to give an outdoor speech in what, back in those days, they referred to as a "racially mixed" neighborhood. In Indianapolis. He was urged to cancel the speech, but refused. There were riots elsewhere in the country that night, but not in that neighborhood.

People thrive on hope; they crave it like a drug. In Bobby, the country saw a chance to recover the promise of youth it had lost in the blood and gore of Dallas. A great tide roared up and swept Bobby along on its crest. Bells pealed; this time, whispered the tide, we will keep Camelot.

Bobby won lots of primaries. Then he descended on California, knowing the outcome would make or break him.

On June 4, around ten o'clock at night, the three of us were sitting in front of the television watching a local Star Trek rerun when they ran a news banner across the bottom of the screen that Bobby was projected to win the California primary. Jeffrey let out an uncharacteristic whoop. He got up and twisted the dial on the TV, looking for the San Francisco evening news.

At that moment, Jeffrey, Daria, and I experienced something quite strange. It wasn't at all like the ripples in time we felt whenever we encountered people and places that might turn out to be significant in the future. It was completely different. It was like being sideswiped in your car—it was like you might feel walking right next to some railroad tracks while a freight train roared past you—*going the other way*.

"What the hell was that?" cried Daria.

I looked at the others in dismay. "I don't have a clue."

We were completely stumped. We couldn't begin to figure out what on Earth had just happened to us. When we recovered from the shock and Jeffrey finally managed to find the news on TV, nothing remarkable had happened.

We stayed up late to watch Bobby give his victory speech at the Ambassador Hotel in Los Angeles. He was so tired he looked like he was going to keel over, but he got up there on the podium and gave quite a nice little talk, considering the circumstances. Then he said to the crowd of jubilant supporters, "My thanks to all of you, and now it's on to Chicago and let's win there."

Jeffrey started cheering again. On impulse, I went into the kitchen to break out some genuine French champagne we had gotten at a bargain down on Columbus Avenue, and were keeping for a special occasion. Daria followed me, and we filled three glasses. We were guzzling away when the people on the TV screen started screaming and milling about like ants boiling up from a hill somebody'd just stepped on.

I didn't get it at first. Then Daria, on the couch, let out a cry, and it dawned on me what had happened.

I couldn't accept it. I thought I could stop it, if I only refused to believe it had happened. I stretched out my hands toward the television. "No," I pleaded, over and over again.

Bobby died about twenty-four hours later. But it didn't stop there. Shortly after the attack on Bobby, someone killed Richard Nixon in his New York apartment, a third gunman shot Vice President Humphrey campaigning in Colorado Springs, and a fourth shot Eugene McCarthy at the Beverly Hilton in Los Angeles. They were real pros.

They didn't go after Johnson; he was holed up in the White House and too hard to get to, even for them. And they left Nelson Rockefeller, George Wallace, and the perennial Harold Stassen alone. Evidently, the assassins considered those guys small game—their major mistake.

It turned out that all the killers were Arabs—two were from Syria, one from Egypt, and one declared he was from

Palestine (it was later determined he had been born in Jordan). When captured, each said the American candidates were assassinated to avenge the Arab peoples' humiliation in the Six-Day War of 1967.

The country went into a convulsion of rage. Lyndon Johnson pleaded for a calm and considered response to the atrocities, but nobody wanted to hear it.

Having no other choice, Johnson re-entered the presidential race. To the astonishment and furtive delight of the Arab world, he did nothing to retaliate for the assassinations. He was like a man lost in the fog; he had lost control of his life's rudder, just at the time when the country wanted blood.

For months rumors flew fast and furious that the Soviet Union was behind the orchestrated killings, and many Americans believed them. People simply could not accept the notion that a few "fucking ragheads," as the assassins were oft described, could pull off such a stunt unaided. Sam Yorty, the mayor of Los Angeles, said it best: "Evil Communist organizations played a part in inflaming the assassinations of our finest citizens."

With Nixon gone, the Republicans ran Nelson Rockefeller. George Wallace ran as he'd always planned to, as an independent. He had a real hard time choosing a vice-presidential running mate. After waffling between the actor John Wayne and Colonel Harlan Sanders of fried chicken fame, he finally settled on that nuclear warrior, Curtis LeMay, who had so strongly advocated the invasion of Cuba back in October 1962. The voters liked that. LeMay was a fellow who just might give them their pride back.

The Wallace/LeMay campaign consisted of a five-month denunciation of American feebleness. They harangued the people for having let the country grow so soft that it was now the laughingstock of the entire world, and the Arabs in particular. They accused the USSR of having put its Arab allies up to the assassinations, and promised full retribution if they were elected. They whipped the electorate into a frenzy.

They won. And they kept their campaign promises.

Having lived through one nuclear crisis, we could see another one coming—and quick. Then I happened to remember the strange sensation we had felt in the living room just before Bobby Kennedy's assassination, the one that felt like a freight train passing you at full bore.

"Oh, Christ!" I said as it dawned on me what that sensation must have been. I reminded my comrades about the incident and said, "That had to be us—passing ourselves as we went back in time. That means there *is* going to be another war. When the missiles start flying, we're going to have to jump far enough back in time to have room to work to prevent it."

"And meet ourselves? Right here?" cried Daria.

I shook my head. "Apparently not. I don't see our doubles running around the apartment just now."

"Jesus," whispered Jeffrey. "Do you realize what this means? By jumping back again, we're going to create still another alternate world."

Daria put her face in her hands. "A *third* Earth. That means *this* world, the one we're living in here and now, is doomed. The war will come, everyone here will die, and there's nothing we can do about it. We can't keep on creating new Earths, just to watch them burn up. It's like somebody who keeps on having babies, even though they know the babies are going to die of some awful disease!"

That rocked me back. I thought long and hard, and wished I had Father Alexeyev to talk to. On the first jump back in time, when we'd gone to see John Kennedy and created a new world in which no nuclear war had followed the Cuban crisis, I'd felt like such a hero. Now we were going to have to abandon that second world, which we loved so dearly, to the fire. We would have to jump back in time yet again, with no guarantee that the next alternate Earth we created would not suffer the same fate.

I wanted to live. And my heart, ever cooperative, told me the right thing to do was jump back again, but I was not entirely sure I was right, and I shrank from making such a decision. "Comrades," I said, "we have to face the fact that every time we jump back, we create a new host world that can fall prey to war. I have to ask this—is it right for us to go on? Morally?"

Jeffrey made an emphatic gesture. "Yes, we must! Somewhere, we'll find a world that won't always destroy itself!"

Daria laughed. "No matter how many other worlds die? I think maybe you just want to save your own skin!"

There was a long silence. Then Jeffrey said, "I do. I also know our elders wanted us to use the time machine to save Earth in 1962, even if that meant wiping out everybody in the timeline that gave birth to the Bunker—including you, me, and Anna. I don't think our elders would have given the machine three more jumps if they didn't want us to use it again, if necessary. They gave us three more chances to create a viable Earth out of the flames of the last. I don't think we can just throw those chances away."

"All right, then," I said, drawing a deep, shaky breath, "It's battle stations, everybody. We don't know yet exactly when and how the next war's going to start. We've got to identify all the events that led up to it, verify what the branch points are, and figure out how we can get at them after we jump back in time. Right now, I suspect the main branch point is the presidential candidate assassinations. That's when we felt ourselves going back. But we can't be sure until we've seen the whole scenario play out."

We didn't have much time to prepare, as it turned out. Less than two months after Wallace's inauguration, he and LeMay launched a massive invasion of Egypt and Syria, tossing in Jordan for good measure.

The Soviets had an estimated twenty thousand advisors in Egypt in late 1968. In the course of the invasion, many of them were killed. The USSR lost no time rushing to the defense of its client state, and sending prodigious amounts of arms and supplies to Syria and Jordan to assist them in repelling the Western imperialist offensive. Soviet and

American battleships and air carriers poured into the Mediterranean.

At first the invasion went well. Then, thanks to Soviet aid and fierce Arab resistance, it stalled. The American people got really frustrated. After all, they had practically tasted victory, and then somebody just up and snatched it away.

LeMay had said during the campaign he would prefer not to use truly nasty weapons, but if it were necessary, he would use "anything we could dream up, including nuclear weapons." Now, his back to the wall, he decided the time had come.

Wallace, scared to death by the forces he had set in motion, tried to put the genie back into the bottle. But LeMay and the rest of the military had set their hearts on a "limited nuclear surgical strike" that would take out Cairo and Damascus, as a surgeon would excise a couple of troublesome tumors. (They weren't going to touch Amman; it was far too close to Jerusalem, and even LeMay realized you never could be sure just which way the fallout was going to go.)

The Soviets gave our guys an ultimatum. Shoot, and we'll nuke Ankara. LeMay laughed. He said they wouldn't do anything, just as he had said during the Cuban crisis—and he'd been right then, hadn't he?

Wrong. While mushroom clouds lofted into the stratosphere of the former infrastructure of Cairo and Damascus, the Soviets detonated a ten-kiloton nuclear warhead over the capital of Turkey. Turkey, of course, was a NATO country. NATO was bound to us by treaty. So we responded.

You can take it from here. Please, do. I'm feeling too queasy right now.

We did conclude that the candidate assassinations were directly responsible for the war. So Jeffrey compiled from media reports detailed files on the movements of each presidential candidate on the night of the assassinations— Bobby at the Ambassador, McCarthy at the Beverly Hilton, Nixon in New York, and Humphrey in Colorado. He traced every known movement of the four assassins on the night in question and identified the moments at which they would have been most vulnerable to someone else stalking them. Curiously, he uncovered no evidence that any of the assassins had had a backup. Pros or not, these Arabs had been on a budget.

Jeffrey programmed the machine to send us back in time a week before June 4, 1968. We packed light. We took printouts of all Jeffrey's research (which, obviously, would not be retrievable from his computers back on May 29, 1968); a few lethal, featherweight Bunker weapons that James Bond would have killed for; all our big bills and gemstones; and several sets of fake IDs. This was so we would still have the money, firepower, and papers to enable us to move quickly, just in case we miscalculated and all our tools and resources weren't waiting for us in the apartment after the jump. I mean, if we ended up back in our apartment before we'd bought the damn thing, it would have been murder to prepare for saving the world from scratch.

The moment we arrived back in our living room at the end of May, that second Earth, the one that we had saved from the Cuban missile crisis, was sundered in twain. A third world was born, because the universe could not allow two sets of youthful nuclear Bunker superheroes to co-exist in the same space and time. The only way out was to create a new place, our third Earth. To us, it felt like being flattened by a giant flyswatter.

When we recovered, we found that everything in the apartment was just as it had been on May 29—and nobody else was there.

We flew into action, and set priorities. My assignment was to save Bobby. I insisted on having Bobby. I didn't get too much lip from Jeffrey, who arguably had a slight edge over me for title of "Best Fighter." His mission was just as important—to kill Nixon's assassin. That way, even if the rest of us failed, there would be a Republican left who could beat Wallace.

We didn't think it necessary for one of us to take out Humphrey's assassin. Humph was, after all, vice president of the United States, and if the Secret Service got tons of warning, they could take care of it. We arranged for the Veep to receive anonymous telexes from all over the country outlining exactly how he was going to be assassinated in Colorado. That, surely, would do the trick. And, in fact, the service never let the assassin get a crack at Humphrey, and nothing about it ever made the news.

So Daria, our only arguable lightweight, got assigned to save Gene McCarthy. (Sorry, Gene; honest, it was nothing personal. You just didn't have that good a shot at winning.)

We prepared very, very carefully. Early on the morning of June 5, we headed to the airport, plane tickets in hand, and headed off to our respective destinations. Jeffrey hugged Daria and me before we boarded a plane for Los Angeles. Then he gave Daria a funny look and said, "Be very careful, darling. Don't get hurt. Nobody'd go to war over just McCarthy."

I had disguised myself to blend into the crowd at the Ambassador Hotel. I was costumed as a Kennedy campaign worker with a complete set of ID, a short little dress with an attention-getting scooped neck, a jaunty hat, lots of eye makeup, and a demeanor as perky as Marlo Thomas in *That Girl*. I had a soft fringed leather drawstring purse, that little touch of counterculture couture every liberal needed in 1968, which was coincidentally big enough to hold all my stuff. My two favorite weapons nestled cleverly within what appeared to be a plastic hairbrush and a plastic rat-tail comb—two indispensable girlish accessories in the spring of 1968.

I knew what the Arab looked like, and that he meant to shoot Bobby in the pantry corridor behind the hotel's Embassy Ballroom. It was obvious to any observer that Bobby, after his victory speech, could not make his way through the massive crowd in the Embassy Ballroom to the press conference scheduled elsewhere in the hotel. The

crowd was so thick, he would have to go out the back way.
The assassin had taken up a position in the pantry, and was
waiting for him there.

As it grew late, I made myself part of the milling crowd
in the ballroom. I scanned the crowd like a hawk cruising
for a mouse. Several times I skipped down the corridor all
the way to the Colonial Room, as pert and goofy as they
come, keeping an eye out for the Arab. I knew he wasn't
scheduled to show up just yet, but I had to be extra careful
for my own peace of mind.

When Bobby's victory in the California primary was
announced and he went up to the podium, I wormed my way
back to the corridor behind the ballroom. I turned right,
went through a set of swinging doors, and tried to engrave
the scene on my memory.

The pantry was hot, dingy, and smelled bad. On the left
were three desk-high warming counters. On the right was a
row of ice machines. On one wall some unknown person
had taped a most curious, hand-lettered sign that read "The
Once and Future King."

The place was mobbed. Everywhere there were waiters,
cooks, busboys, and campaign volunteers hoping to see
Bobby. For one tense moment, I thought my man had gotten
there early. I saw a small, swarthy young guy sitting on top
of one of the desklike warming counters, holding a rolled-up
Kennedy poster. But he was talking most animatedly to a
young miniskirted girl, and when I got a good look at him,
it was clear he was not my target. I hadn't committed the
bastard's features to memory for nothing.

I walked on. A roar went up from the ballroom behind
me, and I knew Bobby had begun to speak. I started
walking, very quickly. I went all the way to the very end of
the corridor. I didn't go into the Colonial Room; it was full
of press, and we knew the assassin had not entered the
corridor from there. Instead, I kept going, bearing left,
always left.

Then I saw him, and at once went into my act. I sang to

myself, fished around in my purse, and at last extracted a
pack of cigarettes. I placed a smoke between my teeth, and
continued to paw through my purse like a ditz-brain. All the
while, watching everything from under my dime-store false
eyelashes.

Heart hammering, I giggled and fluttered and went up to
him, eyelashes going a mile a minute, and said breathlessly
that I had lost my matches and would he please light my
cigarette.

Yes, I know it's corny. I know it's the oldest trick in the
book. It got to be the oldest trick because it works. Face it,
men from his background in that era, killers or not, were
still not completely used to women walking around in
public with naked faces—let alone legs and the rest of it.

I only had to throw him off guard for a fraction of a
second. I peppered him with twitters and movements. I took
out another cigarette and pressed it into his hand, I laughed
and chattered and fussed and stood very close to him. He
had his mind 99 percent on his mission and I think he was
on the verge of backhanding me to clear the way. But he
wasn't expecting trouble, and the other 1 percent of his
mind got flustered just long enough to give me the opening
I needed.

I decided the rat-tail comb would be enough. With an
apologetic little titter, I took it out and slipped it cleanly
between his ribs. He didn't even realize he'd been hit until
the poison flattened him.

It was very fast acting. I put everything back in my purse
and cried out, "Oh, this poor man, he's sick! Somebody
help!"

I ran in feigned terror back toward the ballroom. But there
was no need for theatrics, for although people were around,
nobody had been right there in the corridor to see me kill
him. They were all down the hall, waiting for Bobby.

Now I began to shake in earnest, having never killed
anybody before. I pushed back to the Embassy Ballroom, to

see Bobby once more and remind myself why the murder was necessary.

He had just finished speaking as I wormed my way to the front of the crowd, not ten feet from the podium. He had just spoken those last words, ". . . it's on to Chicago and let's win there." As he stepped back, he caught sight of me, standing there amid his army of supporters. A wisp of mortal fear flickered in the depths of his eyes, as if I were Death, and he knew I was there to convey him to our appointment in Samarra.

Our gazes locked, and I threw my arms open wide, as if I could embrace him across the distance that separated us. Then I raised my left hand above my head in a "V," in the sign that meant peace to the young people in that room, and victory to their fathers. I didn't jump up and down and scream like all the others. It wasn't necessary. He got the message.

He gave a quiet, happy smile. I thought he framed the words "Thank you." Then his shoulders slumped, for it was okay for him to be tired now. His people took him through the gold curtains behind the podium into the anteroom, and he briefly vanished from my sight. I shoved my way through the door to the right of the stage, and was standing right by the swinging doors when he and Ethel and their entourage went into the pantry.

I knew I should get out of there before somebody, somehow, linked me to the body at the far end of the corridor, which was going to be discovered any minute. It was not inconceivable that, earlier, someone had spotted me heading in that direction. But I couldn't help myself; I stayed to see more of Bobby.

He made his way through the crowd, greeting people. He came level with the warming counters and shook hands with one of the hotel dishwashers. Suddenly a man burst from concealment behind the large ice machines, crossed the corridor, steadied his right elbow on the counter nearest to Bobby, and began firing.

I did scream then. Bobby fell. People piled onto the gunman, one after another. Still he kept shooting, and wounded half a dozen others. Then two Kennedy supporters, Rafer Johnson, the Olympic champion, and Roosevelt Grier, the football lineman, kicked the gun out of his hand and slammed him spread-eagled onto the counter. A campaign worker tried to strangle him.

Shortly the bastard's face was covered with blood. Jesse Unruh climbed onto the counter and screamed at the crowd to keep the man alive—"Let's not have another Oswald!" Rafer Johnson had the presence of mind to pocket the assassin's gun.

The worst moment was when I recognized the would-be killer. He was the slight, swarthy man I had seen sitting on a warming counter, talking to a stray girl, with a Kennedy poster under his arm—a poster that had concealed a weapon. I had walked right by him and never suspected.

Later I would learn that his name, Sirhan, was the Arabic word for wolf.

The truth dawned on me. Two men, not one, had been gunning for Bobby. But this second, according to our best intelligence, was not a backup. He had to be a madman—a wild card. Back on our second Earth, he had not gotten his chance to shoot Bobby, for the trained assassin had gotten there first.

I couldn't judge the passage of time with all the screaming around me. It seemed like it took the police and the ambulance an eternity to get there. I sat down against the wall of the corridor and cried, because I was sure Bobby was going to die; I had seen all the blood on the floor and knew his head wound was massive. And just before he was shot, I had waved at him, and made him think everything was going to be all right!

At some point most of the commotion died away, and there were only a few of us left in the corridor. Roosevelt Grier sat on stool, his face in his hands, weeping. A young press aide sat near him on the floor, holding Bobby's shoes

to his chest. When I got up and walked into the lobby, I saw
dozens of men and women on their knees around the hotel's
mock Moorish fountain, which was filled with balloons.
Some were counting rosary beads and chanting Hail Marys.
As I watched, a young black man in a suit picked up a chair
and flung it with all his might into the fountain, where it
landed with a crash. "That's what you get!" he cried. "That's
what you get in white America!"

Sometime later, still in a daze, I went to check on the first
assassin's body. It had disappeared. The Arabs may not have
had backups, but they clearly had a cleaning crew.

My memory of the following hours is fuzzy. I know I
went back to the lobby and sat down and watched all the
people grieving, and that around three in the morning I
asked a man at the front desk to call a cab for me. I went to
the airport, got an early morning flight to San Francisco, and
drank myself into a stupor in our apartment. I knew it was
a dangerous thing to do, as there might still be work to do,
but I didn't care.

At eight A.M. Jeffrey returned from New York. He had
been successful in preventing the attack upon Nixon. When
he caught sight of me, he started yelling, because he thought
I'd screwed up. When he saw how drunk I was, he literally
spit on me. I told him to shut up, because I had gotten my
man, only there had been a madman assassin we hadn't even
known about. When Jeffrey realized that, he sat down on the
couch and started to cry.

We waited and waited for Daria. We knew she had been
successful, for the news had reported no assassination
attempt on Eugene McCarthy. But hours passed, and she
didn't show up.

Then Jeffrey's computers picked up a Los Angeles police
report describing two people the cops figured were the
victims of a murder-suicide pact. The bodies fit the descrip-
tions of Daria and McCarthy's erstwhile assassin.

We concluded Daria had waylaid the assassin as planned,
just before he reached the Beverly Hilton. But her judgment

had been poor. She had used a plain handgun, not the James Bond stuff with which she felt less familiar. Not that she didn't nail the guy. She shot him chock full of lead. But he died too slowly, and was able to shoot her back—right between the eyes.

In the wake of the attack on Bobby, the Los Angeles police were very much on their toes. As soon as they started digging, they realized the ID papers Daria carried were fake, and they had not a clue who she was. When they realized the man who died with her had something of a reputation in the Arab world, they went through the roof. But nobody—including us—ever managed to link his presence in Los Angeles to that of Sirhan Sirhan. And the police never had a chance at figuring out who Daria was.

All this meant that we couldn't go claim her body. We didn't dare. We had to grieve for her in silence, in the dark. We didn't even know what they did with the bodies of unidentifiable people like Daria. Perhaps they burned them.

That August, Hubert Humphrey won the Democratic nomination, as police beat protesters in Grant Park on nationwide TV. Richard Nixon won the Republican nomination and, in November, the election, by a mere four-tenths of one percent of the vote. Wallace and LeMay ran a safe and distant third.

There was no nuclear war.

In December, the *Bulletin of the Atomic Scientists* moved up the Doomsday Clock to seven minutes before midnight.

## 15

## 1968–1972: San Francisco and Austin

History proceeded apace in our third Earth, heedless that Jeffrey and I were walking around in a state of grief and shock. As the years passed, the shape of things to come kept on chugging away like a little choo-choo train, creating itself in the ether just as it damn well pleased, despite all our time-traveling efforts to put things on the right track once and for all.

Jeffrey and I felt incredibly alone in this new Earth. In 1962 we had burst into the Oval Office after our first jump through time, confident, brash, full of energy, believing we could never fail. We had appealed to the President of the United States, saved the world, and found ourselves launched on a glittering new life with plenty of money, a carnival of new experiences to discover, and grateful friends in high places. Now, with only each other to rely on, we faced a world stripped bare of all the friends we had known since leaving the Bunker—a world without Daria, Jack, Bobby, or Rima; a world where I was still cut off from Lavrenti. The first six months in our new home were one of the bleakest times of my life.

Still, I dutifully paid attention to the march of events. While I might *feel* like both arms had just been cut off, we were still responsible for standing vigil over Earth III as the toddler took its first unsteady steps down the new timeline.

The war in Vietnam had become a disaster of enormous

proportions. In 1968, President-elect Nixon talked a lot about putting an end to it, but didn't follow through. In fact, many years later, it was rumored that in 1972 he actively strove to prolong the war through the 1972 presidential election, so no unforeseen screwup in Vietnam could dethrone him.

By April 1969, the death toll from the war topped 33,000, and troop strength peaked at over half a million men. In November of that year we were treated to the horrors of the massacre at My Lai. The year of 1969 wasn't completely bad, though. The first human beings to walk on the moon arrived there in July, and in August five hundred thousand young people showed up at a culturally defining moment in New York state called Woodstock.

Throughout 1970, the news continued to be mixed. Students were shot dead at Kent State. Mississippi educational television banned *Sesame Street*. Janis Joplin and Jimi Hendrix died. But Americans celebrated the very first Earth Day.

In 1971, George Wallace announced still another presidential bid, and Nikita Khrushchev died in obscurity. The following year, former Red-baiter Richard Nixon became the first U.S. president to visit Moscow. He spent an entire week in the Soviet capital and signed a landmark nuclear arms treaty. In fact, so successful was he, that by the end of the year the Pepsi Company was doing business with the Soviets, and the Doomsday Clock got bumped all the way back to twelve minutes before midnight. However, when he subsequently referred to his visit as "the week that changed the world," Jeffrey and I laughed until our stomachs hurt. We weren't making fun of Nixon; he really had a right to crow. It's just that there are some weeks that change the world, and then there are others. The old guy only knew about the first kind.

Thanks to Nixon, I got my hopes up and tried writing letters to Lavrenti at several alternate addresses. But it was no good. I never got an answer. Despite the President's efforts, the curtain that hid Russia was still made of iron.

In March 1972, George Wallace won, but big, in the Florida presidential primary. Having had a taste of what the man could do at the helm of the ship of state, my heart rate went through the ceiling. It did calm down a bit when George McGovern, advocating a quick end to the war, won his primary in Wisconsin. But on May 4, Wallace responded by winning seventy percent of the Tennessee primary vote. He just would not go away! I was starting to sweat really hard when still *another* crazed lone gunman took him out.

Was there a factory somewhere where they made these nut cases? As little fondness as I had for Wallace, I spent the night of May 15 depressed and shiftfaced drunk in a bar on Union Street. Fortunately, the barkeep knew me and my big tips quite well. He sent me home in a cab, thereby preserving a significant portion of his future flow of income.

When the McGovern campaign began to heat up that fall, I decided to put my cash where my convictions were and wrote out a big fat check. I didn't expect anything more than a thank-you letter. To be brutally honest, I just did it to make myself feel better. I still felt guilty for failing to save Bobby. Plus, I was tired of sitting on the sidelines. It was 1972, I suddenly found myself near the unimaginably old age of *thirty,* and I wanted to start being—what's that word that came into vogue in the 1980's?—proactive.

Anyway, to my surprise, I got invited to this dinner in Austin, Texas, honoring "significant" contributors to the McGovern campaign. I went. Hell, I'd never been to Texas. I wanted to see firsthand that strange land where a few of my ancestors had come from; where, after the Civil War, they lynched more whites than blacks—but only because the ol' boys were stealing horses. Hey, from the time it gained its independence from Mexico in 1832 until it joined the Union in 1845, Texas had been a foreign country. Certain people said it still was.

*    *    *

At the dinner I sat in the audience to the left of the podium, where Senator McGovern was holding forth. After McGovern's speech, one of his aides took a few moments to recognize those who "had greatly assisted the campaign's fund-raising efforts." He went on and on thanking people, and I almost went to sleep, but about twenty minutes later, when he mentioned "a lady real estate developer" from California, I perked up my ears. Whoever she was, I knew I should definitely look her up when I got back home.

"She does not destroy old neighborhoods, but preserves them. She is, in the best sense of the word, a conservative," said the senator. This got a good-natured hiss out of the audience. "While saving the heritage of a beautiful American city, she creates jobs, and invests what she has earned back into the community. Because of her, San Francisco is a more beautiful place today. We are pleased to honor her contribution to the campaign. Please give her a hand." Then he called my name.

I was flabbergasted. I didn't think I'd given McGovern all that much money, but evidently my contribution was relatively huge. (*Bad* omen for his ultimate success in the election!) I stood up and gawked at the senator and the crowd like a high school sophomore. I was about to sit down when I noticed a familiar-looking young man sitting up on the banquette four or five places on the other side of McGovern. He was in his mid-twenties, and was staring at me like his life depended on it.

I got a real shock. It was the kid from the Rose Garden back in July 1963. All grown up.

After the thing broke up, he made a beeline for me. "My God," he said, "if it isn't my White House Cassandra, lo these many years."

We shook hands and he gave me this warm, sunshiny grin like I was the only person in the world that mattered right then. He must have worked real hard over the past decade, figuring out how Jack had done it, copycatting all of Jack's best moves. Now he had gotten real good at the Kennedy snow job. Boy howdy, as they said down there in the Lone Star state, did he have charm!

I went weak in the knees. "Nine years, to be precise," I said, to save face. "You have a memory like an elephant."

"So they say. However, I'm a Democrat," he replied.

"What are you doing up there next to the senator?" I asked.

He grinned. He was so young, and so proud of himself. "I'm heading up the senator's campaign in Texas."

I was really impressed. "No kidding?"

He nodded. "With the able help of my girlfriend over there." He pointed to the table by the senator. "We just got out of law school at Yale, and came down here to kick some ass."

I looked up at the podium. I saw a serious young reformer—an intense, bespectacled, intelligent-looking woman who looked feminist enough to satisfy Betty Friedan. "Far out," I said. "Not bad for a poor little Texas boy."

He shook his head emphatically. "Arkansas. Just visiting Texas for the big time."

He was too cocky. I had to take him down a peg. Over the years, I had perfected my cobra stare. Now I impaled him with it. "Yale, huh? Aren't you the hot dog!"

He gave a modest little shrug. "I like school. After college at Georgetown, I even got to spend a year at Oxford."

I was supposed to bite and, like an obliging idiot, I did. "How'd you manage that?"

"Rhodes scholarship," he said casually.

"Oh," I said, outgunned. "*Then* law school."

"Yeah."

I regrouped. I was a woman of the world, and knowledgeable. Shit, I was *older*. "You probably passed up a Wall Street job for this poorly paid stuff. Why?"

"This is more important," he replied. He looked like he meant it. "And a hell of a lot more fun."

"Not many Arkansas boys would say that. What's next? Legal Aid?"

He shook his head. "After the campaign, I'm going back to Fayetteville to teach law at the university. Then I'll probably run for office. Attorney general, maybe, or governor."

"In *Arkansas*? That's bush league!"

He laughed. "Just you wait."

Oh, well. Life is full of disappointments. Despite the considerable talent that the young man, Bill, his girlfriend, and many others brought to the campaign, on November 7 Richard Nixon beat the pants off George McGovern. McGovern carried only Washington, D.C., and the state of Massachusetts. I looked sadly at my checkbook, swore off politics—at least for the time being—and went back to what I was best at: doing my damnedest to frustrate World War III.

## 16

## 1973–1991: San Francisco and Moscow

A year later, in 1973, the Yom Kippur War erupted, giving us some *bad* moments. The Russians were backing the Arabs, we were backing the Israelis, and it looked like the world was about to get dragged into still another nuclear war. As the tension mounted, Jeffrey and I would stare at each other from opposite ends of the couch in our too-quiet living room, the whites of our eyes showing. We could hear Daria's ghost posing the dreaded question: "Are we going to have to jump back *again?*"

"Damn it!" cried Jeffrey at the height of the crisis, his nerves shot. "Where does it say we've got to have a nuclear war every five years? It feels like we're being stalked!"

Truer words were never spoken. I went for a long walk; at thirty-one, I was beginning my acquaintance with despair, and was struggling not to lose hope like poor Father Alexeyev had. I was so afraid that the war was going to come back for a third round, that the atomic demon, once loosed upon the world by the insane rivalry between our parent countries, could never again be caged.

But we got lucky. The war stayed localized, and eventually a peace accord was worked out. The world began to enjoy a most welcome period of "peace," marred only by numerous petty non-nuclear wars, that was to last almost two decades. Jeffrey and I took advantage of the lull to make even more money and dug our tentacles even deeper into the fabric of society. And we did our best to keep up with old friends.

Five years later, in 1978, I came on the following mention of Bill, my Rose Garden buddy, in Jeffrey's newspaper database—specifically in Lloyd Shearer's "Intelligence Report" in *Parade* magazine:

> Political prophets are making a long-term prediction that [Ted] Kennedy's running mate in 1984 will be William Jefferson Clinton, a tall, handsome, 31-year-old former Rhodes scholar and Yalie who is currently Arkansas' attorney general, most probably its next governor and one of the most potentially charismatic politicians in the country.

"Well, I'll be goddamned," I said. Hearing me, Jeffrey came bustling up and peered over my shoulder.

"Is he important? Should I be keeping tabs on him too?"

I nodded. "It sure can't hurt."

In 1982, Jeffrey and I felt an indescribable chagrin as we both turned forty. Not that there was anything the matter with being forty; we just couldn't get used to the fact that two decades had somehow slipped away when we weren't watching.

However, Fate didn't leave us much breathing room to dwell on the course of our own lives. As Lorelei Lee would have said, Fate just kept on happening.

In the mid-1980's change at last came to Russia. A mere spark at first, then its pace quickened, and like magic roared into a whirlwind that swept aside the despotic regime that had ruled that country since the October Revolution.

It happened like this. In 1982, Leonid Brezhnev died at age seventy-five. He was replaced by the head of the KGB, Yuri Andropov. But Andropov himself died a year and a half later, and was replaced by still another aging Party leader, Konstantin Chernenko, who was himself at death's door. In late 1984, the British press reported that a top Soviet official named Mikhail Gorbachev, believed by many to be the next Soviet leader, was to visit Great Britain. Sure enough, in March 1985, upon Chernenko's death, the Party chose Gorbachev to be its next general secretary.

His ascension to power was like a warm wind across a frozen lake. It brought hints of spring—and of danger. In spring come the rebirth of life and the renewal of hope—but also killing storms. In spring, the river ice can crack beneath your feet without warning and send you to your death.

This Gorbachev had come up through the Party just like all the others. He was even a protégé of the KGB-master Andropov. But something was very different about him. Having been born about the same time as Elvis Presley and my lost Lavrenti, he had grown up in a newer era than his predecessors. He would have come to young manhood in the 1950's, after Stalin died. Like Lavrenti, he would have gone to parties, smoked Marlboros, and listened to all the evil forbidden American music of the time; at the minimum, it was a good bet he was a jazz fan. A decade later, he would have watched the convulsive social changes of the 1960's sweep the Western world, and noticed how the music of that decade rattled the very foundations of that culture. Perhaps he guessed a second revolution might someday come to Russia; he might even have dreamed of bringing it about himself.

Never underestimate the subversive power of rock and roll.

The Soviet Union was fond of singing about how their glorious October Revolution had turned the world upside down. However, it took Mikhail Gorbachev to actually accomplish this curious phenomenon. Armed with youthful vitality and altogether too much charm, he put his mind to courting favor with the West, and succeeded beyond his wildest dreams. At the beginning of the 1980's, President Reagan regularly referred to the Soviet Union as the "Evil

Empire." Halfway through the decade, Americans were visiting Russians by the hundreds of thousands and giving them lots of money, and Ronnie was eating out of Misha's hand.

By the summer of 1991, Russia had a lot to rejoice about. The secret police were no longer knocking on doors in the middle of the night and carting people away. Freedom of the press and the arts began to blossom. However, things were not completely rosy. Food was hard to get. Vodka, I heard, was really a bitch. Since the typical human being thinks first with his stomach, then with his groin, then with his ancient emotional lizard-stem brain, and only then (if there is no possible other alternative) with his modern rational brain, the proletariat was royally pissed off at the state of things. A bunch of coupsters who wished to return the country to Communist rule saw an opportunity to oust Gorbachev.

The so-called Gang of Eight weren't terribly creative folks. They must have looked up in the official Commie Coup Manual how the Party bosses got rid of Khrushchev back in 1964, and dutifully copied down the formula like schoolboys. They followed instructions to the letter, even claiming that Mikhail Gorbachev had stepped down for health reasons, and playing nonstop classical music on the state radio station all during the coup.

But, passing strange, they completely neglected to pull the plug on the foreign media. I mean, they had not a clue about the importance of modern telecommunications, let alone the Internet. Consequently, the cameras were tagging along, and rolling full speed, when members of the elite KGB Alpha unit intercepted one Boris Yeltsin in front of the Parliament Building of the Russian Republic.

Earlier, Yeltsin had escaped capture at his home by a margin of five minutes, and had made for the Parliament Building with all due haste. Unfortunately, he didn't have that last minute or so necessary to get inside to safety. Those of his supporters who survived and talked to the media said he had intended to make a stand there and rally the people. But he never had a chance. When the KGB tried to arrest him, he resisted, and his bloody death was recorded live by every Western television network.

I watched the execution—for that's what it was—with a very personal kind of horror, realizing that the newish Russian Parliament Building, the site of Yeltsin's murder, occupied that very spot of land that had been visible from my window in the Ukraina Hotel in 1963, and had given me the shivers. During my visit to Moscow in that faraway year, I had guessed history would one day be changed on that spot. But I had not dreamed how terrible the change would be.

The citizens of Moscow were outraged—that much was clear from the news reports we saw. But with no one to rally them, they were unable to mount any effective resistance. The massacre of the hundred or so student protestors who eventually showed up at the Parliament Building the next day equalled in savagery the events of Tiananmen Square in 1989. The American CNN network lobbed it around the world in all its grisly, gory detail.

What was most disturbing to American viewers was that many of the young people mowed down by the Red Army had taken symbols, signs, and gestures from the American hippie movement twenty-five years earlier. They painted themselves with peace symbols, sported long hair, wore flowered shirts and dresses, and flashed the peace sign even as the tanks bore down upon them and they were crushed beneath the treads.

The hundreds of thousands of Americans and other Westerners who had visited Russia since the rise of Gorbachev were horrified and disgusted. The coup perpetrators suddenly found themselves ostracized and embargoed by the West, and the Cold War resumed in earnest. The Soviet economy, which had been on its last legs anyway, collapsed in a matter of months.

Jeffrey and I, paranoid as ever, had immersed ourselves in

study of the events of August 1991. We read every newspaper and magazine article available that dealt with the
coup. We pored, frame by frame, over every last bit of
television coverage of the event. Always we looked for
branch points—points of great leverage in the web of
events, where a single, well-placed push might direct the
course of history down a different path.

While we studied frantically, events marched on. The
coupsters who took over the Soviet government couldn't
hold on to it. They were in over their heads, and besides,
most of them had severe drinking problems. As the economy
sank into the mire, strikes, food riots, and protest demonstrations broke out all across the country. Viktor Alksnis, the
hard liner well known in Gorbachev's day, the ultra-nationalist
army officer called the "Dark Colonel," seized power from
the Communists. With an iron fist, he reimposed order
throughout the Soviet Union, abolished the Communist
Party, and established a new, nationalistic Russian state. He
preached that ethnic Russians were chosen to rule over
the inferior peoples who actually made up the majority of
the former Soviet empire. The persecution of Jews re-
emerged, members of many races, formerly Soviet but not
Russian, died in pogroms.

Unfortunately for Alksnis, scapegoating and master-
racing could get people's minds off the economic chaos in
Russia only so long. When you got right down to it, the
Dark Colonel needed lots of hard currency, and he needed it
fast. He realized that since he had enough nukes to kill
everyone on the planet at least ten times over, he didn't need
all of them. So he began selling off the surplus to unstable
third-world countries.

The United States demanded an immediate end to this
atomic bazaar, but Alksnis paid no heed. In search of a
massive and drastic infusion of resources, he invaded the
Baltic states, the Eastern Bloc countries, and the German
Democratic Republic, all of which had effectively gained
their independence under Gorbachev. While he was at it, he

occupied West Berlin, which he felt should really have gone to Russia in 1945.

The United States and NATO were not about to hold still for that. And thus the war over Berlin, which John F. Kennedy had so feared thirty years before, finally came to pass.

As I said, Jeffrey and I had been preparing for this eventuality, and were ready to jump the moment the missiles flew. As we fired up the machine, Jeffrey was all puffed up like a toad, ready to go do battle with the forces of evil. But the years had taken their toll on me; almost fifty years old, I was having a hard time staving off despair.

I was starting to accept the notion that our lifelong efforts had only delayed the inevitable destruction of the world. By continually going back in time and patching up history, we weren't bringing about any lasting change; we were only treating the symptoms of a much more serious human illness. And what in God's name did we expect to do when the time machine finally ran out of jumps and still another war came along?

But what could we do? Just thinking about it gave me the willies. To put an end to this recurring cycle of atomic wars, we would have to go so far back in time, and make such radical changes, that the modern world would become unrecognizable.

Think about it. In this brave new world free of atomic terror, there could never be an October Revolution, or a Soviet Union. Neither could there be a First World War to lead to a Second World War and the Manhattan Project. No Hiroshima, no Nagasaki, no Cold War, no arms race, no nuclear genie to let out of the bottle. But who on Earth would dare take responsibility for making such extreme changes to the world we knew?

As we materialized in our living room back in early August 1991—creating a fourth world in the process—we were well aware of the difficulty of our undertaking. To prevent this latest war, we would have to interfere in the affairs of a foreign country on the mother of all grand scales. On the other hand, we were optimistic. It seemed to us that the Soviet junta had succeeded in seizing power in spite of its stunning incompetence. We thought we could take advantage of its many mistakes to destroy its undeserved good fortune. Given a nice hard shove at a carefully chosen branch point, Fate might favor the Russian people instead.

We weren't gluttons for punishment. Our first move was to try to warn Gorbachev about the impending coup. However, we nursed no vain hopes that this would do the trick, because important people had been telling Gorby about the possibility for months, even in the newspapers. But he had paid no attention.

The previous winter, Alexander Yakovlev, Gorbachev's prime minister, had tried to warn him. His staunchest ally, Foreign Minister Eduard Shevardnadze, had specifically told him that "a dictatorship is coming." Shevardnadze had even resigned his post to underscore the seriousness of his belief. But this dramatic gesture elicited little response from Gorbachev, except for a bit of subsequent sucking up to the country's right wing. I mean, in some ways he and Reagan were regular brothers in the 'hood.

We gave it our best shot, we really did. We wrote, phoned, and faxed Gorbachev using half a dozen of the best aliases we had constructed and maintained over the years for use in just such moments like this. We also fraudulently wrote and faxed him using the names of people we knew he held in high esteem. It didn't work. He shrugged it all off and went right ahead with his vacation in the Crimea.

So impervious was Gorbachev to the notion of an imminent coup that many Russians believed he'd actually been involved in the conspiracy. In fact, Gorby's peculiar stupidity was never satisfactorily explained. Still, we never believed he was part of the coup. No matter how you sliced it, there was just no way he could have benefited from it. And there was no way the junta would have gone to prison just to restore Gorby's popularity.

When it became clear that warning Gorbachev wasn't going to work, we moved to our fallback position. Actually, our Grand Plan. After intensive study, we concurred that Boris Yeltsin was the key to crushing the coup. Although he did not command many troops, he had two great sources of power. He was the only popularly elected President of Russia *ever*. Plus, he could call people into the streets and he could evoke strikes.

See, we had concluded that resistance to the coup needed only a spark to set it aflame. Jeffrey and I had had quite a wrangle over this back in our quarters on Union Street. Jeffrey was playing devil's advocate and arguing that events in the Soviet Union needed more of a push then even we could deliver. I disagreed emphatically.

"Remember *The Time Machine*, Jeff?" I asked.

"Of course I do, but this is no time to start discussing great films."

"You're not getting it! Remember the scene down in the caverns where this Morlock is choking Rod Taylor to death? There are dozens and dozens of Eloi there, more than enough to stop the Morlock, but nobody has the balls to strike the first blow! Until this really cute one—Bob Barron, I think his name was—started making a fist over and over and took this deep breath and punched the Morlock's lights out? Literally, if you remember the special effects, how his eyes blinked out—"

"Yes, yes, enough! Shut up and let me think."

"The Russians are like all those Eloi. All they need is for one guy to strike a blow at the right time, and they'll rise up. They did it once before in 1917, remember, when no one thought they would."

"So we keep Yeltsin from getting killed and he gets to the Parliament Building. So what? They'll still send in the tanks."

I pointed out that our research made it clear that few citizens favored the coup. Some of them were so opposed to it, and so determined to speak their minds, that they had died in the streets in protest. Therefore, our strategy was to (a) warn Yeltsin early and get him safely inside the Parliament Building, (b) get the word out to the people, and (c) pray they had enough time to organize some resistance before the repression got tough.

We thought we had a good chance of success. Once enough people rallied at the Parliament Building, it was not at all certain that the army and the KGB would obey the coup plotters. When the tanks finally arrived at the Parliament Building, their drivers would not encounter a confused handful of students in generation-old hippie garb—instead, they would find their mothers, their fathers, and even their *babushkas* on the barricades. At that point, they might just back off. Or join the rebellion, like so many Slavic Luke Skywalkers.

Or so we hoped, and prayed.

We had always made sure that at any given moment, at least one of our many respective aliases was possessed of a valid, current visa to enter the Soviet Union. So, as soon as it was clear our frantic warnings to Gorbachev would go unheeded, we hopped a plane to Moscow.

## 17

August 1991: Moscow

   This time we entered Russia the right way. This time we weren't the kids in a tour group going to visit the fearsome Evil Empire. We were grown-up, savvy, disgustingly rich, and we knew how to work the Russian system quietly. And effectively. We made all the right phone calls, poked the appropriate people with influence, and greased palms when necessary. The guys at Russian customs were downright obsequious. They didn't even look at our luggage. Consequently we, and all our goodies and equipment intended to avert the coup, made it into the country unscathed.

   We rented rooms at our old stomping ground, the Ukraina Hotel, since it was next to the Russian Parliament Building and fated to be right in the middle of all the action. We didn't take the largest suite—we didn't want to be too ostentatious and attract attention—but we booked several more modest adjoining suites, so we had plenty of room to operate.

   On August 18, the day before the coup, we pulled out this extensive computer-generated database we had of Moscow's liberals, reformers, and Yeltsin supporters, set up a clever little automatic dialing device that made one untraceable telephone call after another, and let it work on the database. When someone answered, a voice told them in perfect Russian that early the next morning there would be an attempt to overthrow the government by a group of eight hardliners calling themselves the State Committee for the State of Emergency. They would try to kill Boris Yeltsin, Mikhail Gorbachev would be placed under house arrest at his vacation home in the Crimea, and tanks would occupy Moscow. The voice told them to spread the word of this coup as fast as they could, by whatever means they thought best, and to go to the Russian Parliament Building to show their solidarity for Russia's legitimately elected President.

Then we went to work on Yeltsin. We didn't plan to try to see him in person, because of his guards who were already nervous, given the unstable environment. They were capable of taking out two well-meaning middle-aged types like Jeffrey and me, even if they were no match for the elite KGB Alpha unit. However, reaching him was not hard at all, because we had done our homework and had obtained the names of a dozen friends Yeltsin had made during his various trips to America. Several of these guys had Yeltsin's private telephone number and fax number on their home computers. If those computers were linked up to the Internet or any kind of online service, we could get inside and get the goods. And we did.

Yeltsin was a smart old fox, and took a lot of convincing when I called him. I had to drop names like the biggest social climber in Washington, D.C., and give him so much precise information about the net closing around him, that he finally pegged me as a high-ranking official with the CIA. Desperate for anything that would satisfy him (short of the real truth), I hopped to it. Thereupon, like the emotional Russian peasant he was, he shed tears and slopped over with sugar and said how moved he was that the Bush administration, which had hitherto been so cold to him, should go to such lengths to save his life.

I felt like a real shitheel and cast about for some way to help him more. "Boris," I said, "let me tell you a big secret. These coup plotters don't understand anything about television. Whenever you get a chance, play to the cameras.

Think photo opportunity. Talk to CNN and the other TV networks as much as you can, because when you do, the news reports are beamed not only to the rest of the world, but straight back into Russia, and to your potential supporters. I can't tell you how I know this, but it hasn't even occurred to the coup plotters to pull the plug on the news media let alone the phone lines and the Internet. If things start looking bad, just get on the phone and ask George Bush or John Major or François Mitterrand to go on TV and give you a plug. It'll help, I promise."

"My dear friend," said Yeltsin, "thank you, thank you. Will I ever get to meet you in person?"

"No, I'm afraid not."

"At least tell me your name. Even your code name."

I thought long and hard. "Bunker," I said. "Edith Bunker."

Despite my age, and all the disappointments of wars gone by, I've still got to say there was no thrill like a job well done. Particularly when the other side was so stupid it kept me in perpetual stitches.

Obedient Boris left home very, very early Monday morning, this time missing the KGB squad sent to arrest him there by forty minutes. He hightailed it to the Parliament Building, got his butt safely inside, and holed up for the long haul. In a matter of hours people were referring to Boris's cozy nest as the Russian White House and the Citadel of Freedom. Sometimes I love Russians in spite of myself.

At 8:00 A.M. Moscow time, the group of eight conspirators calling themselves the State Committee for the State of Emergency announced that Gorbachev was gravely ill, and his powers had been constitutionally assumed by Vice President Gennady Yanayev. They tried to make it sound all nice and neat and legitimate, but there was a problem in maintaining this image for long because tanks started rolling into Moscow.

As in the previous timeline, the coupsters made unbelievable mistakes in judgment one after another. For instance, they decided to occupy Moscow with tanks. That was straight out of the official "How to Coup" manual. But they chose to deploy the Kantomirovsky Tank Division, a unit based near Moscow where Yeltsin had done a lot of heavy politicking, and where he was very, very popular. This move was very, very dumb. Especially considering that in this timeline, Jeffrey and I were now armed, dangerous, and determined to keep using the coupsters' mistakes to derail their plans as we had begun to do when we saved Yeltsin.

Well, by Monday afternoon, thanks to our faxing marathon and the diligence of CNN and its colleagues in journalism, the word was out. People were grumbling that Gorbachev's illness was bullshit, and Yanayev and his gang were pulling a plain old coup d'etat. A crowd began to gather in front of the Russian White House; the people—young and old—beseeched the boys in the Kantomirovsky tanks to support Yeltsin, not the coup. Before long, a couple of the kids risked their lives by turning their tank turrets away from the White House, toward the Kalinin Bridge—across which any assault upon the White House would come.

Yeltsin came out of the Parliament Building at noon and got up on one of these friendly tanks to deliver a fiery speech to the crowd, proclaiming all decisions, orders, and instructions of the Emergency Committee unlawful. For the sake of historical accuracy, I have to say the poor bastard was shaking with fear the whole time. I mean, he could have taken a bullet at any moment. Yet his bravery made him a lot of friends around the world. Even people in Washington who thought him an untutored boor and a drunkard could not remain unmoved. If the world could have chosen an epitaph for Yeltsin's tombstone at that time, it would have read, "He had balls."

But even as Yeltsin spoke and the cameras rolled, the crowd still numbered only about two hundred; and that's counting myself and Jeffrey (who kept closing his eyes and whispering, "Go, baby, *go, go!*"). But we could feel the magic start to take shape in the very air over our heads. News of Yeltsin's heroism and his rousing speech spread like wildfire, and sparked demonstrations not only in Moscow, but in Leningrad and other cities. At 5:00 P.M. Yeltsin made another speech, and called on the KGB and all the armed forces to obey his orders, not the committee's."

The coupsters were totally freaked out. They didn't know what to do about Yeltsin. If they could have silenced him before he got to the White House, they might have been able to keep a lid on things. But now that he was barricaded inside a virtual sanctuary, it would take an all-out attack to dislodge him. That would be extremely messy, and a lot of people would notice.

So they gave orders to send ten tanks from the elite Taman Division to surround Yeltsin and the White House. They also told Yeltsin to clean out his desk and vacate the building. Honest!

In the meantime, the crowd was growing, and the Western news cameras rolled nonstop. By late Monday afternoon five thousand people had gathered. These included some ladies bearing a banner appealing to the tanks and troops, "Sons, don't shoot your mothers!" This was a very good sign. People of all sorts surrounded the Kantomirovsky tanks, stuck flowers in their gun barrels, offered the confused teenagers inside vodka, cigarettes, and food, and tried to win them over to Yeltsin's cause. Barricades began to rise around the Parliament Building.

The coupsters, sensing that things were rapidly going to hell in a handbasket, decided to hold a press conference at 6:00 P.M. that Monday evening. We slipped over there with our fake press passes. Vice President Yanayev and the others acted nervous throughout the whole presentation, even apologetic. And at one point, the unbelievable happened. When it was announced that Gorbachev was very sick and that was why the committee was assuming power, people in the audience started laughing.

I happened to be watching Interior Minister Boris Pugo when this announcement was made. The guy who looked like a real thug. When he heard the laughter, he went white as a sheet. In that moment, his world turned itself inside out. It was unthinkable to him that people could laugh at the committee. It just didn't happen. If people were reacting to the coup with laughter, all bets were off; there was no telling what might happen. Pugo, you may recall, was the one who shot himself when it was all over.

Well, after that chuckle we went back to the Parliament Building. The crowd had mushroomed, and the barricades were growing like wildfire. What none of us knew was that later that night, those ten elite Taman Division tanks sent by the coupsters were supposed to attack the White House and kill Yeltsin.

I first realized that things might not be going our way when the Taman tanks pulled up, surrounded us, and pointed the muzzles of their guns straight at the White House. I had been certain that Jeffrey and I, true to the spirit of Ray Bradbury's butterfly, had so upset the course of events that the coup would fail. Now, looking down the dark barrels of all those tank guns, I wasn't so sure. I remembered how easy it had been for the Chinese to crush the rebellion in Tiananmen Square.

Then, like an amoeba, the crowd spread out and surrounded the Taman tanks. When the turrets opened, these fearsome tanks also proved to be manned by bewildered young recruits who responded admirably to vodka, cigarettes, and blandishments.

"Those are just kids!" I cried to Jeffrey. "Don't those fucking coupsters have a *clue*?"

Suddenly I became aware of the blood pounding hard in my ears. I thought I heard a soft moan rise up from the crowd, and in my mind's eye, I seemed to see the train that was our world rushing toward a branching of the tracks. "Jeffrey," I said, almost whimpering, "it's starting to build. Now."

Jeffrey lowered his head and rested it in his hands, as if he were in pain. "I know. I feel it too."

So it was all in place; the tide was poised to turn the other way, if only luck was with us. I hardly dared breathe for fear of upsetting the precarious house of cards we had built, the teetering beginnings of a tide that could turn back the coming war. I cowered, shivering as the branch point approached.

"Oh, no!" cried Jeffrey. I gave a start and cried out too. He was looking over my shoulder, at the bridge. I jerked my head around, and saw a sleek black automobile approaching, the kind reserved for military commanders.

Jeffrey crossed himself in the Russian orthodox fashion, right shoulder, then left. "Oh, God! This is it," he said. "The big guy's decided to check it out himself. If he tells them to fire at the White House, they may do it."

When the car came to a halt, a tall, white-haired, heavyset man lumbered out. Judging from his girth and his rather florid face and nose, he had consumed a great deal of fatty meat and hard liquor in his lifetime. Curiously, despite his age, the medal collection on his chest told me he wasn't one of the Red Army's very top brass, but only a colonel-general—clearly, the tank division's local commander.

"There's your goddamn Eloi," said Jeffrey, voice shaking. "Only you don't know what he's going to do. If he comes over to Yeltsin, he'll trigger mass defections among the army and KGB. But if he orders those tanks to shoot, we're done for."

The officer put his hands behind his back and walked slowly past the deadly machines. The men watched him go by, and nobody moved a muscle. Out of the corner of my eye, I saw that Jeffrey had begun to weep from the tension, although he made no sound.

First the colonel-general fixed his gaze on a Kantomirovsky boy, the one manning the tank on which Boris Yeltsin had stood that morning—the tank that had pointed its guns toward the Kalinin Bridge, not the White House. "What do you think you're doing?" he asked softly.

The boy looked frightened enough to throw up. "Defending the duly elected President of Russia, sir."

The officer did not reply. He stalked onward, toward the Taman Division tanks. "You!" he barked to one of the young soldiers, who had a flower sticking out of the muzzle of his tank gun. The youngster blanched. "Did Major Yevdekemov send you here?" demanded the officer.

"Yes, sir," said the boy.

"Major Yevdekemov was under orders to man these tanks with crack KGB troops."

"He sent us, sir," replied the boy, trembling.

"You—you puny little boys, with no stomach for firing on your own mothers! How are you supposed to take the Parliament Building?"

"I don't know, sir."

For the briefest of moments, there flitted across the colonel-general's face an expression described in the United States as a shit-eating grin. Then he threw back his head and laughed until he had to wipe the tears from his face.

This went on for so long that I realized his tears had as much to do with terror as amusement. He realized this Major Yevdekemov had pulled the granddaddy of all smooth moves, and he approved. But he also knew that if he sided with the rebels and the good major and they lost, he would face a firing squad.

The commander resumed his walk, and as he drew closer, I could better read his expression. Gone was all the laughter, and the tears. His face was like stone.

He was in the throes of a powerful inner struggle; that was plain for me to read. He had come to the crossroads in his life, where he must choose between duty and conscience, and possibly pay for that choice with his life. The poor bastard, I said to myself—if only he could know how important this was to the rest of the world, his decision would be so much easier.

He stopped, surveyed the way he had come, and lowered his head for a moment. I wondered if he were praying. Then he looked up at his soldiers again—and at their tank guns, aimed at the Russian Parliament Building.

I couldn't help myself. I screamed out, "Comrade general, the whole world is watching! Save Russia! Save the world!"

He turned his head and looked at me for a very long time. Then all traces of struggle vanished from his face. Quickly, he turned so that he was facing the Kalinin Bridge, and made a fist with his right hand and raised it high, in defiance of the coup. "Soldiers," he said, his voice low and passionate, "I order all of you to defend the President. Turn your guns on the bridge."

A moan went up from the crowd. As the turrets wheeled around and the boys trained their guns on the Kalinin Bridge, tornado winds screamed along the track of history. A great tear appeared in the fabric of time. This was the branch point; this one officer had struck a blow that would snowball into a death sentence for the coup.

Wrenched loose from its moorings, one reality dissolved into fine mist, and an alternate world took shape and grew strong all around us. People on the embankment wept unashamedly. They cheered, delirious with triumph and joy, and embraced each other.

I burst into tears. "It's over," I said to Jeffrey. "We did it." He gripped my hand, and then let it go. I heard him whisper another Russian prayer.

I did a foolish thing then. I pushed through the crowd and went up to where the colonel-general was standing. There was a grim smile on his face, as if finally, near the end of his life, he had struck a massive blow for all that was right.

I was still crying, but I didn't care. "Comrade," I said, "you have just changed the future. Every man, woman, and child here owes you their life. Thank you, comrade. God bless you. God bless your courage."

He turned. His face was lined and very tired. I guessed him to be ten years my senior, but a lifetime older in disillusion and disappointment.

He looked at me for a long while. Then the hair stood up on the back of my neck as he ran a finger across my cheek. "Thirty years have passed, my dearest Anna," he said, "and see, they have scarcely left a mark."

The battle wasn't completely over. Lavrenti and I stayed on the barricades for two more days, keeping vigil. We thought the coup would unravel, that we had smashed it beyond repair, but we wanted to be sure. We waited, and watched as the dominoes began to topple. One after another, military units declared their loyalty to Yeltsin; in the end, these defections included a third of all Soviet troops. Seeing this, the KGB dragged its feet when the committee gave it orders; the KGB, never stupid, knew that obeying those orders risked civil war.

The next morning, Tuesday, CNN interviewed Viktor Alksnis, the Dark Colonel, the man no longer destined to destroy the world. When asked what he thought about the coup, he said he still supported it, but thought a lot more force should be used.

Tuesday night, thirty thousand people braved cold rain to hold vigil over the White House. They knew that if the coupsters were ever going to try to take the White House, this would be the night. And sure enough, a half-hearted attempt was made. In the middle of the night, protestors trapped a handful of confused KGB tanks in an underpass, where the Garden Ring Road crossed the Kalinin Bridge, and pelted them with Molotov cocktails. Well did I remember that spot from my visit to Moscow thirty years before; that was where, in the moonlight, I'd had a vision that the grease and grime left by passing traffic looked like blood. These protestors were killed—one shot, two crushed by the tanks.

By the next morning, the crowd around the White House

numbered half a million. The coupsters fled Moscow, some to visit Mikhail Gorbachev and ask his forgiveness.

They didn't get it.

If, back in the Sixties, I had imagined what Lavrenti and I would see walking around Moscow after the coup, I'd have been sure I was dropping too much acid. For starters, Wednesday night the Russians held a rock concert inside the White House, called, appropriately, "Rock on the Barricades."

"Ah," said Lavrenti, "this is just like the good old days when we were young, with all this rock-and-roll music playing."

We had a good laugh over that. Then a rumor tore through the crowd that the citizens of Moscow had gotten hold of some heavy equipment and were going to tear down the huge metal statue of Felix Dzerzhinsky, the founder of the KGB.

So off we went to view the action. At one point, my guard down (or rather, with my second sight *on*) I turned for one last view of the Parliament Building. Like Lot's wife.

I screamed, for fire was leaping from all the upper windows, yellow and crimson against the night sky. "Oh, my God, Lavrenti, something terrible has happened! It's burning!"

"What? No, it's not!" cried Lavrenti.

I blinked. The fire was gone. Nothing was amiss. "I must be hallucinating," I said. "I thought I saw fire coming from the windows of the building."

"Nonsense."

"No, not nonsense," I said. My voice shook, because the glimpse of the flames had so unnerved me. What did they mean? Were they a glimpse of a future yet to come? God in heaven, I prayed, have mercy on us all. Whatever chapter in history we were living through, it wasn't finished yet.

"Wait," said Lavrenti. He brought us to a dead stop and looked at me closely. "You believe you saw flames. You care. You are almost in tears. Anna, who are you? *What* are you?"

"Just a high-strung American woman who loves you. Forget it. You know how emotional we women are. It's just nerves."

Being an idiotic traditional, gullible male Russian, he bought it and cheered right up. In fact, I doubt if anything could have contained Lavrenti's high spirits once we got to Dzerzhinsky Square. Sure enough, they were carting off the statue of old Iron Felix. When they were through, they covered the pedestal with spray-painted graffiti, including the names of the heavy metal rock groups Iron Maiden and AC/DC.

In Manezh Square, near the Kremlin, older folks played Big Band Music from the 1940's. When we headed over to Red Square to see St. Basil's Cathedral all lighted up with fireworks, we could still hear strains of Benny Goodman coming from Manezh. Trust me, it was a transcendental experience.

As a particularly bright burst of fireworks exploded over St. Basil's, Lavrenti fished out his wallet and, with a grim smile, removed his Communist Party card. "I've been wanting to do this for a long time," he said. "Just like an American teenager in the Sixties." From a pocket inside his army jacket, he removed an expensive Italian cigarette lighter. "Burn, baby, burn!" he said, and set fire to the card.

We laughed ourselves sick. Then Lavrenti said we should go into the forest again. For old times' sake.

"Oh, my God," I said, "we are too old for that sort of thing! You're sixty and I'm practically fifty. It's wet and cold and damp in the forest, and we'll both get arthritis."

He grinned, reminding me very much of the old Lavrenti. "These days I have a dacha in the forest. It is well stocked with vodka and beluga caviar. Do reconsider."

"Well . . ." I said. "First we have some things to discuss. For instance, are you married?"

"Yes, but if you ask me to go to America with you, I will."

Clearly, we had a lot to talk about.

"Before we cross that bridge, Lavrenti, I think you should fill me in on the last twenty-eight years of your life."

He grinned again. "Yes, of course, I will tell you everything. But in the comfort of the dacha."

So to the dacha we went. "You haven't done too badly for yourself," I said. It was a beautiful little rustic cottage on an acre of forest land about thirty minutes from Moscow, with a lovely stone fireplace and a cozy couch. It was in fact amply supplied with vodka, sour cream, and the finest Beluga caviar.

He gave a short laugh. "You wouldn't have said that in the years after Khrushchev. You realize, don't you, that at my age I should have attained a far higher rank than colonel-general?"

"I suspected."

"Shortly after Brezhnev and Kosygin took power, someone told the KGB that I was an ardent supporter of Khrushchev's reforms—that I had Western friends and Western tastes. Which was all true, of course. But from that, they inferred my commitment to the teachings of Marxism-Leninism was . . . suspect."

"What nonsense!" I cried. "All those kids at those parties you took me to—they had more Western tastes than Americans! Who was it, do you know?"

He shrugged. "It doesn't matter. Probably one of those very kids smeared me to save his own skin. Anyway, I was demoted to the rank of lieutenant and almost thrown out of the Party."

"You obviously climbed back up the ladder. How?"

"I kissed all the right asses. It was easy to do; after seeing that artist girl die in our arms, after seeing all Khrushchev had worked for thrown into the dustbin, after seeing my own friends turn on me, I had no idealism left. I charmed the

stupid, ugly daughter of a high-ranking officer into marrying me, and around 1970 my career began to pick up again."

"So you caved into the system."

"Yes," he said. "I had to. Otherwise it would have crushed
me, like it did poor Nikita Sergeyevich. But I always told
myself that if the opportunity came to stab it in the back, I
would be alive and in a position to do so. When I arrived at
the Parliament to find all those beardless boys in Yevdekemov's tanks, I knew my chance had come." He gave a bitter
laugh, and downed a vodka.

"What's wrong?" I asked. "Why the awful laugh?"

"Because after so many years of kissing asses, I had
turned into one myself. I knew the time had come to stand
up like a man and do what was right. But I was afraid. I
think I would have struck back at the coup even if you
hadn't cried out to me, but I'm not *sure*. I only know that
when I saw your face, I knew fate had commanded me to
follow the dictates of my conscience."

"You changed the future then and there, Lavrenti," I
replied. "You started the ball rolling. You saved us all."

He looked at me intently. "Anna," he said at length, "I ask
again, *who are you*?"

I took just as long to reply. "Your friend and lover."

"Not CIA? FBI? Not American *something*?"

I broke out laughing and had some more vodka. "You're
not even close!" Before he could press me further, I
switched the subject. "So now, after all these years, you're
willing to go back to San Francisco with me?"

"Yes."

My mind was whirling. There was no reason he couldn't
come to America. Hell, if there was another war, he could
even jump back with us in the time machine, since it was
made for three people and Daria was gone. "Do you have
children?" I asked.

"No. I refused to bring a child into this world."

"What about your wife?"

"We live apart. She does not love me, nor I her. I make sure that she lacks for nothing. I hope you are still rich, Anna, because if I go to America, you will have to support me. My wife's father is dead; she must have our apartment and dacha and money to live in comfort as she grows older."

"No problem," I replied. "I'm plenty rich."

"There is one more problem. A reason you may not want me."

I'd had enough vodka to cry easily; tears started running down my face and I cried out, "Like what? You wouldn't go back with me the first time. I never got married for a lot of reasons, but one was because nobody could ever measure up to you. Now you offer me a little bit of happiness when I'm middle-aged, and the next minute snatch it back. What is the problem?"

"I don't have all that long to live."

"Oh, damn," I said, and started to cry in earnest.

"I have had one problem with my heart already. My doctor says I may only have a year or two left."

"Soviet doctors don't know fucking jackshit," I sobbed. "I'll get you the best doctor in the United States. And don't worry about your wife. If things get bad here, we'll send her lots of money, or bail her out, whatever it takes."

So he came back with me. I got him the best care money could buy, I monitored his fat and cholesterol intake like a hawk, I made sure he got regular and—usually—gentle exercise, and procured for us almost five years of happiness. I would have told him who I was on his deathbed, but he died quietly in his sleep, beside me in our apartment atop Russian Hill in San Francisco.

Once again, since Jeffrey and I had set the world straight, things returned to normal. Four weeks after the almost-coup, the brave young tank paratroopers who had defended Yeltsin were out picking potatoes in the fields, like they always did come autumn in Mother Russia.

The Commonwealth of Independent States survived.
"Hey," I told Jeffrey one day, "you realize we can still call
them Commies?" For a couple more years, whenever we saw
coverage of meetings of the Russian Congress, you could
still catch a glimpse of Alksnis' sour puss in the background.
But he never amounted to much. Although I must admit
another right-wing fool named Vladimir Zhirinovsky, the
original Russian loose cannon, a.k.a. the Russian Hitler
wanna-be, gave me many sleepless nights in the mid-
1990's.

Boris Yeltsin proved to be one of the toughest Russians
God ever created. His megabattle with the Russian Congress
in the summer of 1993 was a heart-stopper; before it was
over, he had shed Russian blood on the spot where his
supporters had turned back the coup in 1991, and had
caused the burning of the Parliament Building I had forseen
in Moscow with Lavrenti. But when all the dust settled,
Yeltsin, the onetime boxer, had won the round. He got a new
constitution and a newly elected Congress, and peace was
preserved.

By 1993, *Time* magazine was joking that "A few years
ago, our differences with the Russians poised us on the edge
of Armageddon; now we only wish we could give them
more money." Unfortunately, this lovely friendship came
about too many goddamn years too late. After centuries of
missteps, Russia had finally started to put her house in
order, and was even best buddies with the United States. But
the rest of the world was now going straight to hell, as the
nuclear demon the United States and the USSR had created
during their long and expensive Cold War began to prolif-
erate around the world.

Yet Fate ever retained its droll side. In constructing this
history, there is one tidbit I simply must include before
moving on to the twenty-first century. In 1993, *People*
magazine did a little chuckle of a story on a certain
computer scientist named Sergei Khrushchev. Seems poor

old Nikita's son was living in Cranston, Rhode Island, that year, working as a senior fellow at Brown University in Providence and anxiously awaiting his green card. Considering his dad had told the Americans back in the 1950's that "Your grandchildren will live in a Communist America," I found this state of affairs rather amusing.

## The mid-1990's: Washington, D.C.

Other interesting things happened in the 1990's. For instance, my old acquaintance Bill from Arkansas ran for President. And not only that, he won.

How did Bill do as President? He was a regular tornado. He crammed into one term the number of reforms any other activist President would have spread over two, though he never seemed to get any credit for them. He tended to appoint feisty women to positions of power and was soft on redwood trees. And, most importantly, there were no nuclear wars on his watch.

What British call the "loyal opposition" detested him. I guess it was understandable, in a way. He was the ol' boys' worst nightmare: a baby-boomer male who had protested the war in Vietnam, who had grown a beard and long hair in his youth, and had even experimented with pot—a younger man from the Woodstock Generation who had not only gone after their job, but gotten it! To make matters even worse, in maturity he had become the sort of man colloquially referred to as a "SNAG," a sensitive new age guy, more inclined to declare that he felt your pain than to beat on his chest and holler like Tarzan. The ol' boys fumed—but a lot of us women liked him.

Unfortunately, society never got to render a solid post-presidential verdict concerning Bill's performance. It takes about thirty years after a President has left office and the shouting has died down to examine his record with a decently detached perspective. Unfortunately, in Bill's case, the world didn't have thirty years left to do that.

I had realized this, in my heart of hearts, before the turn of the millennium, even though the final nuclear war was more than a decade away. How did I know? Well, on account of my long-standing acquaintance with the President, one day I was asked to dinner at the White House. The conversation and the wine were good, and the cooking, while low fat, was almost on par with Rene Verdon's. So I had a thoroughly enjoyable time. Unfortunately, I got invited to go jogging the next morning with the big guy, some visiting firemen, and half the Secret Service.

I had kept in shape, and so, despite our age difference, I was able to keep up with him—just barely. While his thighs were admittedly chubby, Bill had the lung capacity of an Inca backpacker. So I had to concentrate all my energies on staying level with the bastard. I had no idea where our itinerary took us; all I knew was that we rounded a corner next to this park and there was a large crowd gathered to watch the Prez chug by. Catching a glimpse of him on a morning jog had become a favorite pastime of Washingtonians and out-of-towners alike.

Well, anyway, as we passed the crowd this middle-aged African-American woman suddenly dashed toward us. I wheezed and got ready to jump in front of the President, or kick the gun out of her hands. I was way faster than the Secret Service.

But she didn't have a gun. She had a little boy in tow, maybe nine or ten years old. She threw her arms around the nation's chief executive and kissed him soundly on both cheeks. It was a common phenomenon; even though his approval ratings were always supposed to be in the toilet, when people actually met him they acted like he was a movie star.

"Mr. President," cried the woman, "please say hello to my son! You're his hero."

"Why, sure," said Bill, turning to the child with delight.

I mean, he really dug this stuff. "Hey, young fella, how you doin'?" he asked, and shook the boy's hand. Then he hugged him.

The moment was electric. My sixth sense went haywire; on my personal Richter scale, we were talking at least an eight or a nine. I looked more closely at the boy. He was beautiful, with big dark eyes that stared up at the President in rapt adoration. There was all the hope and promise in the world in the child's face; I realized that, in the fullness of time, I was looking at the first black President of the United States.

For me, the whole scene gave off a radiance not entirely attributable to the morning sunshine. I shivered from head to toe with sheer joy, watching the course of the future open up like a beautiful flower.

Then, as if a thundercloud had blotted out the sun, I saw that path wither, blacken, and turn to ashes. Everything— the people, the trees, even the sky itself—was suddenly drained of color. That future was not to be; it would die stillborn.

"Why? Why?" I gasped. I stared at the boy, but I could sense in his future no automobile accident, no plane crash, no death by gang warfare.

As if in slow motion, the President turned to look at me, one arm still around the boy. Behind him I could glimpse the outline of the White House. As I watched, there was a brilliant, consuming flash, brighter than a thousand suns, and I saw the White House and everything around us burst into flames.

Then I sank down on the sidewalk in a heap, fainting. I realized I had seen this world's future, like the time with Lavrenti when I thought I saw the Russian White House in ruins. The last nuclear war might not come for years, but come it would.

After the doctors had checked me out at a local hospital, Bill stopped by with an expression of barely controlled fear on his face. "Cassandra," he asked, "what did you see this time?"

There was no use telling him. He couldn't stop the coming war. No one could, except maybe me, after I had seen how it happened.

"Nothing," I said. "I'm a little out of shape, and you're hell to keep up with. I just got winded."

He didn't believe me. He'd seen me in action before.

"God bless you anyway," he said, and touched my hand.

## 18

## February 2013: San Francisco

No matter how many times we jumped back, The War always happened again, even though the last time it gave us a twenty-year breather. I swear, sometimes I felt like it was a vicious, sentient, mocking thing, stalking me with glee. I often wished Sarah Connor in the old Terminator movies had been a real person; I could have used a girlfriend who understood.

Sure enough, I was reading the electronic newspaper one Sunday morning in early 2013, and I saw the first subtle signs of still another approaching nuclear war. I'll spare you the tedious details this time. Relating them would be pointless. They're essentially irrelevant—just the latest manifestations of an inborn, mortal illness of the human race. Let me just say one key word: proliferation. By 2013, nukes had become as easy to get as electric toothbrushes, and everybody in the world who had ever nursed a grudge against somebody else had the Bomb.

"Jeffrey," I said, "it's starting. Again. A fourth time."

To my amazement, Jeffrey said, "Oh, God, I can't deal with it." He got up from his breakfast, went into the living room, and lay down on the couch with his face turned away from me.

"Jeffrey!" I cried in bewilderment. It was so unlike him. "You have to deal with it. You *have* to help me."

"I haven't got the strength anymore."

Jesus Christ! I really thought he meant it. I just stood there and looked at him in shock. Then an ice-cold sensation hit me in the gut. He was old; *I* was old. And the prospect of handling this latest crisis by myself was terrifying!

Since there was only one jump left in the machine, I put the thumbscrews to him and all his whining. "Buck up, Jeffrey! This time we have to go way back and get at the root of the problem."

"To when? The fucking Pleistocene?" I swear, he had gotten so testy in his old age. He jumped up and began hobbling around the living room in a ludicrous dance, singing, "We are stardust, we are golden, we've got to get ourselves back to the Garden!"

"No," I said, "I have a better idea." We glared at each other like two cantankerous old farts, which I guess we were.

"Fine. Spit it out," said Jeffrey.

"No matter how far back in time we go, we can't change human nature. All we can do is go back to the right branch point to make sure human beings never get their hands on the atomic bomb or the hydrogen bomb or all the rest of it."

"The right branch point? Which one is that, pray tell?"

"I don't know yet. I have to find out."

"Oh shit," he said, picking up his jacket. "As always, you have the answers. I'm going down to North Beach for a drink."

"Jeffrey," I bellowed, "what is the matter with you? Why are you crapping out on me? Why are you being such an asshole?"                                    •

To my utter surprise, he sat down on the couch, and started weeping. I became seriously scared. *"What is it?"* I cried.

"Do you remember how we used to wonder if we were doing the right thing—jumping back in time and creating new worlds, only to see them blow up? We didn't put an end to mankind's misery. We just multiplied it!"

I was floored. He was having a massive guilt attack—

now, at his age, after all the water that had passed under the bridge, when it was *too late* to do anything about all that past history shit. "Christ, Jeffrey, you were always sure we could find a better world!" I cried. "You were always certain we should keep on using the machine. This is no time for cold feet!"

He kept on crying. "Jeffrey," I said, "we'll never be sure what we've done was right. We've just done the best we can."

Jeffrey got stiffly to his feet and went over to our liquor cabinet. "Leave me alone," he said. "I need some time alone."

In some people, the will to struggle, to keep on fighting, to keep on living, dies before the body and the mind. Age had conquered Jeffrey; he was like a candle guttering out before my very eyes. That meant the mantle of our group's responsibility was about to descend squarely upon my shoulders.

At that moment, I would have given anything I owned, or any moments of life's sweetness that might still remain to me, just to have Daria at my side once more.

Struggling to keep my own panic and moral qualms in check, I took stock of our situation. We had one last jump in the machine, and one last chance to set things right. Me, I had three courses of action. When the next nuclear war happened, I could do nothing. Or, I could go back and nix the symptomatic events leading up to it—thereby giving birth to still another alternate world, which, if the past was my guide, in a few years would also be consigned to the flames. Lastly, I could go so far back in history, and change things so drastically, that in time a completely different modern history would come into being—hopefully, one where nuclear weapons would never be invented.

It was the only chance humanity had left. Still, I was terrified. Until now, we had only tinkered with Fate in little ways. I was now thinking about playing God. On a grand scale.

If we were going to play God for real, then logically, Jeffrey and I might have to go back in time a hundred, maybe even two hundred years. For starters, we would have to change history so radically that Russia and the United States could never become superpower rivals—at least, not at a time in history when they possessed the requisite technology *and* the fabulous amount of money required to develop nuclear weapons *and* the intense paranoia necessary to induce them to spend such staggering sums on inventing nukes instead of more useful items, such as a no-cal potato chip, a car that never broke down, or a cure for cancer.

It would also behoove us to figure out how to alter history to eliminate World War I. A tall order, since historians have squabbled for a hundred years over the exact interplay of events that led to World War I. But preventing World War I was a key step to achieving a nuclear-free future. World War I sowed the seeds of World War II. In turn, World War II caused the Germans to build the V-2 rocket and the research center at Peenemunde, which led the Allies to think the Germans were also working on an atomic bomb. In that atmosphere, the Americans believed they had to get the Bomb first, and hang the cost. The Americans' success in this endeavor fanned Soviet fears, so after 1945 the Soviets devoted approximately 90 percent of their country's resources to getting the recipe for the Bomb and then building a lot of them. Hence the Cold War, the nuclear arms race, and all the nuclear wars.

Preventing World War I would be no small task for two poor old fools in their seventies. Where to start? Assassinate Einstein as a baby? Pop back to 1913 and take out Lenin—and the Hitler kid while we were at it? Should we ding that idiot Serb student who sparked World War I? The prospect was upsetting. When you got right down to it, I really detested killing people.

There wasn't much time to dither. Unlike our lost Daria, I had not a drop of Irish blood in me, but I could hear the banshee howl and knew the next nuclear war was coming. It was still a long ways off, but come it would. I had to act, even if Jeffrey was still trying to stick his head in the sand. In desperation, I hit the history books, hard. I read voluminously, in a frantic search for usable branch points. I also went for a lot of long drives in my vintage 1988 Porsche, hoping maybe an inspiration would pop into my head.

One February morning, a Monday, I breakfasted early, roared out of the garage in my car, and soon picked up a street that would take me to the Golden Gate Bridge and the coastal highway. On impulse, I had planned to go to Fort Ross, up the coast an hour or so north of San Francisco. Back in the 1830's it had been a Russian settlement. It had never really amounted to more than a poorly funded stab at taking California away from the Mexicans, not that the latter had a prayer of holding onto the state anyway. I'd been to Fort Ross several times. It had always fascinated me, as if an obscure secret lay buried there that I might one day discover. I found it easy to meditate and think there, overlooking the cold, gray-colored sea.

It was a wet, blustery day, with a new winter storm coming in, and I figured the weather was so foul other visitors would stay away and I'd have the place to myself. The drive up to Fort Ross was always wild and rugged, and I found the wind and rain exciting. When a storm lashed the coast up there, you knew something was really happening; you could almost believe you'd run into Heathcliff striding across a Yorkshire moor.

But that day I had no time for foolishness. I needed to walk and brood on the dire problem that confronted me— and maybe get a little help from Father Alexeyev's God, if He—or It—existed.

But luck was not with me that day. The same weather that I so gloried in had led one foolhardy, hurrying driver to his death on the Golden Gate Bridge. All the lanes leading north were closed, so that Marin County commuters driving south would not have a prayer of making it into The City that day.

I could not work myself into a snit, as I was merely inconvenienced, while some poor bastard had lost his life. I gave up on going to Fort Ross and drove into the Presidio National Park, where I parked my car opposite the old Officers' Club building. The Officers' Club was the site of the first and original Spanish adobe dwelling at the Presidio, and somehow felt like a good place to start. I buckled up my nice Burberry raincoat, and got out my matching plaid Burberry brolly, and took off.

I had it in mind to hike over to the foot of Kharitonov's "Golden Bridge," and remember how Jeffrey and Daria and I had cavorted there like children, fifty years and three worlds earlier, and how Jeffrey had mused that the entire western coast of America could have been Russian, if Fate had only rolled the dice a wee bit differently. I would meditate upon the grim Marin headlands and the gray storm coming in from the sea.

Or maybe I would walk to the old Coast Guard station at Crissy Field. Built in the 1890's, it had served as the headquarters for the Gorbachev Foundation ever since 1993. Oh yes, by 2013, we were still real chummy with the Russians. Ironic, since our friendship had blossomed too late to save humanity.

Anyway, I was about to head for the bridge, when the rain let up. Impulsively, I headed away from the sea, into the dark, enticing forest behind the Officers' Club. I was thinking how wonderful the earth and trees would smell after the rain.

I walked in a few hundred yards, and came to a halt. The rain had not resumed, but the wind from the ocean was lashing the treetops, and I could not hear the sound of a single car. I turned in a complete circle and looked around. I realized that there was not a single outward sign in the grove to tell me what year it was. It was a most creepy feeling.

Thunder rolled, far in the distance, and the hairs stood up on the back of my neck, as if lightning were about to strike. I walked a few paces farther, and passed through a spot of intense cold, as one is said to do in the presence of ghosts.

"Who's there?" I cried. The moment I heard my own voice, I felt incredibly stupid. What a piece of work I was—a woman who had rescued the world several times, acting jumpy in a forest during a rainstorm, in broad daylight no less!

The wind slackened, and fell silent. Goose bumps stood up on my wrinkled old skin. Verily, that poor cowardly outward covering of mine crawled like it wanted to get the hell out of there and leave me to my fate.

Then I heard the sound of a woman weeping. The rain-soaked forest around me seemed to waver, as if I were seeing its image in a poorly made mirror, and I felt a veritable earthquake crash through the structure of time. I gasped for breath, realizing I had stumbled upon something enormous. A branch point. A *big* branch point. I was standing on radioactive ground, charged to hell and gone with the lost possibilities of history. I mean, this spot was really *hot*. Next to it, the site of the Russian Parliament Building, or the Kalinin Bridge underpass, were nothing.

"Where are you?" I cried. My voice fell off into nothingness, and the wind resumed with renewed ferocity.

I forced myself to walk onward. Part of me wanted to run away, to get out of the forest, to get back to the safety of the world I knew. But I could not stop myself, and I walked deeper into the dark, lowering trees.

Then my whole mind, body, and soul were flattened as if from a hammer blow. Truly, I was standing on the site of a colossal change in the course of history. My legs buckled. I fell, in all my fine expensive English rain gear, into the mud.

When I looked up, I saw a beautiful young girl on the path ahead of me. She was dark-eyed and proud and wore her hair bound up with a comb—a Spaniard as ever was. I started shaking with fear, because she was wearing an exquisite, ornate dress that brushed the ground, the kind women had not worn for centuries.

Abruptly, in a swirl of sable, gold, and green velvet, a man appeared. He was tall, fair-haired, dressed in a sumptuous uniform, and quite handsome, although he was not a youth. He looked at the girl with desire of ferocious intensity. His heart was plain for me to read; he would have her, or die trying.

"Nikolai!" cried the girl, holding out her arms to him.

*Nikolai?* Dear God and all the archangels, he was Russian! What on earth was a Russian, a nobleman, doing at the Presidio in this faraway, ghostly time?

He ran forward and embraced her. "Nikolai!" she cried again. "Two years—how can they be so cruel? Swear that you will come back for me, or I cannot bear it!"

"I will, Concha," he said, "I will." I knew he meant it; it was clearly written on his face. Only death would stop him.

As I stared at him, my skin started crawling again. Something about him was familiar, though I couldn't place it to save my life. It was as if I had seen his picture years ago, but paid it no mind.

A blast of thunder pealed directly over my head, the rain poured down again, and suddenly the ghosts were gone. There I was, a skinny old crone, squatting in the forest, a mess of mud, leaves, and wet, stringy hair.

Somehow I picked myself up and retrieved my umbrella. Sanity dictated I should have gone home, but I drove to the visitor center instead. Nobody was there but a sullen kid with an attitude.

I tried to forget that I looked like a wet dog and asked if he knew anything about the Presidio's history. Specifically, I asked if anyone had heard any stories about a young girl named Concha and her Russian lover, Nikolai. The kid just looked at me like I was really weird, and shook his head.

"Do you have books on the Presidio?" I asked. He gave a vague nod toward the far corner of the room. I went over there, but could find nothing except a superficial brochure. The parks were real short of money those days.

"Thanks," I said shortly, and stalked out. Now where? City libraries were only open on weekends, due to budget cuts. So I headed for these two used bookstores I knew, and inspected their massive travel and history sections for leads. But to no avail.

Once I had gotten my teeth into the puzzle, it started driving me crazy. I wheeled onto a street that would take me to the Golden Gate Bridge, burning rubber as I went. This time Fate was kind; the traffic was moving smoothly, and there was enough time left in the day to make it to Fort Ross. I had no idea what I would do when I got there. Maybe they had books there that would give me a clue. Or perhaps the visit, and the solitude it would bring, would help me unravel the mystery.

## 19

## February 2013: San Francisco (cont.)

I got to Fort Ross around three-thirty in the afternoon. Nobody was in the toll booth, but I gave the park its money anyway. I didn't go into the visitor center, but hiked around the perimeter of the restored stockade. Fort Ross was right on the ocean, so the wind was blowing in from the sea like a bat out of hell. I wrapped my soiled raincoat tightly around me and trudged out to a grassy hill that overlooked the fort.

This knoll was the site of the old Russian cemetery, containing the graves of settlers who had not lived to return to the *Rodina*. The original crosses had long since decayed, and the site was now marked by a single huge wooden Orthodox cross.

I stood there, looking at it, hoping for a moment of peace. But the wind battered me without mercy. I tried to remember Father Alexeyev's face, and I wondered what counsel he would give me if he could be here now. Was I just a modern-day Sisyphus, giving my life to an utterly futile endeavor? Did I have the right to play God one last time, to go back into time and create still another doomed world? Or was this the very moment at which my nerve must not fail?

I looked up at the Russian cross with misgivings and tentative hope. "Father Alexeyev wasn't so sure about you," I said to it. "Neither am I. But if there has ever been a time in history when the human race needed some serious help, this is it. If you exist, you really shouldn't pass up this opportunity to make your presence known. Please. Please!"

There was no response. Suddenly the wind died, and for a brief moment all was silent. Then, with the force of a pouncing tiger, the wind returned, chilling me to the bone. "Oh, come on," I pleaded, "you must realize what a desperate time this is." In reply, the wind did a little dance and deftly blew a handful of rain into my eyes.

"Shit!" I cried, my eyes stinging like crazy. "Now I've got to go inside and get cleaned up." I turned on my heel and slogged my way back to the visitor center, went into the women's rest room, and had a nice long cry.

When I was a bit more presentable and just a bit calmer, I went into the lobby of the center. It was very warm and cheery, and boasted a well-stocked bookstore and gift shop. As I entered, a girl looked up with a smile and said, "Zdrastvuyte."

I smiled back at her, albeit wanly. "You're Russian."

"Yes, recently arrived. I live nearby in Jenner."

That was no surprise. Since the mid-1980's, every Russian who could hustle had emigrated to America, usually New York or California.

"Nice store," I said. "You know, most park facilities are pretty bare-bones these days."

"We are all volunteers here at Fort Ross. That allows us to stretch our budget and offer a wide selection of reading matter."

"I see." I almost asked her about my ghostly couple back at the Presidio, but it seemed like such a long shot, I blew it off.

Next to the bookstore there was a small museum with exhibits about the history of the fort. I ambled slowly through this, and felt my old muscles start to lose their stiffness in the warmth of the building. I looked at pictures of Eskimos in Alaska and Russians in California, and at far too many Indian pots and pictures of Indians in native dress. Then I rounded a corner and screamed out loud in shock and astonishment, for I had come face to face with a portrait of none other than Nikolai himself.

I dashed forward and almost fell in my haste to read the legend under the picture. He was Count Nikolai Petrovich Rezanov, in 1806 high chamberlain and privy councilor to the young, reform-minded Czar Alexander I of Russia—and the first Russian ever to set foot on California soil!

"Pay dirt, pay dirt!" I cried. "Now I remember! I saw this on my last visit! It just seemed unimportant then—"

The volunteer girl came running, disturbed by my screeching. "Are you all right, *babushka*?" she cried.

In spite of my exhilaration, I winced. I had never been called "grandmother" before. It hurt worse than when Bill Clinton had called me "ma'am" back in the Rose Garden in 1963.

"Yes, yes," I said, taking hold of the arm she held out to steady me. "Tell me, my dear, do you have a book that goes into any detail about this gentleman?" I pointed to Nikolai.

"You're in luck," she replied. "We just received reprints of a most scholarly biography of Count Rezanov from the 1960's."

This was too good to be true. She took me up to the cash register and put into my hands a big blue paperback entitled *Lost Empire: The Life and Adventures of Nikolai Rezanov*.

Lost Empire? My head spinning, I toddled over to a chair and sat down heavily. "What is your name, dear?" I asked her.

"Natasha," she answered.

"Natasha, do you know anything about a romance between this man and a girl called Concha?"

She laughed, almost tittered. "But of course. Everybody in Russia knows about this love story. It is so sad, so romantic."

But of course? This was too much! After all I had been through, after the desperate studying, the ghosts, the portrait on the wall, this Russian child was saying "But of course," as if everyone in the frigging world but me knew about the story!

"In fact, the first Russian rock opera was written about that romance," Natasha said helpfully. "It was back in the 1980's. The great poet Andrei Voznesensky wrote the libretto."

"Rock opera?" I said weakly. It was too droll for words. "Please," I said, "tell me all you know about these lovers."

She was eager to show off her knowledge. "Back in the early 1800's, the eldest daughter of the comandante of the Presidio of San Francisco was a beauty named Concepción Arguello. She was the toast of all California, 'La Favorita' of her day. But not only was she beautiful, she was educated, for her father doted upon her, and in contravention of the traditions of the day, he allowed her to receive the same rigorous education he gave his sons."

"Arguello?" I asked. "You mean whatever guy they named the street in San Francisco after?"

She nodded. "Yes, and the Arguello Gate at the Presidio, too! Nikolai Petrovich Rezanov sailed to the Presidio in April 1806 to open trade relations with California, in hopes of getting supplies for Russia's colonies in Alaska. He met Comandante Arguello's lovely daughter and was smitten with her. He was a widower, you see, and lonely. The two fell deeply in love. They were allowed to become betrothed, but because he was not a Roman Catholic, but a heretic, her parents insisted that he obtain a dispensation from the Pope and the permission of the King of Spain before they could be married."

"A heretic?" I said. "Surely he was Russian Orthodox."

Natasha nodded. "But Russians make the sign of the cross starting on the right shoulder, not the left like the Catholics."

"Oh, I see. Handiwork of the devil, beyond a doubt."

Natasha smiled and politely ignored my sarcasm. "Count Rezanov started back to Russia in late May 1806, planning to go on to Spain and the Vatican to procure the permissions. He was in such a hurry that his common sense deserted him.

He pushed on and would not rest, despite a return of his chronic condition of malaria. Finally, in March 1807, exhausted and in a fever, he fell off his horse into a stream in Krasnoyarsk, in Siberia. It was ten hours before he could reach a warm, dry place. He became gravely ill, and died soon afterward. Concepción Arguello didn't hear what had happened to him for years, but when she finally learned of his death, she took the veil and became the very first nun in California. The American writer Bret Harte composed an extremely moving poem about her story, and the esteemed American author Gertrude Atherton wrote many a treatise about it."

I could see why this romance appealed to Natasha. It would have had enormous allure for any denizen of that gray, chilly country to the east. What Russian could resist a story about the time they almost got California? Nikolai Rezanov must have taken one look at the future San Francisco and coveted it like gold.

"Would you like to buy the count's diary too?" asked Natasha. "We have a reproduction here of the original *Rezanov Voyage to Nueva California in 1806*."

Oh, Lordy. Serendipity was definitely on my side that day. "Let me have both books," I said, before It could change Its mind. I gave her a hundred-dollar bill and stuck the change in the center's donation box, for good karma. "Natasha," I said, "you can't begin to know how much you've helped me."

She smiled. "If you want to see Concepción Arguello's grave, she's buried over in the East Bay, in Benecia. Find the old Catholic cemetery that overlooks all the oil refineries."

"Oil refineries? You must be joking. It hurts too much."

"No, no. I have visited the grave myself."

As always, Fate had a nasty sense of humor.

I took the books, found a table and chair in a lecture hall, and began to read. Before long I was positive I was on the right trail. The more I read, the more excited I got. I kept giggling and exclaiming things like "All right!" and "Oh, wow!" and "Far out!" Natasha peeked around the corner more than once.

I had struck oil, big time. Nikolai Petrovich Rezanov had been a protégé of the Empress Catherine the Great and, later, a very good friend of Czar Alexander I—a Czar who, in his youth, had been rather liberal and reform-minded. In addition, Nikolai evidently possessed a good head for business, for he commanded the Russian-American Fur Trading Company—nowadays, we would have called him the chief executive officer. He had diplomatic experience, having been the first Russian ambassador to Japan. And he had the hots not only for Concha Arguello, but for the beautiful, rich, sunny land that came with her.

This was like Andrew Jackson's manifest destiny, only in reverse, east to west. If Nikolai had had his way, there would never have been a Puccini opera called *The Girl of the Golden West*. But with no trouble at all, I could envision a chronicle of the Russian colonization of California published around 1960 entitled "*Zolotoy Vostok: A History of the Golden East*."

Yes, Rezanov had had it all: the vision, business acumen, diplomatic savvy, the trust and financial backing of the Czar, the motivation of his love for Concha and the rolling hills of not-yet San Francisco, and a window of opportunity *four whole decades long* in which no European power (or the Americans) would have been able to stop a determined Russian push into California.

If there's anything that drives me crazy, it's a wasted opportunity. If the fool hadn't fallen off his horse in Krasnoyarsk and died, he would have come back to the Presidio, married Concha, and in no time California would have been ass-deep in Russians. When the Americans and Russians finally did meet at their common border (wherever that finally came to rest), there would have been fisticuffs. But that conflict would have taken place before atomic bombs were even dreamed of.

And, in the process, the Russians would have been thoroughly contaminated by American democratic ideals and thought. This was a very, very important piece of the puzzle.

See, I already knew for a fact that the Russians were *real* susceptible to that kind of contamination. Exhibit A, my darling Lavrenti and his friends back in 1963. Also, Exhibit B—a droll chapter in a history book about the aftermath of Napoleon's 1812 invasion of Russia. I had just finished reading it back in San Francisco in my frantic search for a viable branch point.

After Napoleon burned Moscow, the Russians chased his ass all the way back to Paris and occupied the City of Light for a year. The young officers who spent that year in Paris got their heads filled with all the whooping and hollering and idealism left over from the French Revolution. When they went back to Russia, they thought it over for a few years, and then mounted the idealistic but ill-fated Decembrist Revolution of 1825.

Hell's bells—if a few soldiers spending a year in Paris could lead to a revolt against the Czar, what would decades of rubbing shoulders with nineteenth-century Americans do to Russia?

Well, upset the apple cart of modern history but good, or Ray Bradbury had no business writing that damn butterfly story.

I've been called a manic digressive. Forgive me, but history is *so* funny. Do you know how romantic little French bistros got to be called bistros in the first place? *Bistro* is the Russian word for "quickly." In 1813, the Russian soldiers occupying Paris would thunder into restaurants, put their hobnailed boots up on the tables, and demand that they be served food now. Quickly. *Bistro*. The Parisians complied and served up the slop muy pronto. In other words, the Russians, not the Americans, invented fast food.

Yeah, history's sure a kick. In the butt. I was about to close Rezanov's diary, when it sort of fell open to this grainy picture of a monument in Krasnoyarsk. Said monument was a large, rather ornate stone urn, covered with all sorts of carved flowers and ribbons and drapes. According to the caption, this was the monument that Czar Alexander had built to honor Rezanov's memory. Said monument had been blown to bits in . . . the Bolshevik Revolution of 1917. That left a bitter taste in my mouth. Ashes and dust; a world that could have been, but never was. Yes, Fate was definitely sending me signs every chance it got.

I closed the book with a snap and got up to leave the visitor center. My heart told me I had found my branch point, but my rational mind knew it had a lot of work to do. Because there was only one hop left in the machine, I had to be sure that I had found the right place to tinker with history — that I was not just in love with the idea of saving Nikolai and Concha's romance. I feared my motives were suspect. Did the pair not bear a bit of emotional resemblance to Lavrenti and me?

As I left, my eye fell upon the old Slavonic cross on top of its lonely hill. A bite of cold air nipped at my heels. I had asked for help, and gotten rain blown in my eyes for my pain. But the rain had forced me to go inside the visitor center, and if I hadn't gone inside, I wouldn't have seen Nikolai's picture.

The whole thing felt eerie in the extreme. I whimpered out loud, "Father Alexeyev, help! Were you right after all? Or is faith just an illusion, the opiate of the masses?" But no one answered.

I mean, there's never a Russian Orthodox priest around when you need one.

So I began another period of frenzied research that lasted a month. Some of what I found out made my hair stand on end.

If the Russians had colonized California early in the 1800's and spread eastward from there, there was no limit to what they might have accomplished. Hell, they might have settled as far east as Texas, thanks to the politics of the time. Really and truly.

A little background, lest you be skeptical. Ever since Texas won its independence from Mexico in the 1830's, it had wanted to join the United States. And U.S. President Andrew "Manifest Destiny" Jackson was itching to get his hands on Texas, not to mention having the United States expand all the way to the Pacific.

Back during the Texas War of Independence, General Sam Houston (later president of the Republic of Texas) and Andrew Jackson cooked up this scheme whereby Jackson repeatedly sent American troops to stand tippy-toe on the border between Louisiana and the Mexican territory of Texas. Each time, Jackson tried to entice Mexican troops to cross that magic border line, so that the Jackson's American troops could say the United States had been invaded, and promptly pounce on Texas, "liberating" it to join the United States.

The Mexicans never took the bait, to Houston and Jackson's unending frustration. And by the time Sam Houston wiped out the Mexican army at the Battle of San Jacinto and Texas finally got her independence, the Northern states had begun to have second thoughts about Texas joining the Union, because Texas was a slave-holding state. For years thereafter, the United States kept Texas dangling. Finally, poor Sam Houston, who was as much of a liberal as you could hope to get in those days, was kicked out of power. He was replaced as president of Texas by a hard-liner named Mirabeau Buonaparte Lamar. Lamar told the United States to stick it, and announced that he was in the market to ally himself with any, repeat, *any* foreign power in the region *except* the United States.

If there had been a thriving Russian colony barreling eastward across the Rockies at that time, who knows what would have happened? Texans might have ended up speaking Russian with a drawl.

But the Russians weren't swarming over the Rockies, so

eventually Mirabeau Bonaparte Lamar cooled off and deals were struck and Texas became a part of the United States in 1845.

If the Russians had invested serious effort in colonizing California, think how history would have changed. Think contamination. Russian peasants would have emigrated to America by the hundreds of thousands. I knew that, because by World War I, there was actually a land shortage in European Russia, and the peasants were screaming for the dissolution of the nobility's huge estates. The richness and bounty of California and the Wild West would have poured into Russian coffers. So would Western ways of thought and government have poured into Russian heads. Russia would have been forced into the modern age much earlier than in our old, familiar world. She would have embraced the Industrial Revolution decades earlier. With any luck, by the late nineteenth century she would have transformed herself into a constitutional monarchy much like Great Britain. After all, she was already on that road in our long-lost Earth, and quite popular with the English, when World War I broke out.

Russian reform would have begun a hundred years earlier than in our world. There would have been no assassination of the liberal Czar Alexander II in 1881, because by that time the Czar would have been merely a figurehead. There would have been no subsequent throttling of Russian reforms, because they would have been too well entrenched by then. Most importantly, such a healthy society would have paid no attention to that dope Lenin.

American cowboys would not have cried "Howdy" upon meeting, but *"Zdrastvuyte!"* Society in Russia would have been altered beyond recognition. Come 1914, Russia's ruler would not have been a wimpy cousin of the German Kaiser Wilhelm, but a parliament. Even if that dumb-ass Serbian student still managed to assassinate Archduke Franz Ferdinand of Austria-Hungary in Sarajevo, in all likelihood Russia wouldn't have gotten dragged into the war. She wouldn't have been so hung up on the notion of being the protector of the Slavic nations of the world (including Serbia), being preoccupied with maintaining her filthy rich colony in America.

She wouldn't have been obsessed with defending the Slavs in Serbia from the revenge of Austria-Hungary, made grave by its alliance with Germany. She would have been disinclined to squabble over minuscule pieces of European territory, having far bigger fish to fry—like California, like half of North America.

The debacle that was World War I would have stayed where it always should have been—a brushfire, purely local in character. A Russia that was hale, hearty, and bursting with American wealth would have counterbalanced the immense power of Germany. The militaristic kaiser might have had second thoughts about using the war as an excuse to blitz through Belgium and attack Russia's democratic ally, the French Republic. Especially with Russia's other democratic ally, Great Britain, sitting right across the English Channel. With any luck, there would have been no World War I as we knew it, and no broken and embittered Germany, lusting for Round Two. And therefore, no World War II, and no Bomb. Heaven!

Of course, I wasn't going to leave anything to chance if I could help it. Once I had Rezanov's ear, I would tell him where the land mines of the future were buried. With a little twenty-twenty foresight and careful planning, Rezanov and his successors could be on the lookout to nip future disasters in the bud.

Oh, I was cooking with gas! For extra insurance, Russia could make sure the best art school in Vienna accepted, rather than rejected, a certain student named A. Hitler. Russia could make sure that a suitably wealthy patron be located to buy every wretched painting the man ever produced, thus distracting him from pursuing other careers, such as becoming leader of the fascist world. The remaining members of the fascist movement in Germany could have been neutralized quite discreetly on the sly.

While I couldn't see how to put a halt to the advances of pure science, as I said earlier, the actual development and implementation of nuclear weapons technology was damned expensive. It seemed likely that only a war to the death involving the whole world, followed by an ultra-paranoid Cold War, could have caused the superpowers of the time to cough up the staggering amounts of dough needed to actually build the stuff. No World War, no Cold War, no budget for such foolish boy toys . . . no nuclear wars, ever!

My course was clear. Now I had to get my wardrobe together—not to mention some thoroughly convincing exhibits for Nikolai Rezanov. And somehow I had to get Jeffrey's cooperation in this monumental venture.

## 20

## February 2013–May 1806: San Francisco

The first thing I did, after my research was finished, was to engage the best theatrical costume maker on the West Coast to construct a complete wardrobe for two members of the Russian nobility—say a wealthy, landed count and countess—in the year 1806. I played myself up as an elderly eccentric, and asked the woman to indulge me and not ask questions. When I gave her a check for fifty thousand dollars, with fifty more to be paid when the project was finished, she eagerly agreed.

I made her sit through the entire 1968 Russian film of *War and Peace* with me and take notes. I told her that the costumes must be absolutely, one hundred percent authentic. No shortcuts could be taken and no mistakes allowed. She was really puzzled, and dying to know what I was up to, but I didn't care. By the time the poor woman got around to any serious questioning, the world would be engulfed in war anyway. I did tell her to spend the money at once on all the things she had always wanted.

I bought genuine antique Russian jewelry when I could, and acquired impressive new jewels, which I had put into settings appropriate to the period. I also prepared lots and lots of leather pouches full of unset gemstones of exquisite quality to use when times got rough.

When I put on my first costume, I felt utterly transformed. I was an elderly, noble Russian dowager, of wealth and impeccable breeding, from the year 1806. When I looked in the mirror, I thought I looked just like a character in *War and Peace*—the elegant, French-speaking Anna Pavlovna Scherer, lady-in-waiting to the Czarevna Maria Fedorovna.

I decided to change my name. I was Anna Ivanovna Zorina, perhaps a distant relative of the Czarevna. Lavrenti and I had never gotten married, since he had never divorced his wife, but I thought it would have tickled him for me to appropriate his name for this great endeavor. To sum it all up, my appearance implied high status in Russian society. I would be so convincing that when I buttonholed Nikolai Rezanov back at the Presidio in 1806, he would have to hear me out. Caught off guard (as I planned to catch him), he would at first be too flustered to show disrespect for such a noble elderly dowager—like asking me what the hell I was doing in California and how the hell I'd gotten there. By the time he'd recovered himself, I would have spoken first. I would have told him what disaster the future held, and begged him to listen to me.

In a frenzy of activity, I collected the documents and exhibits I would need to convince Rezanov I was the genuine article. I had Bret Harte's tear-jerker poem about "Concepción de Arguello" translated into beautiful Spanish. One gander at that, and I could count on Concha being squarely in my court for all time. Always one for overkill, I went out to Benecia and took lots of pictures of her grave, being sure to get good shots of the oil refineries in the background. I took a brutal crash course in Spanish so I could talk to Concha myself; from my reading, I wasn't sure that she'd picked up that much Russian. I was ordained an American Humanist minister, just in case *I* had to perform their marriage ceremony. I packed my reproduction of Rezanov's diary, the better to scare the epalets off him.

I bought a ton of picture books and scholarly history books, some of which were even detailed enough to mention him. I had an enlargement made of that old, grainy photo of Rezanov's monument, the one that was destroyed when the Soviets took over Russia. I took an expensive palmtop computer with videodisc capability and expandable screen, and transcribed a humongous number of modern documentaries about Russia and the Cold War onto a couple of the little discs. I even included footage taken from the Bunker of the 1962 nuclear war. For fun, I threw in a few movies, including the Russian version of *War and Peace*. I bought a genuine antique, detailed, and accurate map from 1849 showing where the gold was in California, in case the Czar needed a little additional convincing to start colonizing. And I took copies of lots of photos showing the growth of non-Russian, *American* San Francisco from the 1840's onward. Those, I felt sure, would chap Rezanov's butt to the max, and make him listen carefully to all my advice.

I bought lots of Russian currency from 1806 at rare coin shops. I had all my teeth pulled and replaced by incorruptible porcelain chompers—after all, I was heading back to an era with no dentists. I got supplies of every drug for every malady I could think of (being an old lady, I was increasingly beset by maladies of the flesh). I bought a stash of the finest French cognac. I got chloroquinine and other wonder drugs, to treat Rezanov if his malaria acted up again.

I found an artsy place in San Francisco that could make good old paper the way they did in the days of the Declaration of Independence. At considerable cost, I had them make up a couple hundred sheets. Then I found one of the state's top experts on earthquake-proofing and went to see him. If I was going to help birth a city called Novaya Moskva on this little hilly peninsula I loved so well, no earthquake was going to knock it all down in 1906 while I had anything to say about the matter.

"I am old, rich, eccentric, and a science fiction fan," I said to him. "Humor me, and I will give you a cashiers check for two hundred thousand dollars for performing a very small task."

At the mention of so much money, he practically genuflected, especially when I showed him the check itself. I handed him my package from the artsy place, a genuine quill pen, some genuine nineteenth-century-type ink, and said, "Here is the sort of paper and writing instruments they used back in the early 1800's, when San Francisco was first being built. I want you to pretend that you are advising the builders of San Francisco during its first hundred years. Remember that they had none of the funky building materials that we do today, and nothing like our technology. They built with wood, hewn stone, and bricks, that sort of thing. Write an absolutely accurate manual for the builders of San Francisco in the years before the 1906 earthquake. Tell them, given what they have to work with, the best way to quake-proof their buildings."

He did look at me oddly, but he was a science fiction fan too—he liked the really old stuff from the Golden Era, like cyberpunk—and was willing to listen to crazy ideas. When I told him I wanted the manual because I was planning to write and electronically publish on the Net a little alternate world novel set in San Francisco, he got really enthusiastic. I promised to give him credit in the book for his earthquake manual.

The really difficult part was deciding when to waylay Rezanov. He had arrived at the Presidio in early April 1806, and after six weeks had ingratiated himself with its occupants and thoroughly scoped out the beauties and bounties of Nueva California. I had to get to him when his influence with the Arguello family, his love for Concha, and his ambitions for California were at their peak.

What complicated this beyond belief was that until 1917 the Russians had used the old Julian calendar, whereas Great Britain and the American colonies had adopted the revised Gregorian calendar back in 1752. If you ever wondered why the Soviets celebrated their "Glorious October Revolution" in November, this is why. When they got around to adopting the Gregorian calendar, they realized they had had their revolution in November, not October. So I had to find out what calendar the Spaniards had been using at the Presidio back in 1806, and whether Rezanov had followed the same calendar in keeping his records. If I didn't allow for a possible miscalculation of ten days or so, I might arrive at the Presidio *after* he'd sailed for Alaska in late May.

As I worked, the next nuclear war inched even closer. Each morning I had to have a stiff dose of Stoli before I opened the paper. I had so much to do in order to pull off this operation! If the war started early, we'd have to jump back without my having done all my homework.

All this while Jeffrey sort of watched from the sidelines. He didn't help; he whimpered and cried a lot about how he couldn't take responsibility for destroying the modern world we knew. One day when he was being particularly maddening, I blew my stack. I pointed out caustically that if we both sat on our hands, other people would destroy our beloved modern world for us. "Lead, follow, or get out of the way, Jeffrey," I snarled.

"Anna," he said, getting to his feet, "I can't handle this. I can't be a part of it. I won't try to stop you; I'll just stay here and take my chances." With that, he went downstairs to retrieve his car from the garage. I never saw him again.

He had gone driving on Mount Tamalpais and had an accident. His car went off one of the steep, narrow, winding roads up there and rolled several hundred feet into a gulch, where it burst into flames. In the back of my mind, I felt certain it had been no accident. Old as he was, Jeffrey was still a good driver, and the day had been sunny and the road dry as a bone.

I almost lost it then, but the war drums were pounding with increased ferocity, and sheer panic kept me going. I kept my anguish over Jeffrey's death locked away in my heart. One day, if I made it back to the year 1806, I would climb up Russian Hill to the spot where our apartment had been, and grieve for him.

Knowing how strange my modern Russian would sound to Rezanov, I had read everything in Russian written around 1806, trying to get a feel for how the language sounded back then. At the same time I actually managed to retain some Spanish from my crash course. It was the best I could do.

I waited until the missiles were landing to jump back. In fact, I waited until the air over San Francisco flashed bright with warning. Then, my eyes full of tears and my heart breaking, I said good-bye to San Francisco and the world I loved, and pulled the lever on the time machine for the very last time.

With the help of Jeffrey's computers, I knew exactly when and where to set myself down in the forest outside the Presidio, alone, on a brilliant May morning in 1806. Or so I thought.

Damn! In spite of everything my calculations were still off. Or maybe Fate just knew what was best, and interfered enough with my aim (or the machine) to plunk me down at the exact spot in the Presidio where I had seen the ghosts of Rezanov and Concha. Only trouble was, Fate plunked me down while they were still there, weeping and embracing, just as I had come upon them in that spectral encounter in 2013. The problem was, this time they weren't ghosts, but real people.

They gasped in astonishment and fear as I materialized out of nowhere and crossed themselves—Concha, a good Catholic, making the sign of the cross starting on the left side, and Rezanov the Russian Orthodox heretic starting on the right side. At any other time it would have been uproariously funny.

Somehow, I blinked back the tears I had carried back through time from the funeral pyre of my world. I had to think on my feet and carry the moment with sheer drama. "Count Rezanov," I thundered, "I have come to give you a message of the utmost importance."

He was flabbergasted and I had given him no chance to recover. So his years of military and courtly training took over. With one protective arm still around the shoulders of Concha, he bowed. I executed a curtsy appropriate to the time, and approached him to make my pitch.

PART IV

1806–1836

## 21

## May 1806: The Presidio of San Francisco

Sure enough, I got nailed as a witch first pop out of the bag. *"¡Una bruja!"* cried Concha. I denied it, and pointed out that any self-respecting sorceress would surely have employed her witchcraft to speak much better Spanish than I did. Concha hesitated. While she wrestled with this concept, I pounced.

"I am here to warn Count Rezanov of great danger," I said. "But I have come to warn you too, Maria Concepción Arguello y Moraga! If you wish your beloved to live, if you wish to marry him and bear his children, if you do not wish to become the first nun in the land of California, listen to me well."

I know I laid it on with a shovel, but it worked. She turned as white as a Spaniard could turn—which, considering that she was European, was pretty white. She was a beautiful little thing, young and vivacious, and—judging from all I'd read—very intelligent. I hoped I'd get her on my side.

"Count Rezanov," I said, speaking now in Russian, "if you wish to see the Motherland again, if you would live to return to California and wed your betrothed, hear me out."

"Who sent you?" he asked softly. "The Czar?"

"You know that is impossible," I replied, just as quietly.

"Then who?"

"No one sent me. I chose to come myself."

"Why?"

"To save your life. And the lives of others."

As I looked at him, I realized the full irony of this last role Fate had decreed for me to play. In human history, there truly was such a thing as an eternal flame. Once before I had known a man gifted with such intense will, with such potential to affect the future of the world. Once before I had known a man fated to stand at a great crossroads in the history of the world. Now I saw another of his kind before me.

Rezanov's portrait at Fort Ross had not done him justice. In the portrait, he seemed tight-lipped, almost prim. In person he was a strikingly handsome man. Tall and slender, he towered over Concha and me. He was elegantly turned out in one of the dashing uniforms of his era, and his bearing was, I must confess, just a bit imperious.

He had been described as "a great but practical dreamer." In truth, he was another Kennedy, possessing all the same magnetism, charisma, and potential that had been Jack's. He was even the same age that Jack had been when he was elected President. In that moment, I knew I would spend the rest of my life making sure this Kennedy lived to change history.

"Where do you come from?" he demanded. "Your speech betrays you; you are not from the Motherland, even though your dress and your jewels would seem to place you in the court of the Czar."

"I come from here, Your Excellency, from this very spot."

"That cannot be. You could not have escaped my notice."

"That is because I come from this place not in the year 1806, but two hundred years in the future."

"Impossible!" he cried.

"I come from a city built on these same hills, called San Francisco. Unfortunately, Your Excellency, that city is not Russian. It is part of the United States of America."

That got his attention. I realized I had a window of opportunity in which to strike. I made a silent apology to the god of political correctness and said, "Count Rezanov, allow me to explain how I traveled here. Suppose you were to journey into the darkest depths of the African continent. Suppose you then took out your finest dueling pistol, showed it to one of the savage men who dwell in that place, and then shot and killed a nearby animal. Would the man not think you a magician?"

He nodded; he was quite intrigued. His gaze never left my face, and I could sense the cogs turning in his brain. So, in these first critical moments, I was making a good impression. He half believed me, and he was beginning to think I was Big Game. He was already wondering if I could help him snatch California.

"Where I come from, Your Excellency," I continued, "people enjoy stories and tales which emphasize the future advances of mankind. There was a scientist, a great writer of such tales, named after that Arthur who was a legendary king of Britain. This man said one day, 'Any sufficiently advanced technology is indistinguishable from magic.' Do you know what he meant?"

A faint smile passed across Rezanov's face. "Not entirely. Not yet. Please continue."

I decided he could handle the straightforward approach. I opened up the backpack that held the time machine and showed it to him. "This is a machine, a device made by men, just like your dueling pistol. It is very advanced simply because I come from the future. Two hundred years from now, men have simply had more time to invent machines to serve them than you have had. We have built thousands of different machines to make our lives easier. This particular device allowed me to travel from the year 2013 to the year 1806, so that I might speak with you. So you see, even though this device seems remarkable to you, it really—"

"I understand, I understand," he interrupted. "*I* am not an African savage."

Touchy, touchy! I gave a little bow. "My deepest apologies, Your Excellency. I did not mean to patronize you."

"If you have so many machines to serve you in the year 2013," said Rezanov, "why have you come back here? Why should you care whether I live or die?"

"Because we have invented one machine so terrible that no man and no nation can control it. Imagine all the gunpowder in the world concentrated in one weapon—that is the power of this machine. It has destroyed our entire world and all the people in it. I have come back to prevent your death, and thereby change the future so this machine will never be invented."

"My death?" he cried. Concha gasped and caught his arm.

"You're going to push yourself too hard on the way back to Russia, fall off your horse in Siberia, and die," I said bluntly. Hearing this, Concha began to weep, and his arm went round her again. I noted to myself that the girl *was* smart; she must have picked up a hell of a lot of Russian in the last six weeks to understand what I'd just said. I grinned inwardly and began to reel him in.

"But how could my death lead to the development of this weapon you speak of?" cried Rezanov.

"With all due respect, Your Excellency, let me ask one thing: In Russia, do children sing that nursery rhyme about the kingdom that was lost, all for the want of a two-penny nail?"

"I have two children, grown now. I remember such a rhyme."

"You are the two-penny nail. If you die, there will be set in motion a series of events, the consequences of which will profoundly affect the history of mankind. In the end, the United States, not Russia, will colonize California."

"The United States?" he was aghast. "Yes—you said you came from a city, built here, that belonged to the United States. But the United States is such a small, weak country— and it is thousands of miles away. The Yankees, as they call themselves, cannot possibly settle California."

"Not now. But give them forty or fifty years, and they will," I replied. "They're already on the move. You purchased your ship, the *Juno*, and all her goods from a Yankee trader who made it all the way to Alaska. And don't forget that three years ago the Americans bought the entire Louisiana Territory from Napoleon. Your Excellency, if you are killed, Russia will do nothing about settling California except for building one puny little fort a few miles up the coast from here in 1812. In 1823, the President of the United States will issue a proclamation called the 'Monroe Doctrine'—specifically aimed at Russia, by the way—warning the other nations of the Earth to keep their hands off America. You'll lose out, I guarantee it.

"Russia will remain Europe's backward giant. She will not realize her potential until the end of the twentieth century, when it will be too late to save mankind. You see, due in part to Russia's failure to advance as other countries, and due in part to her failure to seize the power that should have been hers, in the year 1914 there will come a terrible war. It will devastate Russia, and set in motion other events that in another hundred years will culminate in the destruction of my world. So, Your Excellency, I'm not going to let you fall off your horse."

To hammer home my point, I went fishing into my luggage. "This is a copy of the diary you will keep if you return on your ship to Siberia. This is your handwriting, is it not?" I asked.

He took the book and examined it with the most profound amazement. "Yes," he whispered.

I turned to a page I had dog-eared, that contained his plea to the Czar to reach out and seize California for the Motherland. "These are the words you will write to the Czar on your voyage home." He read the page, and for the first time seemed actually frightened. I had him. "Nikolai Petrovich, you and I are not going to let the future you describe in that diary come to pass."

"California belongs to Spain," cried Concha, black eyes flashing. "It is not yours to carve up like a roast goose!"

I think both Rezanov's jaw and my jaw hit the ground at

the same time. I cursed inwardly, for as much as I had plotted and planned this encounter, I'd never foreseen this angle. She'd learned Russian, all right, and understood every word we said.

"Señorita Arguello," I said, "this will not be pleasant for you to hear, but I must be frank, or all will be lost."

I paused a moment, and she gave the faintest of nods. "I am very sorry to say this, my dear, but Spain's star is no longer rising in the heavens. For centuries Spain has been the greatest country in the world, but those days are gone. Do not grieve; it is the nature of all countries to wax powerful, and then watch that power ebb. Spain cannot hold onto California. Even now, your own colony is neglected, is it not? You are bored here; you have been known to describe California as a land where there is nothing but cattle and dun-colored grass."

She whitened. "How can you possibly know that?" she cried.

"Because a history book in my time recounts your comment."

This time she went red with embarrassment. "We are very much alone here," she admitted after a moment. "At times I think I will go mad with boredom."

"I know. So let us undertake negotiations with your father, get you married to Count Rezanov now, and undertake a slow, careful journey back to the glittering court at St. Petersburg."

She crossed herself. "Mother of God!" She was hooked.

"In a few years," I continued, "Mexico will mount a revolution and break free of Spain. I am sorry, but it can't be helped. Mexico will then be preoccupied with internal problems and even less willing than Spain to maintain the isolated colony of California. So you see, in the next few years lies Russia's chance to colonize California. In the 1830's, Texas will break free of Mexico, and join the United States in 1845. Also in the 1840's, gold will be discovered in California, and the Americans will descend upon Cali-

fornia by the thousands and take it for their own. Unless, of
course, the three of us act—and act now!"

"*Valgame Dios!*" she whispered, and closed her eyes.

In case Concha was still the least bit anxious about the
notion that Spain would lose California, I got out my copy
of Bret Harte's unabashedly tear-jerking poem about her
lost romance with Rezanov. I felt like a sadist, but I had to
do it. The hell with Spain; I had to bring it home to her that
if she didn't fall into line, she would lose Rezanov. Concha
read the poem, and broke into heartrending sobs.

"If you don't help us, Señorita Arguello," I said, "you
truly will end up the first nun in California. You will be
buried in a cemetery thirty miles north of here called
Benecia, that in my time overlooked a very ugly thing called
a refinery."

She nodded. "I will do anything you ask! Only do not let
that nightmare come true for us!"

All this while the gears had been grinding in Rezanov's
head. Like mad. "Tell us more about this gold you mentioned."

I smiled like a cat inspecting a bowl of cream. "I know
where it all is. I have detailed maps."

"I have an idea," said Rezanov, a note of pure, unadulterated relish in his voice. "If gold is involved, the govern-
ments of Russia and Spain could surely be induced to enter
into . . . an alliance. Spain, lacking the manpower, cannot
colonize California by herself. And she does not know
where the gold is located. She needs Russian help, does she
not?"

"Most definitely," I said. Wow—he was operating in
diplomat mode, suitor mode, and businessman mode simultaneously! A true Kennedy forerunner if there ever was one.

Rezanov took out an elaborately lacy nineteenth-century
man's hanky and began to dry Concha's tears. "Dearest,
Russia will not wrest California from Spain," he said gently.
"Russia will help her keep it. Our two countries will be
partners."

Yeah, right, I said to myself as I listened to this snow job—only it just so happens one partner's star is on the rise, and that partner will soon be ten times as strong as the other and able to move in on half the North American continent.

He glanced up, and our eyes met. An electric look passed between us. We both knew what he was doing. But it was okay. It was necessary.

"Is there someplace we can go to examine certain materials I have brought in peace and quiet?" I asked briskly. "Some place where no one will interrupt us? No one but the three of us must ever know my secrets, or what I am about to show you."

"This spot is the only private place in the entire Presidio," said Concha. "Believe me, there is no other place to be alone. If there was, we would have found it."

Then she realized what she'd said, and blushed scarlet. Rezanov looked rather pleased with himself.

"It will have to do, but there's no place to sit!" I exclaimed, thinking of my lovely costume. I mean, gown.

"Yes, there is," said Rezanov. With a grand flourish, he swept off the dashing, beautiful cape that accompanied his Russian officer's uniform and started to stretch it across the ground, Sir Walter Raleigh style.

"No!" I cried. "The dirt!" I couldn't help it. In my era, the cape would have been a fabulously expensive antique.

Rezanov shrugged, as if he had not a care in the world. "Of what importance is a foolish cape, when the future of the human race is at stake?" he said, and proceeded to lay it on the dirt.

I must have still looked distressed, because Concha whispered in my ear, "Don't worry. He knows one of my maids will clean it."

Our eyes met. Now it was our turn to bond. We women understood each other, and we also understood His Excellency. Truly, this was the beginning of a beautiful friendship.

I hauled out all my stuff and gave them a dazzling

battery-powered, multimedia grand tour of the presently scheduled future of the world. When we got to my excerpted documentaries of the Russian Revolution and the assassination of the Czar, Rezanov wept, as he did later when we got to footage of the Bomb. You must remember that Russians have never considered it unmanly to weep when moved.

As for Concha, she looked frightened, but instead of weeping, she set her jaw, and stared intently into space. Talk about being able to see the wheels turning! She was doing some dead practical thinking of her own.

After all that I thought a little light entertainment was called for; Rezanov and Concha had just gotten an eyeful of the worst parts of the future, and a bit of relief was in order. So I fired up the 1968 Russian film of *War and Peace*, and showed them some selected scenes, such as the great glittering ball, where Prince Andrei Bolkonsky and Natasha Rostova danced with wings across the polished floor of a St. Petersburg palace.

Concha was in seventh heaven, because the film was set in a time only a few years hence, and she and Rezanov were reasonably close to the ages of Prince Andrei and Natasha. California was pretty pastoral (i.e., boring) to a young girl back in those days, and she could not wait to get her tiny Spanish dancing feet on a similarly polished floor at the court of Czar Alexander. Verily, Concha was about to expire in a cloud of sighs and large, liquid, sentimental tears. I even got a little carried away myself, since, as I have said, the actor playing Prince Andrei looked so much like my Lavrenti when he was thirty. Then I noticed something bizarre. Rezanov, far from enjoying the movie, looked like someone had kicked him in the nuts. He looked as gray as when he had viewed the nuclear war footage.

"Your Excellency," I said, "what is wrong? Have I offended you somehow?"

"You say this 'moving picture' was actually made in St.

Petersburg and Moscow in 1969, and that no expense was spared?" he asked hoarsely.

"Yes, Your Excellency."

"But it is not accurate. I have seen these palaces with my own eyes. The walls are bare! Where are all the beautiful tapestries that used to cover them? Where are all the paintings?"

Then I understood. "Oh," I whispered, and searched without success for some way to cushion the blow. "I am so sorry, but they must have been lost during the 1917 revolution."

He lowered his head. "You mean looted, sold by the state, or destroyed by the masses for sheer amusement! Damn them!"

I nodded, my heart aching. For Rezanov, the sight of these denuded palaces was the unkindest cut of all.

"Let's ship the masses over here and get them busy farming, and they'll never raise a revolution," I whispered. "No one who has to milk cows and keep up with a garden has the time for it."

"Well," Concha said in Russian when I had shut off the disc player, "our task is clear. But by heaven and all the angels, *what* are we going to tell my father?"

Abruptly, time changed. The train rushed toward me, the earth trembled, and I swayed where I sat, as if I were about to faint. "What is wrong?" cried Rezanov and Concha, in unison.

"Please forgive me," I replied. "It is a malady I have. Because I have traveled in time, I am peculiarly sensitive to the moment when the future changes. It makes me ill— briefly."

"What?" said Rezanov. "You meant the future *just* changed?"

"Yes, Your Excellency."

"That is odd. I had already made up my mind to help you in every way I could."

"I know. But the last piece of the plan had not fallen into

place until . . ." I paused, embarrassed, fumbling for words.

"Until she made up *her* mind," he finished for me.

"That's correct," I said, and looked down at my toes. "We needed her assistance too."

He smiled. "I have always thought she had the makings of a queen." At that, I felt the future shiver again.

## 22

May 1806: The Presidio of San Francisco (cont.)

We thought long and hard about what we would say to Don José Arguello, Concha's father, the comandante of the Presidio of San Francisco. Although Rezanov was confident the Czar would be able to handle the real truth once we got to St. Petersburg, Concha was adamant that her father, Don José, wasn't up to it. We just couldn't tell him Spain was going to lose California, and end up as a place where Americans went for cheap vacations and paella; he would go nuts. So, we had to think up the bullshit snow job of the millennium to explain my presence in California and the necessity of Concha's wedding her beloved heretic *now*.

Concha remarked that her father was well rested after a recent trip to the Presidio of Monterey in the south, and was in very good spirits. Her gut told her that luck was with us. So, we got our stories straight, and headed for the main house.

As we walked, Rezanov looked more and more worried, and at last said to me, "If the Russians colonize California and the western part of the continent, and the Yankees are expanding as quickly as you say, surely, Anna Ivanovna, there will be war between our people when they meet at their mutual frontier."

"Yes, I am sure of it," I replied. "But that war will take place between our nations in their youth, a century or more before the weapon of which I spoke could ever be invented.

In the end, I believe Russia and the United States will become friends and allies. I believe they are destined to be so. You see, from the late 1980's until the year 2013, when my world was destroyed, we were the best of friends. Our friendship just came about too late."

"Wise words. I promise this war will not destroy our own friendship, if we both live to see it," he said, and smiled.

I went weak in the knees. In another time, another place . . . Concha was just lucky I was over seventy. I had this strange weakness for world-changing men who were age forty-two.

We swept into the comandante's house as if all the future were at stake (which, in fact, was true), and we were in the most dreadful hurry to warn His Excellency. We found Don José enjoying a shot of fine Spanish Madeira after his dinner, and he seemed to be in a very good mood, which gave me even greater faith in Concha's womanly intuition. "Your Excellency!" cried Rezanov. His booted feet snapped together, and he executed an incredibly crisp and perfect military bow. "An emissary has just arrived from the court of Czar Alexander. She has important news for you that cannot wait, sire. We must find a room where we may talk in private with Señorita Concepción and Her Ladyship."

The comandante leapt to his feet and came toward me. "Your Excellency," said Rezanov, "may I present Princess Anna Ivanovna Zorina, lady-in-waiting to the Czarevna Maria Fedorovna, and special envoy from our most blessed Czar Alexander?"

Princess? I had been promoted. Well, fine and good.

The comandante reached for my hand, and bestowed upon it a courtly kiss. *Okay,* I said to myself, I can play this one out.

"Your Excellency," I said softly, "you do me great honor."

"Princess," he said, "how is it you were cast upon our isolated shores so suddenly?"

He was no fool. I grasped his fingers a trifle tighter and said, "I came in great haste from St. Petersburg via Alaska, Your Excellency, in a ship from our colony in Sitka. I asked to be rowed ashore that I might find Count Rezanov and come to you at once. There is disturbing news about the Americans that will affect both our countries and must be dealt with immediately."

He clapped his hands at once, like the autocrat he was. "Everybody out!" he cried.

"Do not forget that the Señorita Concepción may stay," I murmured. "This concerns her also." At this, he looked nonplussed, but nodded to his daughter to stay in the room.

"Your Excellency," I said, when the room was clear, using my softest and sweetest of tones, "I bring news of great import."

You must keep in mind that in Spanish society in those years, the aged were *not* despised; to hear such caressing tones from a beautifully coiffed and dressed woman of seventy was honey to a man nearly as old, such as the Comandante Arguello.

"And that is?" he asked, still holding my hand in his.

"An intrepid American explorer recently found gold to the north, in the far reaches of Alta California—a great deal of gold. He drew a detailed map showing its location, which he attempted to sell in the United States. I was at that time a special emissary from His Majesty Czar Alexander to the Americans, and so intelligence of this discovery soon came to me." I looked at him meaningfully, so he would realize I was not only a noble lady, but a very special spy. "I had both the funds—and the able assistance—to acquire the only existing copy of the map. Unfortunately, word still leaked out among the Americans about the discovery of gold in California, although no one is quite sure where it is located. That is why Czar Alexander dispatched me to rendezvous with Count Rezanov—who was in California already—and propose an alliance between our countries to secure the northern territory and take the gold quickly, before the Americans can act!"

"Have you long been an emissary of the Czar?" he asked.

I lowered my lashes for all they were worth—they and the heavy coating of mascara I surreptitiously applied on the way over. "Yes, my lord," I said, giving him a promotion too. "Since I was a young girl, I have always possessed a talent for assisting the Czar in resolving . . . affairs of state." I looked briefly and winsomely into his eyes, and knew the job was done.

He let go of my hand. "You have this map?"

I smiled sweetly. "Yes, Your Excellency."

"It is the property of the Russian government?"

"Yes, Your Excellency." With a dramatic gesture, I reached into a pocket of my elaborate dress and drew forth a leather purse. Upon the table which had recently hosted Don Arguello's glass of Madeira, I released a torrent of genuine chunks of gold retrieved from California back in 1849, which had been beautifully polished back in 2013, for visual effect of course.

As with Pizarro, Cortés, and all the other conquistadors, the mere mention of the word "gold" could drive all rational thought clear out of a Spaniard's brain. Don José, being a 100 percent pure-blooded Spanish male, was a goner. He gasped, overcome by galloping gold lust. I presented him with the largest and most luscious of the chunks. "This one is for you," I said in a soft voice. "I must keep the rest, to show the King of Spain."

"*Madre de Dios*!" Arguello cried. "There is more, you say, in the northern lands?"

I nodded.

"Tell me about this American explorer."

"He was the best," I said. I started having fun, inventing stuff as I went along. "His name was Rogers—Buck Rogers."

"*Buck* Rogers?"

My imagination caromed hard off Daniel Boone and I

couldn't resist the temptation. "Yes," I said solemnly. "Originally he was named Horace, after the Greek poet, but when he killed a full-grown male deer at the age of two with a bow and arrow he himself had made, he was forever after called Buck."

"I see," said Don Arguello. He sounded awfully impressed. "Why do you refer to him in the past tense?"

"Unfortunately," I sighed, "he was taken ill soon after I purchased the maps from him, and died." Arguello's eyes widened; he was seriously impressed. Hell, he was a little scared of me.

Nikolai Rezanov stepped forward. "Your Excellency, we propose an immediate alliance between our two countries, and a joint expedition to secure the northern borders of California and lay claim to her many gold deposits before the Americans do so."

"How long do you think it will take the Americans to find the gold?" asked Arguello.

I gave a long, sad sigh. "Not long. The Americans could arrive any day. You see, it has taken me more than a year to journey from the eastern coast of America to St. Petersburg to confer with the Czar, and from there to Alaska and California. Your Excellency, our expedition must set out at once. If we delay, the Americans may be waiting for us when we arrive."

I allowed my hands to travel wistfully over the nuggets of gold. "We could reach a signed, formal agreement with the Czar and the King of Spain . . . after we secured for Spain and Russia the borders of California and the rights to all gold found therein. I am sure His Majesty would be greatly pleased with you, Your Excellency, for having procured such great riches for Spain."

"Will you take us there?" demanded Arguello.

I played again with the golden nuggets. "Of course. But . . ."

"But?" he fairly thundered.

I turned to him. I approached to within a pace of him and

removed a Rezanov hanky from my pocket. "Alas, sir, I am overcome with the emotions of a mother," I said.

You have to realize, the Spanish took sentimental things with dead seriousness. Of course, so did Americans in my time, but they always tried to act cool about it on the surface.

"What has motherhood to do with this?" asked Don Arguello.

In an age without telecommunications, you could get away with some real whoppers. I dabbed at my eyes. "When I was a young girl barely the age of your Concha, I was married in Russia to a great man, Prince Lavrenti Zorin. I bore him five strapping sons, and then a beautiful daughter, much like your own."

I knew from my intense reading of history that Concha, the eldest of all the comandante's children, was the apple of his eye. He had had her educated like a son, so that all sorts of radical ideas were amix in her head, and he veritably worshipped the ground she walked on.

"What happened to her?" he demanded. He took my hand again and grasped it hard, as if his life depended on it. For the moment, he had forgotten all about the frigging gold.

"Oh, sir, I do not wish your house to suffer the same sad fate as my own. My daughter wished to marry a young Spaniard as noble and distinguished as your own son Luis, but my husband and I—we were too frail to consent to the marriage ourselves. We waited; we sought the approval of Empress Catherine."

"What happened?"

"Czarina Catherine consented, but the poor bride-groom"—I began to weep here—"died before the wedding could take place. Years later, my lovely Natasha married a fine noble of the court whom she did not truly love, and died in childbirth."

Now he was weeping too. "I beg you with a mother's heart," I cried, "to let these two children marry now! Let me see them happy before I die! They both love the one and only Christ! The differences between our religions are so small, they should not condemn our children to eternal heartbreak!"

The poor bastard had no way out. He knew it was dangerous to oppose grieving, emotional mothers; when thwarted they tended to react, as my own ancestors would have said, like hydrophobic javelina hogs. And he had to have my map, because he didn't dare lose his shot at the gold. The King would have Arguello's crown jewels on a platter if the Yankees found it first.

Originally, Don José Arguello, his eldest son, Luis, the priests of the Presidio, and everybody else who mattered had had big reservations about Concha marrying a heretic. But she was determined to marry Rezanov and wouldn't back down. They had reached an uncomfortable compromise that would require Rezanov to trudge back to Europe to obtain not only the permission of the King of Spain for the marriage, but that of the Pope himself. But now this time-wasting folderol might let the Americans get the gold first. What was a poor Spanish don to do?

I had him where I wanted him. So he kissed my hand again and asked, "If we cement the alliance between Russia and the Kingdom of Spain by the marriage of Nikolai Petrovich Rezanov to my daughter Concepción, the expedition will go ahead as planned?"

"Of course, Your Excellency," I said, my eyes overflowing with tears. "The expedition shall be half Russian, half Spanish, and both countries shall share equally in the spoils!"

I was an early nineteenth-century version of a matron of honor when they hurriedly married Concha to Rezanov. Then we promptly packed up and traveled to the region in my time known as the California gold country. It was a wonderful honeymoon for Concha and Rezanov, even without the craft shops and boutiques that had filled the little towns along Highway 49 in my day.

Concha, of course, insisted upon donning men's clothing

for the journey, as did I. We must have enjoyed the most
beautiful spring in the history of the world. Game and fish
were plentiful, and I have to say that no one on Earth ever
perfected the art of barbecuing to the extent the Spaniards
did. It was a blast. When we got back, the little Indian maid
the Arguellos gave me had to let out all my clothes at the
waist.

We found lots of gold by panning in the local streams,
and posted "Keep Out" signs everywhere. After that, we
hightailed it back to the Presidio, where Don José almost
fainted at the sight of all the precious metal we had
retrieved.

It being almost July by the time we returned to the
Presidio, we realized we had the choice of wintering in
California or in Alaska. Since we had put up so many
belligerent "No Trespassing" signs, we felt our claim to
California had been significantly advanced, and decided to
stay at the Presidio and sail for Russia the following April.
There followed a never-ending series of *meriendas* (picnics)
and great balls, because all the Spaniards from Monterey to
San Jose and Santa Barbara wanted a look at the glamorous
new bride and groom—and the noble lady from the court of
the Czar. I was well on my way to becoming a pudge, thanks
to all that good food, port, and Madeira (how Don José
loved to show off his cellar!) before I got hold of myself.

I must say here that although I am making Old California
sound like Paradise, there were a few things missing. For a
start, try Pepto-Bismol, NyQuil, aspirin, gynecologists,
Vick's VapoRub, Tums, Kleenex, lovely white soft toilet
paper, washing machines, cappucino, hearing aids, electric-
ity, microwave ovens, and stoves with dials on them that did
what you told them to.

Plus, one thing they never tell you in all those Hollywood
costume epics set in any era (or the books that inspired
them, either) is how human beings actually smell in a world
lacking deodorants or the notion that one should bathe

frequently. I mean, who ever thinks about Spartacus or Caesar having B.O.?

My maid could not understand why I was always stripping and washing myself off with water from a bowl; I told her that, being Russian, I was unused to the warm California climate and had to wash myself more often. Concha, aware of my discomfort, commanded the Presidio Indians to build me a little enclosure, with a large kettle outside which could be filled with heated water. With the help of a couple of the strong Indian women, I could have hot showers. Concha joined me once or twice, thinking to learn as much about the exotic habits of the European Russians as possible, and soon got hooked on it. Before long she would shower one evening with me, and the next with her husband. First thing you know, I'd started a new fad. I like to think that I made a significant contribution to the well-being of my new world.

Come the last week of March, we arranged for a cautious, orderly voyage aboard Rezanov's ship, the *Juno*, to Siberia, and from there overland to St. Petersburg. We made good time, and were through Siberia before October. When we came to Krasnoyarsk, where, in that other world, Nikolai Petrovich had died, we were all solemnly, silently thankful, and hurried past that grim place as fast as our horses would carry us.

And so it was that we arrived safely at St. Petersburg just before Christmas in 1807, and were presented to the Czar.

Before I close this chapter, I should tell you a funny story. Right after the wedding, Concha approached me with no small degree of embarrassment. What if she were to conceive a child on the gold-seeking expedition, she asked. Even worse, what if she were to bear a child on the long voyage back to Russia? She suspected me of having miracles up my sleeve—as of course I did, since I had done my best to think of everything.

"Never you worry, dear child," I said. "You have many,

many child-bearing years ahead of you. In my day we had a type of medicine that allowed us to plan our children."

Concha was delighted. For the record, she asked if I thought God would disapprove. I said God had worked so hard to get all of us to this point, I believed He would be very understanding. Once they were re-settled in San Francisco, Concha could have lots of kids. *Lots*—to secure the dynasty. So there was no doubt God would be happy in the end.

Just to be safe, I advised Concha not to tell anybody about the medicine. She said she thought my judgment was very sound. So I got out my medical kit and the injector and implanted—out of sight in her left armpit—the minuscule sliver that would keep her from getting pregnant for five years. A gift, if you will, from a world lost to a world newborn.

## 23

## 1807 and Later: St. Petersburg, Russia

Imagine a schoolroom of twenty children who are all eight years old. Imagine that they do not age, but stay perpetually eight years old. For the next several hundred years, chronicle the friendships that are made, the friendships that break up, the cliques that form, the cliques that break up, and always the alliances, the shifting alliances. You will need a flow chart—a very large flow chart—to accurately construct this chronicle.

The foregoing should give you a good general feeling for what European and global politics were like in the centuries immediately preceding the destruction of the world in 2013. To set the stage for my meeting with Czar Alexander I of Russia at the end of the year 1807, let me give you only the following summary of the brief period between 1796 and 1807, the year I met the Czar.

Catherine the Great died in 1796 and was succeeded as ruler of Russia by her son, Czar Paul I, who was apparently mentally ill. He was subject to violent changes of temper and erratic orders but, as one authority points out, probably no more so than Ivan the Terrible or Peter the Great.

At this time in history all the autocrats of Europe, including Paul, were well and truly wigged out by the events of the recent French Revolution, and through strict censorship did their best to keep such horrific liberal ideas from spreading. In an age without telecommunications, this wasn't too hard.

Under Czar Paul I, the Russian-American Company was founded, and set to the task of exploring and (hopefully) settling the far northern reaches of the American continent. As we know, Rezanov soon came to head up this organization, so the reign of Paul I cannot be said to have been all bad.

Paul seriously annoyed the nobility and gentry of Russia by instituting a policy of compulsory military service. Since there were apparently no student deferments available, this ultimately contributed to his assassination in 1801.

Now, in 1799, Russia, England, Holland, and Austria ganged up on France and went to war. The Russian army, commanded by the legendary Marshal Suvorov, fought well. The Russians crossed half of Europe and recaptured northern Italy from the French. However, this fine performance made the Austrians jealous, so they and the other allies deserted Russia. The Russian army had to bag its plans to invade France, and retreated to Russia via Switzerland. Suvorov died a broken man, and the alliance with Austria against France predictably dissolved.

Between 1799 and 1800, Napoleon's actions at home convinced Czar Paul that Napoleon was not the heir to the French Revolution, but a rather autocratic gentleman determined to undo most of its democratic reforms. So Russia became friends with France, and began to contemplate an alliance against England, who by this time was becoming alarmed at the effect of Russia's growing influence on the European balance of power.

Got all that? Just when relations with England were about to reach their lowest ebb in history, Czar Paul was assassinated. A singularly pissed-off clique of the nobility, possibly aided and abetted by England, and reportedly with the cooperation of Paul's oldest son Alexander, fortified themselves with vodka, broke into Paul's bedroom in March 1801, and offed him.

Alexander became Czar Alexander I. By the time I met him, he had been Czar for six years. Despite the fact that he might have helped murder his father, it must be said that in his youth he was charming, imaginative, had been trained in liberal ideas by his Swiss tutor, and possessed both intellectual curiosity and perseverance. Moreover, he gathered about him a most capable group of men as his advisors, including a very liberal thinker named Speransky who would one day draft a constitution for Russia. (Talk about seditious notions!)

Just before his assassination, Czar Paul had sent troops to southwestern Siberia to invade India. Now, that truly would have created massive public relations problems with England. Alexander called back the troops and swiftly sought to buddy up to England. The greater did Napoleon's ambitions wax, the cozier Alexander got with England. Finally, when Napoleon had himself crowned emperor, Russia entered into a formal alliance with England, which soon led to war with France.

And, lest I forget, Austria reared its ugly head, once again eager to gang up with Russia and England against France. (Jeez, you'd think they'd learn.) In 1805, at the Battle of Austerlitz, the allies got their butts kicked. Austria sued for peace. Then Napoleon adopted a new approach, attacked Prussia, and took Berlin. So the Prussians linked up with the Russians, who still got their asses whipped *again*, in 1807. Napoleon, undisputed master of the European continent, impressed Czar Alexander with his magnanimity at Tilsit, where peace was declared. Alexander cleverly brokered this peace into an alliance.

So as I readied myself to meet with the Czar and talk about much more important things, Russia was again allied with France. And I had a feeling the pragmatic Alexander was definitely a man I could do business with.

Rezanov, the consummate diplomat, had meanwhile taken St. Petersburg by storm. He deftly showcased his beautiful young Spanish wife and made sure she charmed the entire court, including the Czar. He did not dress me as a Russian, but positioned me as an elderly Castilian woman of noble birth—not Concha's maid, but her companion and chaperon, or *dueña*, a position of much higher status. Until the time was right, he kept me in the background.

"You really think the Czar is going to go for this?" I asked nervously as we prepared for our upcoming meeting with Alexander.

"Oh, yes. He is a young man. If your tales can make bugles sing in my aged blood, think what they will do to his."

"Aged?" I laughed. "Don't talk to me about 'aged,' you damn forty-three-year-old!"

When there was an appropriate pause in the Christmas festivities, Rezanov paid a visit to the Czar in the most private of the monarch's suites. We had decided we would tell the Czar the whole truth. We couldn't bullshit our way through this one. There was just no other satisfactory way to explain who I was, how I just happened to show up in California at the right time to hitch a ride back to Russia with Rezanov, and how I knew all this stuff about the future. So I waited in the wings while Rezanov showed the Czar the gold and told him about the newly brokered joint venture with the Comandante of San Francisco.

The Czar was impressed, but said, "Now that this Don José Arguello knows where the gold is, why should His Majesty Charles IV of Spain sign an alliance with us? He is as inept a monarch as may be found in all Europe, but even he would laugh at an offer to help him keep that which he already possesses."

"I have just wed the eldest daughter of King Charles' most important official in Alta California, Don José Arguello. Thanks to the recent, fortuitous discovery of gold, Don José holds more actual power in his hands than the *gobernador* of the province. King Charles will not take this proposed alliance with a pinch of salt. Besides, Your

Majesty, he can be bent to our will. He is truly inept; he will lose his throne within a year."

The Czar gave Rezanov a strange look. "How can you possibly know this?"

Rezanov said, "The history books tell me so. I will show them to you in a moment, Your Majesty—or rather, someone else will. For now, you must realize that King Charles' signature on this paper, while desirable for propriety, is fundamentally irrelevant for our purposes. Charles does not have the power to keep California or the gold. Both are ours for the taking, if we move swiftly. I have brought incontrovertible proof."

"Oh?" the Czar was intrigued. "Show me this proof."

On cue, I entered from the adjoining room. The Czar's jaw dropped, for I was not wearing the matronly black of an aged Castilian noblewoman, nor the Russian finery in which I had first greeted Rezanov. No, I was wearing my finest suit and high heels and jewelry and had my hair coiled into an elegant chignon with a small streak of bright purple—the garb of a professional woman straight off the streets of San Francisco in the twenty-first century. I was also carrying my briefcase of high-tech sorcery. If I'd been dressed as a character out of *The Rocky Horror Picture Show*, his reaction couldn't have been more extreme.

"The *dueña*?" gasped Czar Alexander. *"Who is she?"*

I bowed to him—a straight bow, from the waist, like a man. "Your Majesty," I said in Russian, "I am not the Lady Concepción's *dueña*. In truth, I am no one's servant."

"May I present Anna Leah Fall-Levchenko?" asked Rezanov. "She comes from the city of San Francisco, of the State of California, of the United States of America, in the year two thousand and thirteen."

"Count Rezanov!" cried the young man when he had regained his voice. "I have known you for many years, and always thought you the most reasonable of men, but this is preposterous—"

"She can prove who she is," Rezanov said cheerfully. "Please give her your permission to do so."

The Czar gave a decidedly dizzy nod, so I proceeded to put on the dog-and-pony show. I had done this enough times in my life that I was getting really good at it.

Rezanov had arranged for the meeting to last several hours, so I was able to show the Czar many more documentaries than I had shown Rezanov during our first encounter in the woods. I led the Czar carefully by the hand through the terrible jungles of the future. Because he retained the idealism of a man still in his twenties, Alexander was devastated by the events that flashed by on the screen of my slim computer; when I showed him footage of Washington after the nuclear war of 1963, he covered his eyes and begged me to stop.

"The irony, Your Majesty," I said, "is that this weapon is an artifact of the few years out of all recorded history in which Russia and the United States were deadly rivals. We came to be cherished friends before the end. The only problem was, this bastard child that we had birthed had already spread to other countries around the world. When the final lever was pulled that ended the world, neither of our countries was responsible—and yet we both were."

He continued to weep. "So, Your Majesty, you see why I have journeyed here in peril of my life to lay all my wisdom and my wealth at your feet. I need your help to design a future that will not destroy both our mother countries. Together, let us build a wonderful future that will not be destroyed by folly."

"Yes, yes," he said. "You need only ask for what you need."

"In my time, Your Majesty, I could pick up this machine"—here I pointed to my tiny computer—"and talk to anyone anywhere on Earth who had one like it. Machines like this were starting to bring the human race together like a single family, for are we not all the sons and daughters of Eve?"

"Yes," he whispered.

"In the year 1991, a group of evil men tried to take over the Russian government by force. They were prevented from doing so, because we had the machines that let the whole world see what they were doing—and the whole world turned its back on them in disgust. We were so close to Eden, Your Majesty." I, too, began to weep. "Except for the Bomb, in another hundred years all men might have been glad and wise, as the old hymn tells us—"

"Anna," said Rezanov suddenly, pointing to my computer, "does this one disk contain *all* the scenes you have brought of this terrible nuclear weapon?"

I nodded. I was annoyed with him for interrupting my train of thought, but I saw no reason not to tell him.

Rezanov rose to his feet and removed the disk from its caddy. "Your Majesty," he said in a grim voice, "only the three of us in this room, and my wife, have seen these pictures. No one else must ever see what this weapon can do. No one else must ever dream that such a weapon can even be built!" With a dramatic gesture, he attempted to break the disk in two.

But it didn't break, only bent. He glared at it, decidedly pissed. I protested loudly, but he paid no heed. "This truly is forbidden fruit, Anna. It must not survive."

He clenched his jaw. Imperious and determined, he applied his full physical strength to break the disk. It shattered into half a dozen jagged pieces, one of which cut him through his white gloves so they were stained with bright red blood. He didn't care. He gathered up the pieces, strode over to the fireplace, and threw them into the flames. They hissed and sent up an awful stink as they melted.

Then, to my indescribable chagrin, the future changed—again! A blow came reeling out of the centuries ahead so powerful that it knocked me smack out of my chair. Rezanov cried out, helped me up, and ran to fetch a glass of spirits from a nearby table.

I was shaken to the core; I had thoroughly believed I had saved the world for good this time. But despite all the work

I had put into this last and most important mission, I had not changed the future *enough*. Except for Rezanov's forethought, someday someone would have seen that disk—at a time in history when the advances of science would have once again made possible the construction of nuclear weapons. Once again, the nuclear terror would have been loosed upon the world. When would it have happened? A hundred years from now? A thousand?

"Oh, Nikolasha," I said as he brought me a steadying glass of sherry, "you have just saved the world. You were right to destroy the disk. Otherwise, in time, someone would have found it and guessed its significance. Without you, all my efforts would have come to nothing."

Like a modern-day Isabella, I showed the Czar one of the large pouches of gemstones I had brought from home (never worry; I had others secreted here and there in my belongings and in the palace, in case I got cheated any time). I said that I was willing to fund the immediate, massive colonization of western America by Russia, provided a few minor terms were met. Talk about a deal the Czar couldn't refuse!

Now came the hardest part: showing him how to bring the Russian ship of state safe and sound through the storms of the coming years. I had to convince him that he must stand strong in support of the abolition of serfdom; the taming of his reform-resistant noble class; and the rise of democracy. His sons must be equally adamant in the face of burgeoning technology and telecommunications, which eventually would make dictatorship (which ever does its best work in the dark) impossible. I impressed upon him all the things he and his successors would somehow have to accept, and all the changes that could not be withstood, no matter how much special interests in Russia might wish to resist them in the short run.

I warned him about Napoleon and 1812; I showed him where the land mines of the future were buried. I begged that he not let Napoleon's follies distract him from the far more important matter of expanding his empire in the golden east.

We had a real knock-down-drag-out fight over what to do with Nappy. The Czar and Rezanov were all for my killing him with one of my nasty spy weapons brought from the twenty-first century. I didn't want to do that. I had killed a man once, and the experience had sickened me.

I had another reason for refusing, a private one. Back in the early 1990's, there had been this movie, *Terminator 2*, which the unobservant tended to hold up as an example of the gratuitously violent movies that were ruining our youth. (But nary a word did they tend to say about the gratuitously violent leaders of nations who were ruining our youth along with every other living thing on the planet—snarl, snarl.) Well, there was this one point in the movie where my heroine and role model, Sarah Connor, was on the point of killing a scientist she thought was responsible for building the device that would ultimately decimate the human race by starting a nuclear war.

She almost killed him. She had the gun practically shoved up his left nostril like a spoonful of coke. But something stopped her—at the last moment, she chose good over evil. And a damn good thing for humanity. Because if she had killed him, she would never have gotten the final crucial piece of information she needed to stop the nuclear war and change history.

So, in most cases, killing was wrong. Now, back in San Francisco I generally supported capital punishment for the sort of guy who killed children and then polished off their McDonald's burgers after the deed was done, as happened to be the facts in one celebrated San Quentin gas chamber case. I took a lot of shit for that from my contemporaries. But in most cases where there was a viable alternative, I went for that alternative.

I knew that as an emperor and conqueror, Napoleon was partly responsible for the deaths of thousands of soldiers. But the crowned heads of Europe didn't seem inclined to do anything about it just then, and I didn't see Rezanov offering to kill the guy himself. So I wasn't willing to commit another crime by doing his dirty work for him.

As long as there was an alternative, I was going to be true to the spirit of Sarah Connor. Luckily I did find a way out of my dilemma. I nosed around and found a reliable, blackmailable person to give Napoleon a certain mood-altering drug developed in the twenty-first century at regular intervals. It could be shot invisibly into Nappy's neck at a court function from this nasty little cigarette-sized gun I had brought along on the trip. Basically, the drug would just mellow him out for as long as we could keep shooting him up, and get him more interested in making love than making war. I'm sure Josephine would have thanked me, had she only known I was responsible for her spouse's mysterious and persistent good humor. (Sigh. No imprisonment of Napoleon in Elba in years to come; and therefore, no tale by Dumas of Edmond Dantes, and no delectable Richard Chamberlain in the TV movie *The Count of Monte Cristo*. Oh, well, everything costs something.)

That disposed of, there were other important matters to attend to.

"About the gold, Your Majesty," I said, choosing my words carefully, for maximum effect. "There is truly a great deal of gold in California, and I prefer that it grace the palaces of St. Petersburg and the churches of the Kremlin than the pockets of rough Americans. But there is another source of great wealth in California that no one yet knows about."

"Fur-bearing sea animals?" asked the Czar eagerly.

I shook my head. As far as I was concerned, my dues to the World Wildlife Fund were still paid-up and current. "No. My terms require that you leave the animals alone. They are nothing, mere kopecks. I am speaking of the interior of California—a great fertile valley which makes the Ukraine look like a serf's cottage garden. In my time, the value of all the gold ever brought out of California did not match the value of the crops grown in her central valley in a single year."

The Czar's eyes did a good imitation of popping out of his head. "Yes, Your Majesty," I said. "*That* is the true wealth of California. Do not be distracted by the sea otters. Or, for that matter, the enormous, stately red-hued trees you will find. Both the otters and these trees are more valuable as sights that, soon, all the world will come to see—and will pay handsomely to see."

I was also a paid-up member of the Sempervirens Fund and the Save-the-Redwoods League.

"Your Majesty," I continued, "in our great universities, one of which I attended, they universally taught us the art of conservation of resources. Do *not* be distracted by the quick and easy money that is to be made in California. Do not allow industries to grow up that exploit such exhaustible resources, for the men drawn to such industries must in the last days starve." I gritted my teeth, knowing I had to toss him one bone, at least, to get the ball rolling. "By all means, do mine the gold. But as regards the rest of the state, take the long view, the wise view, and thereby maximize the enormous wealth that will flow to Russia."

He nodded. "Shrewd words. Your university trained you well. I accede to your terms."

I grinned inwardly. Chalk one up for the spotted owl. I could feel that a lot of twenty-first-century ghosts were pleased, and a lot were pissed, and the reactions of both groups delighted me equally.

"Oh, and another thing, Your Majesty," I said. "A hundred years from now, there will come a great, shattering earthquake to the area where now lies the Presidio of San Francisco." I hauled out all my seismic stuff and showed it to him. "These materials will guide the builders of your new St. Petersburg or your Novaya Moskva to make the city as safe as possible in the face of this danger. Have your artisans study these materials as if the lives of their grandchildren depended on them."

"Which they shall," whispered the Czar.

"Yes, Your Majesty."

On the way back from the meeting with the Czar, Rezanov asked out of the blue if I thought it was a good idea to import African slaves to help colonize California, like the Americans were doing in the East, since the native California Indians were reported to be rather lazy and shiftless. I winced at this double breach of political correctness, and braced myself for a tongue-lashing from somebody in the near vicinity. But then I remembered there was no resident of Berkeley around to witness Rezanov's ingrained chauvinism. So I started to give a pat answer, "No, absolutely not!"—and then panicked.

Playing God was one frightening job. Of course slavery was morally wrong. But in my peregrinations through the twentieth and twenty-first centuries, I had made many friends who were descended from those African captives. They had studied their ancestors' suffering, and grieved for those ancestors, but they were also Americans with their minds firmly fixed on the modern era. Some of them were as hooked as I was on caffe latte as it is made only in San Francisco (and in Berkeley by Fanny, the daughter of the great twentieth-century chef, Alice Waters). How could I dare to presume to speak for them, to make a choice for them, to arrogantly assume I knew what was best for them, long before they were even born?

Shit, you just can't make everybody happy, no matter how hard you try. I was wistfully reminded of Bill from Arkansas.

I drew a deep breath and resolved to do the best I could. The way things were going, the way I was fooling about with the path of future history, few people I had known back home were likely to be born, African-American or not. I would let morality be my guide, let the pieces fall where they might, and just hope one of them didn't squash me. Plus, I prayed a little.

"Don't do it," I said to Rezanov. "Slavery is wrong. The

Americans will fight a bloody war and abolish it in 1865. In your own country, serfdom will be abolished in due time."

"Then I will use Russian serfs," said Rezanov, "whose freedom we shall buy with your abundant gemstones. I think it better anyway to fill California with men of Russian blood."

When we got back to Rezanov's apartments, we were ready to party. Since it was December, all Rezanov had to do was put a bottle of vodka outside on the window sill to get it chilled.

Vodka never freezes, no matter how cold it gets; it just turns ice cold and syrupy. At that point it goes down easily, and hits you hard.

Rezanov, Concha, and I all had a couple of shots. A few. All right, we had a lot. When Concha walked carefully and slowly out of the room to find a permissible place for a lady to pee, Rezanov started gloating about how he would start outfitting ships for California the following morning. By February he would have several thousand serfs heading eastward across Siberia to arrive in California by the summer of 1808. "I will be very generous in my terms," he said. "I will give them farm equipment, oxen, and enough acreage to support a family."

Drunk as a skunk, I remembered *Gone with the Wind*, and giggled, "Ah believe the Yankee term for that about eighteen sixty-five was 'forty acres and a mule.'"

He didn't understand, but smiled indulgently. "There is no reason to wait for the signature of that fool Charles IV on this alliance to begin settlement," he said, with his wife safely out of the room. "We will act whether he signs or not."

We downed a couple more swift ones before the proper Concha had returned, almost killing the bottle. "By Christ, we'll have ten thousand serfs in California by summer," vowed Rezanov.

It was the booze, I admit it. My subconscious mind had been freed from its moorings to make all sorts of bizarre connections. Suddenly I started laughing so hard, you'd think at my age I'd have had a heart attack. Concha returned in time to be distressed, but Rezanov, while thoroughly puzzled himself, assured her that I must be responding to a private joke.

I stumbled over to my computer, set it on music mode, and did a quick search, all the while cackling to myself.

"Are women of good family allowed to get this drunk in the twenty-first century?" Concha asked Rezanov, with some interest.

"I can only assume so. Here in Russia, it is allowable on special occasions, and this is a very special occasion. Besides, she is old, and among Russians, eccentric behavior is customarily tolerated to a greater degree when one has attained old age."

I put on the music to a certain 1960's Beach Boys song and started dancing around the room like a madwoman. "What are you doing?" cried Rezanov at last.

"This is a song from my youth," I cried. I tried to do a cartwheel, and landed in a heap, scaring the hell out of Concha, who was certain I had just broken every bone in my body. She didn't know about my years of doing Jane Fonda aerobics tapes.

The refrain sounded one last time, and I sang along. "Everybody's gone serfing," I bellowed, "serfing U.S.A.!"

"What is this?" asked poor Rezanov, bewildered.

I collapsed into helpless giggles again. "Serf," I said. "In Russian, '*krepostnoy.*'"

He merely looked blank.

"Oh, hell," I said, "I'll explain when I sober up!"

Our path was not entirely smooth, and I admit that there were a few bad moments along the way, but we made it. We got Napoleon to behave in a properly laid-back fashion, much to the relief of the European continent. In London, they never named that midtown square after the Battle of Trafalgar, and there was never a monument to Lord Nelson in it. He, by the way, not being famous, got to go off and live happily ever after with Lady Hamilton.

King Charles IV of Spain was a real asshole, like most insecure people. He had a hunch he wasn't very good at kingship and was about to be pink-slipped. He was an absolute beast in our negotiations in Madrid. I mean, he was a butt and a naysayer just for the fun of it. Rezanov, the famed diplomat, almost lost it and told the King to stick the treaty where the yellow don't fade, but our little Concha came to the rescue. Long black eyelashes fluttering, she knelt at the King's feet and pleaded the Russians' case. Occasionally a dewy tear inched its way out of one midnight-black eye, causing the King's courtiers to fidget. The King didn't really give in, but as the minutes passed, the Queen, a rather jittery sort, decided she wanted the lovely Concepción out of the throne room—and away from her husband—as fast as possible. Also, I think she was thrilled by the sight of so much gold. So she whispered something to the King (perhaps along the lines of "Say yes, or I'll break all your fingers when we get back to the royal bedchamber") and he said, "Oh, all right," and signed the treaty.

Concha, at one point, got uppity. I had given her that contraceptive back in 1806 when she married Rezanov. She still wasn't out of her teens, and while in Madrid she started to get ideas about going to the university just like a man, since she had this ability to put off child-bearing indefinitely.

I didn't blame her one bit. In future years I did everything in my power to teach her how to emancipate the women of Novaya Rossiya. But right then and there, I had to give her a talking to on the grand scale. "Doña Concepción," I said, "we do not have four years to spend in Madrid while you go to school. We must return to California *at once* to secure it against foreign interests. Every second we lose makes us more vulnerable to the United States and to the other powers of Europe, who have not failed to take note of our joint venture in the New World."

"Politics," snapped Concha. "Always I am to be sacrificed to politics!"

Reality check time. I said, "Listen, Concha, without me you would have no husband, you'd never have gotten to see Europe at all, you would have waited for years until you finally got word of Nikolai Petrovich's death, and when you were old you would have taken the veil. Surely things are better off this way?"

"Well . . . yes," she said.

"In my time, women had the freedom you crave," I said. "You and I will work to secure that freedom for your daughters and all the women of California—far earlier than they got it in my time! Given a little luck and my medicine chest, which you will inherit, you're going to live another fifty or sixty years. I daresay a few more trips to Europe can be arranged for you."

She began to perk up, so I pressed on. "Concha, you stand at the crossroads of history. I am counting on you to become—in all but title—the queen of a new country. I will pay whatever is necessary to bring the finest European tutors to you, in California. You will literally be a second Isabella. Without the first, the Americas would never have been discovered. Without you, they would never have survived past the year 2013."

"Yes, you are right," said Concha reluctantly. I saw her saying good-bye in her mind to the bright lights and promise of Europe, and my own heart ached for her. But this was deadly serious business.

"God being so merciful, you should bear many children," I continued. "There are many mistakes my own people made that Novaya Rossiya must avoid in the future. To help the colony avoid them, to secure the future, a large Rezanov-Arguello dynasty will be needed. You will train them to give their loyalty to their common blood, their country, and Count Rezanov's vision of the future, not to individual ambition. That is the greatest contribution you can make to the world."

She squared her shoulders. "You are wise, dear Annichka."

"Anyway," I added, "it's not like there isn't a lot of fun and excitement to be had along the way. I'm quite good at bending the rules and loading the dice. We'll dress up Novaya Moskva like a queen—not to mention the exquisite home you and the count will build. With the money we've got to spend, soon there will arise a glittering marble city over which you will preside: the capital of the exotic land of California. It is blessed with a Mediterranean climate in which one may feast on vine-ripened tomatoes at Thanksgiving—I mean in November! The likes of Voltaire and Madame de Sévigné will flock *to you*."

"What's a tomato?" asked Concha.

"Delicious. You'll see. I brought seeds."

At that, her eyes danced. "And you will be around to enjoy the delights of this capital, I hope."

"Oh, yes. I'm looking forward to my retirement—surrounded, of course, by books, music, painting, intelligent visitors from around the world, fresh food, and your father's wine cellar. You're not the only one who's going to have fun."

"Anna Ivanovna," she said, "I love you."

From the Journal of Anna Leah Fall-Levcheko
Novaya Moskva, California: May 1836

At times I am overcome by a homesickness so piercing, so agonizing, I think the pain of a Toledo steel sword run through my vitals would be more bearable.

I have almost reached the hundred-year mark, due perhaps to good genes or clean and virtuous living—but, I think more likely, thanks to my moderate, persistent indulgence in the ports and sherries in Don José's fine cellar. And a shot of Russian vodka and Mexican tequila now and then. Yet I know that death will visit me soon, and give me some sorely needed rest.

It is said that the very old who retain their health treasure each additional day granted them as if it were made of pure gold. But there are times when I would gladly give what little remains of my life to be a girl again, for only an hour or two, and walk the length of Columbus Avenue in the American San Francisco I loved so very much, and can never see again.

In that time there was this funky-looking building called the Transamerica Pyramid, which at first everyone hated, but after it was built, every newcomer enjoyed. It covered almost an entire city block, and I used to stand at the corner that lay at the foot of Columbus Avenue by the north side of the Pyramid, and sniff the air with delight. There the aromas of hot peppers, oil, and heavenly stir-fried meals from

Chinatown collided head-on with the smells of pasta, garlic, onions, and tomato sauce from the old Italian quarter of North Beach. No matter how hungry you were, it was torture deciding which way to turn.

If you chose Chinese, you could go to a little hole in the wall, a real dive run by a man who had fled Shanghai in 1989 (I think he was somehow connected with the students massacred in Beijing's Tiananmen Square in that year). Anyway, this place looked so disreputable that no uninitiated tourist from Oklahoma or Texas would ever dare go in. But once you got past the crowd of locals (mostly neighborhood Chinese and financial district suits) choking the entrance, you were treated to a delightfully clean interior and an entire wall of framed ecstatic restaurant reviews, some from as far away as Frankfurt and London. Then you were served exquisite fresh Shanghai cooking at rock-bottom, dirt-cheap prices—my personal idea of nirvana.

If you chose Italian, there were too many choices for me to describe here with any semblance of impartial justice. But if you were in a pissy-poor mood and just didn't want ethnic that day, there was a little retro-chic black-and-white tiled diner around the corner that served the most exquisite heart-attack-inducing hamburgers, fries, and malted milks in the Western world.

Then you could pop into Tosca's, an old-time bar which had remained unchanged since the 1940's, complete with dark shiny wood everywhere, whorehouse-red plastic cushiony booths, formica tables, and a delicious lethal drink called a "White Nun." You could go over to the jukebox and choose between "Waltz Across Texas with You in My Arms" or half a dozen arias from *Turandot*.

Then, once it was dark and you were pretty lit, you could amble down Columbus and rub elbows with the counterculture at City Lights bookstore, where they published Allen Ginsberg's poem "Howl" back in the heyday of the beatnik era. You could head on downhill toward the sea, past more bars, restaurants, brick ovens with pizzas, and chickens roasting on the spit. You could see espresso cafes and bizarre boutiques and stores selling beautiful but fabulously expensive Italian country pottery. If you felt in the mood to be forgiven for your gluttony, you could pop in at the church of St. Peter and St. Paul, in Washington Square, and launch a prayer into the soft, balmy skies of a San Francisco evening. Or you could go to this nearby cafe with a back patio and sip espresso and listen to the church bells chime the hour, just as if you were in Europe.

I can never have those experiences again. From the vantage point of my little house atop the former Russian Hill (I had it built on almost the same spot as our old apartment building), I look around at the rolling landscape that is not my San Francisco, but Novaya Moskva, the magnificent capital of Russian California, and my heart catches in my throat. In my mind's eye I can see the ghostly outline of the city that will not be. *There*, I say to myself, *there* was Columbus Avenue. *There* was Coit Tower, atop Telegraph Hill, and that ludicrous statue of Christopher Columbus, facing WEST across the Pacific—toward Russia and China! *There* was my favorite cookie shop. *There* I had bought maps to hike the coasts of California, Oregon, and Washington. *There* had stood San Francisco's Pacific Stock Exchange and the financial district—the economic engines of the American West. Now they are all gone, all gone, burnt up.

I must stop this wallowing in sorrow. I must remember that even if I had *not* journeyed back to the year 1806, my beautiful lost world was still no longer mine to enjoy, or anyone's. Hydrogen bombs were blasting it into radioactive dust, even as I pressed the buttons on the time machine to send me on my last desperate journey into the past. I am certain it happened. When I close my eyes at night I can still see the first flashes in the sky.

Last night I dreamed the ghost of Joseph McCarthy had tracked me down, and was going to kill me for giving America over to the Commies. When I woke up I felt so stupid—but I was covered in cold sweat. I had been trying to persuade him that there weren't going to be any Commies since I had changed everything, but he wouldn't listen. Somehow I hadn't thought to tell him that, taking into account the kick in the groin I had just given history, there was probably never going to be a Joe McCarthy either. I think that would have shut him up but good.

It is now the year 1836. Right on schedule, Texas got her independence from Mexico. Terrifically cognizant of all the Russian colonists pouring eastward over the Rockies, the United States didn't stop to fret and pontificate for a decade or more over the fact that Texas was a slaveholding state, as it had been in my world. The United States admitted her into the union *muy pronto*. So Texas never got to be an independent country, and I think the Russian-American border will end up somewhere around the eastern edge of what I knew as New Mexico, rather than in East Texas.

Already there are signs of tension. Russia has made the United States more united. Faced with a common enemy, the Americans suddenly seem to be willing to resolve the slavery question peacefully. In all likelihood there will not be a Civil War. No Confederacy, and no bloodied South, hammered to its knees, handicapped and poor for the next hundred and fifty years.

Jesus, it really makes you wonder about human nature. This amazing and sudden tractability on the part of the United States government apparently means the Civil War was not all that "necessary." Maybe a lot of other wars were not really necessary either . . . hmmm? Is anybody listening? *Any of you boys who murdered my world?*

Recently I did some checking up on history in the making. Ha! A child named Abraham Lincoln *was* born back in 1809 near Hodgenville, Kentucky. It does make sense; in the early part of the year 1808, when Lincoln was conceived, I clearly had not yet sufficiently disrupted the course of American history—at least as it was playing out in rural Kentucky—to negate his birth.

If he becomes President in another twenty-five years or so, he probably will not be assassinated. At least not by John Wilkes Booth. See, I checked again. John's older brother, the magnificent Edwin Booth, the greatest American actor of the nineteenth century, was not born on schedule three years ago in 1833. So, unfortunately, it seems that Edwin, that specific person, that singular union of sperm and egg, can now never be born. I'm so sorry; he was said to be a wonder on the classical stage. But, since I've thrown such a monkey wrench into the march of history, it is highly unlikely that his kid brother John Wilkes Booth will be born in 1838 either. See, the daily life of the Booth family timetable has been so altered that papa Junius Brutus Booth and his wife will almost certainly not make love at the crucial moment that resulted in birth of the John Wilkes Booth we knew.

God alone knows how many other credits to the human race we have now lost, and how many benefactors we have gained. God alone knows how many villains we are now shed of, and how many new scoundrels we must endure.

Rezanov's oldest boy, Alexei, is of a contemplative and scholarly bent. I think he will write the first history of Zolotoy Vostok, or the Golden East. Rezanov's second son, Dmitri, has a taste for management and will undoubtedly follow in his father's footsteps and become governor of Russian America. Both boys studied at universities in Europe, and Rezanov's four young daughters are also scheduled to attend. Concha and I have insisted to Rezanov that when the girls are grown, they too will be given positions of responsibility in the colony. What Concha wants, Concha tends to get, so I foresee an early flowering of women's liberation in this society.

War will come. I can feel it. It has a most distinctive smell. If God is kind, I will die soon; I will be spared the brutalities of this particular conflict. I have had my fill of war; the very thought of it sickens me. It grieves me that Nikolasha, Concha, and their children must watch it.

But our two countries will survive this early war, and grow past it into friendship. Most importantly, the race will survive this war—as it will survive all future wars, which will not be fought with atomic or hydrogen bombs.

Of that I am certain, in my soul.

# THE FINEST THE UNIVERSE HAS TO OFFER